About the author

Margaret was born in Glasgow in 1931 and brought up in Shettleston.

She had a passion for reading and "devoured" books from the age of eight.

Margaret married quite young but sadly her first husband died at an early age. However, there were two daughters to this marriage.

She married Gerald Wiener in 1985, an animal geneticist. Margaret tragically died in 2020 after a long illness.

Throughout her life she felt she needed to work, first to help supplement family income and later for the satisfaction. To that end she undertook teacher training and after some years in different schools in East Kilbride was appointed head-teacher of a 120-pupil primary school in Kirkfieldbank, Lanarkshire. She stayed there for about 17 years before "retiring" but continued teaching for a further few years in a school for gifted children in Peebles.

In addition to her teaching qualifications, she obtained a first-class honours degree in English and Philosophy from the Open University. She was also a member of Mensa.

Margaret was multi-talented. Apart from writing she painted, knitted, quilted – all to a high standard – played the piano, was a member of the theatre workshop in Biggar, a cook of exceptional ability and an enthusiastic world traveller.

On top of her lifelong passion for reading she had hopes of writing but felt her life's circumstances never gave her time or chance. Not until she was already in her seventies when she was encouraged to attend a writer's course.

The result was eleven stories awaiting compilation and three books. The first of these, "Marching in Scotland, Dancing in New York" was praised by Tom Devine, the Scottish Historian, as "the real history of Scotland in its time and full of human interest"

The next book, "Blind Date in Gibraltar" (on Kindle) is an entertaining story set in Spain. It involves the expatriate community, and is given its authentic feel because Margaret had lived in Spain for months at a time over a period of years.

Her third book "Goodbye Berlin – the biography of Gerald Wiener" was published in Edinburgh, by Birlinn Ltd. and is available in hardback and paperback.

"Snakes and Ladders" was found on Margaret's laptop, as a complete novel, after she had sadly passed away in July 2020. Hopefully it will be a fitting memorial to her writing skills.

Margaret was the best wife in the world. She was also a wonderful mother to her two daughters, grandmother to seven children and great-grandmother to eight, all of whom miss her greatly for her love and inveterate story-telling.

SNAKES AND LADDERS

Margaret M. Dunlop

SNAKES AND LADDERS

Vanguard Press

VANGUARD

PAPERBACK © Copyright

2023 **Margaret M. Dunlop**

A CIP catalogue record for this title is
available from the British Library.

ISBN 978-1-80016-721-6

Vanguard Press is an imprint of
Pegasus Elliot Mackenzie Publishers Ltd.
www.pegasuspublishers.com

First Published in 2023

Vanguard Press
Sheraton House Castle Park
Cambridge England

Printed & Bound in Great Britain

PREFACE

This novel is timeless. Set in the 1960s, it could as easily have been set in the 2020s. People still fall in love. People still worry about their finances and, at times, how to make ends meet. Attractive young women can still fall prey to the desires of powerful men who, as their employers, have a hold over them. It still is everyone's hope that the "ladders" in life take them up further than the "snakes" pull them down.

This is an absorbing story of love, seduction and unfaithfulness and its aftermath in the more sexually strict days of the 1950s. Set in Glasgow, London, Paris and Rome, the book tells of the highs and lows in the lives of Maggie, and the decisions she has to make to balance out her career, to cope with husband Jamie and the encroachment into her young life of a powerful seducer.

Margaret M. Dunlop (aka Margaret M. Wiener) was a gifted writer. Her use of dialogue is superb. Oft-times, the reader feels part of the conversation and thinks of joining in.

Margaret was born and brought up in Glasgow. She had a passion for reading books from early childhood on and a desire to write books and stories. Unfortunately, circumstances prevented her from doing so until she was encouraged, when already in her seventies, to attend a writers' course. Her trial book, *Marching in Scotland, Dancing in New York,* received this appraisal from her tutors: "Had you started to write earlier in life you would now be an acclaimed best-selling author." When published, that book received further public praise, most especially from the noted Scottish historian, Tom Devine. Two other books followed before a prolonged illness overtook her.

Sadly, Margaret died in 2020. I found *Snakes and Ladders* on her laptop after she had passed away. This book will be a fitting memorial to a short but successful writing career.

Gerald Wiener

Chapter 1

The sound of jazz music filled the air in the little living room —
Bix Beiderbecke playing a trumpet solo from his album, "Singin'
the Blues." Jamie held his breath in wonder as he absorbed the
yearning and melancholy of the music. The soulful sound drifted
round the room reflecting his mood. A coal fire was burning low
in the fireplace, and on the coffee table lay a letter he had read
several times, while around him were the cardboard-sleeved
records from his precious collection. His right leg, stiff and
bandaged under his trousers, was supported on a footstool. This he
moved now and started to replace the records in the wine-coloured
record case, bought for him by the family to compensate for those
long months in hospital.

Sent home now from the sanatorium, the doctors having
declared him cured, he was trying to acclimatise himself to the
normal world; two years older and estranged from his former
friends and sporting pursuits. When he had been in the local boys'
football team, his thick, sandy-red hair had earned him the
nickname of "Rusty". With his ready smile showing uneven teeth,
his strong broad shoulders and muscular, goal-scoring legs, Jamie
had been a favourite in the neighbourhood. Then at just twenty-
four, excruciating pain in his right leg was diagnosed as a serious
bone infection, and on that September day in 1954, his life of
football and all adolescent shenanigans had been brought to an
abrupt end.

He heard his mother at the door, returning from work. "That's
another day, another dollar, Jamie." She put down her shopping
bag. I brought us some fish for tea. How's your leg feel today?"

"Oh it's great. I'm definitely on the mend now. All ready for the interview tomorrow. I've pressed my suit and ironed a white shirt."

Mrs London sat down heavily, out of breath. "Make us a cup of tea, son. I need a pick-me-up before I go into the kitchen." Jamie was quickly off to fill the kettle, while Jessie London, chest wheezing, dozed in her chair, dreaming of the past, the better days she had known, and the fun of a happy family and a good-natured husband. She was a tall, heavily built woman whose jet-black hair, now streaked with grey, was permed and styled neatly. In her youth she had been slim and good-looking, devil-may-care, full of fun, easily winning the heart of John, Jamie's father. But the past few years had brought her much pain and sorrow. First her husband's sudden death and, within eighteen months, her three daughters, all in their twenties had all left home, two to be married and one to emigrate to Australia. Then the tragedy of Jamie, the light of her life, had struck. His illness had almost finished her. Her husband had been manager of a big transport firm, and they had been well-off, before his death. Now the car was gone and the coffers were empty. She had found a job as a cashier in the local underground station, but she had to work sometimes until eleven o'clock at night, and life had few compensations left for her.

Jamie's release from hospital was a great joy, and she watched him carefully, praying that he really was cured. He was her only son, a miracle to her when he was born after three girls, and she had spoiled him. Sadly, had she but known, the untreated milk she heated and gave him every day after school, while she caressed his sturdy young legs, was almost certainly the source of the tubercular infection which struck him in his teens.

"What's this letter, Jamie, son?"

"It's from Catherine. You can read it if you like."

Jessie read the letter, her face growing hard. "So she's going to Canada after all?"

Jamie came in with the tray of tea and biscuits. "Yes. For two years she says. But I wonder if she'll ever come back."

"It's them, you know. Her parents. They want her to go abroad so that she might meet a better prospect." Her voice was bitter.

Jamie's face was non-committal. "Oh, well, it's a chance for her. She is only twenty-one. She has relations there."

"She is your fiancée, Jamie."

"Oh, that's more-or-less finished now. I told her when she mentioned Canada, that we shouldn't hold each other to the engagement."

Mrs London was upset. "It's a crying shame. You were both so happy. They've turned her against you." Under her breath she hissed "Bastards!"

"Don't get upset. I've accepted it, and it's for the best. She's coming round at eight to say goodbye, so I don't want any recriminations or tears. It's all over. If I get this job with Rodger and Russell's then I'll start a new life, and we'll have a bit more money through our hands, Mamma." He caressed her rounded shoulders as she sat slumped in front of the fire, teacup in her hand, and touched her wiry black hair. He loved her very much.

"Well, I'm glad I won't be here when she comes. I've to be at Betty's at eight for a game of solo, thank goodness. She'll get no goodbyes or good wishes from me, that's for sure."

In truth Jamie was dreading the farewell scene. Catherine had been a regular visitor to the hospital, and their young love had been tender and strong at first. But both of them knew that it was not surviving, when the months dragged on, and Jamie was still bedridden. They had grown apart. Maturity had come to him, and in contrast, the pretty, curvaceous Catherine had begun to seem young and shallow, and gradually her visits became less regular.

In all those hours of enforced immobility, he had read widely, and he had met and talked to many older and more experienced men who were in hospital as a result of the war. Jamie became interested, and eventually crazy, about traditional jazz. He read magazines on the subject and acquired pen friends with the same interest. Sophisticated, and keen on politics, he came to have left wing convictions through his wide reading of recent history and current affairs. Catherine shared little of his interests.

11

That evening, when his mother had gone to her card-night, Catherine's parents waited outside the house, while she called to say goodbye to him. In spite of knowing that this was how things had to be, Jamie felt a pain in his chest at the idea of this sweet young beauty who would have been his wife, leaving, and whom he would probably never see again. "I'm going to miss you, Catherine, and I'll think of you often." Her hair fell in thick curls to her shoulders, and she smelt sweet and exciting.

She said, "I'll write to you, Jamie. As soon as I get there, I'll drop you a line and tell you all about it. It's great that you are home and on the mend."

"Sure. I've got a job interview tomorrow. I'll write to you and let you know how I'm doing."

"I'll always love you, Jamie London. Always." She ruffled his wavy hair and wiped her tears. "Think of me sometimes. Will you?"

"You know I will. You'll do well. You're a lovely girl. I'll never forget you. And who knows? If miracles still happen, I might make it to Canada, too." The car horn tooted in the street, a warning, raucous sound.

"Goodbye, Jamie. They're waiting for me."

"Goodbye, sweetheart. All the best."

He stood at the window and watched her pretty head, and shapely legs disappear into the back of the car. A tearful sad, young face was the last he saw of her.

"You will be on a month's trial in the invoice department." Golden words. Jamie breathed a silent sigh of relief. The announcement was emanating from the thin lips of his new employer, Regional Manager, Lewis Benton. The older man was leaning towards him across the large desk, his manner quite solicitous. "Your football injury is completely healed, now. You're finished with the hospital altogether?"

Jamie nodded, "Yes I was declared quite fit last Friday, thank goodness."

Mr Benton stood up and held out his thin hand to Jamie. "We'll see how you get on, then. I'm sure it will work out. I knew your father slightly. A fine man! I remember reading his obituary in *The Glasgow Herald*." Jamie was silent, the memory of his beloved father hidden under many protective layers in his mind. Mr Benton surveyed his empire, a busy old-fashioned place where telephones rang constantly, manual typewriters were being pounded and young girls moved round absorbed in their work, or gave that impression, as they went from filing cabinet to desk.

Adjoining the office was a huge warehouse repository of stock — steel tubes and flanges and fittings, held there to be ordered by plumbers and house builders. All day long, great lorries arrived and departed loaded up with supplies, the warehouse staff being kept busy checking off order sheets, hopefully ensuring the success of Rodger and Russell, a busy, thriving company.

"This is Mina. She takes care of wages so you'd better give her your papers. Salaries are paid at the end of the month. She'll give you your duties. Keep you right." Suddenly the thin, dry face broke into a smile. "Good luck. I hope you'll be happy at Rodger and Russell's." He shook hands with the young man, and departed to his heated office, behind a heavy, oak door.

Mina chattered on pleasantly about the firm, and Jamie tried to look attentive listening to the mountains of information she was attempting to communicate. She held up a sheaf of invoices from various suppliers, addressed to 'Messrs. Rodger & Russell, Steel Stockholders, Pipes and Flanges.' You check the prices and discounts according to this manual, Mr London."

"Oh, listen, call me Jamie."

"Right, Jamie. If you find any mistakes in the invoices, you must let me know. As you see, the phone rings all day long. Don't answer it until you've got the hang of things in the office. Just let it ring." She smiled up at him, a plump, blonde lady, warm and efficient.

"Thank you, Mina."

"And if you are puzzled about anything…" Her words were interrupted by a tall fellow with a shock of red, curly hair and a flushed face, breathless and slightly dishevelled. Mina turned in mock disgust to the newcomer. "Not again, Gregor. It's ten minutes past nine. You know I've been here since eight-thirty, and the boss came in at five to nine."

"Did he notice I wasn't in?"

She raised her eyebrows, "I don't think so, but you'd better get busy before he gets back."

Gregor looked at Jamie. Mina said, "This is Jamie London. He started this morning. Doing invoice-checking and generally helping out."

"Oh, great! I'm Gregor McFarlane." They shook hands. "I chase up orders, you know the sort of thing." Suddenly his eyes fell on his shoes. "Christ, I've come all the way on the subway in odd shoes — and I thought that girl sitting opposite to me was flirting with me, smiling all the time." He slumped on to a chair, "My God, she was laughing at my odd shoes!" He put his head in hands. Mina and Jamie looked down to see two size-nine feet, one pushed into a brown buckle-shoe, and the other into a black brogue.

Mina shook her head, "How can you do things like this, Gregor? You're completely nuts."

"Prudence and I overslept again. It was eight-twenty when we woke — the baby was up half the bloody night, and then the alarm clock didn't go off. It was quarter to nine before I opened my eyes. I just dived into my clothes and ran for the subway." He looked at his feet again. "Oh God! I can't go out for lunch like this."

"Don't be silly, Gregor," Mina said. "They'll be so busy looking at that red hair on your head and that ghastly yellow tie, they won't have time to get to your feet."

They settled down, Jamie at a desk, which butted against Gregor's. Soon he was engrossed in calculations involving long additions of money. He concentrated hard, anxious to hide how rusty he was at this kind of thing. In the outer office, three girls sat bashing away noisily at typewriters, seldom lifting their heads from their work. Each time the phone rang, Mina or Gregor, or sometimes Malcolm the podgy office boy, answered it.

The mood of activity was interrupted when Mr Benton appeared, his funereal face still white and pinched, a cigarette in one hand. He dropped a pink memo onto Gregor's desk, grunted a, "Good morning, Gregor!" gave a half-hearted smile, and shy as a badger caught out in the daylight, vanished into his luxurious lair.

Gregor picked up the pink memo and glanced over at Mina. "Let's see! What's the old bugger saying now? Another of his crazy instructions, no doubt!"

In a voice of mock seriousness he read:

MEMO 45 5 September, 1956.

FOR YOUR PERUSAL AND RETURN:

I wish to bring to your attention that there have been complaints about the staff toilet. Someone has not been flushing the lavatory efficiently, and solid matter is appearing intermittently. This situation must be remedied. Will ALL staff please give this matter their best attention.

Faithfully yours,

LEWIS BENTON

(General Manager.)

Jamie started chuckling, partly at the popping eyes and incredulous voice of Gregor as he read the message out. "You can laugh, Jamie, but I tell you the old buffer's deranged. No question about it."

At this, the overgrown schoolboy who was the office boy, Malcolm, appeared, his face agitated. "I say Gregor," he whispered out of Mina's hearing, "I've just done something in the toilet, and it won't go away."

"What?" Gregor hissed. "Won't go away?" He jumped up "Let's see."

"He'll know it was me," whined Malcolm as he trotted along behind Gregor. "You wait and see. He'll be sure to know it was me." Jamie felt drawn to the scene and followed the pair into the men's toilet. There was a stunned silence as they looked down the toilet pan, and Gregor and Jamie retired to their desks, creased with mirth while the panic-stricken Malcolm shouted, "He'll give me the sack for this!"

By two in the afternoon, having shared Gregor's lunch, Jamie felt more relaxed, although his head was swimming with figures and percentages. Yes, he could cope with this, he was sure of it. Then, suddenly he stumbled upon a total that was in error. "Gregor, this bill from Stevenson and Co for tubing and angle-bends is wrong. It doesn't add up."

Gregor hurried over to him. "Let me see, Jamie. Great stuff! Your reputation's made. You found an error in Stevenson's bill. Good for you! You're quite right, too. I'll let the old fella know. He'll be delighted. He'll phone them up with relish. It will make his day, boy."

Holding the paper in question, Gregor stood at the oak door and knocked and entered on command. "Just want to bring to your attention, Mr Benton, this bill from Stevenson's is wrongly totalled. Detected by Jamie."

Mr Benton took the bill from Gregor and glanced over it. He smiled slyly. "Well done! Well done, indeed Jamie," he called from the door. "Good work! I'll see to this!" And he shut the door to his office.

"You're in the good books now all right, Jamie. Found an error on your first day. I'm impressed."

They settled down again for ten minutes when the boss's door burst open. A livid Mr Benton stood, framed by the gleaming oak of the door, and the flame of the fire within. "The other side, Gregor McFarlane! There was more written on the other side!" the voice thundered. "Six items appear on the other side of the paper. You put me in the position of having to apologise to these Stevenson people." His yellowing teeth were bared behind the thin, drawn lips. "I'd appreciate it if you would take more care in the future." He dropped the invoice disdainfully on Gregor's desk, and about-facing, marched to his domain.

"Sorry, Mr Benton. Sorry!" Gregor held the paper his face red and miserable.

Jamie was devastated. "My fault, Gregor. Very sorry."

"Never mind, Jamie. Keep the old bloke from falling into a coma. Just forget it. All in a day's work." He leaned over and picked up the ringing telephone. "What? *What?*" His red hair seemed more up on end than normal while he shouted into the phone, and he ran his hands through it. "The chimney's on fire? How long? Ten minutes? Burning for ten minutes. For God's sake! Keep calm, Prue. Just keep calm. I'll be home in five minutes. Take the baby next door." He replaced the phone. "My chimney's on fire!" He announced to the three or four people whose eyes were on him. He picked up his jacket and knocked at Mr Benton's door.

"Sorry to disturb you, Mr Benton. Phone call from home. From Prudence. Domestic crisis. Got to go home."

"What kind of crisis, Gregor?"

"Fire. Chimney on fire. Prudence is having a nervous breakdown. Got to rush!"

"Of course, Gregor." Mr Benton stood at his door looking serious. "Hurry home. Phone me when you can."

The distraught Gregor flew out of the office, and Jamie and Mina looked at each other. "How awful for Gregor and his wife! And they have a baby, too?" Jamie enquired solicitously.

"Yes. Little Jack." Mina's face was resigned. "Don't worry, Jamie. It's situation normal as far as Gregor's concerned. His life is just one crisis after another. Just adds to life's rich tapestry." She pulled the cover over her typewriter and smiled at him. Taking out her powder compact, she dabbed at her nose, and applied some bright red lipstick at the same time saying. "I'm going to the Palais tonight. Sandy and the Stranglers are playing. They play bebop. Do you dance, Jamie?"

"I haven't danced much lately." He felt embarrassed at the thought.

"My boyfriend, Charlie and me, we love dancing. We go three nights a week. Do you like Johnnie Ray? I've got his latest record, "Somebody stole my Gal." It's terrific."

"Yes, I've heard it. It's very good." He left his desk and wandered over to the window to look down on the great open gates of the warehouse. "This is the fastest-passing day I can ever

17

remember. It's been great." He tidied his desk and smiled at Mina. "Thanks for your help."

"You're welcome. It was a quick day. That's the best kind of day at work." As she spoke, Mina tidied her desk, throwing unwanted sheets of paper in the waste-paper bin. "So, you think you're going to like working here?"

"I think I will." Jamie smiled.

"It's okay. Only now and again you'll find it's the craziest place in Glasgow."

A minute later, at five o'clock exactly, the oak door opened and the boss appeared. "Phone call from Gregor. The fire brigade has gone now. All is well. Fire is out." He looked at his watch. That's five o'clock now, folks. I shall retire to the Three Bells. I have to meet a customer there. Mina, be so kind as to phone Mrs Lindsay and say I shall be home for my evening meal by seven o'clock."

He passed grandly through the office, his dark overcoat highlighting the pallor of his face. He carried a black, rolled umbrella. "Good night, all. See you tomorrow, Jamie, I hope."

"Yes, yes, Mr Benton."

"Well done! Well done!"

Jamie looked at Mina, unable to think of a remark.

"Well, that's him off on time, as usual. He'll be well oiled by seven o'clock. Mrs Lindsay is his landlady. He's a bachelor. Comes from Aberdeen. He's got no family in Glasgow. Lonely old soul, I'd guess."

She made the phone call and they put their coats on. See you at eight-thirty in the morning, Jamie. Good night!"

"Goodnight, Mina. Enjoy your bebopping."

"Can you do it? Bebop I mean?" She had turned to smile at him.

"You can show me how tomorrow at lunchtime, Mina."

"Right!"

By the end of the month, Mr Benton informed Jamie that, as his work was satisfactory, and that he would be put on the permanent staff. He was elated. A steady job, and working beside Gregor, who kept him permanently amused was a godsend. They became firm friends and when Gregor heard Jamie raving about trumpet solos and so-and-so's improvisation he became caught in the enthusiasm of his colleague and Jamie invited him to his home one Friday evening to hear some jazz.

"My mother will be out at a whist drive, so we can play the records loud."

"Friday night, fella? Dunno!" Gregor's brows furrowed. "Usually take Prue on a pub-crawl, Fridays. Have a bite to eat, you know. Baby-sitter comes on a Friday."

"Well, bring Prue along."

"Really?"

"Maybe she'd be bored."

"Not a bit of it. She loves music and fun. Anything that resembles a party."

Mina joined in. "Hey, Jamie. I'll lend you my Johnnie Ray record, and I've got 'Rock around the Clock.'"

"Thanks, Mina. That'll be great. You and Charlie can come if you like."

"No we're booked up. But you and Gregor have a great time."

Jamie looked at Gregor. "I'll make some sandwiches. And maybe we could rise to a bottle of gin or some beer or something."

"Great idea, J. Listen I've seen your eyes stray to young Maggie in the typists' room, she of the large bosom." He illustrated his remark with his hands. "How about asking her to make it a foursome."

Jamie paled. "I don't know, Gregor. I'm a bit out of practice. Anyway, she's probably got someone she goes out with already."

"Well, just ask her. Go on! I'll tell you what. I'll give her some invoices to put in order and tell her to pass them on to you. She'll have to come to your desk with them, and I'll call Mina outside on a pretext. That'll give you a chance to chat her up."

At the approach of the shapely Maggie, Jamie felt his heart quicken. Instead of the calm, world-weary, twenty-three-year-old he wished to appear, he was hot and bothered, and tongue-tied like a sixteen-year-old. She handed the invoices to him.

"These are for you, Jamie. You wanted them in alphabetical order, Gregor said."

"Yes, thank you." Her breasts were round and full inside her white lace blouse. A little posy of violets was pinned to the collar and her earrings, too, were violets. They picked up the colour of her eyes. Her lipstick was pink and shiny on her perfect mouth. He smiled broadly at her to keep her there for a second longer. It's about three weeks you've been here now, Maggie, isn't it? How do you like it?"

"Oh, it's fine. They're teaching me to type. It's my first job, if you don't count odd jobs in the school holidays."

"Really?"

"Yes, my dad wanted me to study to be a dentist, but I couldn't bear the thought of all those years of scrimping and scraping to get through university, so I got a job here in the meantime. I'm learning a lot. I like it."

"You've just left school?"

"Yes. In June. My parents are mad at me for not going on with my education, but we can't all be brain-boxes and swats. I suppose I could have done it, but… well, I've made my choice now." She shrugged, smiled and turned in her ballerina-type shoes and walked to the door. "See you, Jamie."

He jumped up. "Wait a minute, Maggie. Would you like to come to a party? Gregor and Prue are coming up to my place tomorrow evening. Do you like jazz? I'm going to play some of my jazz records. Have a drink and so on. Would you like to come? Oh, and Mina's lending me some of her rock-and-roll records."

She looked uncertain, but answered, "Sounds fun. Trouble is the other girls in the typing department are going dancing and they've asked me along."

His face fell. "Well, think it over. I'm sure you'd enjoy it."

A dazzling smile crossed her face, so that Jamie had to look away to hide its effect on him. He looked up shyly. "You'll think about it?"

"I have thought about it, Jamie. I'll come. What time?"

The front room had been polished and a bright coal fire burned in the grate. On a side table, covered with a red checked tablecloth, stood sparkling glasses, plates of sandwiches, bottles of beer, a bottle of gin and some bottles of tonic water, lemonade and orange juice. Mrs London had gone out to her whist, warning Jamie to keep the sound down, and he was in a state of great anticipation as he put on his first record, "Twelfth Street Rag."

From the minute the three guests arrived, dancing as they came into the room, his party went with a swing. They joked and laughed about almost everything. They danced to the toe-tapping music, changed partners and danced again. The sandwiches and drinks went down as the party progressed, until, towards the end of the evening, they calmed down a little, and Jamie put on a dreamy version of "There will never be another you." Jamie held Maggie close, and Prue and Gregor, too, moved like young lovers to the mellow music. In a sweet, uncomplicated way a mutual feeling had grown up between Maggie and Jamie.

"Great party, Jamie!" Gregor winked at Jamie, his face a study of alcoholic contentment.

"Yeah, right, Gregor!" Jamie danced with his face close to Maggie. "It's been a great night. We must do it again, sometime." By eleven when Maggie had to go home, Jamie had the old, starry-eyed feeling he remembered from his teenage days that suggested he might be ever so slightly in love. He walked home with her, and when they reached her block of flats, he put his hands on her waist, saying, "I must see you again."

"You will see me again, dopey. You'll see me on Monday in the office."

"Not before that?"

"I'll see you on Monday. There's just two days in between." She gave him a flirty sideways glance. You'll last until then, for sure."

"Two long days," he answered in mock despair.

She was delighted at her conquest, and touching his hair said, "You have lovely golden waves in your hair. Under the street light it just glows."

He pulled her closer. "You're truly fantastic. Everything about you."

"Oh Jamie. You're crazy. But I must tell you; you're a great dancer. I've never enjoyed dancing so much. I didn't know I could do that jitterbugging. Your records are just terrific too."

"You like jazz?"

"Sure, I love it. It was a real fun evening. I don't think I ever stopped laughing. You and Gregor are so funny when you get together."

"Yeah, he's a great guy. A laugh a minute."

She giggled. "Everything seems to happen to Gregor. He's so accident-prone, and Prue just looks on in amazement at his stupidity."

"He's crazy about her. She's quite a looker with that black hair, and what a shape! She pretends to be kind of cool towards old Gregor, treats him like an idiot, but if the truth were known, he's really extremely intelligent, and she looks up to him for that — in spite of his long gangly legs and that hair." He laughed, "Those corkscrew curls! Anyway, he's been very good to me since I started in Rodger & Russell's."

Maggie giggled again remembering Gregor's attempts at jitterbugging. "Those long legs of his, Jamie! They look they're made of rubber. It was such a fun night. I really enjoyed myself."

"That's the way life should be, you know, Maggie. Wouldn't life be great if it were just one long party like tonight."

"You're dreaming, you idiot. Ninety per cent of life is struggle and strife. People wanting you to do what they want, follow their advice — do what they tell you."

"Well just listen to life's little victim! The voice of experience!" Jamie shook his head and looking into her young face said, "You know, Maggie, maybe with you around I could turn the tables on life, make it into ten per cent of struggle and ninety per cent fun." He kissed her quite chastely on her almost virgin lips, and gently drew her body close to feel her soft curves blend into his own hungering body. "Goodnight, Maggie. It's been wonderful. I'll dream about you, sweetheart. See you!"

"Good night, Jamie. I had a very nice time." She turned and ascended the stairs without looking back.

Chapter 2

"I tell you…" Gregor's face was animated, his voice high and excited, "…everything's free! A night at the theatre, the meal, and as much booze as you can drink." He eyed Jamie across their desks, his face frank and incredulous as he told his tale, and taking another swig from his coffee cup, fleetingly wishing he hadn't stopped smoking again. "It's the best thing about Rodger and Russell's. Once a year, they push the boat out. I've been to three, and I tell you, Jamie, each one's better than the year before."

"What theatre?" Jamie asked.

"Oh, the Pavilion, usually. You know, a pantomime — the first house of the 'Five Past Eight Show.' What a show!"

"Yeah!" Mina agreed. "Last year it was a wow! We laughed till the tears ran down our faces. My Jerry loved it. We look forward to it all year. Rodger and Russell's are the envy of all the other offices around for their great night out."

"Tell you what, Jamie," Gregor had found a cigarette butt in his pocket and was lighting it. "Prue and I will meet you in town about five-thirty, so we can have a drink together before the show. You and Maggie. You're still seeing her?"

"We've had three dates. Gone to the pictures three times. She is a nice girl, but I don't know, she's a bit young for me, you know," he whispered to Gregor, "Strait-laced, you know. Goody-goody!"

"Oh, they're all like that at first. Feel it's their duty to show how pure they are. You'll just have to work at it, mate," George whispered back.

"Yeah, if you say so."

"Speak to her about it today. Just in case she partners some other bugger. There's a few have got their eye on her — if I weren't married, I tell you, Jamie boy, you'd have some competition."

The great day of the annual beanfeast was approaching, however, things for Gregor took a wrong turn when the phone rang in the office and he answered it. "Rodger & Russell's Steel Tubes, can I help you?"

It was Prue. "You'll have to come home Gregor. We've got mice in the house. I opened the oven door and two mice ran out. I'm dead scared! You'll have to come home and deal with them. I can't go into the kitchen."

He hissed down the phone, "Oh, not now, for God's sake, Prue. I can't leave the office. I'm very busy."

"But what will I do? The baby's hungry and I'm too frightened to go in there to get his food." He heard her inflated sobbing, and little Jack crying in the background.

"Oh, *okay*! I'll see what I can do. I'll try and slip away. Keep calm! I'll be home soon." Gregor banged down the phone. He looked round the office trying to control his frustration, mentally counting to ten before he spoke. Jamie sat opposite, his head held low, trying to look sympathetic to his friend.

"Women! Never get married, Jamie boy. It's hell on earth, believe me. Look!" He glanced at his wristwatch. "It's nearly lunchtime. I'll just slip away. If old Benton's looking for me, tell him I had to go for aspirins or something. Probably need them before the day's out, I'd say."

"Something wrong at home?"

"Bloody mice in the bloody oven. Would you believe! Women! Bloody useless! Bloody women!" He left the office, still cursing, his red curls bouncing on his high forehead, his coat tails flying behind him. On reaching home he found Prue cowering behind the kitchen door, clutching the baby, tears of hysteria not far away. He opened the door of the kitchen, stamping his feet to scare the mice, and banging the oven door with a poker to make sure they would flee. He set two mousetraps and then put the kettle on for a cup of tea.

"I think we'll have to get a cat, my love." He found another fag end and was attempting to find a light for it. "I'll see if I can get us a cat. That would chase them. Come and sit down, love. I'll make us a cup of tea. You'll be all right," and he took the baby in his arms, kissing him fondly.

"Oh, a cat might be bad for Jack. It might sit on his face while he's asleep."

"For God's sake, Prue. Get a grip of yourself! Hundreds of people have cats. They're bloody harmless."

"Don't swear at me, Gregor."

"Don't swear!" His loud voice frightened the baby who started bawling loudly. He handed him to his mother. "I'm the laughingstock of the office. I can't get my work done for you phoning, 'Come home, Gregor, there's mice in the oven! Come home, Gregor, the chimney's on fire!' Next it will be, 'Come home Gregor, my drawers have fallen down!'"

This last remark brought the tears and sobs from the girl. "Well that's it! I can't stand your vicious tongue any longer. I've had it! My mother tried to warn me what men were really like. Bullies every one of you! She told me you looked the self-centred type."

"Bully? Self-centred? If you were any use at all as a housewife, we wouldn't be in this mess. You can't manage anything yourself. I can't be at home and out earning a living at the same time. Your mother will say I caused the Second World War next!" He watched her mesmerised as she strapped the baby in the pram and put on her coat. "What are you doing?"

"I'm taking Jack on the bus to my mother's. I can't stand you, or this infested house any longer."

"Don't be silly, Prue. Come on, I was just a bit angry." Gregor was alarmed.

"You get angry too easily, and Jack and I have to listen to you and your foul tongue, Mr Perfect!" She was almost screaming now. "Well, no more! You're just a fool! That's it, a born fool!"

"I'm a fool?" He followed her down out of the house and into the street, his face contorted with frustration. "Why am I a fool? At least I'm not terrified of some harmless little mice."

She swayed along the street in high dudgeon, her red high-heeled shoes clippetty-clopping on the pavement, and her red handbag swinging from her shoulder as she pushed the pram.

Gregor cupped his hands to his mouth and bellowed after her "And at least, I don't set chimneys on fire!" A few heads popped out of windows to stare at the crazed man with wild-red hair. He stood oblivious to the neighbours, rooted to the spot as he watched his fast-disappearing wife, until she rounded the corner, headed for the bus stop and the solace of her mother.

Next morning, seated miserably at his desk in the office, Gregor waited until Mr Benton was busy elsewhere and made a phone call to his mother-in-law. His stomach was churning as he heard her voice. "Prue's not up yet. I'm giving the baby his breakfast. My girl's exhausted, and you, shouting and swearing at her doesn't help matters. She was quite ill last night after your abominable treatment of her."

"Ill? What's wrong with her?" He tried to keep his voice low so that the office people wouldn't hear him.

"You find out. I have to go. The baby's crying." She slammed down the phone, and Gregor put his head in hands, misery engulfing him.

Full of the joys of life, Jamie appeared throwing down his newspaper and hanging up his coat. "You'll never guess my news, Gregor. Maggie's going to be my partner at the office 'do'! God, I can't wait till Saturday!"

"Christ, the office do!" Gregor looked up at Jamie and put his head back in his hands.

"What's up?"

"Prue's left me!"

Mina and Jamie stared in disbelief.

"We had an argument and she's gone back to her mother."

"Oh," Mina jumped up. "I'll get you a cup of coffee."

Gregor lit a fag.

"You're smoking again?" Jamie's face was suitably solemn.

"Yeah! Three weeks I was off, and now I'm smoking like a lum. A house full of mice and no wife. I'll have to get a cat."

"I'll go with you, if you like, to the cat-and-dog home. You get cats for nothing there."

Mina came in with the coffee. Malcolm, the office boy, arm in a sling, face doleful, stopped to stare at the distracted Gregor.

Gregor stared back trying to take in Malcolm's bandaged arm.

"What's wrong with your arm, Malcolm?" He hoped he had found someone in a worse plight than himself.

"Oh, I was playing nine-pin bowling last night. I've done something to my wrist. It's very painful. It's the third sport I've tried my hand at. The fat boy slumped down in a chair after looking round to see Mr Benton was not about. "First a golf ball in my eye, then my knee done in at football, and now this. Everything I try turns out to be a disaster. And I can't get anyone to be my partner at the night-out. I've just got no luck!"

"Tell me about it, Malcolm. My heart bleeds for you, I *don't* think. You don't know you're bloody living!" Gregor sat up and began moving papers about when Mr Benton appeared.

The boss man shouted from his office door, "Malcolm. Take this letter to Rabbie in the warehouse." He looked round. "Everyone all set for the annual shindig? Mr McTavish is coming from Head Office, and the director, Mr Green, and their wives are coming too, of course. They all just love the Glasgow pantomimes. You three are all set with your partners?" They nodded dutifully.

"I, of course will be unpartnered," he said in a gloomy voice. "But that's just how it goes. One can't have everything," he announced pompously. "Work has always come first with me." He scanned the papers on Jamie's desk until Malcolm returned from his errand, when he sniffed disapprovingly on noticing that the boy's trousers were too short for him and that a good stretch of red socks was showing beneath them. He looked at the boy's arm in the white sling. "You have a partner, Malcolm?" he enquired lugubriously.

"No, Mr Benton."

"Well, see what you can do, boy. There surely must be somebody spare in the typist room. There's dancing, you know after the meal."

"Yes, Mr Benton."

Gregor flinched under Mr Benton's critical stare, and gave him a plastic smile.

"Got a baby-sitter, Gregor, for the little one?"

"Yes, Mr Benton. All fixed up."

"Good, good." He studied Gregor's work over his shoulder. "Our Mr Green from Head Office took quite a shine to your wife, Prue, last year. He'll want a dance with her, this year, no doubt. Right, carry on, carry on!" he ordered. "Invoices are two days behind. Lots of work to be done! Work to be done!" and he escaped again into his den.

"Mr Green from Head Office! Lecherous old bastard. Took a shine to Prue. That white-haired old money-bags would go for anything in skirts. Poncy old bugger!"

"You're really cheesed-off today, Gregor." Jamie said. "You are not yourself at all."

"I know I'm a pain in the arse. I can't live with Prue without fighting, and I'm miserable without her and the baby."

"We'll go to the cat-and-dog home tonight, anyway, Gregor and pick up a cat. At least that's a positive step."

"Yeah, positively entrancing, Jamie. I can't wait!"

That evening, they took a black cat home to Gregor's empty flat. As they gave it some food and milk, it eyed them with malevolent suspicion. "No gratitude, that's your trouble, mate," Gregor told the cat. They shut it in the kitchen, their minds on a sandwich and a beer in the local hostelry. "Do your worst now, cat. Kill. Kill, you clever animal!"

"You'll have to call it something," Jamie said as they left the apartment.

Gregor thought. "I'll call it Harry after my mother's brother. He was an evil-looking black-haired bastard, too. Yes. Harry. Good name." Jamie nodded in puzzled agreement. 'Harry, the cat?' Sounds good."

From the pub, Gregor went to the telephone and once again tried to speak to Prue. At last she came on the line. "What do you want?" She sounded very severe.

"I want you to come home."

Silence.

"I've solved our mice problem."

"How?"

"We've got a lodger, now. It's a cat. He's called Harry."

"What colour is he?"

"Black."

"Oh!"

"And the chimney-sweep's coming tomorrow, so no more chimneys on fire. The fire brigade will be relieved."

"Yes, that's true."

"How are you feeling?"

"Not great."

"What's wrong?" There was a pause.

"It seems I'm almost five months pregnant, I didn't know."

"Pregnant?" he shouted down the phone, so that the whole pub looked round.

"It's his wife." Jamie assured the customers.

"Oh!" They smiled and went back to their conversations.

"I'll catch a bus to your mother's. I'll be there by about half-past eight."

"OK!"

Gregor put down the phone and stared blankly at Jamie. "Congratulations, Gregor" Jamie said, "Another baby? That's great!" and to the barman, "Bring us two large whiskies, please."

"Jesus!" Gregor was shell-shocked.

"To your growing family, Gregor. Remember your troubles are only little ones."

"Christ, I've got to face the old war-horse, my mother-in law. She'll be warming up with her advice. 'Stop smoking! Stop drinking! Time you had a better job, my boy! When are you getting a car? So-and-so's got a television set, you know! When are you and Prue getting one?' I can hear her now."

"Never mind. You're right there in the thick of it, you're a lucky man!"

"Exactly what am I in the thick of, Jamie?"

"Oh, you know, life. You've made inroads on the great wall of 'out there', you know, 'other people' — you've got relationships. You're really living, Gregor."

Gregor made a face. "You're havering, man."

"No, really." Jamie gulped at his whisky. "You've thrown yourself manfully in there. You know, Gregor, the other day I met an old tramp, you know a real down-and-out, smelling of wine, stopping passers-by and begging for money. In Argyle Street it was, and he said to me, 'Lucky man! Money in your pocket, and places to go. See me! See the world! Ah canny catch it.' And, you know, Gregor, I can't get that old tramp's words out of my head. Sometimes the world is hard to catch, you know. But you with a wife and soon two children, I envy you."

"Oh sure, I'm awful well-off, what will it be like with two children, and a cat, and a lot of bills to pay, and a very bad case of nervous debility." He held up his whisky. "Look, I'm shaking!"

Jamie put his arm on Gregor's shoulder. "You go and bring her back. That's what she's waiting for, a knight in shining armour."

Gregor looked down at his shoes. "Do my shoes match, Jamie?" He felt his head swim with the quick downing of the whiskies.

"Yes, they're fine. Very nice."

"And my hair?" He took out a comb and tried to tame the corkscrew curls while looking in the bar mirror. "Have I got a bus fare?" He checked his pockets.

"Good luck, Gregor. See you tomorrow."

On the evening of the office Christmas night out, Jamie and Maggie met Gregor and Prue in a pub in Hope Street, O'Malley's Bar. There, the doting Gregor stood, a happy smile on his face, intimately close to his wife, Prue, as she sat, beautiful and poised, on a barstool, mistress of all she surveyed. His silly smile was partly due to alcohol, and partly due the fact that he and Prue had escaped from the domestic scene, and were out on the town. It seemed almost like the days when they were courting.

"When's the baby due, Prue?" Maggie looked in awe at the self-assured mother-to-be.

"Oh, not till the end of May, so I don't show too much yet." She patted her stomach.

They all looked at her bulging breasts. "Well, maybe just a little," Gregor said, his eyes travelling from his wife's bosom to her eyes as she returned his loving look. The two were completely reconciled. Sweetness and light had returned.

"How's Harry doing, Prue? Catching any mice?" Jamie smiled in reminiscence of the malevolent-looking cat.

"Oh, he's great. The baby loves him, and he caught two mice this morning."

"Great!" Jamie turned to Maggie. "Do you hear that, Maggie? Remind me if I ever ask you to marry me, we'll have to get a cat first thing."

Maggie was startled at this throwaway remark.

Gregor shook his head good-naturedly. "You've embarrassed our little schoolgirl, Jamie. Look, she's blushing."

Jamie put his arm around her. "Drink up, my sweet. We're going to have a great evening. I'm going to dance you off your feet."

At the theatre, they laughed almost non-stop at the comedians with their local jokes. The pantomime lived up to its tradition of colour and fun, together with the titillating lines of near-naked dancing girls. The staff of Rodger and Russell were in celebratory mood when they reached the hotel where the meal would be served.

They felt like lords and ladies as the food was brought in, food that was richer than any these young folk were used to, the austerity of the war being so recent in their memories. The free-flowing wines and spirits, for which generosity their firm was renowned, put from their minds the daily grind of the nine-to-five routine in the office.

"You were right, Gregor. This annual night-out was worth waiting for! Here's to Rodger and Russell's. May God bless them and all who sail in them!"

"Yes, Jamie, and we have the Christmas and New Year holidays to look forward to. Can't be bad, mate! Can't be bad!" Gregor gave a smile that encompassed the whole room, and placed a fat cigar in his mouth, which he proceeded to light from the candle burning at their table.

The band started up, and soon Maggie found herself being spun round the dance floor in a fast-paced quickstep. Jamie was a good dancer and while he danced he sang in her ear, "Toot, Toot, Tootsie, goodbye!" And they spun, locked in each other's arms, as if they had been practising dancing together for years.

The four friends sat down when the evening was well advanced to have a quiet drink together, when two middle-aged gentlemen stopped at their table. "You four seem to be having a whale of a time." It was the big boss, Mr Green and another of the directors, Mr McTavish. "And how are you, Prudence? As lovely as ever, I see."

"I'm fine, Mr Green. Just fine." She gave him a wide smile. "Long time, no see."

"Quite, my dear, and this is our bright, young man, Gregor." He shook hands with him, and turned his attention to Jamie. "And this is…?"

Jamie stood up. "Jamie London."

"Pleased to meet you, Jamie. Settling in all right, are you? Mr Benton's told me about you."

"Yes, fine. It's a pleasant place to work." Jamie swayed slightly from the cocktails he had drunk, and his words were just slightly slurred.

"Not too pleasant, Jamie, I hope." The director thought he had made a joke.

"And who is this young lady?" Mr McTavish leered over Maggie, his white hair and moustache and round pink face contrasting with the young freshness of the object of his attention.

"This is Maggie, my girlfriend."

"Maggie, eh?" McTavish took her hand and his eyes swept over her. "Would you do me the honour of dancing with me, Maggie." Mr Green did likewise with Prudence, and the two boys were left a bit shocked at this take-over. The dance seemed to last forever, as they watched their partners being sweet-talked by the two old codgers.

When the music stopped, their boss, Mr Benton stood at the microphone, and gave a little speech, telling everyone what wonderful evening they were all having. "And now, since I believe we have a first-class singer in our company, I will ask Jamie London to sing for us, this evening."

"For God's sake, Gregor. Did you do this?" he hissed through a false smile.

"Not me, mate. But you'd better go and get it over with. They won't take no for an answer."

The band slowly picked up on Jamie's old-time jazz classic, and within a few seconds they were making music together as if it had been rehearsed. Jamie ended on a loud, rhythmic line, to the cheers of his audience, with "Tomorrow night at the Darktown Strutters' Ball." a big smile creasing his good-natured face. Maggie, clapped along with the rest as they called out "More! More!" And Jamie went into another old favourite of his, "I can't Get Started with You."

He looked straight at Maggie as he sang, and she drew envious looks from the other women. Still the audience had not had enough, and he finished with a heartfelt rendering of: "You Stepped Out of a Dream."

Jamie sang directly to her, and she tried to keep a poker face, but her blushes gave her away.

Within a few weeks, Jamie and Maggie were inseparable, and were talking of becoming engaged. They planned to go on holiday the next summer with Gregor, Prue, Jack, and baby Melanie, to Ireland, to a place advertised in the newspaper, and to buy the ring there. After months of anticipation and planning, of scrimping and saving for the great event, the time for the summer holiday arrived.

With great excitement they set off on the ferryboat crossing to Belfast, from there to travelled to a remote location in the south of Ireland. The bus dropped them with their luggage, Gregor carrying Jack, and Prue pushing a pram, at a little white-painted hotel, in a village called Dunlough, sixty miles from Dublin. Weary from their long journey, they were shown into a small guest sitting room, while Mrs O'Hare, the proprietor's wife, called a boy from the kitchen to carry up the bags.

They relaxed in a sitting room beside a well-polished dark-wood fireplace, where shelves held gleaming brass ornaments. Victorian photographs of grandfathers and grandmothers vied for attention with a collection of ornamental plates. The four of them felt relieved to find that their random choice of a holiday had turned out to be a welcoming and comfortable place. With her broad Irish accent, Mrs O'Hare made them welcome, and very soon turned her attention to Jack and the tiny baby, Melanie.

"Oh, what a lovely little chap we have here!" she cooed. Just eighteen months now, Jack was turning into a fair-haired little angel, gurgling his own language, and pointing and smiling at everything, alert and bright as a button. She pronounced the baby to be, "Gorgeous." when the child clasped the fat finger she held out to her. "Well, you are all welcome to our corner of Ireland, and to this house. I hope you have a good holiday, and that the weather is kind to you. Patrick will show upstairs, now, and I'll see you all at dinner." She bustled out and left them to make their way up the staircase from where they could see the dining room with its tables covered in white tablecloths, set for the evening meal. "Hurry along there, now. I know you'll be tired after your long journey from Scotland, but the dinner will be served up in one hour, so you haven't much time."

Gregor and Prue, and the children were given a nice room overlooking the street. Maggie and Jamie were put in separate rooms, on each side of the long upstairs corridor. At the end was the O'Hare's room where, at night, the door was left open and the mirror of a great dark wardrobe gleamed at them. Both Maggie and Jamie thought it must be a deterrent, Mrs O'Hare's "magic eye" that watched out for adventurous, young, single people who had thoughts of wandering in the middle of the night.

Their dinner was a hearty, three-course meal, plain cooking and plenty of it. Bowls of potatoes and other vegetables were set on each table to accompany the generous portions of roast pork. Used as they were to years of austerity and food scarcity after the war, these guests in Ireland thought that everything Mrs O'Hare sent out from the kitchen to be mouth-watering and the portions of meat to be lavish. From their places at table, they caught glimpses of large hams, hanging from the rafters in the old-fashioned kitchen.

In the morning, they were served ham and eggs, and the quality and quantity of the platefuls were unbelievable to them. Sliced by hand, the ham was served in flavoursome half-inch thick slices, and the eggs were freshly laid. After breakfast, the four of them and the children went out walking, and found sand dunes and a deserted beach where they relaxed in the sun for an hour or so, while the bluey-grey waves broke on the shore. They paddled at the edges of the water with little Jack, a bundle of excitement at the new sights and sounds of the place.

"What do you think we'll have tonight for dinner?" Gregor was skimming a stone along the water as he spoke. "I tell you, folks, I could take a lot of Mrs O'Hare's cooking." He dropped down onto a sandy hummock. "Hope it's the same as last night. I could eat that roast pork to a band playing!"

It was Saturday evening, and the dinner was steak pie followed by apple sponge. Then, while they were being served cups of tea to finish the meal, Mrs O'Hare dropped the bombshell. "Breakfast's earlier tomorrow morning, everyone, so we'll be in time for the eight-thirty mass. So remember, half-past seven if possible." So saying she left them alone in the dining room.

"Mass?" Gregor whispered. "Does she think the whole world is Catholic?"

"Listen, the lady really means what she says! I don't think she'll be pleased if we don't go to church."

Gregor decided for them. "Oh, just let's all go. It'll be an experience, and it will be good for our souls. It will be worth it, if she keeps coming up with these fantastic meals."

Next morning, in an incense-filled, old stone church, the four of them with the children sat bemused as the fat old priest chanted away in Latin. They stood when everyone else stood and tried to sing the hymns along with the rest of the congregation. It was as if a spell was cast on the people, as their eyes followed the rich robes of the priest as he moved on the altar beneath the many vases of fresh summer flowers.

Most of the congregation had weather-beaten, country faces, contrasting with the coloured woollen hats of the women, and dark suits and white Sunday shirts of the men. Some of the girls wore berets, pulled far down on their heads, making them look like dull-witted peasants of a past age. There was the occasional better-dressed, fine-featured lady or gentleman, no doubt the local gentry, praying devoutly throughout, all the time telling their rosary beads while gazing on at the age-old ceremony. The visitors felt like interlopers at this theatrical scene. They listened, bemused, as the people fervently answered the priest's calls with their well-learned Latin responses, and watched amazed as the circle of bread, the Eucharist was held aloft by the priest, and the congregation went on their knees before it.

It was with a feeling of relief that Jamie, Gregor and the girls spilled out of the church into the bright summer sun. Gregor immediately lit a cigarette. "Unbelievable! Did you see the faces of those people? They were in a different world!"

Maggie said, "They're lucky to have such faith."

"I suppose so." Prue sat Jack on the end of the pram. "But it's so kind of medieval, really. It was like no church I've ever been in."

"Let's go down to the pier and fill our lungs with some good sea air. Give us an appetite for Mrs O'Hare's lunch!" Jamie was walking ahead away from the church.

"Trust you, Jamie," Maggie said. "Always thinking of your stomach."

They capered about for a while, watching some skin-divers whose boat was just a few yards out from the pier. "Let's get back to the hotel." Prue was getting impatient with their larking about. Jack's getting hungry." Jamie kicked hard at a pebble as a last farewell to the scene. They watched in horror as his shoe flew off, soared above the choppy water, and disappeared into the brine.

"Good God, Jamie! You'd do anything for a laugh." Gregor stared unbelieving.

"These are my only shoes!" Jamie was devastated and stood at the edge of the pier staring down at the choppy water, while the others creased up with laughter. There was nothing else for it. Shamefaced Jamie had to limp back to the hotel where he found himself the centre of interest and merriment.

"Don't worry, Jamie. It'll be all right!" Mrs O'Hare's great chest heaved with laughter. "You're the first visitor we've had, who's kicked his shoe off into the water, and I can't help but laugh. You're in such a state!" She looked at his shoeless foot, and put her little fat hand on his shoulder. "I'll ask Seamus, the bus driver, to get you a pair in Sandy Rock. He'll do it for you tomorrow. What size do you take now? Sure, he'll do it for you tomorrow. He does all the errands for the village."

"Size eight."

"Black or brown?"

"Brown."

"Right!" She just managed to keep her chortling to herself. "I'll tell him, but you'll have to stay around the place until tomorrow afternoon when Seamus gets back".

Maggie and Jamie were a bit worried at this turn of events as they had secretly planned to take a trip to town on the following Saturday, to buy an engagement ring. Jamie had saved just £30. However, they were too young and happy to let this bad luck affect them, and once the shoes were purchased by Seamus, and miraculously found to fit, they took off the next Saturday morning, visiting a few small jewellers before choosing a ring with two small diamonds in a twist.

Beaming with happiness, they returned to the hotel, Maggie now claiming the limelight. She shyly held out her left hand for the ring to be admired, and the dinner that evening turned into a party. Jamie and Maggie were toasted in wine by the half-a-dozen other guests, and at the end of the evening, Mrs O'Hare treated the company to a tremulous version of "This is My Lovely Day." She sang with great sincerity, her voice being uncommonly good. When she had finished, to much applause, she turned to the four of them said, "You two boys can take the girls to the dance that's on tomorrow night in Limban. I'll look after the children. They'll be fine with me. What do you say?"

"It's very kind and thoughtful of you, Mrs O'Hare. Are you sure?" Gregor said, humbly.

"Sure, I'm sure! So that's that settled. You'll have a great time. It will make a nice end to your holiday."

The following evening, they were treated on all sides to the customary village greeting, "There you are now!" and pushed into the back of a car that looked as if it had only a few miles left in it. Six of them took off amid much jocularity, driving along winding roads in the semi-darkness. After about twenty minutes, they knew they were near the event when they heard loud accordion, drum and fiddle music as the ancient car drew to a stop at an old farm building.

Maggie and Prue stood by the door in nervous anticipation gazing at the wild scene. Ruddy-faced young men and women thumped their way from one end of the room to the other at terrific speed. That all were enjoying themselves there was no doubt. Soon, the visitors found themselves joining the crazy throng of floor-bashers in reels and whirls, the wildness of which left anything to be seen in their native Scotland in the shade. The music was fast and furious. Each dance seemed to last for an age so that at the end, they flopped breathless on the chairs that lined the side of the room.

Never allowed to sit out for even one dance, the girls were snatched by the unflagging farm boys and whirled on to the floor as the other couples skirled around them. Jamie and Gregor were manoeuvred outside to the back of the building, where, lit by the lights from the windows of the hall, could be seen the whisky bottle being passed from man to man, where they stood in friendly groups taking a breather from their athletic capers in the hall. Then back they trooped for another half-hour of frenetic Irish reeling. There was none of your customary close-held quickstep, or smoochy waltzing. Here the sight of the girls as their bosoms jumped and swung, and their long curly hair flew out behind them, seemed to be sufficient excitement for the young bachelors' Saturday evenings.

At the end of the exhausting night, the two couples were squeezed back into the rattly old car along with at least six others, so that there was no room to budge an inch. They were a happy, giggling party in their closeness, the smell of whisky mingling with the perfume of the girls. Everyone was just tipsy enough not to care about the state of the car or the driver as they careered along the dark, country road. By some unseen guiding hand, they arrived back at the village and Mrs O'Hare's hotel at two o'clock in the morning, tired and happy with their unforgettable revelling.

Chapter 3

Mrs Fisher looked at the wedding dress, a mass of white tulle and lace as Maggie pulled it out of the box. Holding the lid of the box was Nancy, Maggie's sixteen-year-old cousin, a smaller, slighter girl, with dark brown curls. The two girls in their high-heeled shoes and fashionably full, flared skirts, spread the dress out for her mother to see. Then Maggie held the dress against herself, and this brought tears to Mrs Fisher's eyes.

"Oh, if only your father could have been here for your wedding, Maggie. He would have been so proud and happy."

"I know, Mum, but there's nothing we can do." She wished her mother would snap out of this eternal grieving and yearning for her late husband. It had been almost two years now.

"What colour will I wear, Maggie:"

"I'm not sure, Nancy. Pink? Pale blue? We'll go for your dress next Saturday. You can come too, Mum. Lewis's have got some lovely bridesmaids dresses. And you can look for an outfit for yourself."

Mrs Fisher looked startled. "I suppose so," was all she said.

"Yes, mother, the wedding invitations are going out next week, and the wedding cake is ordered."

Her mother dried away the tears. She felt strangely lethargic in the face of all this activity. "I know I'll have to get a new suit." She looked down at herself, seeing clothes she had been wearing for too long. I know I need to smarten myself up, but I just can't be bothered shopping. I'm sorry I'm no help to you, Maggie."

Putting the dress down, Maggie went over to her mother's side. "I'm not leaving the country, mother. I'll still be your daughter even when I'm married. You'll see me regularly."

"Nineteen is so young to get married — to be tied down. You were so good at school, Maggie, and we had such ambitions for you. It's a shame you gave it all up."

"Oh, I'm doing what I want to do, Mum. Jamie and I are very happy together. Anyway, you got married when you were nineteen, didn't you?"

"You're right. And your dad and I were very happy. But, mind you, I never got the chance of an education. However, I should be happy for you, and I am really." She stood up wearily. "I'll make some tea."

Jamie's and Maggie's wedding was a fairly quiet affair. Rivalled by her cousin, Nancy, so pretty in her in rose-pink taffeta, Maggie was a radiant bride, her thick dark hair showing up against the virginal white of her gown and veil.

The honeymoon was a week in a little hotel in Port Patrick on the Solway Firth. They were the only guests there, it being out of season, and they were given VIP treatment by the indulgent proprietor. They roamed the village and cliff-tops, engrossed in each other, needing no one else.

They returned to start their life together in a tiny, rented room. Then their luck changed, and they were offered accommodation in the bottom half of a town mansion, a large house which was owned by friends of Jamie's family. The people had a dance hall in the centre of Glasgow not far from the house, and Jamie and Maggie were to occupy the semi-basement flat. It had a large Victorian kitchen with an old-fashioned range and a coal fire, which heated the water for the whole house. For the cost of keeping the fire going all the time, they lived rent-free. It was a happy situation, and Jamie suggested that they should have a house-warming party.

Maggie was excited at the prospect. "The front room is ideal for a party. With that low ceiling, and the lovely polished wooden floor, we could take up the rugs for dancing, and then there's the window seat. It could hold about six people." To Jamie's amusement she chattered on excitedly. "A party would go with a swing." She spring-cleaned the house, moved furniture and

42

cushions in her enthusiasm. In those days, in the first flush of their marriage, the smallest events gave them great happiness.

"I think I'll paint the bathroom, Jamie," Maggie announced one morning. I found some paint in the cellar. There's some black paint and some pink."

"You've never painted anything in your life, Maggie, you idiot."

"It's easy. I'll do it. I've seen my mother paint things, often."

"Well, you can do that and I'll decorate the cupboard that leads off the sitting room with the magazine bathing beauties I've cut out." Mmmm… Brigitte Bardot! What a body! And Sophia Loren." These will make a nice backdrop to the booze. We can use it for a bar."

A week or two later, all preparations made, the awaited day dawned. Guests arrived, the girls in their wide full skirts, held out by stiff taffeta petticoats, and the boys in narrow trousers and bright sweaters. They danced non-stop, rocking and rolling the night away. The best dancers gave demonstrations of the new steps, and in the interludes, when the dancing stopped, Jamie was asked to sing for them some of his jazzy favourites. He was having a whale of a time, passing round drinks with great aplomb. Everyone was getting tight and more outrageous in their antics as the night wore on.

Around eleven o'clock, they caught some of the older generation, the people who lived in the flat above and some of their friends, trying to peek through the chinks of the curtains on the basement windows, from the pavement outside. The throbbing beat of the dance music and the full colourful skirts of the girls as they whirled around in their frenetic jiving, left the older people amazed. The new fashions in clothes, with total disregard to wartime austerity and economy, the new music and style of dancing, the free-and-easy attitudes of the young people seemed to have spread like wildfire through the country, and to have left them in some wartime backwater. It was, to them, like the dawn of a new era.

"Play 'Manhattan' for me Jamie. It's my favourite," Maggie pleaded. They were standing together beside their large, highly polished radiogram, which Jamie had bought second-hand from a hotel which had gone bankrupt. It sat in splendour in a corner of the low-ceilinged room. They danced close together, delighted with the success of their first party, and so happy in each other.

Maggie sang with feeling the well-known tune about New York, the Bronx and Staten Island, even though the streets of Glasgow were just outside. "I love that tune, Jamie."

"I love you. You're the loveliest girl in the room."

"Yeah, yeah," she mocked.

"You are. You're the loveliest girl in the whole world, you are. You've made me so happy. By the way, did I tell you that I'm thinking of buying a car?" He saw her amazed expression. "What do you think, sweetheart? Do you think it's a good idea?"

"A car, Jamie? I don't know. Can we afford it? It's sounds a great idea, but you haven't even passed your test yet."

"A mere detail. I'll pass the driving test all right." He put his arm around her. "Then we'll be on our way to being toffs. I've wanted a car ever since Dad died and we lost everything. We always had a car of sorts when I was young. First, Dad had a motorbike and sidecar, then he bought a Hillman. We went everywhere in that car."

Maggie smiled at him. "Well, it would be fun right enough."

"I'll never get fed up with driving you around and showing you off to the world. Can't you just picture us — not a care in the world, taking off for picnics at the coast? I'll be the envy of all the boys."

"Well, we will have to share it with Gregor and Prue."

"Oh, I know. But it will be a start to have a share in a car."

She nodded and looked at her young husband frankly. "I've got a plan of my own to help us in the future. I'm going to try for a job at that restaurant that's recently opened around the corner. It's called Mario's. They're advertising for a secretary. I thought I could do it, and it would be a change from Rodger and Russell's."

Jamie returned her gaze with a doubtful stare, but he was distracted from making a reply by the party starting to break up and some of the guests preparing to leave.

Some were a bit unsteady on their feet. As they waved goodbye, the girls covering their curls with scarves, their skirts bouncing around their calves, their flat ballerina shoes pattering on the quiet pavement, they sang tipsily little snatches of tunes, still in their heads from the music of the party.

In mock sadness, they sang their ways along under the lamplights seeking out taxis or buses to take them home. Gregor and Prue returned to his mother's house, a short walk away, where they had left the children. On sitting down, Gregor fell asleep, and his mother and Prue decided they'd best roll him into bed.

"My God!" Mrs McFarlane exclaimed as she saw the black paint from Maggie's toilet seat, which had made a perfect ring around Gregor's buttocks. "What kind of house do these people keep if their toilet seat's as black as that."

"It's only black paint. Maggie painted the bathroom the other day. It couldn't have been dry." Prue had to laugh at the apparition and soon Mrs McFarlane too saw the funny side of it. Gregor's father rose from bed to come to find out what the commotion was all about. The three of them stared at sleeping Gregor in disbelief at the perfect black ring decorating his bottom. Eventually he woke and sleepily eyed the three faces looking down on him. Pulling up his trousers he managed to slink away unable to grasp their interest in his nether regions.

After checking her face in her handbag mirror, and taking a deep breath, Maggie entered the new restaurant. Mario Pacitti's father had come to England from Italy in 1918 when Mario had been ten, and made a living selling ice-cream from a handcart in the streets of London. When Mario was twelve, to please his devout mother, he had been sent away to college to study for the priesthood. The boy had been unhappy, having had no real vocation, and at fifteen he got himself a job as a commis waiter in one of the big London hotels. There he learned the catering trade and after ten years the hotel chain offered him promotion to head waiter if he were willing to uproot and move to their top restaurant in Scotland, The Jacobean Room, in Glasgow.

Now, at the age of fifty-one, he had saved enough to open a place of his own. Beautifully designed as a restaurant-come-night-club, the place was expertly run by this cockney-Italian, and on the city's famous Sauchiehall Street, had opened in a prime location. Daily it was gaining in reputation for delicious gourmet food, Mario overseeing the work in the kitchen and being responsible for buying only the best ingredients. With the country's recovery and the wish to make the austerity of post-war rationing a fading memory, there was a fast-growing trend towards eating out. This new interest of people in food, coupled with the novelty, for ordinary people, of dancing afterwards, just like in the pictures, made Mario's restaurant a winner from the start.

The staff were picked with great care. His chef, Frederico was volatile, but an artist in the kitchen. His waiters were top-notch. In the office was a middle-aged lady, Mrs Greig, a careful bookkeeper of the old school, and Diana, a girl of eighteen who worked as her assistant, and now Mario had decided he needed a secretary. He liked the look of the brown-haired Maggie as she presented herself for interview.

"You do shorthand as well as typing, Mrs London?"

"Yes. I have a certificate for one hundred words a minute."

"Good! And you are used to answering the phone?"

"Of course."

"You think you will like working in a restaurant? It gets a bit noisy and chaotic at times."

"I'm sure I'll like it." Maggie looked around. "It's a lovely place."

"Thank you." She had said the right thing to the proud proprietor. "And your husband? What does he do?"

"He works beside me… for Rodger & Russell's Tubes. He's in the office too. We've been married for only two months."

"I see."

"Your advertisement for a secretary seemed a challenge, and just the sort of thing I've been looking for. I'm sure my boss, Mr Benton, would give me a good reference, if I asked him."

"Well! I can't think why I shouldn't give you a chance. You seem to have the right qualifications. How about we try each other out?"

"That would be fine, Mr Mario."

"When can you start?"

"Two weeks. I have to give notice to my present employers."

"Two weeks? That's a long time in a restaurant." He looked at her young face and made up his mind. "Oh well, we will wait for you. That will mean you will be starting on Monday, the seventh then, at nine in the morning." He stood up and, smiling courteously, showed the girl out of the tiny office. He watched her figure and shapely legs as she made her way down the stairs to the street, and felt pleased with that morning's arrangement.

From the start, Maggie loved the work. The waiters teased her, and she had to keep a close watch on their wandering hands whenever she found herself alone with any of them. But the job was a lot of fun. After the first few weeks, Mario called her into the kitchen to speak to her.

"We need a receptionist-cashier for the restaurant. There's more money in it, and I think you are just right, Maggie, for the job. Only it will involve working in the evenings, with afternoons off. What do you think?"

She felt tempted. She knew there was music at night, and well-dressed people to see. It sounded like an exciting prospect, and "receptionist" sounded good. "I'll have to speak to Jamie, Mario. He might not like the idea."

"Of course, Maggie. You must speak to him. You bring him in to see me if you like. I'll put his mind at rest and let him know that you'll be safe in our hands."

That evening, Jamie listened to Maggie's description of the interview, with mixed feelings. Her face was rapt as she described the lovely pink tablecloths, and the bandstand and the bright flashes as the waiters flamed the food in front of the customers. "I'd love to try it, Jamie. I think I would enjoy seeing how the other half lives. And it would mean a bigger pay cheque. You can pick me up at night when I finish at eleven."

"Well, I'm not too sure I like the idea of all those waiters hanging around you, but I suppose you know what you're doing. If you really want to give it a try, we could certainly do with more money."

It was a step into the world of night-time entertainment, which did not seem like work to Maggie. Her clothes had to be more glamorous, and she took more care with her hair and make-up. In the rosy candlelight of the restaurant, at her round desk she sat in a spotlight where the waiters handed her the bills to add up and to work out the percentages for their tips. Pencil-slim in the new fashionable long tight skirts, her hair in a short curly style, she was the beauty of the establishment.

"I can't play the music for looking at you, Maggie," the bandleader, Matt McLeod was leaning over her rounded desk leering at her shape. "You should be in pictures." Flattered, she flashed a broad smile at him and tried to carry on with her work. "The next song we play is for you, sweetheart."

The band started to play "Moonlight and Roses," and Matt ogled her from the bandstand as he sang. Mario came out of the office, and seeing this he was not pleased. "Listen, my dear, just you keep your eyes on your bills and money and pay no attention to that Romeo type. He flirts with all the girls, the kitchen women, the barmaids. Don't believe a word he says." Mario walked up and down in front of Maggie's desk fuming at the bandleader for flirting with his protege. Although not a tall man, Mario cut an imposing figure, his rotund build fitting well into the evening suit he wore, his thick black hair perfectly groomed. He was proud and fiery, and very Italian, and he fascinated the young girl.

Now he was looking fondly at Maggie. "Are you hungry, my dear? Can I get you a sandwich or something from the chef? It's a long evening for you on your own here."

"No, thanks, Mario, I'm not hungry. I'm loving this job. It's exciting to see all the dresses of the women, and everyone having such a good time. And the band is really good." She saw the doting look in his eyes as he listened to her, and she blushed to the roots of her hair.

"You are a very nice girl, my dear. You must not be taken in by types like Matt. He is only out for a good time."

As the weeks passed, Maggie found that Mario seemed to spend more and more time around her desk, helping her with the bills and money, and fending off any waiter who had more than a few words with her. At night he helped her lock up the money, and got down her coat for her. She knew that he had some feeling for her, and she found herself hot and bothered under his brown eyes. "You are like the daughter I never had, Maggie. Your husband, Jamie, is a very lucky man." Such open compliments left her tongue-tied. Without doubt she had a growing affection for him. She would have said that he was like the father she no longer had, and whose affection she missed greatly, but she felt unsure of herself, and kept her thoughts and feelings to herself.

One evening when the meals had all been served, Frederico, the chef slipped into the bar, still in his tall hat and long white apron, for a drink. On passing Maggie's desk, he stopped, his large black eyes taking in her shapely young figure. "Would you like a lift home tonight, Maggie? It would be a great honour if you would sit in my car. You would add a touch of class to it." And he kissed his fingers theatrically as he tried to hold her eyes with his. "Do you know you are very beautiful? You are a beautiful flower. You are wasted on that husband of yours."

"You are drunk, Frederico, and my husband is none of your business. And you have a wife and children. Go away! I am a married woman."

"Ah I could make you so happy, my darling!" His eyes were looking closely at her neck, her bust and down to her legs. "I would never let you out of my sight if you were mine." Frederico glanced up to see Mario approaching, whereupon he straightened up swiftly, and bowing and smiling ingratiatingly, walked backwards, giving a token salute to his boss.

Mario scowled darkly at the tall man, and turned his back on the comic antics and attempts to placate the big boss. "Take no notice of that scoundrel, Maggie, my dear. He will keep you off your work and lead you astray if he gets a chance. I should not give him permission to leave the kitchen."

However, the chef did not give up. Any time Maggie had to go to the kitchen, or pass him, he would look at her as if she were the Mona Lisa. "You are really stupid, Frederico! Keep your eyes on your work. You will burn your steaks!" But she could not help laughing.

"He's in love with you, Maggie. He talks to us in the kitchen of nothing else but you." The spotty commis chef was laughing too.

The chef came and stood very close to her. "Is Jamie coming for you this evening? I could easily drive you home. I just want to talk to you. I love to watch your lips move over your beautiful teeth."

"No, Frederico!" She moved away, totally out of patience with him. "Jamie'll be here all right."

"He's not good enough for you. You need a big man like me, Frederico." He spoke with an Italian accent, and pushed out his ample chest to show his strength. "Frederico knows how to love a beautiful woman." He leaned down so that his great eyes were close to hers and whispered, "And listen, *chérie*. I give you a piece of advice. I don't like how you let Mario hang around you all the time. I know he's the boss, but he's an old man. He must be fifty."

"I don't let him hang around me. He's just showing me how to do the job, that's all. He's kind and friendly to me! He shows me how to do the bills in the restaurant, and how to talk to the customers and so on."

"I bet he would like to show you more than how to do the bills, sweetheart!"

"Really, Frederico, you're impossible."

"Well, listen, my little flower, he has a very jealous wife, and if she catches him playing around, she will not be happy, I assure you."

"Oh, go and fry your sausages, Frederico, and leave me alone."

Next day at lunchtime, Maggie had a cup of coffee with Mrs Greig and Diana in the office.

"How is Jamie doing this weather, Maggie?" Diana was a small, thoughtful girl who admired Maggie, and her ability to deal with the lady-killer Italian waiters, and to move around the restaurant with confidence and composure.

"Oh, Jamie's fine, Diana. He's talking about buying a car, for holidays and things."

"What a nice, good-natured young man he is." Mrs Greig had stopped poring over books to drink her coffee. "Not many husbands would sit at home while their wives were out at night."

"Well, I am working after all, Mrs Greig, and we need the money. We're saving up to be able to buy our own house. And my money keeps the wolf from the door, you know." Maggie was on the defensive. She felt guilty that she enjoyed being in the restaurant every evening, all dressed up. "Anyway, Jamie's very busy in the evenings himself, you know. He and Gregor are busy trying to start up a little printing business of their own. They've bought a home press — you know, they do printed stationery and things like that. They also write popular songs. Jamie's quite talented, musically. They've written a couple of songs which they're trying to get published."

Mrs Greig stood up and straightened down her tweed skirt. "Well, things are very different from when I was a newlywed. Then we stayed at home and started to raise a family. My husband would have been horrified if I had worked at night in a restaurant. What age are you now, Maggie?"

"I'll be twenty-one next year."

The older lady lifted the tray of coffee cups to return them to the kitchen. "You just think about what I've been saying, Maggie. Someone may come along and steal that nice husband from you, if you're not careful."

When the door closed, Diana whispered, "Never mind that old busybody, Maggie. She came out of the ark. How are you getting on with Mario?"

"Shh! He might come in. Oh, he's really nice to me. I think he's such a kind man. He's always there to help me with the restaurant bills, and keeps that Luigi, the lech, away from me, and of course, Frederico."

"You're so lucky, Maggie. Oh, to have a figure like yours, and your good looks. You look so confident as you greet customers. I bet you could get a job anywhere, now."

"Rubbish, Diana. I was just in the right place at the right time. And Mario has been very patient training me and showing me the business."

"I've seen the way Mr Mario looks at you, Maggie. He's gone on you."

Maggie blushed and looked down at the papers on the desk. "I'd better be getting out to my desk," she said.

"I think you're a bit gone on him."

"He's very nice to me. I can't help liking him. And sometimes I'm thinking about him… I can't stop thinking about him, Diana. Oh, I know it's wrong and I shouldn't, but he's such a… a gentleman."

"I know, Maggie. I can see the attraction. But he's so old. Past fifty. He's probably just a father substitute."

"He's so… so… commanding, confident and…"

"Rich?"

"Oh, Diana. Don't suggest that! That's not fair!"

"Well, promise you'll tell me tomorrow what happens tonight. The restaurant is fully booked. There's a party of Danish students have booked a table for eighteen. There should be fun and games."

Maggie laughed. "Every night is different. You never know what new antics the customers, or the band, or even Luigi and Frederico will get up to."

"Just as long as Jamie turns up at eleven to take you home. That's the main thing."

"Oh, don't worry I'm not a silly little girl. I can look after myself!"

But that evening as Maggie got herself ready, she turned to look at Jamie as he tried to improve the picture on their new little television set.

"I think I'll give up the job in Mario's soon, Jamie. It's not as good as I thought. And the hours are long. I'm fed up with constantly having to go out again every evening." Maggie looked at her husband's back, her face serious and bothered.

"Give it up?" He turned round. "But we've saved almost enough for a car. We need the money, Maggie."

"Don't you think you and Gregor will ever make some extra money with any of the schemes the two of you think up?"

"Our latest song is definitely a winner. "When I think of you." it's called. Gregor is getting it arranged, and just maybe our luck will be in. We're going to send it to some of the singers on the radio. If it sells, then you could stop work and maybe we could think about starting a family."

"Oh, it will never happen." Maggie returned to her mirror and her eye make-up.

"No, really. I've been round at his house three nights this week. We've worked hard on the song, and the home printing might just take off. There are six orders for stationery. Prue's got a job in the evenings as a receptionist in the George Hotel. She finishes at eleven like you. Maybe we could visit them tonight and see how they are getting on."

"But it would be nearly midnight before we got there."

"Never mind. It will be fun."

"Okay! I'll have to go now, Jamie, or I'll be late. See you about eleven."

He came to the door, and hugged and kissed her. "Don't work too hard, and don't let those waiters push you around. It'll all turn out all right, you'll see."

The evening was a whirl of diving and weaving waiters, dance-band music, steaks being flamed dramatically at the dining-tables, to the delight of the diners, intent on having the time of their lives.

The Danish students, noisy and outrageous sat at a long table on the left of the room. Fourteen tall, blonde Nordic young men, thumping the table, and harassing the four blonde female students in their party, anytime the opportunity arose. They whistled and called after Maggie if she moved from her desk. Maggie ignored them and looked over to Mario who was seriously displeased. He came and stood alongside Maggie, eyeing the Scandinavians with distaste.

"That's the last time I take their booking." His romantic Italian soul was outraged. "No woman is safe around these wild men."

Like Viking warriors, with their fair, youthful looks, when they stood up to call a toast, they towered above Mario and the waiters. They were throwing back pints of beer with amazing speed.

"I wonder when they'll ever go home," Maggie sighed.

Jamie appeared at eleven o'clock and stood where the rosy glow of the table-lights and the perfume from the dining room hit the door. Maggie waved to him between counting cash and adding up figures in the dim light. The band played "The Dark Strutters Ball" and Maggie said to Mario, "Jamie's arrived. He's over at the door waiting for me, and what do you know, they're playing his song."

"He sings?"

"Yes, he's a great jazz singer. Brings the house down."

Mario quickly approached Jamie. "Maggie tells me this song they're playing, Jamie, she says you sing it pretty well."

"Oh, sometimes I sing it, yes, Mario. It's a good jazz number."

"Will you sing it for us now?"

Before he could protest, Mario had taken Jamie's coat and was leading him up to the bandleader. "Play it again, Matt. Our friend, Jamie here would like to sing along with your music."

When Jamie's voice filled the room, the diners sat up and took notice, and in no time were swinging along with the catchy tune.

At the end, Matt shook Jamie's hand smiling all over his face, and everyone, including the band clapped and cheered Jamie's swinging version of the old song. Mario, standing beside Maggie, was also applauding. "I can see he has a lot of charm, Maggie and a very good voice, your Jamie,"

"Yes," she replied wistfully looking at her husband. He's really a lovely person. It's just that... if only...."

"What?"

"Well, he never gets anywhere. He doesn't seem to have any ambition. I mean everything's got to be turned into a joke."

"And this little girl would rather have someone who wanted to make money, or be somebody?"

"Sure! Making ends meet seems to take all our energies. I mean, I love this job, and Jamie works hard, but we're never going to get our own house and be able to have kids, the way we're going on."

"You are young, my dear. You have plenty of time."

Jamie stepped down from the bandstand. Smiling broadly, he approached Maggie and Mario.

"Well done, Jamie! That was sensational!"

"He writes songs, too," Maggie beamed.

Mario turned serious. "Look, Jamie. I suppose you could use a little pocket money. I'll speak to Matt and see if you can sing a few songs with the band on Saturday nights, perhaps Fridays too. Does that appeal to you?"

"I'll say it does. Great, Mario!"

"Well, the customers like you, so we'll give it a try. See Matt about the kind of songs you can do."

Later at Gregor and Prue's, they talked excitedly of the future, and the songs they would write, and of how rich they would be. Eventually, Maggie and Jamie decided to walk home, and waved from the street to the third-floor window to their friends. It was two o'clock in the morning, and the city was very quiet.

"I've forgotten my black sweater, Jamie." Maggie gesticulated to Gregor who was still at the window, to throw over the garment. They watched as the sweater came sailing down from the window, and then stopped on a branch of the only tree for miles around. It hung there while the four of them looked on speechless.

"I'll come down and help you get it down." Gregor opened the window and called to them. Tipsy and tired they looked up at the tree. "Tell you what, Jamie. If you stand on my shoulders, you would be just at the right height to pick up the damned thing."

"Oh, do you think you can do that, Gregor? That would be good. I really need the sweater for Monday morning."

"Take heart, Maggie. Gregor to the rescue!"

He crouched down against the great tree, and Jamie stood on his shoulders, then they slowly stood erect all the time with their hands on the tree. A giant, almost twelve feet high now swayed about in the road, and a late-night bus almost crashed into the pair, the top-deck passengers thinking they must have drunk more than they had thought when they found themselves gazing into the eyes of the giant, red-haired Gregor.

After ten minutes of this stunt, they gave up, their hilarity getting the better of them, and Jamie and Maggie said goodnight while the sweater remained in the tree. Next day, the lady who occupied the first floor leaned out of her window, and picked up the sweater, and, with a disapproving, "Normal people do not throw clothes out of window, Mr McFarlane. I hope you and your wife won't make a habit of it," before handing it over.

"Sorry, Mrs Smethers. It seemed like a good idea at the time."

She shook her head and closed her door, saying, "That's your trouble, Mr McFarlane — too many good ideas." Gregor trudged up to his flat mumbling to himself, "Too many good ideas, Mr McFarlane! Too many good ideas!"

Chapter 4

The January wind was keen, and it blew Maggie along Sauchiehall Street and through the muffled-up shoppers until she reached the doorway and the warmth of Mario's restaurant. This was her new world — a world apart from the grey stone buildings and overcast skies of Glasgow. Brass sparkled on the doors of the hallway and large potted plants had been artfully placed around. It was new, modern, stimulating. Taped music played semi-classical tunes and immediately the girl felt her mood lighten. The whole place was like a stage-set, and she relaxed in the warmth of this decorated palace. Mario stood looking on at the waiters, while pink tablecloths flapped in the air, as the room was set up for Friday's customers. With his tanned Italian complexion and dark hair, Mario appeared exotic in comparison with the Scotsmen Maggie was used to. Dressed in a well-cut dark suit, his nails manicured, he stood holding a sheaf of papers, the epitome of the efficient manager.

"Many bookings for lunch today, Mario?" Maggie hung up her coat in the office.

"About twenty or so, so far." He hesitated on his course to the kitchen just long enough to answer her. "But this evening we're fully booked." He stopped in his tracks and returned to join Maggie at her desk. "You look fresh and pretty, as usual this morning, Maggie. How are you? Is your Jamie going to sing for us tonight?"

She beamed back at him as she arranged her desk. "Oh, yes. He's quite excited about it. You'd think he was appearing at the London Palladium to hear him. Every time I see him he's studying song sheets." Mario listened to her enthusiasm indulgently, his eyes playing on her face as she spoke. "He's got four numbers rehearsed already, and they sound great. I hope it goes well." She gave a nervous smile to convey her apprehension.

"Of course it will. You have nothing to worry about. You have brought me luck, Maggie and I've a feeling he will, too." He looked at her in a fatherly sort of way "And every day you are getting to know the business better."

"Yes, well…" she blushed. "I can count the bills better now when there's a push on. You get used to it."

He smiled, patted her hand, and caressed her bare arm. "I am very pleased with you." He rushed away on his rounds, almost bumping into Diana as she carried out a pile of neatly typed menus.

"Hi there, Maggie!"

"Well, look at you, Diana. New shoes. Stilettos? My goodness! You look miles taller." Diana raised her left hand up to Maggie's face in display, her face shining. "You're engaged? How lovely, Diana! Congratulations!" She hugged the other girl.

"Yes, I've kept it a secret for three weeks now. And I have another surprise for you, Maggie. I'd like you to be my bridesmaid. Well, matron of honour."

"Oh, no. Really, Diana?"

"Yes. It's to be on June the eighteenth. Will you do it, Maggie?"

"I'm really honoured, Diana, and flattered. If you want me to, I'll do it. Oh, Gosh! I'd better go on a diet or I'll spoil the photos." They both giggled at the thought of the whole event.

Diana said, "I'll have to watch you to make sure you don't steal the show."

"Nobody steals the limelight from the bride, don't be silly, Diana." Maggie put down her pen and bill pad, and becoming serious said, "You've been so tolerant with me, Diana. I know I've been a pain at times, mooning around and telling you how wonderful I think Mario is. Maybe I can do this for you to make up for me being a pain in the neck. If Jamie knew how often I talk about the boss, he'd be devastated"

"I know you love Jamie really. You're just a bit star-struck on Mario — you know — the older man. He's so well… powerful."

Diana gave a broad smile as she shook her head. "And he's certainly gone on you! But, for goodness' sake, Maggie, he's an old man. You'll get over it." Diana sat down on the edge of the rounded desk, her eyes on the slim waiters as they hurried to lay cutlery on the tables. "Listen, can you manage to come shopping with me tomorrow afternoon. I've seen a beautiful wedding dress in Pettigrew & Stephen's. You could tell me what you think of it."

"Gosh, what colour will I wear?"

"Well, maybe pink, or midnight blue. That would be mysterious. Give you a sophisticated air that always interests men. Not that you need that! What do you think?"

"We'll look tomorrow afternoon, Diana. I can't wait to see your dress. Who's going to be the best man?"

"An electrician, Roddy Bell. He's John's mate at work. They're going to hire morning suits, I think. Oh, Maggie. It's so exciting."

"Where are you going to live?"

"At my parents' house to start with. But Daddy's talking about helping us to buy a little place."

"Lucky devil!"

"Well, if he's got any money left. He's just bought a Ford Anglia. He's thinks he's joined the upper classes now that he has 'wheels'. Any news about Jamie and Gregor getting a car?"

"No, not yet, unfortunately."

Mario returned to the scene of their tête-à-tête. "Right girls. To work! What is this? A mother's meeting? I have an important guest coming here soon. A friend of mine, Mr Valente is visiting us today. He's a very important man. Owns a lot of restaurants in London. I want to make a good impression on him. He's up from London for a few days. He wants to see my restaurant and how we do things." As he spoke he straightened cutlery and smoothed out tablecloths.

Diana took off to the office leaving Maggie gazing at Mario as he perfected the appearance of the room. "Your friend, Mr Valente sounds quite… quite efficient and a bit scary, Mario."

"Sure. Plenty of money." He rubbed his thumb and two fingers together to illustrate his point. Loads of dosh! We were at school together in Naples, long, long ago. He's opening a new place in London and is looking for some tips from us. His eyes will be everywhere, so look smart and pretty." He clapped his hands and rushed forward to greet the first of the lunchtime customers.

Dominic Valente proved to be an enlarged version of Mario. Darkly good-looking, and also in his fifties, he exuded power and personality. After warmly greeting each other, the two men sat down to lunch, talking very seriously throughout. Towards the end of their meal, Maggie felt their eyes on her as she wrestled with the bills while the impatient waiters stood at her desk. As they rose from the table, she heard Mario say, "Come and meet my little Maggie. Then you can see the beauty of the kitchens."

She stood up and leaning over the desk, shook hands. "Pleased to meet you, Mr Valente."

"Charmed to meet you, Maggie." And turning to Mario he said, "Where did you find such a nice girl, my friend? We don't have many as beautiful in London. *Bella! Bella!*" He continued to smile his eyes holding hers.

Mario smiled broadly. "Maggie is my little jewel. And she's efficient. Very clever, Dominic! Can add up bills like lightening, and keep the waiters, calm." Both men unashamedly studied the girl. "And she's a good girl, too. No time for guys who try to chat you up. Eh? Maggie."

There's no answer to this, Maggie thought, but she said, "Well, I try my best!" and felt that she must sound really foolish, and added, "You'll make me sound goody-goody — too good to be true." She smiled and tried to go on with her work.

Mario patted her on the shoulder, "Really, you know, Dominic. This little girl found me. Just walked in the door one day looking like a million dollars, and stole everybody's heart. Right Maggie?" She was embarrassed as Mr Valente's eyes held hers for a few seconds before he looked back at Mario and they moved on to the kitchens.

That evening was Jamie's big chance. At nine thirty he made his debut as a singer with Matt McLeod and his band. His voice was good and he carried the room along with him as he swung to the old jazz standards. He drew applause, which grew more enthusiastic with each number. At eleven-thirty, he stood, his face wreathed in smiles, his arm around Maggie, in the foyer of the restaurant. Departing diners congratulated them, as they waited to say goodnight to Mario.

"Move over, Frank Sinatra!" He looked down into Maggie's eyes. "All this and you get paid too. What a night, sweetheart! It was unbelievable."

"Well, you deserve it. You have a great voice. I was proud of you up there swinging away." And she stood on tiptoe and kissed her husband on the cheek. Mario with Dominic Valente came quickly out of the office together, and seeing the pair, stopped to speak to them. "This is my husband," she said shyly. "Meet Mr Valente, Jamie."

"I enjoyed your singing, Jamie. You have talent. Some of my favourite songs, too. You certainly can put a number over. It was a very pleasant evening."

"Thank you, Mr Valente. Did you have a good journey up from London?"

"Sure, came up by car." He turned to Mario, "Got my own driver, these days. It's fantastic." Then his eyes found Jamie's again. "I'm here to see how my friend here makes so much money." He laughed showing a mouthful of strong, even teeth. "And you have a very nice girl for a wife, Jamie. Lucky man!" He turned his attention to Maggie, and she felt a nervous shiver as his eyes searched her face.

Mario put his arms around Jamie and Maggie and moved them gently towards the door. "You go off home now. You both deserve a rest. It's been a great night. See you tomorrow, Maggie." They were being jostled by the customers, picking up their coats and leaving the restaurant. "Goodnight! Goodnight Jamie." In high spirits the young pair left, and the two restaurateurs slowly made their way to a corner table where they ordered a pot of coffee.

"A nice couple, Mario."

"Yeah. I like them."

"Your place is terrific." Dominic looked round appreciatively. You've made a good job of it. You've got a winner here, I should say, my friend."

Mario was flattered and smiled modestly, at the same time protesting, "It's not as big as your place in Chelsea or your first one, Ferrari's in Kensington. You're big-time Dominic."

The coffee arrived and there was silence for a few minutes, as they viewed the quietening down of the place, and watched the band pack up. Then Dominic spoke slowly and quietly, "What would you say, Mario if I asked to borrow your Maggie to help to open my new place in Albemarle Street?"

Mario was startled. "I'd say 'no'."

"Let me speak to her. It would just be for a few weeks, to help me to get things started, and a couple of other girls trained."

"You must be crazy, Dominic. She's a nice girl, and she's married."

"You like her, don't you, Mario?"

"Sure I like her. She's a fabulous girl." He took out a cigar, his face troubled.

If Vera finds out about her, she'll not be very happy, my friend."

"There's nothing to find out."

Dominic face was enigmatic, then a broad smile appeared on his face.

"What are you smiling about? This is stupid, Dominic. London is full of good-looking girls. You don't need to take mine."

"I want this one, Mario."

Mario's face changed. He was angry. "You can't just walk in here and take a young girl away. Anyway, she wouldn't go to London on any conditions. I know her. She's got too much sense."

"Let me speak to her. She might just be persuaded."

Mario puffed on his cigar. "You're a crazy man."

"You still owe me thirty thousand, remember."

Incredulous Mario took the cigar from his mouth. "You wouldn't?"

"Sure. I'll call it in. Business is business!"

"For Christ's sake, Dominic!"

"You agree to let me talk to her?"

"You can try, but I tell you, you are wasting your time."

Across the luxurious carpet a fashionably dressed figure in a greyish lilac suit was advancing towards them. From her ash-blonde hair to her expensive purple leather shoes she was groomed to perfection. Her face as she approached gave nothing away. She was neither happy nor unhappy. Her eyes were dark and serious.

Dominic quickly stood up, "Ah, Vera. What a surprise! Long time, no see!" He kissed her on both cheeks. "I was just asking this man of yours about you. How are you? What a pleasure! What a pleasure! You must be very proud of your beautiful restaurant."

She smiled a tight smile. "Good to see you, Dominic." He was holding out a chair for her, and Mario rose and kissed her cheek.

"This is a surprise, my dear. Friday nights you don't usually venture out. Would you like a drink?"

"Campari and soda, please, if the bar is still open."

"Of course! Of course!" Mario hurried away.

Dominic looked at her. "You like living in Scotland, Vera? You must miss all your friends in London."

"Oh I have some friends up here now. You know, Dominic, it's much more peaceful than the rat race in London. I go down about every second weekend to Marge and Derek. How's Myra these days?"

"Oh, she's in New York. Has been for almost a year. Nicki went first and she followed. She loves it there. Nicki's got a good job with a law firm. He may pay me a visit soon, or so he says."

"Not married yet?"

"Afraid not. Looks as if we're going to have to wait a while for our grandchildren."

"That's too bad, Dominic. I do miss London, sometimes." She lit a cigarette, then looked more serious. "I am trying to talk Mario into retiring back down south, maybe to the south coast. I'll talk him into it, someday. Right now, he just wants to make some more cash while he can."

"Sure, sure, my dear. We must go where the money is."

Mario returned with her drink. "You are late arriving, Vera. Your bridge game was finished?"

"Yes, I got Mary to drop me off, just to see you were behaving yourself." She sipped her drink and smiled. "Can't be too careful, you know!" She gave an almost imperceptible wink to Dominic. "I hear you have a singer now with Matt's band. You didn't tell me this."

"Yes, Jamie. He's good, too. Eh, Dominic?"

"Sure is. Got the crowd going tonight. A real nice personality."

"He's Maggie's husband, you know, Vera."

"Who's Maggie?"

Mario took the cigar out of his mouth. "You haven't met Maggie yet. She's the cashier."

"Really!"

"Yes, you should have been here an hour earlier, my dear. You would have met both of them. They're a nice couple. Agreed, Dominic?"

"Sure, sure. Very nice! Very nice!" Dominic lifted his bulky frame from the seat, the satin lapels of his evening suit gleaming in the glow from the table light. He took out a white handkerchief and wiped his perspiring face. "I have to go, Vera. Sorry to have so little time with you, but it's after midnight. I'd best be off. I'll see you tomorrow night, Mario… probably about nine."

Vera lit another cigarette. "When do you go back home, Dominic?"

"Sunday afternoon. My lawyer's with me. We've got to be back by Sunday night. He's back at the hotel. I don't know when I'll see you again, Vera, but I have to get back. I'm opening a new eating place in Albemarle Street."

"Good for you!" she said. "Too bad you're going back so soon. You could have come out to our place for a drink."

"Oh, I'm sad about that, Vera. We could have talked about the old days, but sorry to say it's impossible. I must say you're looking great, though. You haven't changed a bit, and still playing bridge?"

"Yes, three nights a week. But you may see me sooner than you think. I might also come here tomorrow evening to hear this Jamie. My curiosity's aroused."

Mario looked at her hard for a split second, then standing up he put his arm on his old friend's shoulder. "I'll walk with you to the door, Dominic."

Dominic whispered, "Is she keeping tabs on you suddenly, Mario?"

"Who knows? Maybe somebody told her about our new singer. She very rarely visits like this."

Dominic laughed. "Watch out. Remember Frederico and Vera used to know each other well. Maybe he told her."

"Yeah, anything's possible. Who understands women?"

The main kitchen of Mario's hummed with activity on the following evening. Frederico called out orders and the under-chefs, their tall white hats bobbing madly, worked fast, preparing for the heavy Saturday evening ahead. It would be a gruelling five-hour marathon of chopping, mixing, whisking, baking and grilling. Now it was six thirty and all was noise, movement and concentration.

Two men in evening dress moved into the space and broke the spell of frantic preparation. Frederico looked up to see Mario and a handsome, smooth-faced man of about thirty approach him leisurely.

"Frederico, I want you to meet Andre Ferri." The chef put down his large knife, wiped his hands on his apron and greeted the stranger. "He's going to be Assistant Manager."

"Yeah?" Emotional confusion rushed in on Frederico. Assistant Manager sounded ominous.

"Yes, I want you and Luigi and Robert to show him the ropes. For tonight, he will stay with me, just to see how the dinner-dance routine works. But on Monday he'll have some time with you in the kitchen. You can talk about menus and so on. Andre has experience in Manchester and London, so you can help each other."

"That's good," Frederico forced a smile, and as they started to leave, he gave Mario a long look, "Can I just see you privately for a few minutes, Mario? I have a problem."

"Okay! Okay, Andre, you go out and check the table-settings, and try the lights. We want a nice rosy glow about the place. Luigi, you go with Andre and give him a hand."

Mario retired with the chef to Frederico's semi-private cubicle off the kitchen.

"Who is this guy, Mario? What are you springing on us now? You said nothing about an Assistant Manager." His voice was indignant.

"It's been on the cards for a while. I discussed it with Vera. She wants me to train someone up so that we can go back to London, after Christmas. Besides that, she wants to go on a cruise. What can I do?"

"I am your cousin, after all, Mario. I know you don't want people to know that, but what about me? I thought I had a chance of taking over when things got going. I've worked with you for ten years now."

Mario paced around in the small space. "I know, Frederico, but…"

"But, I'm not reliable. Is that it?" Mario looked uneasy. "Just because I lost my temper once or twice."

"Lost your temper?" his voice was rising. "You nearly killed that kitchen boy."

"You never forget, do you? The boy has forgotten. He is my friend now. Amando would do anything for me."

"Yeah, I know." Mario's mouth was turned down, and he looked unseeing at the work going on in the kitchen.

"You could give me a chance if you wanted to."

"I can't, Frederico. There's your gambling, as well. Remember? How can I trust you with thousands of pounds when, in the past, you have gambled away all your wages." The accused was crestfallen and hung his head. "Your poor wife could tell a story or two, I'll bet. Poor Mary, she's had a lot of trouble from you."

"She hates me, anyway. You know that."

She's had a lot to put up with."

"What about Vera with you?"

"What about her?"

"Does she know how you're crazy about your little Maggie."

"Enough! That's enough! You know it's not like that." Mario turned to the door.

Demoralised, Frederico followed him, "Please, Mario. I'm older, now. I hardly ever gamble. I drink much less than I used to. Say you'll think about me this time. I could easily manage this place. I'd put everything into it. I'd work hard."

"You're a good chef. You work long hours. But you know yourself how you can lose the place at times. How about that five hundred pounds I lent you to buy a car? You lost that."

"It was stolen from me."

"It was taken out of your pants pocket in a brothel, you mean." Frederico was close to tears.

"Listen! It's Saturday. Valente is coming here again tonight. I've got enough to think about. Just get on with your work." Mario watched the chef wipe the tears from his eyes with the dishcloth, which hung to his belt. He felt sorry. "Okay! Okay! Listen, business is good. I'll give you a raise this week. And if you keep out of trouble, who knows, things might get better for you." He put his hand kindly on his old friend's shoulder. "Tonight is important to me. I want everything to be first-class." Frederico looked blankly back at him, unable to speak. "Listen we'll talk again about this next week. There's no time now." His face was strained and serious as he declaimed, "And to crown it all, my God! Vera is coming to hear Jamie sing."

"Vera is coming to the restaurant? I'd like to speak to her for a little while, Mario."

"Okay! If she turns up, I'll tell her to look in on you. You're all right, now?"

"I'm all right now." But he felt deflated and tired although the evening was just beginning.

Chapter 5

Diana stepped out of the shining, new car, just outside the entrance to Pettigrew and Stephen's, where Maggie stood waiting on the pavement. Her father drove off with a wave, to his bookie's shop, while the two girls teetered on their high stiletto heels through doors of the shop, making straight for the escalator to the Bridal Department.

The hours of excitement the girls spent there trying on bride's dresses were the greatest fun of their young lives. When the choice was made, the shop assistant drew back the curtain on Diana in the dress. She stood like a fairy princess on a little dais, a fake diamond tiara on her head, her thick fringe of fair hair gleaming under the lights.

"That's it, Diana. You look sensational! This is definitely your dress!" Maggie was enthralled with the sight. The assistant cooed and fussed around them and the sale was made. There was no way Diana wasn't having this film-star dress.

When Maggie's turn came to make a choice she picked out a bridesmaid's dress of palest blue, and, feeling happy, the two friends made their way to the tea-room, to calm themselves down with coffee and cream cakes.

"What a great morning, Maggie! And I haven't told you, yet. My father's treating us to a honeymoon in Spain."

"You're so lucky, Diana. What a great start to your marriage! Most of us have to struggle for everything from day one. Money is always a problem for us."

"Oh, come on, Maggie! You're not doing so badly. Now that Jamie's singing on Fridays and Saturdays at Mario's you must be a bit better off."

"Well we seem always to have difficulty paying the bills, and I worry about money constantly. Mind you, we're not as badly off as Gregor and Prue. They've got two kids now and they're always broke."

Diana gave a short laugh at the thought of the pair. "Oh God! Those two! They're always in some dire strait, but they're such good fun with it. It never seems to bother Prue."

"I know. The other day, at lunchtime, Gregor came round to borrow a fiver from me. I had just spent all my cash on some cheap, unskinned whiting at the fishmonger. All I could think of doing was to give him half-a-dozen fish to take home."

Diana giggled, "Oh, no!"

"I know it's funny." She looked round at the well-heeled ladies in the tea-room, eating their cakes and engaging in carefree gossip. "Poor soul, he left with the fish, and it was just as well, as his mother had come to visit, and there was nothing to eat in the house. He just handed Prue the fish, and she took them as though she had expected them all the time and proceeded to cook them! A close shave!"

"What a pair! They're too alike. One's as daft as the other."

"I know. I think Mrs McPherson often keeps tabs on Prue. She often visits unexpectedly about mealtimes to see what's going on. She thinks Prue's so much of a scatterbrain. Anyway they're getting out tonight. They're coming to Mario's for dinner and to hear Jamie sing."

"I wish we could come, but John plays football on Saturdays and then goes out with the team for a drink."

"Well, he'll give that up when you are married, won't he?"

"I hope so. He loves his team-mates. You know, there's no one like 'The Boys'." She made a face to show her discontent.

"He loves you, Diana. You'll see. He'll settle down."

"Oh, I expect you're right, Maggie." She picked up her handbag. "We'd better be getting home. Look at the time!"

When Maggie arrived at her flat that Saturday afternoon, a large, black, Glasgow taxicab was standing outside the door. Puzzled, she turned the key of her door to hear loud jazz music coming from the sitting room, and to see Jamie standing in the hallway ready to greet her.

"Who's the taxi for, Jamie?" she called through the music. Jamie came quickly from the sitting room, his face a study of good nature and happiness.

As he embraced her, she said again, "Who's the taxi for?"

"It's for us."

"What?"

"Gregor and I bought it this morning. We're to have it for the first two days, then Gregor and Prue will have a turn of using it."

"You mean this is to be our car? This is the car you've been talking about for so long?"

"Sure! Lovely isn't it? Gregor and I are going to clean and polish it tomorrow. It's out of date for commercial use, so we got it for fifty pounds. It goes like a bomb."

"I wish it would blow up like a bomb. How can I tell Diana and Mrs Greig, and all the others at Mario's, our car's an old taxi?" She sat down despairing "What make is it? They'll want to know."

"A Beardmore."

"A Beardmore? I've never heard of a Beardmore."

"Come on sweetheart. It's four wheels, isn't it? It will be fun. I want to take you out in it. We could go right now."

They went outside, and Maggie stared at the monster in distaste. Next to the driver's seat, there was an inset where luggage could be secured. "But I'll have to sit in the back while you drive!"

"So what! That doesn't matter." They drove around the city, Jamie proud and pleased with himself. Maggie, feeling a fool on an endless taxi journey, sat with face immobile, expecting a crash at any moment."

"Get over to Hampden Park, mate! They're crying out for taxis there." Another cab had drawn up alongside them at the lights. Jamie gave a little salute at the man, and turned round to grin, but Maggie looked away in disgust. They arrived back and Maggie stumped out of the car in a fury of frustration and humiliation. "I've got to shower and change for work tonight, and you're not taking me to Mario's in that thing."

"Don't be such a snob." Jamie was hurt and disappointed. He looked bemusedly at the old taxi, wondering what he had done wrong.

"Diana's father's got a brand-new Ford Anglia. Who ever heard of a Beardmore?"

That evening, when she arrived at the restaurant, the carefree look had gone from Maggie's face. She went to the kitchen to pick up a cup of coffee before the crowds started to arrive.

Rows of dishes, ready to be filled, were in place, and a slight lull was descending on the workers before the tyranny of the evening started, when waiters would be shouting orders and dashing around at high speed. Frederico was unusually morose, and hardly looked up from his little screened-off cubby-hole, when she came through the door. She wandered to the back of the kitchen, poured some hot coffee and stood thinking about what she would say when they asked her about the car.

Luigi came towards her. He was the same height as herself with broad shoulders and dark good looks, the best-looking chef in the kitchen. Maggie fumbled with her cup and tried to smile. She had seen him polish a car in the alleyway at the back and knew that cars were his passion. "How is our pretty little receptionist tonight? Stunning as usual." He stood very close, his eyes on her face.

"I have to go, Luigi. The first customers will be arriving any minute. I have to be at the door to say good evening. Mario will be looking for me." She put down her coffee cup.

"What is the matter, *chérie*? You look unhappy." He moved even closer to her, so that she saw his tanned skin with little droplets of perspiration standing out. His black curls hung around his face, and his eyes burned dark and soft.

"I'm all right, Luigi."

"No, you are not. Come to Luigi. Tell Luigi what is wrong." He put his arm around her and pushed his body forward in such a manner that she was suddenly aware of the danger of the situation. He pressed his large mouth on hers, and she felt him push even more closely against her, while his hands moved down her back to her thighs. She felt his hot desire and panic rose in her. Someone

72

would see them and think she wanted this. She pushed hard on the broad chest.

"Stop! Stop it, Luigi!"

"You're magnificent, Maggie. I have been watching you for weeks now. You drive me crazy."

"Just leave me." She pushed him away and rushed through the kitchen and through the swing doors into the restaurant, blaming herself for getting into such a vulnerable position. "Always it's my fault," she said to herself, bitterly. She arrived at the dining-room entrance still shaking, but hiding her discomposure as she smiled at the customers now crowding the foyer. "Good evening, sir! Good evening, madam!"

Gregor and Prue arrived looking like kids going to a party. Prue's smile was her best feature, her perfect, white teeth gleaming against her red lipstick. Tonight she was beautiful in a close-fitting, black dress and diamante necklace. Gregor in his best suit, pressed for the occasion, with his red curls springing up and his gaudy, red and yellow zigzag tie flapping around, was like a hen on a hot girdle with excitement at being out on the town. "I say, Maggie, do I look all right? They're not all in bow ties etcetera, are they?"

"No, no. It's optional, Gregor. As long as you have a jacket and tie on, you're all right. I see you have on one of your famous ones." She looked down at his shoes. "Suede shoes! Really, Gregor. You're not half with it tonight!"

"You can do anything but keep off of ma blue suede shoes." he sang and jived around. "You'll dance with me later on, won't you?"

"Oh, the hired help are not allowed to dance, I'm afraid, sorry Gregor." He raised his eyebrows in disappointment, and she relented laughing. "Well, you never know. Maybe just a little dance when no one's looking. Have a good time, the two of you. See you later!"

Soon the room was a hive of industry as the orders for drinks and meals were taken and the waiters got into their stride. Walter, the oldest of the waiters, small, fat and with a drink problem and a wobbly, rolling gait, kept a plate of soup next to the grill, from which he took a spoonful or two every so often. The soup was whisky, but the other waiters kept his secret, and he had got away with this comical practice for years. The band started up and a few seconds later a striking-looking lady, a vision in a long scarlet dress, walked by herself into the room.

A little stunned Mario greeted her with a polite kiss. "May I introduce Maggie to you? Maggie, this is Vera, my wife." The older woman watched the girl's face as Mario spoke, and read her as naive, but intelligent and extremely pretty. Maggie had not expected this meeting.

Her first thought was, *Attractive but old enough to be my mother*. But Vera's perfume and her expertly made-up face marked her out as a million miles away from the middle-aged woman who was Maggie's mother. She had the sophistication that leisure and money endow, and her beautifully cut dress made her figure youthful and curvaceous. Vera had seen pretty waitresses and receptionists like Maggie come and go over the years, and she had little to learn about straying husbands.

Slightly fazed and outclassed, Maggie stood back feeling less sure of her own appearance, while her eyes took in each detail of the new arrival. Mario led his wife to a side table, and sitting down with her, called to the waiter for two brandies. The two sat back as Jamie made his entrance and sang in his happy, rhythmic voice, "Sweet Georgia Brown", his arms swinging, and his fair waves falling over his boyish face. The diners tapped their toes and kept time with him and at the end of the song, called out for more.

"He's good, Mario." Vera's eyes were studying Jamie.

"I know he's good, but don't tell him too much. I want to keep him."

Jamie went into "Manhattan", and Vera caught the look he gave to Maggie, as she sat smiling at the cash desk. The words were sung straight to the girl, and it was obvious to Vera that the singer was crazy about her.

"That kid, Maggie, she keeps the figures right? She doesn't make mistakes?"

"She's as good as you were, Vera. She's reliable, just like you were in the old days."

"But prettier?"

"She's young. Everybody's pretty when they're young."

"Where's the new guy?"

"You mean Andre? Oh, I'll get him. He's in the office." Taken from his book-work, Andre appeared before his boss's wife to be introduced, and he bowed low kissing Vera's hand with a great show of respect.

"You've been in the trade for a while, Andre? In Manchester, I believe?"

"Eleven years, Mrs Pacitti. I've worked in the kitchen and the bar. I've been a waiter, a headwaiter, and also I've done a year in the office. So I know my way around. All aspects of the restaurant business, I know. My father has a little place of his own."

"You like our restaurant?"

"It's sensational. I love it!"

"Yeah, it's not bad." She smiled. "You've got a wife or a girlfriend, Andre?"

"She's in Manchester. I plan to bring her and the baby up, if the job works out, Mrs Pacitti."

"Let's hope so, Andre. My husband works too hard. He needs a rest."

"Oh things are going very well, Mrs Pacitti. We're booked out for weeks. Your husband's eye for detail is so obvious, he has hit just the right note." Mario smiled at this open flattery and the conversation stopped as they applauded Jamie's song.

"I'll let you get back to your work now, Andre. It was very nice to meet you. Good luck!" Andre stood up and waited attentively as Vera spoke. "Will you tell that young man, Jamie, the singer, I want to speak to him?"

Elated from the cheers of the crowded dining room, Jamie shook hands with Vera and was asked to sit down beside her. "I hope you'll sing some more, Jamie. I love these old tunes."

"So do I, Mrs Pacitti." He accepted a drink from the waiter. "I play them all the time. I collect jazz records. It's been my kind of hobby for years."

"That's very interesting. Very interesting indeed. Maybe you'll let me hear some of them some time."

Jamie looked at her. "Sure, any time."

She stood up, "Well, now I've met the famous Jamie, and I've also met your pretty wife, I'll know who Mario's talking about from now on." She picked her evening bag and straightened her dress. Now that it's a bit quieter I think I'll just go into the kitchen and see Frederico. He should have a bit of time to see me, now. We can talk about old times. That's me, an old-timer now."

Jamie shook his head and smiled, "Oh, no, Mrs Pacitti. Don't say that!"

"Goodbye Jamie. It was nice to meet you."

He held out his hand as she proffered hers. *What a woman!* he thought and watched her in fascination as she picked her way among the tables to the kitchen.

As she walked through the swing doors, all eyes turned to greet the boss's wife. Things were slackening off now and Frederico appeared from his cubby-hole. He had taken off his hat and had just poured out whiskies for his cronies, Luigi, Roberto and one for himself. His face lit up with a broad smile. "Vera! My dear! Come in! Come into my castle! Now my evening is made. Come in!" The other two chefs picked up their hats and their drinks, and left, nodding to Vera as they passed. "Sit down, honey, you look like a queen! Have a whisky. You look so swell, Vera."

She was pleased and gave the chef her full attention. "It's a new dress. You like it?"

"Like it? Who wouldn't like it? Your beautiful figure has never changed, not since all those years ago. You remember when I first met you, when you were waiting tables and I was peeling vegetables in Battersea? My God! That was what — thirty years ago."

"Nineteen thirty. Those were hard times, Frederico."

"Oh, if only I had met you first, before Mario!" He shook his head and smiled wistfully, still looking at the line of her long thighs encased in the scarlet crepe of her dress.

"How's life been treating you, Frederico?" She accepted the glass of whisky.

"Listen, Vera! Will you speak to Mario for me? He's brought in this Andre character. Mr Know-all. From Manchester. I don't think I can take orders from a boy like that."

"I've seen him, Frederico. Smooth customer, and very sure of himself."

"It's not fair, Vera. You know that I know the business as well as anybody. But still he won't give me a chance to run things when he's away. He thinks I can't do it. You ask him, Vera. Ask Mario to give me a chance."

She finished her drink and he poured her another. "I'm tired, Frederico and so is he. I want him to take a rest. For the past four years, I've been at home every night by myself."

"You should have had children Vera." Her eyes became sad and she said nothing. "Do you ever speak to him of the child you had in Italy?"

"No." She mused for a few seconds. "Marianne. My sister in Palermo's had her since she was three weeks old. Her face grew sad. "She'll be twenty-four now. I haven't heard for a year or two. She went to college, I know, but she wouldn't know me if she saw me."

"It's a shame, Vera." He patted her hand kindly and she drew herself up.

"How's Mary?"

"She's... oh, you know, getting old like everyone."

"And Vincent? And the girl? What's her name?"

"Liza. Vincent's Okay. He's studying to be a doctor. He's quite steady. Not like me," he laughed ruefully, "but Liza's a worry. She's nearly sixteen and wouldn't you guess it, a bit wild."

"Really? Is she pretty?"

"Sure! And boys round the house all the time. It's a worry!"

"Which is worse, Fred, too many worries or not enough?" She knocked back her drink.

"I think not enough worries is best — you can always make up some worries if you haven't got any real ones. Money worries, for instance."

"I'll speak to Mario."

"Vera, you are a good friend. Listen to me. Instead of this cruise you want to go on, you should go to Sicily and find your daughter."

Vera was wistful. "She's not Mario's, Frederico. You know he wasn't the father."

"Who cares? She's yours, and he loves you. So he would love your daughter."

"Does he love me? I wonder."

A tall youth walked into the kitchen door and found them. "Can I speak to you, Dad?"

Startled, Frederico stood up. "Vera, this is my son, Vincent."

"I haven't seen you since you were about five. Hello! He's like you, Frederico, only more handsome." She stood unsteadily on her feet. "I'll go and find that husband of mine, Cecil B.de Mille."

"Come and see me again soon, Vera." Frederico called as she swaggered out of the door, giving a backward wave.

"*Ciao*, Frederico. Don't work too hard!" he heard her before the door swung back.

As he sat down again the folds and wrinkles of Frederico's swarthy face seemed to have grown deeper. "What are you here for, Vincent? I would have been home in an hour."

"It's Mum." The boy poured some whisky into a glass, and took a gulp. Frederico watched in horror. "Mother has gone. She's taken Liza."

"Taken Liza? Where have they gone?"

"Manchester, to her sister, Frances. She said to tell you she's not coming back. She's packed her cases and…" The boy put his head in his hands, then looked up at his father. "I have to tell you this, Dad. It seems Liza's pregnant."

"Pregnant? No!"

"Sure, up the spout! You know:"

"Who did this?" Frederico's face was black.

"I don't know."

"Christ Almighty!" Frederico took the bottle and poured himself a large drink.

Dominic, suave and polished in his evening dress arranged himself in a chair in the little windowless office of the restaurant, while Mario stationed himself behind him coughing nervously. Maggie entered, a little dishevelled with the effort of balancing the cash against the bills that Saturday evening.

"Come in, my dear. Take a seat. You have had a busy evening. You must be tired." She touched her curly hair, puzzled at this summons and switching her eyes from Dominic to Mario, tried to guess the reason for her summons. Dominic spoke. His accent was almost cockney with a hint of foreignness. "Jamie was a big hit again tonight, Maggie. You must be proud of him."

She smiled, "Yes. I am, Mr Valente."

"Well, Look, Maggie. It's midnight, so I won't waste any time. Mario and I have a proposition to put to you. I am opening a place in central London, similar to this, maybe a little bigger, and…" he stopped to look at the unsmiling Mario. It has been agreed for Mario to lend you to me to help me to open up the new restaurant in two weeks' time. What do you say?"

Maggie opened her mouth to speak and all that came out was, "London?" Then she dried up.

"Yes."

"For how long?" She felt flattered and wary at the same time.

"Perhaps four weeks."

Mario spoke then, "You don't have to go, Maggie."

"But… where would I live?"

Dominic's dark-complexioned face creased in smiles, his double chin appearing more obvious, "Oh, don't worry about that. I have connections. That would be no problem. You would be very comfortable. It would be good experience for you, and your salary would be about double what you earn here."

Maggie looked at Mario. She was puzzled. "Who would do my job here?"

Mario's eyes were enigmatic. "Don't think about that, I'd find someone."

Mr Valente came round from the other side of the desk. He put his hand on her shoulder. His dark eyes were magnets holding hers. "You're tired, now, sweetheart. Go home and talk it over with Jamie. I will phone on Monday morning to find out your decision. Have you ever been to London?"

"No, never."

"Oh well, then — think about it. This is an opportunity for you. You'll learn a lot from my staff. You'll broaden your horizons. And after four weeks, you come back to Mario, and maybe he'll give you a raise in salary." He laughed as his eyes found Mario's.

She tried to think of something to say, but felt awkward and tongue-tied.

"Go home, sweetheart, and think about the opportunity. It will be a chance for you. You've got the makings of a top-class receptionist. I know what I'm talking about." Dominic Valente had become serious as he stood and held out his hand to her. She saw that she was dismissed, and she gave a final glance at Mario. He was not happy, even though he gave her his fond smile as he said goodnight.

Chapter 6

"It's quite simple, Prue. There's eighty-five pounds in my pay packet. When I pay the rent and the television rental and the hire purchase on the furniture, there will be around sixty left. So we take four envelopes and put fifteen pounds in each one." He raised his voice. "If you don't touch the second one before the second week starts, then everything will work out all right."

The smells left from the evening meal of boiled potatoes, sausages and onions still hung around the flat, and Prue was engaged in sloshing hot water and a pan cleaner around the final pot at the finish of the washing-up.

She removed her apron and sat down, "Okay."

"You don't look convinced."

"Well, you know, last month, there was only two pounds left in the last envelope when I got to the fourth week of the month."

"Why was that, Prue?" Gregor's voice had taken on a threatening tone.

"And there's something else..." He followed her into the sitting room as she spoke. "Oh, let's talk about it another time," she said, "I'm not in the mood." Her face was drawn. She watched him sit down at the piano. He played an arpeggio, his face blank. Then he turned round to face her.

"What else, Prue?"

"I have a bill for twelve pounds for that dress I got for going out last Saturday night." Her voice faded at the end of her sentence, and Gregor's head sunk down to his chest, "and..."

"And?"

"I think I'm pregnant."

He stared at the keys in disbelief, then turning in fear and trembling, whispered, "You think?"

Her face puckered. "I'm almost sure. All the signs are there. My breasts are bigger. I feel sick and my you-know-what has not come this month."

He rose and put his arms around her. "O well! A family of three. That puts everything else in the shade." They clung to each other as the tears started up in his eyes. His stomach turned over at the thought of the future, and he could think of nothing else to say. The doorbell rang and Gregor made a face. He disappeared to the front door returning with Jamie wearing his usual benign expression.

"Hello there, Prue. Is this a good time or a bad time to call on you?"

"You're always welcome, Jamie."

"Yes, come in, boy! We were talking about money — filthy lucre — subject normal, you might say, household budgeting, and Prue has changed the subject and would you believe…" his voice was rising and his face was a bit manic, "we think… or rather Prue thinks she's expecting again."

"Oh, that's nice, Prue." Jamie looked at both of them, nonplussed. He'd obviously walked in on a crisis.

Prue smiled as she picked up some toys from the floor. "'Nice' is not exactly the right word, Jamie, not to describe six months of a gross, fat body, and a year of sleepless nights."

Gregor paced the floor in mock hysteria, "My God. I can't stand it!"

"Congratulations, old man! It'll work out all right, you'll see." He slapped Gregor on the back and gave Maggie a hug saying, "I'll just nip down to my car. There's a bottle of gin and a bottle of bubbly there, too, I think. We have to celebrate your news." Later they toasted Prue, and Gregor soon mellowed with the effects of the wine, deciding to let the future take care of itself.

"Are you picking Maggie up at eleven at Mario's, Jamie?" Prue had relaxed into an armchair with her feet up. Already her clothes felt tight on her body.

"Yes." He looked serious as he settled his glass on the side table.

She smiled sympathetically. "You're fed up with her working at nights, Jamie, aren't you?"

"It gets a bit lonely on your own at times. My mother is never in at nights, and everyone is always busy. I'm not sure this job in Mario's is a good idea."

"It's time you two started a family." Prue swigged the sparkling wine appreciatively. "Give you more point in life."

"Oh, some day, when we gather the money together. Maggie wants to buy a house first."

Gregor had found some beer in his cupboard and poured out two glasses for himself and Jamie. He lit a cigarette. "Cheer up, Jamie. Maybe that song we wrote will be bought by somebody. I sent it off the other day. Then we'll all be in the money."

Jamie continued to look glum. "It's not just that. It seems that Mario has agreed to lend Maggie to Dominic Valente for a month to help him start up his new restaurant in London."

"Good Lord. A month? Bloody hell, Jamie!"

Prue sat up. "Lucky Maggie! I wish it were me."

"I think Maggie's flattered by it all. She's going about kind of dazed. She hardly sees me at times." Jamie sunk further down in the armchair.

"Is she going to do it?" Prue was entranced at this news.

"She wasn't sure at first, but last night he phoned and increased the money he was offering. They seem to be impressed with her."

Gregor smiled knowingly and said nonchalantly, "Good Scottish brain she's got. Good looks, too. Always said she was a smart kid!"

"She says she won't go, if I don't say it's all right, but... I wonder if she really means that. I don't think so. She's started folding her best clothes up in preparation." He looked at them both helplessly, "What can I do? I feel as if I'm losing her, somehow."

"It's only for a month, Jamie. It will fly by." Prue's voice was soft.

"I hope so." He looked at his watch. "I have to leave. Maggie asked me to invite you to Sunday lunch, and bring the children, of course. That will be something to look forward to. She's asked Diana and John."

"Oh, that's nice. She'll have to be back from London for Diana's wedding, anyway, Jamie." Prue rose and put her arm around him in a motherly way, pulling him close so that her warm body reminded him of rising bread dough.

"Yes," he smiled, shrugging off his low spirits. "Thank you for listening to me, folks. Talking to you two and the drink was just the job. I feel much better now."

Maggie had prepared a delicious lunch of roast beef with Yorkshire pudding. Afterwards as the children played around, they relaxed with some beer, discussing Maggie's trip to London, then moved to talk about Diana's and John's wedding. John, especially, got fed up with talk of toasts and speeches, of menus and shows of presents. The girls were in their element, but the men decided to take a Sunday stroll along the quiet streets.

"Gosh, Diana! Just think. It's only two months away. You'll be an old married woman." Prue nursed her youngest child who had fallen asleep.

"I know. Married and settled down and I'm just nineteen."

Maggie turned to Prue. "And by Christmas, you'll have your baby, Prue. Three children under five. It's unbelievable."

"Don't remind me. Luckily Gregor loves kids. He's secretly delighted. If he wasn't, I don't know what I'd do."

"Well, these two are lovely anyway." Jack played with his toy cars while the baby slept. In the flickering firelight, in the large, low-ceilinged sitting room, and feeling the effects of the beer, Maggie felt wistful. "What about you, Diana? Do you think you and John will have a family quickly?"

"Who knows? I love babies, so maybe." She turned her gold bracelet as she spoke, and Prue and Maggie took in her fashionable outfit. Her clothes always seemed new, straight from a fashion-rail. "But I have to watch John. He's got a wandering eye. You know you can never really trust a man."

Maggie and Prue laughed at her. "What nonsense!" Prue said. "He's crazy about you."

Diana knelt down on the rug to play with Jack. "My mother says all men are the same. You can't trust them if temptation is put in their way, and John is so, so... male."

"Oh, get her! Tell us more!" Maggie and Prue bent up with laughter.

"Oh, I wish you weren't going to London, Maggie. You've no right. You're my matron of honour. I need you here." Diana pouted and threw back her shoulder-length blonde hair. In her frown could be seen traces of the indulged child she had been.

"I'll be back in good time, Di. This is a chance to make some money for me and Jamie for the future. It's all right for you. Daddy's little girl."

Diana lifted Jack on to her knee and looked at Maggie, "Poor Jamie! He'll miss you." But Maggie grew impatient, and stood up quickly walking to the big bay window which looked out on the grey terraces of the city, bathed in a weak sun.

"Jamie knows it will mean more money. That's why I'm going. We can't live in this semi-basement all our lives. We could be put out with a couple of weeks' notice. My mind's made up. I want to buy a house out of town where we can make a good start, and not be counting the pennies all the time."

Prue looked at her friend's determined face as she spoke. "You're so sensible, Maggie. I wish I had my chance again. I would have waited before I had the kids. Money is a worry."

"Sensible. I don't know about that. But Jamie's head's in the clouds. So I have to be well, you know... I have to think ahead."

Prue deposited the sleeping baby in the bedroom, and returned, relieved, to her armchair where toddler, Jack leaned against her knee. "Well, I tell you. I wish I were going to London. Anything for a break! Just to have some days to yourself without cooking and kids climbing all over you. What bliss! And staying in a hotel. No cleaning to do! And a full night's sleep guaranteed!"

"Oh, don't, Prue. You'll put me off getting married!" Diana said.

When the men returned, Gregor sat down at the piano and played over some popular tunes. Jamie sang the latest song the two had composed, a sweet melody:

When I think of you
And of the things that we could do,
I know our love would grow
With every hour of every day,
If only you could learn to love me too.

Jamie sang it in a yearning sort of way which was very affecting, but at the end the authors shrugged off the compliments, cynically. They had tried too long to sell their work.

John said, "You boys are really talented at song-writing. I wish I had your gifts." Diana's fiancé was handsome, a broad-shouldered bruiser who loved sport, thought about little else, apart from playing sport or watching sport... and beer, and then beer and more sport... and maybe girls.

"Just another one to add to the list of unpublished works." Jamie smiled shyly and shoved both hands in his trouser pockets. Gregor continued to pick out tunes on the piano as the others talked, and presently, as the fire died down, he launched into "Paper Doll." Jamie stood beside him and picked up the tune.

Maggie flinched uncomfortably through her smiles, as he seemed to direct the words at her. His face was unusually serious.

"When do you go, Maggie?" Prue asked as they were getting ready to break up.

"Next Wednesday. I think I have to start work on Friday. Dominic's personal assistant is coming to meet me at the station, someone called Mrs Page."

Jamie put his arm around his wife. "Maybe, I won't let her go." He held her tight.

Prue said, "Don't be silly. It will pep up your marriage. Just think how great it will be when she comes back."

"It doesn't need to be pepped up." He looked adoringly at Maggie. "She knows I'm her love-slave." And he kissed her neck.

When their guests had gone and the clearing had been done, Jamie prepared for bed and, seated on the bed in his pyjamas said,

"I'm dreading Wednesday morning, you know, Maggie. Why are you doing this to me?"

Maggie paused creaming her face to say, "You know why, Jamie. We need the money."

He winced at this direct reply. Watching her remove her jewellery, his feeling of unease increased. She was living in a world of her own. Her thoughts were miles away. The idea of their separation was sinking in now, and for the first time in years, his frank, happy face was creased in sadness. The flowery perfume she was using drifted over to him, and in a voice distorted a little by emotion, which Maggie hardly noticed, he said, "Well, if you don't like it, you'll phone me right away. You promise?"

"I promise." In bed they clung to each other, Babes in the Woods, each lost in differing thoughts of the future.

Dominic's personal assistant was Arlene Page. Maggie recognised her almost immediately on arrival at the railway station. Of medium height, in her forties, she was dressed in a dark suit with short stylish dark hair, and as arranged she was carrying a copy of *The Times* in her right hand. Arlene was the wife of Dominic's accountant and from her accent, she was French.

"I'll take one of these bags," she said. If you follow me, I have a taxi waiting. You have a room in the Irena Hotel. It is next door to Dominic's new place, Ristorante Dominic. We will stop there to let you have a look at it."

With an efficient, self-assured manner, Arlene led the way to the taxi; her quick steps had Maggie trotting along beside her. In the taxi, the long beautifully painted nails of the woman amazed Maggie. She searched for a sensible remark, but found herself dumbstruck by the sophistication and reserve of her companion.

They arrived, and with a quick smile, Arlene told Maggie to wait with her bags in the foyer of the restaurant. She stood alone and self-conscious as the workmen eyed her curiously. She saw Dominic emerge from the kitchen, all the time arguing and talking to a younger man, and followed by Arlene Page.

"Ah, it's Maggie." He spread his arms wide and embraced her as if she were his long-lost daughter. His smile was slow and intimate. "You made it! This is wonderful! Meet Nicki, my eldest son. He's over from the States for the opening."

Nicki was taller than his father and more reserved, "How do you do?"

The French accent of Arlene cut in, "Okay, Dominic. I will take Maggie to her room in the Irena, and see she's settled in. Then, perhaps I'll see you tomorrow. I have much work to do."

"Sure, sure! Thank you. Thanks a million, Arlene. What would I do without you?" Dominic was obviously abstracted with all the activity around him, and also in a hurry to be someplace else. "Tomorrow at nine thirty in the morning, my dear Maggie. You must meet me here, and we'll have a good talk about things. You, too, Arlene. I have some plans for you also."

"You have plans for me?" Maggie looked mystified and smiled uncertainly.

"Of course. Nicki and I have left the architects in the kitchen. We must go." He lifted Maggie's hand and kissed it. "Delighted to have you in London, my dear. Just delighted."

Embarrassed, her eyes moved from Dominic to Nicki. A cynical look on his face, he quickly hid behind a smile, "Nice to meet you, Maggie," he said. She nodded politely and, carrying her travelling case, followed Arlene out of the door.

Next morning the meeting took place over coffee. "Take her up to the West End, Arlene. She'll need perhaps three outfits, dresses, shoes. You know, smart and sexy."

Arlene nodded and Maggie's eyes widened as she listened. "You're buying me clothes?"

"It's the custom, sweetheart. You'll be on show all the time. We want a first-class image. You will help me with the reception of the guests." He turned to Arlene looking serious again. "Her hair, Arlene? He lifted the thick dark waves which sat on her shoulders."

Arlene lit a cigarette. "Yes?"

"What do you think, Maggie?" His dark eyes played on her face, "A little shorter? A little smoother?"

"You don't like my hair?"

"It's lovely, but maybe a new image, less curls would be more sophisticated."

Arlene stood and proceeded to walk around Maggie, then in her sexy French accent she said measuredly "I think you're right, Dominic. We'll see what we can do with it. You agree, Maggie?" Her smile was direct, friendly and charming.

"If you think so. Maybe a change would be nice."

Dominic continued. "And on Tuesday, you two can interview the girls. We need three smart girls to deal with the cash and cheques, and also a cloakroom attendant."

Arlene took out her notebook. "You still plan to open on Saturday evening?"

"Yes, but it will be mainly invited people, so there won't be too much work with cash and so on. They'll be my guests. The real business starts next week." Brief and to the point, Dominic left them.

For the next few days, Maggie, accompanied by Arlene had an insight into the high life in London as she was taken to the top stores, and saw how the people with loads of cash behaved. By the end of the week, dresses of exquisite cut and detail were in her wardrobe, her hair was restyled, and she was the owner of shoes which previously would have cost more than her week's wages.

Every evening she ate with Arlene in the hotel, or at a smart restaurant in the heart of London. Tonight, Arlene had taken her to her flat to eat with her, and to meet her husband, Paco. He proved to be friendly and easy to talk to. He asked her about Scotland and seemed interested in all she had to say. "How do you like London? You've been at Harrods today?"

Maggie sat, sipping red wine, at the long, polished dining table; "Harrods is amazing! I've never seen anything like it."

"Yes, it is impressive the first time you see it. Are you nervous about Saturday night at Dominic's"

"Well, I am a bit. I don't feel like myself any more."

Paco poured some more wine in her glass. Well I don't know what you feel like but you look good. You'll be a wow!" His familiar stare brought a blush to Maggie's cheeks. The luxury of the table, the soft leather of the chairs, the whole ambience of their home impressed her, and their suave manners, made her feel awkward and untutored. She looked at Arlene to see if she was annoyed with her flirting husband, but she was leaving the table to stand at the fireplace where she lit a cigarette.

"Paco and I will be diners on Saturday. We're to sit with some of the invited guests. But I'll be there to give advice if you need it."

"You've done receptionist-cashier work before, Arlene? In one of Dominic's restaurants?"

Paco interrupted, "Sure she has! That's how we met. She was working for Dominic, alongside me in La Mirage in Soho. She was his protege from France — a model of experience and efficiency, weren't you darling?"

"And you were a very small-time clerk in those days, Paco."

He straightened his Rolex watch so that it showed below his white cuffs, "Yes, we were all small-time then."

It had been a tiring day, and pleading sleepiness, Maggie asked to be excused to go. As she was leaving, she said, "I love your apartment, Arlene. It's beautiful. And thank you for a lovely dinner."

"Thank you for being such a pleasant guest in my home. Sorry I can't be company for you tomorrow evening, but Paco and I have a prior engagement. The hotel food is quite good. So you should be all right."

Next evening, feeling lonely and just a bit homesick, Maggie dined alone, and then, in her bedroom, the telephone was too much of a temptation for her to ignore. She phoned Mario in the Glasgow restaurant and was immediately cheered up to hear his voice. "You'll have a great time tomorrow evening, Maggie, down there in the Big Smoke among all the swells… don't worry. It will be terrific. I'm sure everything will go great for you and for Dominic."

"Yes. I hope so. How are things at your place? Is Jamie there:"

"Sure! He's singing, now. You phoned at a bad time."

"Oh!"

"He'll be through in a minute. I must phone Dominic later and wish him well for the opening. He's sunk a lot of money into that place."

"You should see it. It's really beautiful, Mario."

"You like it? You are happy to be down there?"

"Well, it's exciting. I've got lots of new clothes, and a new hairstyle."

"Yeah?" His voice sounded non-committal.

"You know Arlene Page. She's taking me around London, and showing me the sights. We've been in all the big shops, Harrods, and Harvey Nicholls. It's been great. And I've had dinner at her lovely apartment. She's very sophisticated."

"Yes, I know." Mario was non-committal again.

"And there are three new girls starting as cashiers. So I won't be hard-worked."

"It sounds... fine, Maggie, but I hope you remember you're just on loan to the fleshpots of London. We're waiting for you to come back."

"Oh, don't worry, Mario."

"Have you seen much of Dominic?"

"No, not really. He's up to his eyes in work. Every night there are workmen in the place, until two in the morning sometimes."

"But he wants to see me this evening. I've hardly spoken to him since I arrived. I've met his son, Nicki."

"Oh yes, he's there, is he?"

"Yes, just for a visit, you know, from America."

"Yes. Look, Maggie. Take care of yourself down there. Don't go changing, as they say."

"I won't."

There was a pause on the line, then he said, "You want to speak to Jamie?"

"Yes, please."

"Hold on."

She waited for Jamie to come to the phone, then heard his tentative, "Hello!"

She felt happy to hear the familiar voice. "Hello, Jamie. How are you?"

"Great! How are you?"

"Oh, I'm fine."

"The big opening's tomorrow evening."

"Yes. There's lots of important people coming."

"I'm sure."

"You sound funny."

"No, don't be silly."

"Well, that's my first week finished, so that's good isn't it?"

"Yes."

"You're managing okay?"

"Of course. I visit Gregor and Prue, and my mother, and you know, there's plenty to do."

"You miss me?"

"You know I miss you."

"How did your singing go tonight?"

"Great. Lots of applause. I've added two new numbers."

"I wish I could be there to hear you."

"I wish I could be with you." There was a pause on the line. "You'll phone again soon?"

"Yes. I'll phone on Sunday and let you know how the first night went."

"I'm due back with the band now, Maggie. Just remember, I love you."

"I love you, too, Jamie," her voice broke. "Goodbye!"

"Goodnight, my love."

She hung up. There was a knock at the hotel room door, and resplendent in a new evening suit, Dominic stood there... He took in her dejected position by the telephone. "What's wrong? You look a bit sad, my dear." His face was all concern, and he put a broad, tanned hand on her shoulder.

"Oh, I've just been speaking to Mario and Jamie on the phone."

"I see." He sat down on the bed. "Jamie misses you?" His aftershave was heavy and musky. He looked out of place, almost alien in her room.

"A bit, I think." She sat down on the only chair.

He spoke softly, "I don't blame him, my sweetheart. We're lucky he let you come to London. Just you wait until you see the excitement tomorrow night. You'll see it has all been worthwhile. Maybe I could see your new dresses while I'm here."

"Of course, Mr Valente. They're in here." She took out her handkerchief and gently blew her nose and, rising, opened the closet door.

"Ah! Lovely! Why don't you put one on to show me?"

"Now?"

"Yes. I would like to take you down to see the restaurant. Everything's completed. I want you to see it."

Maggie changed in the bathroom, and when she appeared in front of him in the bedroom in a dark plum-coloured velvet model, he whistled. "Beautiful! Just beautiful." His smile was wide and he shook his head as if he could not quite believe what he was seeing. "Here put on this jacket, or you'll be stopping the traffic."

It was eleven o'clock as he opened the door, and two or three waiters were busy putting the finishing touches to the tables. At the far end was a dais for the orchestra, and this was surrounded with large flower displays. The tables glittered with new cutlery and glassware, and on each one there was a mushroom-shaped lamp throwing pools of romantic light.

"How beautiful it all is, Mr Valente!"

"I want you to call me Dominic. Say it, 'Dominic'."

Shyly she repeated, 'Dominic' and felt the colour rise in her face under his powerful gaze.

She walked around a few of the tables. "I've never seen anything so fantastic. The table linen, the cutlery, the lights, they're all so... so... luxurious. And this carpet is so thick. It's just wonderful."

"Take off your jacket. I want to see you walk among the tables."

Shyly she did as he asked, and when she returned to his side, he kissed her cheek. "Now I am happy. You were made for the place. Or it was made for you."

He went behind the cocktail bar, and she heard the pop of a champagne cork. He emerged with two glasses and handed one to her. He looked around the room, his face beaming with anticipation and excitement, then his eyes were on her, and he raised his fluted champagne glass. "To you, Maggie. My little Scottish baby. You are my inspiration. Good luck to both of us!"

She caught his mood and with a sideways glance at him she said, "Good luck to Ristorante Dominic!"

Chapter 7

Frederico awoke, his eyes narrow slits in his face, his chin dark with stubble and his tongue, dry and furred. He moved his head and knew he had a monumental hangover. The empty space in the bed beside him made his heart sink, and he remembered Mary had gone. The bedroom seemed plain and drab without her, and a coldness filled the air. He found he was still dressed in his thin cotton shirt and trousers from the restaurant kitchen, as he rose to go to the bathroom. Then he remembered the other thing. Liza was pregnant! A great groan of frustration escaped him. He felt a ceiling of despair descending. Throwing himself back on to the crumpled bed, he gave way to sobs of hopelessness.

"Dad! Dad!" a hand was on his shoulder. "I've brought you some coffee. Here." Frederico opened his eyes and looked at the tall outline of his son. He took the cup and sipped the hot liquid. "Here," Vincent gave him a lit cigarette. "I'll bet you feel awful."

"Bloody awful! Son, this must be one of the worst mornings of my life." Miserably, Frederico stared at the carpet in disbelief, holding the hot mug. "Just where did I go wrong? I couldn't have done any more?"

"I phoned Manchester. They've arrived. I spoke to Liza."

Frederico looked at the boy guardedly. "And?"

"She's okay. They're both okay."

"I'll phone her."

"You'd better not just now. It's Sunday. She'll be at mass, and she was in a state. Mum wants her to book into a clinic to have the abortion, but she… she's not sure what to do."

Frederico paced the floor. "My poor girl! I had such hopes for her! Who has done this to her?" There was a silence and he continued, spitting out the words in anguish, "I will kill him!"

"Listen, Dad. She would be best to get rid of it. Then she can go back to school. She wanted to go to university."

Frederico looked at his son. "Who could believe this could happen? She could have had a great career. She could have done it, too. She could have made it if only... if only she wasn't such a stupid, stubborn spoiled... idiot!" Pain and disappointment were on his face as his eyes fell on his son. "You are so lucky, Vincent. You have brains. You are steady. You are like your mother. But, Liza is made like me." He shook his head as he recalled bits of his youth. "I was wild too, but for a man, it's different." His face grew fierce; "I will kill whoever did this to my child."

"It's not all his fault."

Frederico turned and stared hard at Vincent. "You know who it is?"

The boy moved across the room to look out of the window. "The sun is out."

"Who is it?"

"I can't tell you."

"Tell me. He's a friend of yours?" Frederico stood threateningly over his son.

"I can't let you loose on him. I can't do that." He pulled away from his father's grip.

"I said I would kill him, but first of all, I will talk to him. Who is he?"

"You won't touch him?"

"No."

"You've met him once. He's a good friend. At medical school. He's been going out with Liza for a few months now. Paul Sakowski."

"That little Polish bastard!" Frederico sucked in his breath between his teeth. His face grew dark.

"Paul's okay."

Frederico's eyes were popping out of his head. He turned quickly to the wardrobe and picked out clothes from his wardrobe at a furious speed. "We'll see about 'okay' when I get my hands on him."

"Dad! Please control yourself!"

"Messing about with my daughter."

"They phone each other all the time. They're… I think they're in love."

"Love? Love? She's a schoolgirl, for Chrissake!" Raging, Frederico banged his way into the bathroom.

Vincent, alone and miserable, for want of anything else to do, started to cook some breakfast. As his father emerged from his toilet, clutching a bottle of aspirins and a glass of water, there was a ring of the doorbell. The young fresh-faced friend of Vincent, the tall, good-looking Paul came into the room. He stood nervously near the door of the room. From the silent atmosphere, he could see that Frederico knew the whole story. He pressed himself against the wall under Frederico's fearful gaze.

"You are my son's friend, right?"

"That's right, Mr Santini."

"And you are studying medicine along with him?"

"Yes."

His face seething, Frederico came towards the boy, a knife in his hand. He clutched him by the throat. The terrified boy was struck dumb, and Vincent's entreaties to his father were useless. "And you are so stupid as to make my daughter pregnant?" Giving a great push, Paul managed to free himself. He was white and shaken. Frederico stood seething with anger. "I want an answer."

"It just happened. It was an accident." Paul stood four-square in the middle of the room. He was near to tears.

"Don't you see what you have done? My wife has left me, and my fifteen-year-old-daughter is pregnant to some… bloody nobody! She'll have to have an operation. My life is in ruins." He was screaming at the end of this outburst.

"An operation?" The boy whispered.

Vincent led his friend to a chair. "Mum has taken Liza to Manchester. She wants her to have the baby aborted in the clinic there." His friend was stunned. "It's for the best, Paul." The poor boy sat in shock on the chair, unable to think straight.

Frederico started up his raging again. "She's not sixteen yet. Liza is a schoolgirl. She is a brainy girl. She had a future, like you and Vincent will have. Now it's all been taken away. God damn you for a bastard!"

Vincent sat on the arm of the chair beside his friend. Paul's head was sinking lower and lower as Frederico got into full flood. He strutted around the room like Mussolini, his eyes flashing, unable to control the passion he worked up. At last, he sat down and after a silence, he spoke in cold measured tones. "Today is Sunday. I have a day off tomorrow. I will phone Mario and tell him I won't be at work on Tuesday. I have to do something. I must go to her."

The two boys watched the demented man make his plans. Now he was striding about in a trance around the room. I will phone Luigi and ask him if I can borrow his car. I will drive to Manchester and take charge of this mess."

"Liza says Mum's in a terrible state. She's insisting that she was going to leave us anyway, and this has just been the last straw. Do you think she'll come back?"

Frederico changed from outrage to abject grief. Taking a handkerchief out of his pocket, he wiped his eyes. "I have tried to please her. I was going to buy a family car soon. She has a lovely home, two clever children. I have provided for her for twenty years. I have tried my best." He sobbed quietly into his handkerchief.

Vincent moved over to his father's side. If Luigi lends you his car, then I'm coming with you."

Paul stood up. "I'd like to come Mr Santini."

A scathing look crossed Frederico's face, a look of bitter dislike was directed at the young man, but within seconds his face changed and the look had passed. "So! You want to come! Okay! You want to come to Manchester, you come. You are responsible for the whole mess. Give me the phone."

The boys listened to the conversation, part of which was in Italian. They heard, "She's gone to Manchester. She's running away from me. Also she's taken my beautiful girl, you know, Liza. She's got herself in trouble."

Luigi replied, "Trouble? What trouble?"

"You know the usual with girls."

"Christ! And Mary has left you?"

"Yeah, and I'm gonna get her back, don't worry, Luigi. Can I borrow your car to go and bring them back?"

There was a pause, then, "Okay! If I drive. Can I come, too?"

Another pause. "What about Mario, Luigi? Mario will go mad if we're both away."

"Oh, he can cook for a day. What's the problem? I'll be at your place by twelve o'clock."

"Okay, Luigi. I'll phone Mario and tell him."

The car with the four men, Luigi at the wheel, pulled up several hours later at the brick-built semi-detached house in the suburbs of west Manchester. The four men sat there immobile like a squad of Mafioso waiting to make a hit. After some minutes, Frederico took a deep breath and broke the silence in the car. "You wait in the car. I'll go in first. We don't want to shock them."

A dark-haired woman in her forties answered the door. It was Wilma, his sister-in-law, tea towel in hand. Behind her, further down the narrow hallway he could see Mary, his wife.

"Frederico!" the exclamation from Wilma was involuntary.

"Yes, It's me, Wilma. Long time, no see. Can I see Mary, please?"

She pulled the door open wider and he stepped into the warmth of the house. "Go into the lounge. It's on the left."

Mary was standing by the stone fireplace amid the silver photograph frames and potted plants, her handkerchief in her hand, her eyes red and swollen with crying. "You shouldn't have come here." She turned her back on him and stared into the fireplace.

"This is terrible, Mary. You shouldn't have run off like this. We'll sort it out. The boy, Paul's here too. And Vincent. He told me about Liza." He sat down in the plush armchair, and leaned his head on his right hand as a sob escaped him.

99

"Don't give me those Italian dramatics. If you had been at home more often when she was growing up, this would not have happened. I've had to do all the bringing-up of these children. How do you think I feel?" she shook with emotion. He put his arm around her, but she pushed him away. "Where is Vincent?"

"He's in the car. In Luigi's car. He's here, too. And the boyfriend, Paul."

"Good God!"

"You shouldn't have run away like this, Mary. It wasn't fair on us. I've been out of my mind."

She broke down then and cried inconsolably "What will I do, Frederico? She's a child of fifteen." He put his arms around her, his ageing face solemn and they sat by the window, humbled and saddened.

Soon she said, "You'd better tell the others to come in. They'll need some coffee or something."

Weighed down by the seriousness of the situation, Mary and her sister with the four men sat round the dining-room table, their conversation stilted, when the plump, pretty Liza appeared in the doorway, her face flushed pink, her expression quite blank. Frederico rushed to embrace her. *"Cara mia!"*

Tears welled up in his eyes. Then she turned to Paul who stood beside them, his face pale and strained. The boy took her in his arms, and without a word they left the room together.

Outside the little brick-built terrace house, the two young people looked at each other, troubled and shocked by their situation. Liza said, "Let's walk in the park. There's a bench there under the trees. We can sit down for a while."

When they got there, he faced her, searching for words. "What do you want to do, Liza?"

Her face was contorted. "You don't want to be a father, do you, Paul?" He didn't answer. "I don't want a baby either."

"I don't know what I want. I'll do whatever you say." They hugged each other.

Then the boy said, "If my mother finds out she'll go mad. My father, too. But especially my mother. And she's against abortion, I know. She's a devout Catholic and takes the church's line. How would your family be about the idea?"

"Mother was all for the idea at first but, I see now she's not sure, and her relatives will be shocked."

"Will it cost a lot of money to have it done?"

"Oh, yes. A lot." Liza stood up. "Let's walk on a bit, Paul. I'm getting cold." They strolled along the deserted path of the park, feeling like actors in a play that had nothing to do with them. The first heavy blow of their lives had hit them, and they were numb.

"Mother's brought more than one hundred pounds for the clinic." Liza's voice was thin and ethereal.

Paul took this in then asked quietly, "How far on are you?"

"Three months."

"God! It must have happened the very first time."

"I know. But we must decide today what to do. The operation's booked for tomorrow morning."

He shook his head in disbelief and looked sadly into the leafy trees.

"Don't feel too bad, Paul. I'll get over it. I don't want to be tied down with a baby. I'm just lucky my mother agrees with me." They walked slowly on, hand in hand, without speaking, as stray dogs hurried past through the darkening park, intent on some secret destination.

An air of crisis hung over Wilma's house. Luigi and Vincent, feeling like bit players in the great drama, had some food, went out for a smoke, then decided to stroll down to the local pub. Frederico sat with his wife, his face stricken with puzzlement and misery.

"So you think she should get rid of it?" he said at last.

"I'm just glad I've got the money to pay for it, that's all. She has an appointment at the clinic for ten o'clock tomorrow morning. Then she'll need a couple of days to get over it."

"Then you'll come back home?"

As she made to reply, the door was opened and a man of about fifty, slightly built, handsome and intense entered. He hesitated and

Mary rose and stood beside him. Frederico's eyes followed her as he tried to make out the situation. "This is George. He is a friend of mine. He drove Liza and me down here."

Frederico remained sitting as if glued to the seat. He said, "Your friend?"

"Yes. He lives quite near us, in Hillhead. He's taken me out a few times when you were working. At the weekend." She watched Frederico's face harden. "Well do you think I can stand to be alone all the time while you're in bloody Mario's?"

The stranger spoke. "She's coming to live with me, Frederico, when this is all sorted out. We love each other."

Frederico struggled to control the turning in his stomach, and the panic in his chest. "You must be joking!" he spat out.

Mary's voice was raised in protest almost to a scream. "You know how miserable I've been these last few years. You must have seen this coming."

Flashing across Frederico's mind was a picture of the two of them, locked in physical love, and he felt sick. He stood up, looming head and shoulders above the smooth-faced, finely built man. With a look of disgust he faced his wife. "Leave me alone. Go on! Go! With your so-called friend. I don't need you! I don't need any of you!" They left him staring miserably down at the polished dining table. After some time, he stood up as if pushed into action by an unseen force, and soon found himself out of the house, striding down the avenue, walking on and on, through the brightly lit streets and busy shops of the city. Through bustling crowds he went, his brain a blank, his motive only to keep moving. For perhaps two hours, he strode unseeingly through the unfamiliar town, and then without any forethought he turned into a public house, ordered a large whisky and twenty cigarettes.

He looked at the glass of whisky and the packet of cigarettes as if they were from another planet, and then he looked up at the curious barman. "I don't smoke. Haven't for seven years." Like a crazed man, Frederico opened the packet and put a cigarette between his lips. The barman lit it for him, and he took a deep draw. Then he lifted the whisky and drank half of it down. "That's better!" He eyed the surprised barman. "Strategies! You've got to have strategies in this life. To deal with fate and bad luck." He finished the whisky and called out, "Same again, please."

The man behind the bar, smiled as he filled the glass up again. "You lost your dough at the races or something?"

"No, guess again."

"Your dog just got run over?"

"No."

"Your mother-in-law's coming to stay?"

"No, my wife's leaving me, and my daughter has got herself pregnant, and she's not even out of school yet." Frederico lit another cigarette.

The barman gave him another whisky. "Here, have one on the house. And just think, it could be worse. I can't stand my wife, but she would never leave. Just think of that."

"You've got a point there, friend."

"Just call me Ralph."

After an hour or so, and more friendly banter with the barman, the whisky had done its work, and chucking the half-empty packet of cigarettes at Ralph, his now firm friend, Frederico swayed himself out of the bar. "Goodbye, Ralph! Thanks for all the advice. See you again, sometime!"

It took him a long time to stumble his way back to Wilma's house for he had walked several miles right across the city. All was quiet and subdued when he arrived, only Mary and her sister being there, sitting by the fire drinking coffee. Wilma, when she saw her brother-in-law, rose and escaped saying, "I'll bring you some coffee, Frederico."

He looked at his wife's still-young figure, her well-shaped breasts, and thought of her in someone else's hands. Slumping down in an armchair, he spoke in low, sad tones. "Where did I go wrong, Mary? I thought I gave you everything."

Guilt flooded her but she hardened her heart. "George loves me. He makes me feel like a woman again. He wants to take care of me. He saw I was miserable, always at home, the never-ending housewife with nothing to look forward to. No holidays for years, and nothing new in the house, no car, having to watch my friends and neighbours getting on. All because of your drinking and gambling. I'm getting out of it all, Frederico. I've had enough. George is trying to get me a job, and I can be independent. He's divorced and he needs someone in his life."

"Haven't I taken care of you for twenty years? Don't I need someone in *my* life?"

"You haven't cared about me for years. You love your job, your kitchen, your little whores at work. You don't love me."

His voice was hard and bitter, "You're wrong, Mary." He got up and stood in front of her. "Please, let's give it another chance."

But she looked away from his pleading eyes into the flames of the fire. "Go home, Frederico. I'm staying on here for a while. I'll get in touch with you." She did not turn to look at him.

After ten minutes of stony silence, Wilma entered the room quietly, tight-lipped and serious. She put her hand on his bowed shoulders, "There's some supper for you in the kitchen, Frederico."

After a while, he looked up, "Thanks, Wilma. That's very kind." Rising and following his sister-in-law into the kitchen he presently asked for Liza. "Where is she, Wilma? I want to speak to her"

"She's a good girl, really, Frederico. She'll be back soon. Don't worry."

Later, father and daughter stood in the twilight at the front of the little house, Frederico's face strained and unhappy. "Your mind is made up, then, my sweetheart?"

"I think it's for the best, Dad. I can go back to school. And Paul can be free of any responsibilities. It will be a long time before he's through his education. It's just not on to have a wife and baby round his neck at his age." Her poise amazed him.

"It's such a terrible, sad to start your young life, Liza. 'Abortion,' the very word is horrible." He was feeling the divided feeling of wanting to be rid of the problem, and not wanting to take the action necessary, both at the same time. He hung his head in misery.

"I have got to be single-minded. Mum has got the money for it so I'm luckier than some other girls I could tell you about." She put her arms around her father. "It will be over quickly, you'll see, Dad."

"Well, you know we'll be leaving in an hour or so. Got to get back to work. You'll phone me as soon as you can, sweetheart."

She threw her arms around him once again, "Of course I will, Daddy. I'll phone you."

"Your mother tells me she's staying here or else she's going back with this new friend, George. What do you say to that?"

She looked at her father sadly, unable to think of what to say.

"I can't take it in!" His face crumpled and his voice broke.

Liza looked at the slumped, rounded shoulders of her father, and bending down gently kissed his hair. "She's been unsettled for a long time, now. You must have known that, but I think she still loves you underneath it all. Don't give up hope, Dad."

He managed a smile for the girl saying, "And you? You'll be all right with your mother? What about Paul?"

"Oh, I'm not staying with mother. I'm coming home to live with you. I'm going back to school. Paul loves me and I love him. We're both hoping to be together in the future when we've finished university. I'll be back to stay with you when this is all over."

His face lightened. "You're coming back home?"

"Sure. Of course." She gave him her best smile.

He hugged her, "Oh, I love you so much. I'm so sad you have to go through all this."

"Well lots of girls do. I'll survive."

The four men got themselves into the car once again, Luigi at the wheel. Just then, Mary appeared at the front door beside Liza. Frederico struggled with his hurt and mixed emotions, as he looked at his wife and daughter together.

Finally, he got out of the car and held out his hand to her. "I don't think I deserved you doing this to me, Mary. You should have told me how unhappy you were. I would have done something." He looked at her sadly. "When you want to come back, I'll be waiting." Their eyes met until she looked down in confusion. "You'll let me know how things go about Liza? Look after her." He tried to read her expression.

She said, "I'll phone you tomorrow night. She will have had the operation by then." She managed a smile. "Don't worry!"

It was a long, quiet journey back, the four men subdued and thoughtful as they drove through the border hills, and up the never-ending road. The following evening found Frederico hanging over the telephone, waiting for it to ring, Vincent and Paul by his side. Every so often he poured himself a little noggin of whisky, and sipped at it slowly, silent and introspective. The two young men, impatient of this inactivity, went outside to the garden at the back of the house, furtively smoking, and at the same time listening for the phone. Then they heard it.

"Yes. My darling Liza! Are you all right?" He held back the disappointment at the loss of the unborn child, mixed as it was, with relief at the loss of a burden.

"I'm all right, Dad. I'll be out tomorrow, and I'll be home on Saturday. Is Paul there with you?"

Frederico handed the telephone to the apprehensive young man, and watched the worried face relax into a relieved smile. "I love you, too. Of course. Good night. I'll put you back to your father and I'll see you on Saturday." His body was crumpled with relief as he handed to telephone to Frederico.

"This is wonderful, Liza. I'll get home early on Saturday from Mario's. I'll finish up early. Oh, I'm so glad you're coming home."

"Me too, Dad. Goodbye until Saturday."

Chapter 8

"Well you've done it, Dominic! What a night! What taste! The place is a triumph." Around the well-padded restaurateur, a small crowd of smartly dressed people bobbed and chattered. He beamed satisfaction back at his customers under the chandeliers. "Must have set you set you back a fortune. And such a generous dinner, old man. Two hundred guests! Best food in London! Well done, old chap!"

"Thank you. You're very kind, Harry. You enjoyed your dinner, Mrs Fortescue?"

"Delicious, Dominic. It was a delightful evening." Diamonds sparkled at her ears and on her hands. "Champagne on the house, my dear, Dominic. How generous! It's been wonderful."

The plaudits continued for some time, and the well-wishing showered on Dominic and Maggie as they stood by the cashier's desk, bidding goodnight to the guests. The orchestra was playing "Moonlight and Roses" as Maggie was called over to one of the few tables left with people. She hurried back to Dominic. "They want another bottle of champagne, and they want you to join them. Go on and sit down, I'll go and get another bottle."

He smiled broadly at Maggie, glowing with the excitement of the evening, "Of course, but you must join us, too, my dear. There's not much to see to now. The place is nearly cleared. Come on sweetheart, I want to tell you how proud of you I was this evening. You look like an angel." He kissed her lightly on the cheek. "Go and get a couple of bottles and join us. Now where is he? Where's Buick?"

Businessman and *bon viveur*, Henry Buick sat at a table with his wife, Maria, and daughter, Clara, and her current boyfriend. All were high on champagne, exotic cocktails and liqueurs, their table a mass of festive streamers and other debris. Holding a fat cigar, Buick jumped to his feet when he saw Dominic.

"Come on, Dominic! What's keeping you? Congratulations! What a night! Best meal I've had in London in twenty years. Where's Nicki? I hear he's over from the States. You know Maria, Clara and Ferguson."

They smiled and said something like, "Thanks for a wonderful meal."

Nodding and smiling, Dominic shook hands all round, then indicated, "This is Maggie, my right-hand woman."

Buick threw an arm around Maggie. "Come and have a glass with us. Ah, I see you've brought some supplies."

They all sat down, Dominic and Maggie the two sober people among their tipsy guests. Maggie tried to get on the same plane as them but their exuberance and intoxication was hard to match. Between taking large sips from her glass she surreptitiously massaged her ankles, and soon had slipped off her shoes.

Dominic asked the pianist and a couple of the band to stay on, the reward being free drinks. Some of the staff waited behind too, and bathing in the rosy glow of a successful night and their employer's good mood, they sat around relaxing and easing their tired feet.

"How's Nicki, Dominic? Has he settled down in New York?"

"I think so. He's doing something in the Stock Market. Last time we spoke he sounded quite confident. Lives in Greenwich Village. You know, arty-farty. They think they invented everything, free love, theatre, literature. He'll be a nice boy if he ever grows up." As he spoke two young men were approaching their table from the darkness of the door. It was Nicki and his friend.

Buick saw them first. "Come here, Nicki, my boy. Great to see you! Your father's done it again!"

"Oh, he's a big success. I'll give him that." The boy's complexion was smooth, his appearance handsome. He seemed well-bred and refined in his immaculate evening dress.

"And how's your mother?"

"She's enjoying life. She has lots of friends in New York. Let me introduce Patrick. He's a lawyer. Earns big bucks. He came over with me for the trip."

"What are you two boys drinking?"

Nicki surveyed the wreckage of the table. "Campari and soda, Mr Buick."

"Same for me, sir." Fair and serious the boy looked a bit like a fish out of water standing beside Nicki.

They sat down and Nicki, seeing Maggie, smiled sardonically at her. "How is our Scottish friend? Is London impressing you, Maggie?"

"Oh, I'm having a great time. Tonight in the restaurant was unbelievable. The atmosphere was just great, and the clothes and the jewellery were like nothing I've ever seen." She stopped, realising everyone was listening to her. "But I still miss home."

Maggie smiled politely at Nicki, trying to work out something that puzzled her about him. She felt no friendliness coming from him. He was cold and remote. Did he think she was a little upstart, or worse still a gold-digger? What was it with Nicki? As for the fair-haired Patrick with his soft American accent, he didn't give her a second glance. She watched them as they sat together sipping their Camparis, and the slow realisation that these two were a couple dawned on her.

Some people were dancing and having a ball on the dance floor, and Maggie found herself in the arms of Dominic as the band played, "Let's take it nice and easy, It's going to be so easy for us to fall in love." Maggie caught the soulful look in Dominic's eyes and a little panic started to rise within her. She hoped the others couldn't see him, and put his manner down to natural elation and too much champagne. Later she danced with Buick and when she sat down at the table, giggling at his compliments, she saw Nicki watching her in amused tolerance.

He leaned over and said, "Will you move in with my father in London, Maggie?"

"Move in with your father? What do you mean?"

"Oh, well when I get back home, my mother will be full of questions. I just want to know what the score is."

"I'm down here for four weeks to help out. That's all!"

She watched a smile cross his face. "We'll see," he said. "Don't you know when somebody's got the hots for you?"

She stared him. "You are mistaken, Nicki. I have a husband in Scotland."

"Never mind. But you must have noticed how he treats you as his favourite, and how the waiters and other men around clam up when you appear. You're marked down as Dominic's property."

"You're wrong. This is not New York, or a Hollywood movie, Nicki."

"Am I?"

"I'm friendly with all the staff. There's nothing between your dad and me."

"Well, we'll see. Buick here already thinks you're Dad's girlfriend."

Maggie was ruffled now. "Oh really? Well, he's wrong. Do you know, you look at me as if you hate me? What's the matter with you? Can't a girl get a job in the limelight without fingers pointing at her? I'm just earning my living. Do you hate your father, too?"

"I don't hate him. I know him. He knows how to make money better than anyone I know. He just gets carried away at times."

Deflated and sullied by this conversation, Maggie hardly looked up when Nicki and Patrick left soon afterwards. She sunk into a mood and wished she were home in bed.

Dominic saw her looking unhappy and came and stood beside her, and between answering the bantering of his friends, he leaned down and said, "I'll take you to your hotel room. You look all in, Maggie."

She picked up her bag and her wrap, and when they got to her door he said, "May I come in for just a minute?"

She hesitated. "No, Dominic. I'm tired and…" In her new high-heeled shoes she found herself looking down into the deep, black waves of his hair, and at the pale brown sheen of his Italian skin."

"You're moody. I don't understand you tonight. Has it all been too much for you, Maggie? Have we been working you too hard?"

"Oh, it was just something Nicki said. He kind of upset me. You'd better come in."

She dropped her things and sat down on the bed. "Never mind Nicki. He's a bit screwed-up and likes to burst people's bubbles. He's got his own troubles." He threw his arms wide, a happy smile on his face. "Tonight was a triumph for both of us. It went like a bomb, way above my expectations. You should be happy, along with me."

"Oh, I don't know, Dominic. Maybe I'm just homesick."

He went over to the French window and opened it. He stood looking down at the lights of the city, then lit a cigar. After a few minutes, Maggie joined him and he put his arm around her. "You know I'm in love with you, don't you?"

"Dominic, please!"

"Don't worry. I'm not going to attack you or anything."

"Nicki said…"

"Yes?"

"Is he queer? You know effeminate? Homosexual?"

Dominic looked hurt and bitter. He flashed her a look. "Why do you say that?"

"His attitude."

"You mean he doesn't make you feel like a desirable woman?"

"Well, yes, and…"

"Do I make you feel desirable, Maggie?"

She took a step back, searching for a suitable answer, and he pulled her to him and kissed her lips, a long passionate, hungry kiss. "My little flower. You are perfection. I have fallen for you completely."

She was shaken by his passion, and turned and walked to the other side of the room. "Nicki thinks I'm your mistress."

"Nicki thinks? Damn Nicki! Of course he's a homosexual! A poof! A waster! He goes through money like water. He's only over here to see what's going on. To see what money he and his bitch mother can screw out of me. Forget him."

"He made me feel cheap."

"You could never be cheap."

"He says all the staff give me a wide berth because they think I'm your…" She sat down on the bed.

He pulled her up and took her arms and put them around himself. "Forget everybody. Do you like me just a little?" He smiled. "With your shoes off, we're able to look into each other's eyes."

"I like you, Dominic. But what about Jamie? He's a nice guy, my husband. I can't hurt him. I just can't." She was near to tears.

"I know you love Jamie. That's another story. Another time. Another place. Look, my dear little one. I am happy just to look at you. You don't know how good you are. You are that rare thing, a girl who's gorgeous, smart and nice with it. Most good-looking girls, by your age, have worked out how to get what they want. They use everything they've got. You… you're different." His eyes were hypnotic and she looked away.

"You seem to have experience of good-looking girls," she said.

"I've had my moments, but you, my dear, are something else. Do you think I would have brought an ugly, unattractive girl down from Scotland to London to work for me, to be on show in my stylish new place? No, I found you a knockout, so I knew everyone in London would find you a knockout."

"Mario gave me a job. He's good to me. He likes me but not the way you do."

"Look, honey. Mario didn't touch you, I know, but do you think he didn't want to. He's crazy about you."

"I know he likes me a lot, but he doesn't want to spoil my life."

"He's an old man. Forget Mario. Just say you like me a little and I'll sleep well tonight. I'll not touch you."

Her sleepy eyes twinkled, "I like you, Dominic. You're solid, kind and affectionate. You're like my father would have been, if he had lived."

"Your father?" He burst out laughing. "You really know how to turn a compliment! That's rich — your father! May I kiss you goodnight, sweetheart?"

His kiss was stirring, and he lightly caressed her body as he whispered, "I'm crazy for you." Then he dropped his arms suddenly, and whispered, "Goodnight, my darling."

Each night of the next week was as busy as Saturday had been. Maggie took more and more responsibility for things, supervising the girls and paying them on Saturday evening, paying the band and making sure they were given dinner and had no complaints. The pace was hectic, and the phone never stopped ringing with people booking tables. Sometimes, Arlene Page would be there to help out and to prime Maggie if any VIPs or blue bloods were to be entertained, and gradually she was learning who was who, and even what they liked to eat and drink.

"You are becoming more skilful every day." Dominic was admiring her answering the phone. "Have you phoned Mario's tonight?"

"No, I thought I'd do it at ten when Jamie takes a break from singing."

"You haven't had a drink, this evening, or a thing to eat."

"No, the time's just flown."

"Would you do me the honour of eating with me, your Royal Highness?

"Oh, well, I'll think about it, since no one else has asked me."

Dominic gave a mock scowl. "Just let them try."

"Won't it make the staff talk if we eat together?"

"Let them talk. Who pays them?" He gave her a serious look. "You don't care about them, do you? They envy you. Anyway you've done nothing wrong. You've worked hard. I depend on you, and anyway, you've nothing to hide, have you?"

She grinned at him. "If you say so, Dominic. I'd love to eat with you."

He ordered two steaks from the kitchen and they ate at his special corner table. The wine was smooth and red, specially chosen by Dominic. They were left alone and Maggie felt pampered and flattered after her week of hard work. She chattered on about the affluent customers and the way they threw their money about, and about the laughs and misunderstandings in the kitchen, and other happenings of the day. He knew she was keeping the conversation light, and he indulged her by listening to her humorous remarks, while she grew a little heady with the wine.

"Come on, smile Dominic." She leaned towards him a little tipsy. "You're so serious tonight."

"I have to see the kitchen staff in five minutes. Will you wait until the end, let's say one o'clock, so that we can have coffee and a night-cap together? I'll be free in about half an hour. I'll have to wait to see the Biltons' party off the premises. They've spent a lot of money tonight. He'd be insulted if I didn't show him out. The Biltons are money-on-legs."

"Okay, Dominic. I'll tidy up in the office until you're ready."

It was almost two o'clock when he took her to her hotel. Out of his coat pocket, he produced a bottle of champagne and two glasses. "To celebrate our association of two weeks. You make me happy, Maggie. You bring me luck."

Well, you've made me happy too. I've never worked so hard or enjoyed myself so much." He helped her remove her coat and smelled the perfume of her soft dark hair as she threw it back.

"And you're getting paid for all this enjoyment, darling."

"Well, I bloody well hope so."

"Oh, she swears, too. Drink up your wine, love. You are improving with age." She giggled and fell back on the bed.

"I think I'm a bit tipsy. Too much wine." She sat up again looking at him with a flirting smile.

His eyes, dark and luminous followed her as she rose from the bed, and he took her hand and pulled her close to him. "Tonight, I do not beg." His voice was thick and urgent. "Tonight I want you." His hands caressed her breasts, and looked into her eyes. "You want me, don't you?"

She placed her long slim arm on his shoulders and threw back her head so that her breasts were pushed forward. She heard herself say a little shakily, "I want you, Dominic."

He unbuttoned his jacket and shirt, his eyes never leaving the girl he had inflamed. He embraced her again, his hands searching her body, and she knew she was in the hands of an expert. "My God, how you shall have me, *chérie*!" is all he said.

Chapter 9

The sound of water splashing in the bathroom wakened Maggie, and the face of Dominic and the night before flooded back to her. Her mind was a confusion of guilt and pleasure at the memory, and suddenly Dominic was there gazing down shyly at her. He was dressed in dark trousers, his broad chest and shoulders bare. As their eyes met, his face became wreathed in smiles. He came and sat by her side, straightening the ribbons of her night-dress and pushing back her hair.

"Good morning, sweetheart. You have wakened up at last!" He kissed her briefly on the lips.

She sunk back on the pillows. "Oh, Dominic! What have we done?"

He kissed her neck. "You did not like it?"

"How can I face people, now?"

"What people?

"Oh, you know. The people in the restaurant — Arlene, the waiters, Victor the chef. And all the others. They'll suspect. And when I go home, there's Jamie and Mario to be faced. How can I hide what happened last night?"

He stood up. "You're not going back for weeks. I won't let you."

But her face was frowning as she got out of bed. He embraced her and she felt the fire of the previous evening returning, "No Dominic. I must get dressed. Do you think we can keep this a secret? Do you think we'll be found out?"

He approached her again where she stood at the door to the bathroom, his face amused. "So! You want to keep me a secret?" And he tried to put his arms around her again.

She pushed him away laughing as he bore down on her. "No, I'm going in here to the bathroom."

"I can't keep it a secret. I love you. You are so beautiful." His hands were caressing her hips and breasts. Call me an old fool if you like, but I want to shout my love from the rooftops."

"Crazy man!" she shouted and, with difficulty, escaped.

When she was dressed, he said, "Today we'll go to the country. I have friends who live in the Chilterns, near Wycombe. I want them to meet you. Forget facing people, my darling." He looked into her eyes. "I know I am too old for you. Old enough to be your father. But I cannot help loving you. We have today together. Let's enjoy it. Let's live for the moment, *chérie*."

Maggie's face coloured. His little heartfelt speech had silenced her, as varying emotions crowded in on her. Dominic's love was palpable. His declarations seemed to charge the air with excitement. His masterful personality excited her whole being. She was thrilled and flattered and yet, at the same time, full of dread. She held him back from her, placing her hands on his arms.

"You have made me into a wicked woman, Dominic." Then, on seeing his face fall, she smiled sadly and her right hand strayed to his thick dark hair. "I am a lost soul." Each of them felt the desire rising in the other, as they stood close in the little bedroom looking into each other's eyes.

He paused, kissed her cheek, and said huskily, "If you are a lost soul, Maggie, what have you done to me? Let's go."

After a pleasant drive from London, they drew up outside and old inn, gabled and timbered with a cobbled courtyard at the side and back, and a hanging sign announcing, The White Swan. Heads turned at the sight of a girl not long out of her teens, slim and pretty, being escorted closely by a foreign-looking man in camel-hair coat, aged at least fifty. In her first two weeks working with Dominic, and walking behind him, carrying papers and notes, Maggie had felt no embarrassment. Now, however, his proprietorial air, and the closeness of him to her, made people speculate about their relationship.

The hotel was a fairly old building, mainly Victorian in design, warm and cosy with much polished wood, shining brass, doors with little windows, leading on to narrow corridors, and everywhere pictures and ornaments. A log fire flamed and sparked in the main lounge, and there was an appetising smell of roasting meat on the air, and the whiff of spirits from the bar. The girl at the desk recognised Dominic. "Mr Valente!" She smiled broadly. "Are you here for lunch? How wonderful to see you! Mr and Mrs Marshall are here already. They're having a drink in the lounge."

A tall, fair-haired man in his fifties, fit and athletic-looking, his features slightly foreign, with dark, very curly hair and green, intelligent eyes, together with a shorter, female figure, rounded and homely, her hair a dark frame round her face, rose to greet them. They were introduced as Rudi and Ruth.

Ruth was Jewish and had come to England in nineteen thirty-nine on a ship with many other children escaping from the terror of the Nazis. She had spent the war with a family of devout Christians, and had eventually become a Christian herself. At that time she had been in her own bed-sitting room and making her own way in London. She already had a regular boyfriend, but Rudi had just bowled her over.

Every day, after their first meeting he would come into the restaurant where she worked as a waitress and ask for tea and scones with jam. Regularly, from three in the afternoon until four, he sat reading his paper and smoking a cigarette or two, trying to snatch some conversation with her. "You are busy today, Ruth. Your feet must be sore." His accent was attractive, and his voice was deep like a Russian's. His face with its high cheek-bones and soft green eyes seemed to follow her, and his smile was open and charming.

"When are you going to take pity on me? When can you come out to the pictures with me? Can't you see I'm a lonely old soldier left over from the war in this den of iniquity called London." For he was truly a war casualty, an ex-flying officer of the Polish air force in London who had never gone back home.

"I'm sure you have plenty of girls who would go out with you, Rudi."

Then he would flick back his hair and repeat, "It's you I like. I can't see anyone but you. I want only you. No one else will do."

"I have a boyfriend, Rudi. He drives a van in this area. He will be in soon to see me."

"And you are promised to this driver. You are engaged?"

"No."

"When are you going out with him?"

"We go out Thursdays and Saturdays."

"Well, this is Monday. How would like to see a Fred Astaire movie?" There's one on at the Odeon. I'll pick you up and take you home. Please, just this once. To make an old man happy." He was forty-two, and she was just twenty-one.

She looked shyly at this handsome man and tried to put up a resistance to his charm. "I'm sure you are only kidding me, Rudi. You should leave me alone."

Then later when she passed his table again, she stopped to say. "Is it Polish you said you were?"

"That's it. Polish and proud of it! And I know you came from Berlin at the beginning of the war. You have no family now in Germany?"

"No."

"Please come out with me. Just one night. I'd like to get to know you."

He picked her up at her apartment block, and after the pictures they went to a little restaurant in Soho. They talked and talked about their pasts, their childhoods, and soon he was asking her to go out with him again. "The theatre, Ruth, and a little supper afterwards. I'll get tickets for a show. I must take you out again."

"I'll have to put Robert off." She was worried at her infidelity.

"You do that, honey. We'll have a wonderful time."

After the film they ate a Chinese meal, a whole new experience for her. Then after some drinks, she spoke of her parents and Auschwitz and how the war had been nearly over when they were killed. She spoke of the support of the good-living, kind people who had fostered her. He too was sad, but luckier than she was, as his family was still alive, although living a desperately poor life in post-war Poland, behind the Iron Curtain. He had not seen them for eight years, and longed to see his mother most of all. But this was impossible, as, if he went back, he might not be allowed out of the country again.

"Someday, when I have enough money, I will buy car, and maybe I can find a way of driving across Europe to see them all again. It is one of my ambitions."

"Your business, your laundrette business is doing quite well?"

"Sure, I'm going to open another one around the corner. We're very busy. It's very good business. I am making money okay."

And so they had come to know each other, and to have feelings for each other.

Within a month, they were lovers, and her romance with Robert was a thing of the past. She had been seduced by his deeply uttered love declarations, his green eyes shining with desire, urgent and passionate as he broke down her resistance. "You are so beautiful, my Ruthie. You make me terrible. I am full of love for you. You are a beautiful ripe fruit. I love your eyes, your hair." And as he caressed her he declared, "You are my princess. No one else must have you. You are mine and I want to marry you."

Within a few months they were married. They moved into a flat near to his businesses, and Ruth took charge of the new shop. They worked from morning to night, but they were blissfully happy. Next, Rudi bought a bingo hall, another great success. His bank balance was swelling, and he expanded into the property business, buying and selling flats and houses. Within a few years he was well on his way to becoming a millionaire. When their son was born, Ruth was fulfilled and happy. To her, Rudi could do no wrong. She worshipped him. The happiness that marriage had brought her showed in the sweet serenity of her face. They were the perfect couple.

"Dominic, you old devil! How are you? I heard about your new place and the one in South Kensington. How are you doing?"

"Great! Just great, Rudi! You must come and see it. Posh! You wouldn't believe it! And you too, Ruth. How are you, Ruth?" He embraced the smiling lady. "Beautiful as ever. Glad to see this old crook's looking after you. This is Maggie, my right-hand man. She's been helping me get the new place off the ground."

"How do you do? You're from Scotland. How nice to meet you!" They were gracious and warm in their greetings to her, and she liked them right away. Drinks were ordered and they sat before the crackling log fire, the only occupants in the hotel lounge, Maggie mostly silent as the three reminisced about their struggles in the old days. She saw that they assumed that there was an intimacy between herself and Dominic, but they asked no questions, and made her feel comfortable and relaxed. Neither did they enquire about Dominic's family in America, although they must have known about them.

"You must come next Sunday. Can you make it, you and Maggie, Dominic?" Ruth looked pleadingly at Dominic. It's our wedding anniversary, and we're having a celebration. Do you think you can come?"

"Sunday is a good day for me." He looked at Maggie. "Would you like that, my dear?" His loving expression when he glanced at his young companion caused Ruth to give a quick, knowing glance at her husband. They saw that their old friend was well gone on his young Venus of a girlfriend.

"That sounds very nice, thank you."

"Yes, thanks Rudi and Ruth. We'd love to come. What time?"

"Could you make it for six? We will eat at about seven-thirty. It will be just about ten people, some really old friends, together with one or two people from the village," Ruth said.

"Yes, Dommie," Rudi became more animated. "We've asked Paddy and Louie and their wives, and Harry Weeks. He's big business now."

"Still doing Catering Supplies?"

"Yes, and Paddy and Louie are in the wholesale fruit business. They seem to be doing really well. Changed days from their fruit barrows, down the East End. Never mind. They're just as much fun as ever."

"Oh. It will be good to see all that lot again. Those were the days, Rudi." Dominic put down his coffee cup. "That was real work. Sixteen hours a day. How did we do it? Seven days a week. "I really envy you two, retiring to the country like this. And by the way, you both deserve it."

"Yes Dominic. We've been very lucky. Mind you, I still keep my finger in a few pies. I haven't completely thrown in the towel. I even thought of giving you a run for your money and opening a restaurant in Marlowe or in some place like that. There's no doubt, eating out is becoming very popular with ordinary people. Around here you've got to book a table a week in advance, sometimes two or three weeks in advance, if the place is popular."

"Is that so?" Dominic took the cigar out of his mouth and Maggie could see his mind working overtime."

Rudi laughed. "See! I knew I'd get you going if I mentioned business. Maybe we could try it as a team. You and me, Dominic. What do you say?"

"I say, very interesting, Rudi." He laughed his chesty laugh. "Very interesting indeed. I will think it over — a country restaurant — a nice little hideaway? Maybe, maybe."

"Oh, business, business. Can you men talk of nothing else?" Ruth scolded good-naturedly.

"Come now, Ruth, my dear. Remember what pays the rent." Dominic turned to Rudi. "Whatever happened about your planned trip to Poland to see your mother, Rudi? Are you still thinking about it?"

Rudi stood up and lit a cigarette. "Yes, Dominic. Do you think if I took a couple of pep pills, I could drive to Poland without stopping, after I got across the Channel?"

"Don't ask me, Rudi. Sounds dangerous stuff to me. But I know how you must long to see your homeland again. I don't blame you. It's been one helluva long time. Will you take Ruth and your little boy?"

"Of course, he'll take us. Peter and I want to go. I want him to meet his grandmother. We have no family here. It's a great loss, you know, Maggie. I suppose you have a family in Scotland?"

Maggie looked down, blushing deeply as she thought of Jamie. "Yes, I come from a large family. I have two brothers married and away from home and one younger brother, Lawrence. He's sixteen and still at school. My mother, sadly, is widowed. My father died three years ago. I miss him a lot."

Ruth smiled, "I miss my father and mother. They died in the war."

"I am sorry, Ruth. How very sad!"

"Yes. It is sad." She shook off the dark memories their polite conversation had skimmed, and smiled. "But now I have Rudi and Peter. I am very fortunate. They are my family, and I love them very much. Maybe one day, we'll have another one or even two, before I get too old. And we have lots of good friends down here in Stokewood, and we get great joy from our house and garden. I'm becoming quite a gardening fanatic. You will see it next Sunday."

"And your little boy? What age is he?"

"Peter? He's four. He's like his father, although he has my straight hair. He's becoming a little spoiled I'm afraid. You'll see him too next Sunday, Maggie."

"That's nice. I'll look forward to that."

As they drove back to London, Maggie sank back into the passenger seat lost in thought. "They're nice people, Dominic."

"Sure, they're very happy now, but they've known hard times, both of them."

"Were you happy in those days, with your wife and son and everything:"

"Oh, when we were young, I suppose, yes, we were happy. We worked together in the business. Just like Mario and Vera did. Damned hard. But I don't know what happened. We just grew apart. As we got older, we just had nothing in common."

"What's her name?"

"Maria." He was silent for a while, then said, "I think she has someone else in New York now. I pay her plenty of money to live over there. She makes sure of that."

"You sound so bitter."

"I suppose a lot of it was my fault. There were other girls, and I was always at work. Night and day. If only I'd had someone like you. You're a totally new experience to me. You're so, well... I can't explain, sympathetic, so soft and vulnerable, and at the same time so efficient." He stole a glance at her to see how she was taking his words.

"Dominic, you won't want me to say this, but I miss Jamie. I feel bad about him. And I miss home."

He sighed and after a pause he said, "Listen, I won't stop you going home. Don't worry."

They drove on in silence for some time. Eventually he spoke again, his voice serious. "I'm going to Paris next Thursday. There's a chef there I want to try and hire for the new place. How would you like to come with me? I'm coming back on Saturday. We can go to Rudi's party on the Sunday, and then, after that, it will be your last week in London. You can get ready to go home — if that's what you want."

"You know I have to, Dominic. Besides everything else, I have to be bridesmaid at Diana, my friend's, wedding. And Jamie expects me home."

They arrived at her hotel. "Let's have a little supper together, darling." He leaned close to her in the car so that she could smell his maleness mixed with the sweetness of his toilet scent. "Can you bear me to stay with you one more night?"

She kissed the pleading, schoolboy expression on his handsome face. "Well, I might as well be hanged for a sheep as a lamb, Dominic." And she smiled tearfully at him. Their conversation on the journey had moved her, so that she felt fragile and emotional.

Over dinner, he said. "Please come to Paris with me, Maggie. It will be part of my dream of you when I'm old and grey. I know

I can't have you. I'm a silly old grandfather, but my theory is we should grab what happiness we can when we can."

"I'll think about it, but, it's very risky. It's a real temptation. I've never been abroad, but, well, if Jamie should phone and I'm not here... what then?"

"That's easy. I'm on a business trip and you're my personal assistant. It happens all the time, nowadays. Believe me. Ask Arlene. She used to accompany me on business."

Involuntarily, Maggie flashed him a questioning look. She felt a stab of jealousy.

He smiled. "That was all a long time ago, my sweetheart. Believe me. And I tell you, you haven't lived if you haven't been to Paris. Especially with someone who is crazy about you." His voice was hoarse as he drew her towards him, lightly kissing her face, until he reached her parted lips when she felt his passion rise, so that she was a puppet in his hands. She felt out of control of herself, powerless to make decisions, subject to the dominance of his magnetism.

The next few days in the restaurant flew in, and on Thursday morning, she had packed her bags, and high with excitement she was whisked off to the airport to take the short flight to France. On the plane she sat petrified, her hands clutching the arm rests as she awaited take-off, much to Dominic's amusement. After half an hour of nerves, she managed to smile at Dominic, and sipped the champagne that was served, her eyes glowing. By the evening, when they had dinner in the restaurant in the Eiffel Tower from where they could see all Paris, lit up and spread out before them, she felt truly special.

"What a wonderful experience, Dominic. The view is magnificent! I had no idea Paris was so magical."

Dominic was very happy. "I'll always remember this night, Maggie. Paris by night with the most beautiful woman in the world!"

"You're spoiling me, Dominic. How will I fare back in my poor little basement flat at home, once more counting the pennies to get through the month?"

"That's your choice, my dear." He poured out some more wine. "You could stay with your old sugar-daddy. What is it they say? 'Better an old man's darling than a young man's slave.'"

"I won't be a slave, exactly. But I'll miss all this. Do you know, Dominic, I think I'd like to try a cigarette. What do you think?"

"It's not good for my darling, but why not? Let's be as wicked as we can for tonight. We have two nights together in a glorious hotel in the most romantic city in the world. Let's make the best of it." He called the waiter who soon produced a packet of tipped cigarettes for her. "And two cognacs, *s'il vous plait.*"

They got tipsy, she giggling and flashing her cigarette at all angles, puffing and blowing out smoke wildly. He laughed at her inane jokes, and saw something of the young Maggie that Jamie knew so well. The fun-loving, carefree girl she had been before she took the train to wicked London. "What a lucky man your Jamie is! If this were the Italy of my father's time, or we lived in the Middle Ages, I would have him killed, and you would be mine, no matter how you protested."

"And you would keep me locked up, like in a private harem of one, so that you could visit me and make love whenever you felt like it?" She giggled at the thought.

"Something like that."

"Sounds like it might be all right for a week or so."

"You could stand me making love to you for a week?"

"Perhaps?" She grinned teasingly at him.

"I will kill you if you tease me any longer. Then no one else will have you."

"What shall we do now, Dominic? I feel reckless tonight."

"Well there's dancing at the hotel until midnight. We could go there and have another drink, if you like."

A taxi along the Champs Elysees and then they were in each other's arms, dancing cheek to cheek, high on champagne and love. "I wonder if I'll ever be as happy again, Dominic."

"Sure you will. Life is what you make it. You will have a great life. How could it be otherwise? You are young and talented. The world is your oyster. You just have to go out there and grab happiness. You work hard and the rewards will come."

They sat down and sipped their wine, a slight cloud descending on them. "I will miss you, Dominic."

"Well if you do, *chérie*, you must call me. I'll always be there for you. You know that."

"What will you do? After I've gone home?"

"Oh I have lots of work still to do. But I suppose I might take a trip to New York and see how Maria and Nicki are doing. Maybe there is something left for me there, or maybe not. We haven't spoken for months. She never writes, but you never know. She is still my wife."

That night, their love was sweet and wonderful. He could arouse her to great passion. His experience with women was evident in the control of his desire, so that she cried out in ecstasy at the force and power of his body. Afterwards, she lay on the bed drowsy and fulfilled, then moving slowly she put her silk night-dress over her breasts, then touched his muscled arms and caressed his thick black hair as he lay smiling up at her. They stared at each other in disbelief at the depths of their passion.

"I know what you want. You want me to do it again, don't you?"

She smiled, "You make me sound insatiable."

"And are you?"

"Yes."

Then he laughed and he made love again with no preliminary until they both shuddered to a climax of pain and pleasure. "You are an animal," she said.

"And what are you?"

"I am what you have made me. A shameless, wicked…"

"Beautiful, hot child. You are all woman, and I will love you forever. Do you know you are the love of my life?"

"Please don't, Dominic. You are making it more difficult to face next week, and the time when I must go home." A few tears stole from the sides of her eyes. "I'm going to try to have no regrets, I will just blame you and your love every time I feel guilty."

He looked at her as she lay there, her lovely brown hair spread over the pillow, the swell of her breasts with their pink nipples showing through the sheer gown and said, "Okay, sweetheart. That's a bargain. No regrets. And no strings attached."

The next day was warm and sunny and after a light breakfast, they went sightseeing. "I want to show something of the paintings in the Louvre. It is a few years since I was there." Maggie was amazed at his appreciation of the great paintings on show.

"This one is by Georges de La Tour. Look at the child's face, and how the candlelight shines on his face. And the old carpenter, see how beautifully his face is lit. Wonderful!" They moved on stopping now and again while Dominic explained the merits of his favourite pictures, Fragonard's *Women Bathing*, and Delacroix's *Portrait of Frederick Chopin*. "See how he has portrayed the anguish of Chopin's creativity. The work of a master, Maggie."

She was enthralled at seeing the actual painting of the famous *Mona Lisa*, and he pointed out to her the shading of the colouring on the beautifully modelled face. "I must come back here one day and see these things again. Maybe, I'll bring Jamie. He would love it."

"Yes, why not? Bring Jamie one day," he answered, his face inscrutable.

"Dominic, you have really surprised me today. You know so much about art, I had no idea."

"Oh well, I used to know a lot about painting. But that was a long time ago." He took her arm. "Let's get out into the sunshine, sweetheart, and have some coffee. Then we can go to Montmartre. We'll see what's doing up there. The view is wonderful, and you will see the church of Sacre-Coeur."

Montmartre was as busy as ever with artists and tourists everywhere soaking up the ambience beneath the steps of the great, dominating white church. When a street artist pleaded to sketch her portrait, Dominic relented and let her pose for ten minutes. The drawing made her look like a Hollywood queen, but there was just a slight resemblance. A little crowd of admirers formed around her and the artist as he worked, and when he had finished, he proudly handed her his picture and gave a good-natured bow. "It's wonderful!" she grinned at the Frenchman. "He has flattered me I know, Dominic, but I love it anyway."

"This atmosphere is getting to you sweetheart!" He put an arm around her and pulled gently away from the friendly Parisian men who surrounded her. He held her hand and they walked around like sixteen-year-olds, their delight in each other apparent to the whole world. That second night they hardly slept. They had drunk ice-cold champagne and talked and laughed in a cocoon of happiness until eventually they were tipsy and sleepy, but still they couldn't sleep. Between lovemaking they ate chocolates and danced to the hotel radio, or played silly games with pen and paper. At last, at six in the morning they fell asleep close together, exhausted in the heady perfumed air of the bedroom, five floors up above the streets of Paris.

Chapter 10

Lewis Benton walked the half-mile every morning along the streets from his lodgings in Mrs Travers's boarding house to the office of Rodger and Russell Tubes Ltd. Past schoolchildren trudging to school, past other office workers hurrying to be at their desks by nine o'clock. Alongside the thick traffic in the uncertain early morning light of the industrial city he went. Buses, lorries and cars passed him within touching distance, all impatient to be somewhere else on this Monday morning. His weekend at his sister's place had unsettled him, and his step was a little slower and less confident than normal.

Lost in thought, briefcase in hand, he decided to cut through the park for a change. It would take him away from the endless grey tenement buildings and little shops, which, on this day he found depressing. On a hill above the park stood the magnificent pile that was Glasgow University. From his path through the great old trees alongside the river he could look up and see the students making their ways to their classes. He should have done that. He should have listened to his father when he told him to work hard, to pass his exams and try to be a doctor or a dentist, or a lawyer even. Perhaps he would have met a nice girl and settled down to raise a family.

But all these chances were in the past and would not come again. He had flunked school, losing heart after the death of his mother. He had gone for a job as a clerk all those years ago. Now, sure, he was manager of the Glasgow branch, and he had a lot of privileges and enough money. There were forty-five people whose jobs and fate were in his hands, but still he wasn't happy — well, not really happy. Life seemed to have passed him by. He was nearing retirement age, and felt he should have made a better go of things. He could have had a home and a wife if he had made more of an effort. He could have had it all — the girl, the job and the money, as Philip Larkin had said.

As he strolled along, lightly swinging his briefcase, through little groups of blackbirds hopping on the pathway, he mused on these things while looking unseeingly over the railings at the ducks on the river making their watery journeys. Then, he remembered what that briefcase contained and felt a hot flush steal over his face. He said to himself, "I must get rid of the damned thing today. Damned general manager, Charlie Ross thought he was doing me some kind of favour giving me it. Pornography! A man at the top of the tree, large salary, member of the golf club, stalwart of the church with a real lady for a wife, and he spends his spare time devouring such filthy books!"

Arriving at the office, Lewis mumbled a good morning to the staff who were early arrivals, and closed the door of his own private room. The fire had been lit and burned brightly. The mail lay ready for his inspection. He hung up his coat and stared at the briefcase. After a minute or two, he extracted the magazine and laid it on his desk. The book with its lurid cover lay there, an alien object in the room that had been more of a monk's cell than anything else. Not even Mina, who took his letters in shorthand, came into that room, at least very seldom, for he dictated his letters to her in the outer office. Only the occasional commercial traveller or the odd visitor from Head Office was ever received here.

He opened a drawer in his desk and, taking out a bottle of malt whisky, poured himself a nip. Then he lit a cigarette, staring all the time at the offending piece of print. He'd have to get rid of it, but how? He couldn't leave it in his waste-paper basket in the rooms at Mrs Travers's, nor could he chuck it in the basket here. It would stick out like a sore thumb. At his sister's house, he had had to keep it hidden.

With the whisky glass in one hand, he gingerly opened the book quarter of the way through. A dark-haired, beautiful, nude girl stared back at him, her legs spread out, her private parts on display to the camera. With two fingers of her right hand she held open her vagina, an inviting smile on her lips. Colour drained from his face as he sat mesmerised, studying the photograph. He tried to think what possessed such a lovely, young woman to pose for such a picture.

On the next page she had changed her position slightly and now was looking at a man, a bronzed hunk who stood with an erect penis eyeing her lasciviously. Lewis sat back in shock at the sight. "Good God!" for he had never been with a girl. Sixty-two years old, he was untried, virginal. He poured a larger glass of spirits and turned over the pages in disbelief and amazement. So engrossed did he become at this world of shameless sex display that he almost jumped out of his chair with guilt when the telephone rang.

"Mr Muldoon to see you, Mr Benton." The door burst open and in came Freddy Muldoon, the chief representative of the firm, travelling salesman for Rodger and Russell's.

"Lovely morning, Lewis! Oh, having a nip? Good idea! Just the thing to get you going. God Almighty! Lewis. What have you got there?" Lewis had shut the book and tried to put it in his desk drawer.

"Come on, boy. Don't be selfish. Let's have shufty!" Round of face and stomach, high colour in his cheeks and nose, with a perennial smile of jollity on his face, Freddy Muldoon was the epitome of a commercial traveller. His heavy dark blue suit fitted well round his ample stomach and beneath his dark rimmed spectacles, friendly, if myopic eyes, stared out in eternal amusement. On his daily rounds to customers, he carried jokes from one firm to another, ever welcome as a caller for his fund of funny stories.

"Christ Almighty, Lewis! Look at the tits on this one. You're a dark horse. I didn't think this would be your style. Good Lord!"

"It's not mine, Freddy. Old Charlie Ross in Aberdeen gave it to me at the weekend. It's disgusting."

Freddy picked up the book. "Sure it's disgusting. Never seen the like. My wife undresses in the dark. I didn't know she looked like this. Good God! What a show, I say!" His round eyes almost popped out of his head. Give us a little nip out of that bottle, there's a good chap."

Resignedly Lewis poured Freddy as drink. "Give me back the damned thing. I'll have to find a place to get rid of it. Perverted old bugger, keeping such trash in his house. He's got a dozen of these in his den at home."

Freddy slumped down on a leather chair, "Well, I thought it wasn't your style. You never were one for the ladies."

"No. Let's have it back. I don't want anyone else to see it."

"Just a minute, Lewis." Freddie, boggle-eyed was now reading the letter page. "Listen to this, I don't believe it! Dear Irene. Can you enlighten me on whether male sperm is fattening? I am trying to lose weight and—"

"For God's sake, Freddy! Shut up, will you. I've got a day's work to do here. You can take that piece of trash with you, if you like."

"No fear! Molly would kill me if she caught me with this. She's the original prude from way back. Thinks sex stops when you get to thirty-five or so."

Lewis pushed the magazine into a drawer and looked up wearily, "Did you want to see me about something?"

"Yes." Freddie slumped in a leather chair on the other side of Lewis's desk. Been working up to this for some time, I have to say." He looked candidly at the manager. "It's a matter of the job, you see."

"The job?"

"Yes, Lewis, my job as representative of Rodger and Russell. As you know I'll be sixty-five in July, and I'll be retiring"

"Oh God, I'd forgotten." Putting his chin in his hand Lewis thought what a bore this was. He liked Freddy and looked forward to his weekly visits. He admired his jokey attitude to life's brickbats, his bad eyesight, his inability to drive a car, his childlessness. These disappointments were all accepted by Freddy as his share of unavoidable handouts from fate. "Oh, Freddy. The place will not be the same without you."

"Well, thank you, Lewis, but I'm slowing up, you know. And Molly wants me at home. Don't ask me why." He smiled wanly. "We've worked together for a long time, Lewis. It will be strange not to come in here regularly to report to you. Have the odd drink together. Have you thought of a replacement for me?"

"Well, I have to say, Freddy, you'll be hard to replace. You've brought a lot of business to the firm. Thin on the ground, you know, people with your well-developed sense of humour."

"Well, coming from you, that says a lot. I'm very flattered. Molly and I, we want to put our feet up. Like you, we had no children. I have my painting as a hobby and the piano, and well these cold mornings, I'm not so anxious to get out of bed. But I have a suggestion for you."

"Yes?"

"How about Jamie?"

"Jamie? Jamie London?"

"Sure. He's got a nice personality. You have to admit that."

"Yes, that's true."

"And he knows the trade quite well."

"Yes. He's quite bright."

"And you have got to admit, Lewis, he's got a lovely wife. My job would be a great boost for him, especially if you added the company car. I'm sure he'd work his socks off."

"Mmm. Well, I suppose you have something there."

"I could take him round the customers before I leave and introduce him. He and Gregor have bought an old van, you know. That's the latest. It will break down and be a wreck in a couple of months."

Lewis laughed and lit another cigarette.

Freddy continued on his mission: "He's a nice fellow, Jamie. I like him. He deserves a break."

"Yes, yes, I agree. I'll think about it. You know Gregor's got a better job with more money? He's leaving the firm."

"Is he? That's a surprise."

Lewis shrugged his shoulders; "He's been offered more money at Tennants Steel, so he's given me notice. His wife's expecting number three. Poor bloke, he can't get on for falling off."

Freddy's smile disappeared for a few seconds. "We'll miss Gregor. He's always good for a laugh."

"Yes."

Freddy stood up. "I'll leave you now with your reading matter, Lewis, but just think about what I say."

As he was going out, Freddy stopped to speak to Gregor and Jamie. "You boys doing all right? I hear you've bought a van."

Gregor looked animated. "Yes, you can see it from here, Freddy. Look out the window. What do you think? We painted it green last night."

"That's what the bridegroom said when he painted it green."

"What?"

"It's a good standing colour."

"Your jokes get worse every day, Freddy."

Lunchtime saw Gregor and Jamie off to the centre of town to buy some paint for Gregor's sitting room. They sat together in the front of their second-hand van with Jamie at the driving wheel, like two schoolboys out on a spree.

"How's Maggie getting on in the Big Smoke, Jamie? Soon be time for her to come home, won't it?"

"Oh, you know Maggie. She seems to be a big hit wherever she goes. I can't keep up with her."

"Yeah. She's a smashing looking girl. You must be missing her."

Jamie steered the old van round the corner. "I miss her. She phones nearly every night, though. She's coming back in about ten days. There's Diana's wedding. She's to be bridesmaid. It's to be a big do, you know. Father's a bookie."

"I know. Prue and I have been invited, too."

"So, Maggie's a big hit in London?"

"Well, they seem to like her down there."

Gregor was silent.

Eventually Jamie said. "Never mind. Things will get back to normal when she gets back. It was bad enough when she was here at Mario's with all those dagos eyeing her, but down there, who knows what goes on? Never marry a good-looking woman, Gregor. Oh, I shouldn't be telling you that. Too late for that advice." Jamie laughed.

"Don't I know it. They set you going round in circles. Prue's got a twenty-pound dress bill this month. And soon there'll be the expense of the new baby."

"At least you're getting out of Rodger and Russell's to fresh fields and more money."

"Money! Don't mention it. This paint and wallpaper Prue's ordered will cost the earth and this baby's going to cost me a fortune, the way Prue's buying. Think of that! I tell you, Jamie, sometimes I wish I was back in the air force where I had no worries except how to get out of it. Life's a grind."

When they came out of the store, they loaded the decorating material into the old van. "Watch it! That paint is not quite dry." Gregor touched it with his fingers. "It's still a bit tacky. Did you manage to get the road-tax disc yet?"

Jamie shook his head. "Not yet. I'll get it on Saturday. I'll ask Mario to pay me on Friday. My singing money."

They jumped into the van and Jamie turned the ignition key. The engine chugged and spluttered and would not start. The street was very busy, and Gregor looked around. "Christ, Jamie. Look! There's a policeman. What's that disc you've got on the windscreen? He's looking at it."

"It's a Guinness label. I thought it looked quite like a tax disc."

"God, we're going to get arrested. Look he's coming over."

The burly policeman looked into the van as Gregor wound down the window. "Having trouble boys?"

"Yes, officer," Jamie answered with a smile. "She refuses to start. Going fine this morning."

"Here," the policeman said, "I'll give you a little push. It might just start on that little incline."

"Right," Jamie nodded. "Thank you."

The van moved with the policeman's push and this time the engine leapt into life. Jamie accelerated and they shot off into the stream of traffic. Gregor sighed with relief. "God, we were nearly in the soup there, boy. Driving without road tax! He'd have locked us up!"

Glancing quickly back, he saw the policeman in disbelief looking at his hands, which were covered, in green paint. "Ho, ho, ho, keep going, Jamie, don't stop for God's sake." As they sped away from the irate policeman, Gregor put his hands together in mock prayer, his eyes turned to the sky. "Oh, thank you, God. Thank you St. Antony and all the saints."

Back at the office, their good luck at escaping the law made them light-headed with relief. "Wait till I tell Prue about this one!"

"Don't tell her Gregor. She'll just start again about how we're a couple of clowns, risking our lives and our careers, breaking the law. You know what she's like."

"Oh, Prue's all right, really. In her own way she's just as crazy as you or I. Come home with me for supper. I think she's making steak pie tonight. You must be fed up with cooking for yourself."

"To tell you the truth, I'm going to Mario's house tonight. Vera has invited me for my supper. She's asked me to take some records to play to her cronies. She has a card school on a Monday night. But I'll come home with you and have a cup of tea and help you up to your flat with the paint and stuff."

"Please God, my mother won't be there." Gregor had cleared up his desk and was putting on his coat.

"Your mother? What's she been up to?"

"You know, she keeps trying to help us furnish the bloody flat. We need a carpet for the sitting room and you'll never guess. She turned up with a big rug, beautiful carpeting it was from a shop that was closing down."

"Sounds good."

"Good? There were four holes cut out of it. No kidding. Each hole was about fifteen inches in diameter where the carpet had been round the pillars in the shop. It was ridiculous, but she couldn't see it. She kept moving our furniture to try to hide the holes.

Eventually Prue started to giggle and it got to me. We ended up helpless, but the old lady still couldn't see what we were laughing at."

They reached Gregor's place and picked their way through the toys and building blocks surrounding the plump toddler. Jamie sat on the floor, good-naturedly playing with the little boy. "Still got your cat, eh, Prue?"

"Yes, and no mice, thank goodness. What do you think of Gregor getting a new job?"

"It's terrific. He deserves it. More money, too, I hear."

"Yes. It will be great to get some bills paid and get on our feet again."

There was a ring on the doorbell and Gregor answered it, soon returning with his bustling, hyped-up, buxom mother. She was carrying an awkward brown paper covered parcel, which she quickly unwrapped. "I got these two deck chairs from Johnny's second-hand shop, Prue. Look at them. They've hardly been used. Ten shillings each. Quite a bargain."

Gregor stood looking at them, his hands in his pockets. "Mother, what will we do with deck chairs? It's armchairs we need."

"Well, they'll come in handy. You're so ungrateful, Gregor." A plump little lady with grey hair and rosy cheeks, she sat down exhausted after carrying the deck chairs into the house, "Isn't that right, Jamie?" Jamie nodded, afraid to disagree with her.

Her plump bosom heaved with breathlessness, and she accepted a cup of tea from Prue. Turning to Jamie for sympathy she proceeded to harangue him about how she was never done trying to help her son and his family. "You know I brought them a beautiful carpet the other day. Real Wilton it was, and they didn't want it. It had a lovely pattern. Admittedly it had been cut up a bit." She took a sip of her tea, still trying to get her breath back.

Jamie felt the mirth rising inside him and he was scared to look at Gregor or Prue. "Really, Mrs McFarlane?"

"Five pounds. That's all the shop was asking for it. It would have been lovely in the front room. They could easily have covered up the empty circles."

Helpless laughter engulfed him and he could not restrain it any longer. The more he tried to stop, the more he dissolved in chuckles and the little lady eyed him coldly. "They've told you about that carpet, haven't they?"

Soon Prue, Gregor and Jamie were laughing uncontrollably, so much that a smile broke on the once-pretty face of Mrs McFarlane, and she had to start laughing herself.

Home to shower and change into his black shirt and white tie, the outfit Jamie liked to wear to play his jazz records. As he tied his tie he sang to himself.

He lifted the photograph of Maggie, and seeing her carefree smile, sadness crossed his face. He put down the photo frame, and picked up Maggie's perfume and a pretty scarf, thrown carelessly over the mirror, and after frowning, continued singing.

Picking up the phone he dialled and waited. A voice told him, "Maggie will be back tomorrow, Mr London."

"Back tomorrow? Where's she gone?"

"Mr Valente had an urgent business meeting in Paris. Maggie went along to help with the negotiations. It is very fortunate that she can speak French, as you know."

Stunned Jamie answered, "Paris? Speaks French? I see. Thank you. I'll phone tomorrow night." His expression had changed from yearning to anger. He looked unseeing in the mirror for several seconds, trying to cope with the information. Gone to Paris and hadn't even phoned to tell him! He looked at the little pile of records he had chosen from his collection, and they seemed dull, worthless objects to him now. What was the point? What was he doing? Where was he going? His spirits in his boots, he walked slowly to the door.

Mario's and Vera's flat was luxurious. The chairs were covered in cream-coloured leather and the drapes were of expensive-looking oatmeal coloured material. To Jamie it seemed just like a Hollywood film-set. There were expensive ornaments, mirrors and pictures in the spacious sitting room and a large, arrangement of flowers on a table at the side of the fireplace. On another table stood crystal decanters and several bottles of liquor.

"What will you have, Jamie?" On her home territory, Vera looked younger and prettier, and more relaxed than he had first thought in Mario's.

"Whisky, please, Vera."

She fixed him a drink. "Supper will be in half an hour. We're almost finished our game. Come and meet the others." There were seven people, mostly in their fifties or sixties, well-dressed and relaxed as they sat holding their cards, and giving only half their attention to him.

"This is Jamie, folks. I told you about him. He's brought some records to play for us. Put something on now, Jamie." The company made him feel young and out of place, but he did as she said and soon jazz filled the room. Enraptured by the music, he stood over the radiogram and was startled when one of the ladies came up close to him and asked him to dance with her. She was light-footed and fun, and a really good jive dancer. At the end the others applauded them. *No one will believe this story tomorrow*, Jamie thought, *Wait till I tell Gregor about my evening with the oldies.*

Supper was quite a casual meal — soup in bowls and little sausage rolls and meat pies with vegetables and salad to which you helped yourself. There was also a table with several sweet dishes. People just found a place to sit while they chatted as they ate. The lady who had danced with him, cornered Jamie, and enquired about his job, his family, and flirted with him just a little, in spite of her sixty-odd years. At about eleven they started to leave, and Jamie prepared to leave, too.

Vera put her hand on his arm when she saw this. "Oh, hang on, Jamie. Mario will be home soon. He'll expect to see you here." She pulled him back and closed the door after saying goodnight to her guests. Standing up close to her, he saw that her eyes were heavy with black mascara and eye-pencil. Although she was good-looking for a lady of nearly sixty, close up her rouge showed thick on her face, and there were wrinkles around her mouth.

She held a glass in her hand. "We could dance to this one, Jamie." Frank Sinatra was singing something, and she swung her arms around him. She was a surprisingly good dancer, and although he had drunk quite a lot of whisky, Jamie still felt embarrassed at being alone with a sophisticated woman. He kept looking at the door, expecting Mario to arrive at any moment.

"Let me put on one of my records," she said, and he saw that she was quite drunk as she swayed over to the radiogram. "A Nightingale Sang in Berkeley Square" started and she held him close and sang the words, softly, to him,

Her perfume was strong and disturbing, and the closeness of her slim body was not unpleasant, but Jamie's mood did not match hers. He sat her down on the great, cream leather couch by the glowing electric fire and suggested he made some coffee.

She jumped up. "Oh, come into the kitchen, Jamie. I'll make it. And stop looking at the door. Mario wouldn't mind us having a dance. He knows you're coming here tonight."

"Look, Vera. It's after midnight. Maybe he's been held up. I'd better be going."

"Sit down. Have the coffee first. Tell me about Maggie. I suppose she's a big success in London. When is she coming back?"

"Supposed to be on Saturday. That's in five days."

"Why do you say, 'Supposed to be'?"

"Oh, I don't know. I phoned earlier this evening and she'd gone to Paris with Dominic."

"Oh?"

"Exactly. Supposed to be on a business trip."

"Well, maybe it is."

"Yes, and maybe it's not."

"She's got a lot of sense. I think you can trust her."

"I used to think that, too."

"Do you never look at other women, Jamie?"

"Oh, I look but — she's..."

"I know you're in love with Maggie."

"Anyway, nobody else ever looked at me. Unless you count the half-drunk diners on a Saturday night in Mario's when I'm doing my numbers."

"I look at you, Jamie." He looked down in embarrassment at his coffee. "I know you think that's ridiculous, but I think about you a lot. You know, you're, well, you're... how can I put it, charming and well... gentlemanly, I suppose. I love it when you sing." Jamie opened his mouth to say something but was lost for words. "You think I'm a silly old woman?"

"Oh no, Vera. No, you're attractive, and you're... you're vivacious, and you have a great personality."

"I have everything but love."

"Mario loves you."

"I suppose he loves me. We have a kind of affection for each other, but that's all. We sleep apart."

"I see."

"Yes. That side of things went ten years ago. He has his little romances, which seems to keep him going. He was really gone on your Maggie. But he's... he wouldn't let it go further."

Jamie looked serious. This new world he found himself in through Maggie was perplexing and beyond his experience. "Mario's a nice man. You get the feeling you can trust him. He's got principles"

She rose impatiently and lit a cigarette. "Principles, yes, but he needs to get out of the catering trade. I've had it with sitting alone most evenings. I want to go on a cruise. I want him to retire. I want to go to Italy. Did you know I had a daughter?"

Jamie raised his eyebrows, "I didn't know."

"Yes. I haven't seen her since she was three weeks old."

"You and Mario have a daughter?"

"No. She's not his. I had her when I was sixteen, and she was adopted by my cousin who brought her up. They moved to Rome during the war, and I lost touch with them. I heard that she was clever and went to college, but then my cousin died, and I don't know what happened to the family. She would have been fifteen at the end of the war. Marianne, she's called."

"Haven't you ever tried to trace her?"

"Not really. At the end of the war, there was no money, nothing. Europe was in such a mess. Me and Mario were working night and day in our jobs just to make a living. We had so little. But now, I see I should have tried to find her and my cousin's family. Mario has some relations in London, but none of my family is here."

"I had no idea, Vera."

"Let's have a night-cap. Mario's later than usual." She poured two large whiskies, added soda water and handed him one. "If only Mario would let go of the business, then we could go and try and find her."

"Frederico is anxious to manage the new place I hear."

"I know. Mario should take a chance on him. He has a lot of experience. It might be the makings of him."

They heard a noise of the front door opening. Slightly stooped and looking tired, Mario appeared in the doorway, dressed in his eveningwear. "Ah, still here, Jamie? Good! We can have a drink together. Play one of your records for me. Play something smooth and soothing."

"Here's Bing Crosby singing 'Deep Purple'." Just your era, Mario."

"Yes, that's nice. Tell me, what do you hear from Maggie?"

Vera had placed herself on the settee, her slim body relaxing, her silvery grey gown spread around her, her blonde head leaning on the couch as she watched the two men.

Jamie said, "Oh, Maggie's fine, thanks."

Vera interrupted. "She's gone to Paris with Dominic."

Only a momentary pause as Mario lifted his drink to his lips would have revealed his surprise at this news. "Paris? Oh, yes. I seem to remember him telling me that he was after the chef, Pierre, the French guy at 'La Morena' for his new place. So he took Maggie with him?"

Jamie looked a bit crestfallen. "To tell you truth, I'm a bit worried."

Mario rose and started to walk around carrying his drink. "I'll phone Dominic tomorrow. It would be a business trip, Jamie. He would want to show off with Maggie as his secretary. That's all." He stopped behind Jamie's chair and leaning down whispered in his ear, "It'll be all right. I love her too, you know."

Jamie rose and emptied his glass. "She's due back next Saturday evening. I just hope she turns up, that's all."

"Hasn't she been phoning you?"

"Oh, now and then, a quick call. But she didn't tell me about the Paris trip. I found that out by accident."

Vera, who had been musing on the attractions of Dominic, and the thought of a few stolen days in Paris, interrupted her reverie to say. "She'll come home all right, Jamie. She'll settle down, you'll see. You two should start a family. That would help."

"Yes, but Maggie wants us to buy a house first. That's her ambition anyway. Then we might be able to start a family. It's getting late, folks. I've got to go. I'll pick up the records later in the week."

"I was telling Jamie about Marianne, Mario." They were walking to the door to show their guest out.

"Oh, yeah?"

"He thinks we should have tried to find her long ago."

Mario bowed his head. "Maybe we should. Maybe we should." He patted Vera's hand sympathetically and pulled the door open for Jamie. "Nice to see you, Jamie. Thanks for coming round. Goodnight."

"Goodnight, Mario. Goodnight, Vera."

Chapter 11

Frederico stood in his office at the back of the kitchen combing his hair. He had stripped out of his chef's outfit, and put on a pair of corduroy trousers, a checked shirt and a sports jacket, strangely diminished from the towering white figure he had been earlier in the evening. He looked at his melancholy face in the mirror as Luigi came up behind, ready to leave the steam and noise of the past six hours.

"You going home to that empty house, Frederico?"

"Yeah, Liza still hasn't turned up. She promised she was coming home. Maybe she'll phone tonight. Or maybe even Mary might want to talk to me."

"At eleven-thirty?"

"They know I work late."

"Listen, I said I would meet Dolly and Alice in the bar."

"Dolly and Alice? You mean those two waitresses Mario hired yesterday. No thanks, do me a favour."

"Come on Frederico. They're nice girls."

"They're both married. I've got enough problems."

"So what? A little drink. A little talk. That won't do any harm."

Frederico sat down and gave a sigh. "Luigi, you have a wife at home."

"Oh, come on, give me a break, my friend. She won't miss me for a couple of hours. Anyway, she's got religion. Every night, when I get home, she's reading holy books, the Bible, prayer books. Rosary beads! I can't stand it. She's lost her charm."

"Oh, Luigi. You and Myra are a scream. I don't know what I'd do for laughs around here if you weren't here. This religious kick will pass, you'll see." Frederico's face had broken into an amused smile at his friend's downcast expression.

Luigi slumped down at the table. "I hope so."

"If she sees you in a bar with two women, she'll soon forget about the Bible, the Holy Ghost and all that." Frederico laughed. "I know Myra. She'll throw you through that big mirror out there."

"Oh, Frederico," Luigi gave a wan smile. "I just try to cheer you up, that's all."

"I know, Luigi." Frederico looked into the kitchen, all shipshape and quiet now. Empty — like his life."

Luigi was watching his friend, trying to read his thoughts. "What's happened about Liza? What's the story? She has had the operation? She got rid of it in Manchester?"

Frederico's face became dark again and he looked at the floor. "Yes," he said.

"She's definitely coming back home?"

"She said so. Soon, I hope."

"And then?"

"I don't know." Frederico shook his head glumly. "Where did things go wrong, Luigi? I did my best. Sure, I was a bit wild sometimes. I wasn't always there when Mary and the kids needed me. But most of the time I was working. I'm no saint, but this abortion business has thrown me."

"Better than an unwanted kid at her age. It's for the best in the long run. You'll get over it, and Mary will come back to you, you'll see."

"You think so? This boyfriend she's found, he's got a car to drive her around in, and he doesn't work late every night like me."

"Why don't you buy a car and pay it up? Hire Purchase? That's what everyone does nowadays. I did it. It's easy to get an agreement from the car people."

"You think so, Luigi?" Frederico looked interested, then he shook his head. "No, I couldn't afford it."

"Nobody can afford it. They just do it," Luigi's face was incredulous at Frederico's attitude. "You find the money somehow."

"You'll help me to buy a second-hand one? You'll come with me?"

"Sure I will. Come on, life's too short to waste time talking. We'll go and see the girls. Have a laugh. No strings, eh Frederico?"

Frederico rose reluctantly, "No strings," he repeated.

They found the two waitresses in the cocktail bar at the back of the restaurant. They had removed their caps and white aprons and had added another layer to their make-up. Dolly was the plumper of the two. In her late forties, she had brown hair, good legs and wore long dangling earrings. Frederico sat next to her.

Alice was prettier and maybe a bit younger. Her hair was blonde and she smiled a lot. "Come on boys. Have a seat." Her voice was cosy and persuading.

Frederico started the ball rolling. "You two look as if you're having a good time. You always have a drink after work?"

"Well," Dolly crossed her legs and smiled. This is our first Saturday here, so we're just getting the lie of the land. It's a lovely restaurant. Is he good to work for, this Mario?"

"Sure, he's a good man." Frederico said. "I've known him almost all my life."

Alice looked round the table, "Of course. You're Italian, too."

"Yes, so is Luigi."

They both giggled at this while the barman placed another four glasses on the already crowded tabletop. He removed some of the empties and walked away with an inscrutable expression on his face.

The conversation and laughter grew steadily louder as the rounds of drinks went down. Luigi said, "Listen here, Alice and Dolly. There's a new Indian restaurant opened just round the corner from where I live in Kelvinside. You two fancy some Indian nosh? Have a few laughs?"

They looked at each other and Dolly said, "My Brian will kill me."

· Luigi had his arm around Alice. "Don't be silly. Ring him and say there's a party on at Mario's. You'll be a little late."

Frederico knocked back another whisky. "No, Dolly, don't do that. He'd probably come right over and beat us up if you ring him."

Luigi said, "What about you, Alice?"

"Oh, my man's gone on a night out with the boys. The kids are at my mother's for the weekend. I'm a free agent." She looked pleased with herself, and a little drunk.

Frederico stood up, "Let's go, then," he said.

The Indian restaurant was dark and atmospheric, full of the smells of spices and the sound of plaintive Indian music. At the door stood a large, fat old Indian gentleman, dressed all in white, a turban on his head. He succeeded in drawing in quite a few bemused customers to the world of Indian food, helping people with their coats and mumbling the strange sounds of his language as he moved smiling around the foyer.

Frederico and Luigi drank lager with their meal and the party became quite outrageous and noisy as the night progressed. Luigi whispered to Frederico, "How about your place, Frederico? There's no one there, is there?"

"My place, sure!" Frederico was quite reckless by now. Followed by the other two, he left the restaurant with his arm around Dolly. His heart was not really in the escapade, but her body felt soft and yielding, and the evening took its inevitable course as each couple became hot and lustful in separate bedrooms. The girls stayed for only about an hour, had a last drink with the two Don Juans and asked for a taxi to be called, becoming worried, at last, about the time of night. Luigi said goodnight to Frederico, shaking his hand for ages, then walked unsteadily home by himself, hands in his pockets, feeling at least ten years younger.

Frederico, his brain numb, his body aching from the punishment of a long day in the kitchen, and the unaccustomed efforts he had put in afterwards awoke on Sunday morning, feeling the effects of the curry, and with the usual hangover. He sat at the breakfast table feeling ghastly, while Vincent poured coffee and gave him some aspirin "What time did you get to bed last night, Dad?"

"Quite late." Frederico drank his coffee. Presently, he said, "What time did you get home, Vincent?"

"Oh, about two-thirty."

"Well, I was in bed at two." He felt like an adolescent trying to cover up.

"I found a lipstick in the bathroom."

Frederico looked blearily up at his son. "So you found a lipstick in the bathroom."

"You know, you're too old for this caper, Dad. Who was she?"

"Oh, nobody. Luigi brought a couple of girls up for a drink. That's all."

"Dad, how could you?"

"What do you mean?" His voice was rising as he stared at his son, "Am I a saint? Your mother's got her boyfriend."

"She hasn't." The boy sat down. "She's left him. She and Liza might be coming home. Maybe tonight!"

Tears welled up in Frederico's eyes and spilled down his cheeks.

Vincent put an arm on his father's shoulders. "It's all right, Dad. I think Mum's going to ask you to take her back. To forgive her."

"Forgive her?" his voice was shaking. His eyes fell on the lipstick in his son's hands. "Don't tell her about this, boy. Don't let her know about this. Put it in the rubbish bin." His voice was breaking.

"Of course not. I won't say a word. Now let's get this place cleared up, and have a meal ready for them."

The phone rang and Frederico answered it, "Hello. Mario? What's the matter?"

"Frederico. How are you?"

"Okay."

"And Luigi? I saw you leaving with those two waitresses."

"Oh, that was just a bit of harmless fun. We went for an Indian meal over in Kelvinside. Just for a laugh, you know, Mario."

"Is Mary back yet?"

"She's coming home, Mario. She's coming back with Liza. Maybe tonight."

"That's terrific, Frederico. I knew she'd come back. But listen, I want to talk to you about something?"

"Yeah?"

"I want to discuss your job at the restaurant."

"Discuss? What's to discuss?"

"Well, don't get so excited, Frederico. There are a few things I have to say to you. You know, this Andre character hasn't worked out very well. He's too smart for his own good. He upsets the staff."

"Yes?"

"Well. I've fired him. How do you fancy doing three nights a week as manager, and three nights a week off? I'll do Thursdays, Fridays and Saturdays to start with, and you can do Monday, Tuesdays and Wednesdays. Luigi can take over your job. And the same system at lunches."

"You mean I manage the place three days and three nights a week?"

"Yes. I'd do the rest. What do you say?"

"I…"

"Think about it, old friend. Come in tomorrow about six-thirty and we'll talk it over. *Ciao*."

"*Ciao*, Mario."

Frederico put the phone down quietly and stared at his son in a daze. "Mario, he gives me manager's job."

"Really?"

He almost fell into the chair. "I can't take it in."

"This is great, Dad. Solves a lot of problems. Congratulations!"

As they hugged each other, a car door slammed and they moved to the window to see Mary and Liza paying off a taxi and picking up their bags.

The flat that Gregor and Prue rented was spacious in a red sandstone building in a quiet, middle-class area of town. They were constantly in a situation of trying to decorate the place, no light task. The ceilings were high, and there seemed to be acres of woodwork to be painted. They went about their task in a kind of working silence, each lost in their thoughts of what the future might bring, some inner drive pushing them onwards in search of a better way of life.

Engrossed in their evening of home improvement, they were surprised by the doorbell. Prue opened the door to find Diana and her boyfriend, John, standing on the doorstep. "We've brought some fish and chips." Diana looked fetching and happy, dressed in old clothes and John had put on an old set of overalls. "We're here to help with the painting."

"Oh, you two, you're sent from heaven. We're in such a mess with this decorating." She held a plump child in one arm, her stomach bulging straight out, in advanced state of pregnancy.

Gregor too appeared at the door, smiling, holding a paintbrush in one hand and a still younger child in the other. "Come in, come in! This is great. We can't get on with things, with the kids around all the time."

They presented Prue with the brown paper packages, four mouth-watering fragrant fish suppers. Diana said, "Let's eat these now, folks, and then we'll get stuck in with the painting for a few hours. That should get you on a bit. Let's say until ten o'clock." Her eyes fell on Prue's unbelievably large figure. "Gosh, Prue. You look as if you're going to have that baby any minute."

"I know. It's four days overdue, now. And we so wanted the decorating to be finished before the new baby arrived."

Another knock on the door and Jamie arrived. "I thought you might need a hand with your painting, guys. Here I am. James London, painter extraordinaire!" Soon there was great activity in the place as paint was being slapped on. Diana was clearing up while Prue bathed the children and gave them their supper. Her great stomach got in the way of things, but the talk was good, the jokes flew fast and furious and a semblance of a fresh, sparkling living room was starting to appear.

"What do you want this time, Prue? You've already got a boy and a girl."

"Oh, I'm not fussy. As long as it doesn't take much longer to come. Oh!"

"What is it?" Diana stopped mopping up the floor.

"A pain." She put down the child she had been attending to and held her stomach.

Diana froze. She had never seen anyone in labour. "Give Jack to me. Oh, Prue, sit down. Has it started?"

Prue let out a muffled scream and Gregor came rushing in. Pale-faced, he mumbled, "I'll phone the hospital. Where's your case with your things?"

"It's in the bedroom."

"Oh, I'll have to change my clothes. Oh…" Gregor ran this way and that, still holding on to the paintbrush. "It'll be all right, love. Don't panic. I'll phone."

Prue looked at him in disbelief. "Put the paint brush down, Gregor. Calm down." His red hair was smirched with cream paint and hung in garnished corkscrew curls round his flushed face.

"I'll just get myself cleaned up. Hold on, Prue, love. I won't be long."

Within an hour, a taxi had called for them. Prue ambled out and Gregor, jittering with excitement, the suitcase bobbing at the end of his great long arm, had gone with her. "Phone my mother, Jamie. She'll come and take care of the children." Prue threw at them as she got into the car.

Next morning, Gregor phoned Jamie just before he left for Rodger and Russell.

"It's a boy, Jamie! Can you believe it?"

"Congratulations, that's great. How's Prue?"

"She's fine. I'm just going home to see the kids. I'll go up to the hospital again tonight."

"I'll come too. I'm really pleased for you, Gregor. I'll phone Maggie and tell her the great news."

Some of the euphoria went from Jamie as he reached the office, and waves of nervousness went through him as he dialled London. He had to put from his mind the knowledge of her going to Paris with Dominic, and besides, he shouldn't have been using the office phone. He looked around him surreptitiously as he waited to hear her voice. "Can't talk long, Maggie. Just to tell you, Prue had a little boy last night. They're both doing fine."

"Oh, Jamie. That's great."

"Everything Okay with you down there?"

"Yes. I'll be home on Saturday. I'll let you know the time. If it's late, I'll come to Mario's. Are you at work?"

"Yes. Old Benton'll be in soon. I'd better go."

"Right then."

"Bye, Maggie."

"Bye, Jamie. See you."

Without doubt, Jamie thought that she sounded cooler. Decidedly cooler. Something was missing from her voice. He felt his heart sink although he could not explain what was wrong. He mused on the situation for a few minutes, trying to control the tide of unease that was threatening to overcome him. How could the person who meant most to you in the world hurt you like this? He pushed the thoughts to the back of his mind. She would soon be home. He'd know for sure then.

Mr Benton came hurriedly through the door as Jamie stood looking at the telephone. "Good morning, Jamie. I want to see you in my office in ten minutes. Right?"

"Right, Mr Benton." Jamie panicked. "God! Had he heard him using the office phone to speak to Maggie?"

With trepidation he knocked at the door. Mina held up crossed fingers and Jamie, looking at Gregor's empty chair, longed to see that cheery grin and hear a witty remark that would make him feel less nervous.

"Come in. Sit down, Jamie. How is Maggie? Coming home soon?"

"Yes, oh yes. She's fine. Coming home week on Saturday Mr Benton."

"Good, good." He cleared his throat. "Well, Jamie, as you know, Gregor has left us and we are in the process of interviewing other people to find someone to take his place. I know the work is piling up, and I appreciate how you and Mina are coping, and taking on extra work. However, I have to tell you… God! What was he going to say? …that other changes are in the offing."

"I see." Jamie strangled a cough that was trying to escape.

"Yes. And for you, too. I have been discussing the matter with Mr Muldoon and Mr Charles Ross, our general manager, and they are both in agreement with me, that I should offer you the job."

"The job? You mean Gregor's job?"

"No, no, no. Mr Muldoon's job. He is retiring at the end of May."

"Mr Muldoon's job? Sales Representative?"

"Yes. Now you've got it. What do you think? Can you do it? Of course, you'll have to travel a bit — the Borders, Edinburgh, that sort of thing. You make your own timetable. But there's a company car with the job. You'll have to choose a new car yourself. I know nothing about cars."

Jamie was knocked sideways by this news. "I…" He tried to respond but nothing was coming out.

"Now don't answer without thinking. It's a big step. Perhaps you might want a few days to think it over."

"Mr Benton, I don't need a few days to think it over. I would love to have Mr Muldoon's — Freddy's — job, when he retires."

He said he would give you a bit of training in your first few weeks. You think you're up to it?"

"Absolutely. I'm sure, Mr Benton."

The older man could not help smiling inwardly at the eagerness and delight on Jamie's face. "Your salary will rise by quite a bit, although we do not work on commission in this firm. I'll fill you in about bonuses and that sort of thing later. And you can claim expenses, of course. You will join the management and occupy a different position with more status within Rodger and Russell." Jamie's face was blank with shock. "Let's shake hands on it. And welcome aboard."

Jamie beamed delightedly at the thin-lipped pale face. "Thank you, Mr Benton. I can hardly believe my ears."

"You'll be phoning Maggie tonight, I presume, to tell her about your promotion?"

"Well, no. I think I'll surprise her when she gets home."

Lewis Benton smiled one of his rare, wide, pleased smiles. "Good luck, anyway." He stood up and once again they shook hands. "Now it's back to work for the present. Your new post starts on the first of June."

Chapter 12

Central London and a sunny Sunday morning dawned. The fashionable streets had thrown off their punch-drunk air of Saturday's shopping frenzy and a lull had fallen on the city. In another hour, a new day's traffic would begin grinding into gear.

"Hurry up, my darling. We have a long drive to Oxfordshire ahead of us. I want to make a day of it. We can stop for lunch somewhere nice. I want to make a start."

"Just a minute, Dominic. I want to read this letter. It came yesterday, and I haven't had time to look at it. We shouldn't have stayed so long in bed."

"I wouldn't say that, sweetheart." He put his arms around her and tried to kiss her.

"Please, Dominic!" Maggie pulled away from him good-naturedly. "Can't you think about anything else? I've just put this dress on for Rudi's party. You'll crush it."

"Okay! You win. I'll go out on the balcony and have a smoke. He snuggled a kiss into her neck and ears, and stroked her hair. I give you five minutes."

The letter was from Diana.:

15 Rosepark Avenue,

Glasgow.

Dear Maggie.

I can't believe that three weeks have passed already since you went down to work in London. We are all looking forward to you coming home on Saturday. I have so much to tell you about the wedding plans. The invitations have gone out, and in a few weeks I should be Mrs John Gillan., and off on my honeymoon.

We plan to go to Jersey, but that's a secret, so don't tell anyone. John is getting just as excited as I am. Our house is ready and starting to be furnished. We have had quite a few presents already.

John and Dad are getting on really well. I think Dad is going to help him to start a little business — a garage in Bearsden. Anyway it's to be something to do with cars, so I can soon stop work, if things go according to plan, and start having babies. That's what I'm really looking forward to.

I thought we could try on the dresses once you get home. They look really lovely, and my only worry is that you will outshine the bride. Never mind. I can't wait to see you, and I'm sure Jamie feels the same. We've seen quite a bit of him lately. He's been a bit of a knotless thread since you left, and I know he's dying to see you again. Mario too has been very subdued and quiet since you're not around. I think you brought out the best in the old soul. We are all going to help Gregor and Prue with decorating their living room on Sunday.

I'd better close now as I've still got lots to do regarding the wedding. Mum's having a party for me at home, a week on Saturday, so you and Jamie are, of course, invited.

Lots of love,
Diana

Maggie finished reading the letter feeling sick and guilty.

"What's the matter with you?"

"Oh, just hearing about home and what they are all doing."

"Put it out of your mind. You'll see them all, I suppose, soon enough."

Ruth and Rudi's house was charming, warm and welcoming. There were about twenty guests, most of them round about Dominic's age. The place was graciously furnished with some fine antique pieces and expensive rugs. Maggie looked round, impressed, and then she caught sight of herself with Dominic in the large hall mirror. Slim and tense looking, she stared back at herself. She was at least two inches taller than he was. That cold-faced woman in the mirror is me, and that sallow-skinned, middle-aged man is my lover. My God! What has become of me? She threw back her hair defiantly. She would have to face things, and somehow get through this social gathering. Then she would think things out. Dominic, beaming with happiness, failed to notice her disquiet.

In spite of everything, it was a charming evening with Rudi playing the piano after supper and everyone standing around him, in a sing-song, so that, Maggie warmed up a little and dropped her inhibitions. She had had quite a few glasses of the punch, which had taken the edge off her nerves. Surreptitiously, she had been watching her fellow-guests, the bank manager, the local doctor, the homely friends from the village, and the old friends from London, but she had caught no censorious looks from any of them. No one seemed to be bothered that she was the girlfriend of someone old enough to be her father.

The doting Dominic was attentive, hardly leaving her side. Only at one point, when she had gone to the kitchen for a glass of water, had she had any opportunity to talk with Rudi. He sat there having a cigarette, and quietly sipping a malt whisky.

"Have a seat for a minute, my dear. When do you go back to Scotland?"

"Next Saturday, Rudi. Next week's my last in London."

"Dominic's going to miss you. I've never seen him look so happy."

"Yes, I'll miss him, too. We get on well together." She gave him a frank look, her blue-grey eyes steady. "You two are very old friends?"

"Yes. Before I met him, believe it or not, he had been training to be a priest. Did you know that?"

"No. I can't imagine that." She was a little shocked.

"Oh, yes. It was his mother's doing. But it wasn't to be. He gave up after two years, came to London, and went to study art at the Royal College of Art in London. He's wonderful at drawing, you know."

"He's told me nothing about any of this."

"Well, he met his wife, Maria, about that time, and he gave up art and opened a little cafe along with her. It was lovely, very

Italian, you know, checked tablecloths and lots of spaghetti, all kinds of pasta and pizzas, different sauces. It was all quite new — a fun place to go to in those days."

"I see."

"Yes, they had only one child, a boy, Nicki, but he has turned out to be a disappointment to them."

"I've met Nicki," she said with a smile.

"Oh yes? I haven't seen the boy for years. Anyway, you've been good for Dominic."

"Oh, he's a nice man. He was so good when we were in Paris. He showed me all the sights, you know the tourist things. He took me to Montmartre and the Louvre and I could see he was in his element there."

"Really?"

"Yes. I could see he had a really good knowledge about the paintings, but he didn't tell me he had studied art."

"Oh, yes. He had talent. Could maybe have made something of himself in painting, but like most people, he had to buckle down to making money. What about you then, Maggie — when you go back? Is it back to Mario's restaurant?"

"I suppose so. I should like to take up studying again. Working as a receptionist is a bit of a blind alley."

"Oh, you'll probably be raising a family soon. You're very young."

"Well, I don't want to end up in a rut, with children and not two pennies to rub together. I'm a bit scared of poverty, I'm afraid." She accepted a cigarette from his packet.

He smiled kindly, "Come on, it's not that bad. For some girls, children and a home are enough. You'll change your mind a bit when the time comes. Your husband, Jamie, does he have a career?"

"Well, he works as a clerk. Really, it's a bit of a dead-end too, and not a lot of money in it."

Rudi's voice was sympathetic. "Oh well, things will—"

Dominic came into the kitchen. "So there you are! Come on, they're dancing next door. I need you, sweetheart."

Rudi rose, holding his cigarette in a sophisticated, continental fashion. "Ah, you don't escape his clutches for long." And as she left with Dominic, he gave a little bow to her apologetic gaze.

On the way home, she sat musing in the passenger seat as Dominic drove silently through the dark evening, leaving the country hedges and fresh air behind as they drew nearer to London. "What will you do with yourself, do you think, Dominic — I mean when the restaurant is closed on Sundays, or in the afternoons, after I go home?"

"Slowly die of a broken heart."

"Oh, don't talk so crazy!"

There was a silence, then he said, "I suppose you wouldn't stay for another week? The place is booked solid for two weeks. The new chef's coming over a week today. You could deal with him. He speaks hardly any English."

"No, Dominic. I must get back. It wouldn't be fair."

Another silence, then as he manoeuvred some traffic lights and a right turn. "Will you miss me?"

"Of course."

He gave her a quick glance in the half-light. "You don't regret anything?"

"Yes, I'm sure I'll regret what I've done. But I couldn't seem to stop what happened. I'll just have to live with the guilty feelings. When I think of Jamie, I feel bad."

"It wasn't your fault. I just fell for you that first night I saw you in Mario's. You were so desirable."

"Ah, Dominic, but you've done this before, and, you'll do it again with someone else, no doubt."

"Never like this." As they drove along through the thickening traffic, they sank into a silence.

"Let's stop here and have a coffee, and maybe a cigarette."

"It's eleven o'clock, Dominic. Will they serve coffee this late?" They were outside a hotel, lit up in the bar and dining-room. The place looked very busy.

"I've got something to show you, if we can find a place to sit down."

They found a corner table in the bar, and when the coffee had been served, he drew out a box from his pocket. "I want you to have this. The box sprang open to reveal a ring, a solitaire diamond." Her mouth fell open. "Put it on. Go on try it."

The ring sparkled on her finger, but she didn't smile. "It's magical, Dominic, but I can't take it."

"Why not?"

"Maybe it will bring you back to me."

"No, no." She stared almost horrified at the jewel.

"Please, honey." His face was very close to hers, his brown eyes earnest and pleading.

She took off the ring and looked straight into his troubled face. "How could I go home with such a ring? How could I explain it? Besides, that's not really the point. It would seem to me, and to everyone else like payment for services rendered."

"Don't be stupid. You know that's not true." His tone had changed.

"Well, that's what it would look like. Please put it back in your pocket." She was near to tears now.

"All right, all right! I know when I'm beaten." He closed the box on the ring and replaced it in his pocket.

When they reached home, she hurried out of the car. Turning, she said, "Please don't come up with me tonight. I don't feel well."

"But we have only a few nights left when we can be together."

"Please. I'll see you in the morning." She passed through the swing door of the hotel leaving him standing, camel coat hanging open, a black strand of hair falling over his disappointed face. Somehow, he knew that a spell had been broken.

In the days that followed, she was distant and polite. He didn't ask and she didn't invite him to her room. In the restaurant, the work was hard and hectic. At night she slipped away quietly, and in the lonely bedroom, lay serious and quiet, troubled and sleepless. She saw that he was hurt, but felt that if she relented she would find herself pulled down as in a whirlpool by the strength of his feeling for her.

161

It was Friday morning, just before the madness of the lunchtime crowd, when, as she stood at the entrance of the glitzy restaurant, dressed very correctly, her hair pulled back quite severely, when he appeared suddenly before her. "I must see you tonight, Maggie. I am dying without you. Are you quite set on going tomorrow?"

"That was our arrangement." She stood stiffly, avoiding his eyes.

He looked down at his shoes. The muscles in his face were working to control his emotions. Maggie felt her throat constrict. Her eyes wet with tears she greeted the first of the customers.

"Can I see you this afternoon? It's important to me, Maggie."

"No," she was blushing and becoming flustered. "I have some shopping to do, and I have to pack."

"Will you wait for me tonight?"

She flushed again and his eyes seemed to bore into her heart. She dropped her gaze from his face "All right, I'll wait behind." Then conversation became impossible as the hubbub of the business of greeting and escorting patrons to their tables commenced.

That night it was Dominic's tears that flowed with sadness. The champagne he had brought sat unopened on the bedroom dressing table. He sat slumped and powerless, his evening suit bulging slightly over his middle-aged stomach, his heavy face held up by his rounded hand. He watched her as she carefully and precisely changed into her negligee and removed her earrings. She combed her hair under his watchful gaze, and then when she had finished, she looked seriously at him. "I'm going to go back to studying. I gave up at seventeen, and I shouldn't have done. I've wasted six years, just playing around."

He stared at her without answering.

"You, too, Dominic, you wasted a lot of the time in your life when you could have been an artist, or a scholar, or anything. Rudi was telling me."

"What does Rudi know? I am rich. That is what matters. Who wants to be penniless?"

162

"Then you would have had something to interest you. To fall back on. Not just restaurants, and cutlery and table linen, and ordering food, and chefs and all that work and worry."

"I love my job. I art in it, too."

"But it doesn't seem to be enough for you."

"No, that's true. At least not since I met you." He removed his jacket and took out his evening cigar. "If I open the balcony door, may I smoke?"

"Of course."

"What will Jamie do while you are doing all this studying?"

"Oh, Jamie'll never change. He'll never make a fortune. He has no desire to. It's old jog-along Jamie, I'm afraid. But I'm different."

"What do you want from life then?"

"I don't know. But I'll know when I've got it. You don't blame me, do you?"

"No, I was the same at your age. Divine discontent. I don't blame you. But you should be careful. Things can go wrong. Wrong choices can be made never to be unmade."

"Like you giving up your art education?"

"Well, I felt I had no choice at the time. I needed money badly. In those days that was the only way. One didn't live in sin. One had to battle for a place in the world."

"Do you think things have changed that much? Don't you think the young still have to battle?"

"Well, I suppose so. But, well, the atmosphere is different now. People don't actually go hungry any more."

She threw him a look, her young face strangely strained. "It's still an indifferent world. God helps those who help themselves."

"You don't sound like yourself, Maggie."

"Maybe this is the real me."

"And what I'm offering you is not what you want?"

"This is an unreal situation, Dominic. It is a hiatus out of life. It is not what we should be doing."

"You are wrong. You might never live life so intensely again. Perhaps never in your entire life." He came very close to her, his

163

face close to hers. "Do you realise that? It might never be as good again."

She faced him, paling a little. "You think I should stay?"

"I want to marry you." She stared silently at him. "And perhaps have children."

She shook her head. "You know I have a commitment to Jamie. I couldn't do that to him. I have to go back and sort out my thoughts and feelings. Maybe try to make up to him for… for these last few weeks."

"You'll never do that."

"Don't say that. Don't say 'never'. It's a horrible word."

"Then you must not say 'never' either. I'll always be there for you. I'll always love you, Maggie. If things go wrong when you get home, you only have to lift the phone to Dominic."

Then the tears of suppressed emotion burst forth and Maggie sobbed quietly as she sat, shoulders slumped, head lowered, seated in front of the dressing-table mirror.

"Don't cry, honey. It's not your fault. I must bear most of the blame. I talked you into this." She didn't reply. "And it's Jamie's fault, too."

"How is it Jamie's fault?"

"He should have stopped you. He should have seen the danger signals."

"He's not the type to see danger signals. He trusts people too easily. I suppose he is a bit of an idiot, but… let's not apportion blame. We'd never be finished. It's done, and we've done it. We'll just have to live with it."

He lifted the bottle from its cooler. "Will you have some wine? This will be our last bottle together. At least for a while."

She sat on the bed, her face serious and set, like that of a devout nun, but the black lace on the pink satin of her negligee and the curves of her body were those of a seductive temptress.

"Who can say no to champagne?" A watery smile lit up her face.

He smiled, "And to a rich man who adores you?"

"Well," she smiled. "It's not easy."

They sipped the wine looking conspiratorially at each other. "I wish I were thirty years younger. You'd never leave me then." A bitterness was in his voice.

"Oh, come!" her eyes were mock seductive, and her fine teeth flashed enticingly above the champagne glass. "You don't do so badly... for an old man."

He slapped her playfully and she retaliated. They rolled about on the bed in a mock fight. When they stopped, she said seriously, "What will you do when I'm gone, Dominic?"

"Oh, maybe I'll go to New York for a holiday. Or maybe I'll follow you up to Scotland. I could gate-crash Diana's wedding. See you in all your finery and try to change your mind."

"No, please. I couldn't bear that, Dominic."

He caressed her hips and breasts. "Just once more, darling. Just once more." His voice grew thick with passion. They kissed with tenderness, and his passion inflamed her, so that she succumbed, all thought of the morrow blotted from her mind.

Chapter 13

The taxi driver had carried two of her cases into the cold, and shabby basement flat that was her home. Maggie stood in the large rambling hallway and took in, as though for the first time, the Victorian wallpaper, the low ceiling, and heavy doors of the place. She wandered from the kitchen with its ancient iron range where a low fire glowed, and studied the old-fashioned wood round the sink. It was scrubbed almost white, so that it matched the bare wood of the large kitchen table. From there, she moved as if in a daze to the main bedroom. There her photograph smiled back at her from Jamie's side of the double bed. She sighed. *Well, this is it! This is me, my life.* The phone rang.

"Hello, guess who?"

"Dominic?"

"How was your journey?"

"Oh, okay."

"Glad to be home?"

"Yes. I'll unpack later. Everything seems so strange after being away."

"Jamie at Mario's?"

"Yes, I'm just going to change and go there."

"For the big reunion?"

"Well…"

"I love you."

"Dominic!"

"The offer still stands."

"I'll remember. I have to go now. Time's getting on."

"Yes, well just remember, I'll be thinking of you all the time. Goodnight, my darling."

"Yes, goodbye, Dominic." She stared at the telephone for a few seconds, and with an effort of will she turned round and headed for the bathroom and started the hot water running.

Within an hour she was walking into the noisy, crowded restaurant, where Jamie's voice was coming from the bandstand, tuneful and upbeat. People were quickstepping to the beat of the band. She heard the words of the old tune, telling her that she stepped out of a dream, and within seconds she met his eyes.

He gave her a little nod of recognition, carrying on with the number. Mario came scurrying along out of the kitchen and gave her a joyful welcome. "Maggie, you look wonderful! It's good to see you. When did you get back?"

His face was beaming with pleasure as he led her to a side table, "Come and say hello to Vera. Jamie will be finished in a minute."

"Well, hello, Maggie. The wanderer returns."

Maggie smiled, her eyes turning back to the bandstand to watch the finish of the song. He came towards her, and it seemed as if he walked in slow motion, his eyes now on her, and now on the tables that separated them. They faced each other shyly, and there was just a hint of reserve from him. Then he embraced her and she felt relief and joy in his arms. "Well, sweetheart, so you've come back to us. He kissed her cheek, dropping his arms. "How was your journey?"

"Fine. It's good to see the old place and everyone again." She looked around the room, smiling broadly aware that he was studying her face. "And you, Jamie, you look well. Still singing up a storm, I hear."

"Well, thank you!" his expression seemed guarded. "I've got one more number to do. Then I'll be able to relax and talk to you — hear about your trip." He looked at Mario and Vera. "I've got the sunshine back in my life, folks. Who would believe it?"

Maggie thought Vera stood exceptionally close to him, her eyes flirting, her body pushed against him. "Don't forget, Jamie, dear. You're coming to my little party tonight — directly after the shop closes."

167

"Of course, Vera. Of course." He smiled broadly at the three of them, then hurried back on to the bandstand where they were playing his introduction.

"You'll come, of course, Maggie?" Vera was watching Mario as she spoke. He had not taken his eyes from the girl. "Your fan club will all be there." Mario dropped his gaze. A harder edge had crept into Vera's voice, and she looked Maggie up and down, saying, "I must say, London has put a gloss on you."

"My fan club? What do you mean?"

"Sure, all your admirers. Mario, Jamie, Frederico."

Maggie laughed, "Oh, well, it sounds like a good party."

Mario put his arm around her. "Of course she'll come. It can be a double celebration, for my wife's birthday and for Maggie's homecoming. Two things that make us all happy. And there'll be a few old friends there, like Art Buick and Linda. You'll like them."

By one in the morning, Vera's party was buzzing with conversation while Jamie's record collection made up the background music. He stood talking about jazz with Buick while Maggie stood alone fiddling with her drink. She was feeling a bit chilled, as Jamie seemed not to want to speak to her too much. Mario came to her aid, "Let's go into the kitchen. Vera has prepared a buffet. We'll see if there's anything you fancy to eat. You must be starved after that journey. Come and eat."

In the kitchen, she picked up a little salad and lifted a fork. "What's wrong with Jamie, Mario?"

"Nothing. Oh well, maybe he's just a little resentful at you going away. He'll come round. Anyway, I'm delighted you're back. Was Dominic good to you? He was okay about you coming home?"

She flushed, "Yes... of course."

"That's good, then." He looked around the kitchen. "We all missed you, you know. It will be great to see you in the restaurant again on Monday."

"Thank you, Mario. I missed you, too. It's great to be back."

"Let's go and join the others then, if you're not hungry." He squeezed her, and kissed her cheek, his face beaming.

On a couch in the corner, Jamie and Vera were talking intently. He did not look up as she passed. The warmth of his greeting in Mario's when she had first arrived back from London seemed to have evaporated. Fear and rejection shook her. She saw her reflection in the mirror and found a strange, serious girl with long dark hair staring back. *I must smile and rise above this. I just wonder what he's playing at.*

"Hey, Maggie. Isn't it great about Jamie's promotion?" It was Buick sounding off in a loud voice, half-drunk and super confident. Everyone stopped speaking.

"Promotion?" She looked at Jamie, but Buick was on a roll. "He's to be his firm's representative, executive of the firm — big new car, and lots of leisure time. Time to pull the birds, what my old son?" Buick slapped Jamie on the back.

He rose and crossed over to her side, "I was going to tell you about it later."

"I see. Congratulations." To hide her feelings, she said, "Excuse me," and hurried back to the kitchen. Vera, Jamie and Mario followed her and found her deflated and miserable, sitting at the table.

"What's wrong?"

"If you wanted to humiliate me, Jamie, you've succeeded very well."

"Humiliate you?"

Mario took Vera's arm and they quietly left the two of them alone. "You've practically ignored me since I got back. You could have come to the station to meet me, or at least, have been at home when I returned. I came back to a cold, silent house."

"That's what I've come home to for four weeks, now."

"I couldn't help that. You knew I would be in London for four weeks." She looked up at him with troubled eyes, through her tumbling brown hair.

His face was strained. "You hardly phoned. You didn't tell me you were going off to Paris… and… well, somehow you seem different. You look like a different person to me."

"I am not different."

"Oh no?"

He turned and looked out of the window at the blackness of the night. "You're not like the Maggie who went away."

She couldn't answer. Eventually she said, "Why didn't you tell me about your promotion?"

"I haven't had a chance."

"That's not true. I felt such a fool when Buick came out with it."

"Are you back home for good?"

"Of course."

"You're going back to work at Mario's?"

"Of course."

He walked around the kitchen, looking at the cupboard doors, composing his thoughts. He was hurt beyond measure and yet he couldn't put his feelings into words. Eventually he sat down at the other end of the table from her. Her eyes followed him. "Well, I'll be away for a bit, a week at the least. Rodger and Russell have given me some time off before I start my new job with them, and Vera has asked me to go to Rome with her to help to look for Marianne, the child she had when she was very young. She has some leads on how to find her. Mario can't get away."

"Rome?" she was shaken.

"Yes. Benton has given me the holiday, and Vera and I are setting off on Monday."

"And Mario is in agreement with this trip?"

"Yes. He's quite pleased. It has given Vera a new lease of life. Something positive to do for her at last."

"And you are doing this without even speaking to me about it first?"

"I wasn't sure you'd be interested."

She burst into sobs. "Oh, that's not fair."

He put his hand on her heaving shoulders. "Don't cry, Maggie, please." He did not want the protective wall he had built up during her absence to be breached. "I'm going back to join the others. Fix up your face. Don't give yourself a showing up." His voice was sad and soft "We'll talk about it later."

After this episode, the atmosphere at the party seemed to be petering out. Mario tried to mend the rift, but the ice was there and nothing would crack it. Silently, Jamie drove them home, and they entered the flat, still without saying much. His face downcast he switched on the bedroom light and lifted his pyjamas and robe. "I'll sleep in the other room tonight. You'll be tired after your journey and I have some paper-work to do."

"Is that all you can say?"

"Should I ask about London? Or Paris? Do you want to tell me about it?"

"I had to go — you know that. It was a straight deal between Mario, my employer, after all, and Dominic. I was lent to help get the place started in London."

"And in all London, there was nobody else who could do it? And you just had to accompany him to Paris? Nobody else could do it? Do you think I'm a fool, entirely?"

She bent her head and sobbed. "You are making me feel miserable."

"And he made you feel wonderful, I suppose. I'm sorry, Maggie. I can't help how I feel about it. I'm going to bed now."

"And you won't talk to me? Tell me about your promotion?"

"Well, it's a good break for me. It's an opportunity for me. The car will be great to have. But well…" he broke off. "I think I'll go to bed now."

This withdrawal of his love was new to her. She felt her chest tighten with the pain and anxiety of it, and she didn't know what to do. She sat rigid on the bedroom chair, her mascara streaked, her hair hanging now limp and lifeless round her face. She held her head high and bit her lip.

Staring at him wildly now, and whispered, "And you are definitely taking off with Vera on Monday?"

"Yes. It's all arranged. Can't be changed. Goodnight." He closed the door.

Wearily she undressed, too tired to feel anything. His coldness had hurt her badly. She had never seen his good nature desert him and she dreaded the morning for what new accusations it might bring. But next day she saw little of him. He went out in the morning, and did not return until evening, refusing the meal she had cooked. Afraid to open any further conversations, she retired early to bed, her heart breaking.

As she came out of the bathroom the next morning, she found him standing at the front doorway, ready to leave. He held out his hand, saying quietly "I should be back in about a week or so. I'm sorry things are so... like this, Maggie, but you... well, must understand, it's all been a bit too... oh, I can't explain now. I'm just a bit disappointed, I suppose."

"Just because I went to London?"

"If only that were all."

"And you're sure there's more?"

He looked straight into her eyes. "Yes." She dropped her gaze and said nothing.

"Vera and I should be back in about a week.

"Are you in love with Vera?"

"No."

"Are you having an affair with her?"

"No. That's a silly question. Would Mario condone this trip if that were the case?"

"I don't know."

He lifted his suitcases. "Anyway, I'll see you when I get back." His eyes softened. "I'll miss you." he smiled weakly. "I'll miss your silly, childish, smiling face. Perhaps we can talk things over and try and work something out."

She longed to smile and throw her arms around him, but she found herself saying. "I won't be here."

"Where will you be?"

"At my mother's."

"Oh." He opened the door and was gone.

"Hello, mother?"

"Is that you, Maggie?"

"Yes. Will you be in this afternoon? I thought of coming over to see you."

"Yes, I'll be in. Anything wrong?"

"No. Nothing. I'll see you about three. Bye."

"Bye."

Helen Fisher was a small, thoughtful lady, widowed now for five years. Her two oldest boys had left home, one to work in Manchester, and the other in London, while the youngest boy, Lawrence a boy of sixteen and still at school, was all of her family she had left at home. Maggie had been her father's favourite, never close to her mother. At fifty, Mrs Fisher had settled down to widowhood, trying to content herself with her memories, her dressmaking hobby, and the company of friends and relatives. The house was seldom empty, as she was a sympathetic soul who listened to peoples' troubles. She had never quite matched up to the brilliance of her clever husband, and had spent a lifetime in his shadow, still she loved nothing better than to reminisce about him and his inimitable ways. When Maggie arrived, the table was set with the second-best china and biscuits, cakes and scones.

"So, my dear, you're looking well. Did you enjoy your time in London?"

"Oh, it was fine. Very exciting. The owner of the restaurant bought me some new clothes, for the job, you know. I had to be ultra-smart."

"Well, you always were a smart girl. And how's Jamie?"

"He's fine. He's gone to Rome for a week."

"Rome. My goodness! For his job?"

"No. It's a kind of holiday. He's helping a friend of ours locate a long-lost relative."

"I see."

"Mother, what would you say if I asked to come to live with you for a week or two?"

Helen caught the import of the question immediately. She paused. "Come here? To stay? Of course you can." She saw the agitation in her daughter's eyes and rose to put her hand on her arm. "What's wrong, my pet? You and Jamie having a bad patch:"

"Something like that."

"He didn't like you going to London?"

"No. Since I came back, he's… changed. We seem to have lost something." Her voice shook.

"Well, don't worry. There's plenty room here. You bring your things and I'll get your old room ready for you." She smiled. "Your old mother won't let you down. You'll be a bit of company for me at nights. Lawrence is hardly ever in these days." She was making a great effort to hide her shock and upset at her daughter's news.

"Oh, thanks, Mum. But you're not really old. Fifty's not old, nowadays. You should go out more. You might meet someone else."

"Oh, I don't think so. An old man with plenty of money, and a bad cough," she laughed. "No, no. No one could replace your father. Old devil that he was! Never mind me, anyway. You and Jamie will make it up."

"I don't know."

"Is there someone else? Has Jamie been seeing someone else?"

Maggie shook her head vehemently, "No, no, not that."

"Have you?"

"Not really. Jamie was jealous of my being in London, and sometimes I forgot to phone him. And he didn't like me going to Paris with my boss. But, well… that's over now, and I have to cope with it."

Helen busied herself with the teapot while Maggie stared into the coal fire, which burned in the hearth of the old fireplace throwing out a warming glow. Eventually she looked up said "I'm thinking of applying to university, Mother, to study English Literature and maybe Art History."

"Oh well, that sounds all right. You're young enough, and you have the ability. You're certainly wasted as a receptionist in a restaurant. You were always brainy, just like your father."

174

"I'll have to work at Mario's for the present. That should keep me going financially, and I'll try to save some money. I've still got a little of the money Father left me, but not much."

"You'll be company for me, Maggie while you're here." Her mother tried to sound warm and encouraging, but her stomach was full of butterflies at the situation. She added, "But, remember, I always liked Jamie, and I hope you two can make it up."

"We'll see. You know I'm to be matron of honour at Diana's wedding in two weeks."

"Oh, yes. How lovely! I'd forgotten.".

"We'll see what happens by then."

Two days later, Maggie, cosseted and fussed over by her mother, felt as if her marriage and the last two years had all been a dream. She could feel herself regressing into the gym-slipped girl of yore as her mother served up special meals for her, and washed and ironed her clothes. As she relaxed in the afternoons by the fire, her thoughts full of confusion, sometimes of Dominic and his passion, and sometimes of the hurt face of Jamie, she tried to make sense of her life. She knew that somehow she'd been a fool, but couldn't quite pinpoint where she had taken the wrong step. *Just a stupid cow, I suppose!* she thought bitterly.

Her mother called her to the phone. It was Diana. "Maggie. I heard Jamie's gone to Rome with Vera, so I guessed you'd maybe be back at your mother's."

"Yes, I'm staying with Mother for a week or two."

"Mario tells me you're working at nights only, nowadays, so I won't see you. Is anything wrong?"

"No, everything's fine. How are the wedding plans?"

"Oh, all right, but I would like to see you. It's not long now, you know. Just two weeks. Maybe I could come and see you, say tomorrow afternoon. I'll get off early."

"Sure. That would be great. You can stay for tea."

"Right. I'll be over about four."

A posh, new Morris Minor Traveller car, its varnished wood trim shining in the afternoon sunshine, arrived at the door with the chic Diana at the wheel. "It's Daddy's but he lets me borrow it. He's on the lookout for a little car to suit me."

"Gosh, Diana! You have all the luck. Come in and meet Mother."

"I've brought the headdresses to show you. I hope you like them."

"Oh, they're gorgeous!" They spent the next half-an-hour preening in front the mirror while Maggie's mother fussed around them as they discussed the arrangements for the wedding. "Are you going to keep working after you're married, Diana?"

"Yes, Mrs Fisher. For a while, anyway. I'd miss the restaurant, and all the crises and panics. It's good fun, there's always something happening. And we will have a mortgage to pay, you know."

"Do you plan to have a family, Diana or are you going to wait for a while?" Helen Fisher loved her bit of gossip.

"Well, I hope not for a year or two. I just want to enjoy the first few years of us being together, under the same roof."

She's in seventh heaven, thought Maggie. *It seems like another lifetime since I felt so full of confidence in the future. I hope she's not disappointed.* But she said, "Is John excited?"

"He can't wait. He missed his football on Saturday to go and see about his suit and other arrangements for the wedding and the honeymoon. We talk about nothing else."

Diana drove Maggie to Mario's after tea. When they were almost there she said, "Are you and Jamie all right, Maggie? You seem a bit down."

"Well… Jamie's a bit off me, I think."

"Because of you going to London?"

"Yes."

"He thinks there was something between you and Dominic?"

"Yes."

"You miss Dominic?"

Maggie paused. "He… yes, I suppose so. I'm a bit mixed up just now."

"But you are going back to Jamie?"

There was no answer from Maggie, and Diana took her eyes from the road for a second to catch the pain in her friend's face and see her brush her eyes with her fingers.

"Oh, no Maggie! You and Jamie. You are like the Rock of Gibraltar. Solid. What happened in London, anyway?"

"I kind of fell for Dominic."

"But he's old."

"I know."

"Put him out of your mind, Maggie. He's a Casanova type. Jamie loves you."

"Oh, I don't know." Maggie sat up straighter and flicked back her hair, "Look, you've got the wedding to think about. I don't want to spoil your happiness."

"You've got the wedding, too. And Jamie'll be there. He'll be back in time, and Vera and Mario are invited. I hope they don't let me down."

Maggie gave a half-smile. "Jamie said he'd be back in about a week, so he'll be there all right. Then he starts his new job at Rodger and Russell. That's a great break for him. Are Gregor and Prue going to be able to come to the wedding?"

"Yes, Gregor's mother's going to baby-sit. I'll bet Prue's been shopping for her outfit already, if I know her."

"You're right. Prue just loves clothes. Gosh, just fancy, they've got three children already. I can't believe it."

"Time flies. What a pair they are. We helped them to do up their sitting room. We were helping them, Jamie was there too, the night Prue was taken in to have little Deborah."

"Is that what they called her? So that's Jack, Melanie and Deborah. All the happy families." Maggie sighed and stared out at the traffic.

Diana said, "Things will work out for you, Maggie. You'll see."

That same evening, Maggie went to work, mechanically smiling at customers and answering the phone. By eleven, she was exhausted and demoralised with the effort. A sinking feeling had invaded her, as if her whole life was going down the drain. "I'll phone for a taxi, Mario. Mother will be waiting up for me."

"You don't look so good, my dear. Are you all right?"

"Sure."

"Oh well, things were a bit dull tonight. It's not so good without the band. And you're missing Jamie?"

"Yes."

"Or is it Dominic?"

She answered in a low voice, her face deadpan but her eyes flashing. "Mario! Why would you say that?"

He looked at his shoes. "I don't know. Well, I know you and how impressionable you are. And I know Dominic. He phoned this evening. Asked how you were." She stared at Mario, feeling devastated. "I told him to leave you alone."

Maggie looked away, unable to speak. She could not meet Mario's eyes. "We shouldn't have let you go to London. Where is my sweet, bouncy girl? Where is the lovely young lady that used to work for me?" He saw her distress. "I'll get you a drink."

He returned with a bottle of sparkling wine and two glasses. They lit cigarettes and she said, "You've heard from Vera?"

"Yes. They arrived in Rome this afternoon. They're okay. She sounded quite excited."

"I hope she finds what she's looking for."

"I hope so. It was very good of Jamie to go with her. She's knocking on sixty now, and really needs someone to look after her in this great quest of hers." Maggie did not answer. "He'll come back to you, Maggie, you'll see."

"Well, he's been pretty offhand with me. Very cold."

"He's hurt."

"Yes. Mario, I've been thinking about things, and I'm going to find out about taking up my education again. I've dropped a line to the university."

"You surprise me. I had no idea you had that kind of ambition." He was quiet for a moment, drinking his drink. Then he turned his crumpled face to her; weariness seemed to have invaded him, as he picked up her mood. "So I will lose you too?" She gave him an enigmatic smile in reply, and he hurried on, "No, no, you must do what seems right. You know, you are like my daughter."

As she looked into his emotional, dark eyes and was warmed by his affection. "You'll never lose me Mario. Where would I be without you? You've been so good to me."

He continued to look adoringly at her, then he said, "Try to forget Dominic. Sure he loves you, but he's well over twice your age. You have a life to live. He's done everything there is to do in life. He should go back to his wife."

"I'll phone for a taxi, Mario." Her face was drawn and grim.

"No. I'll phone. You sit there and finish your drink."

Chapter 14

Jamie pressed the button under the name Giannelli. He and Vera stood outside the apartment building in the suburbs of Rome like lost souls peering through the locked glass doorway. They could see a white marble staircase leading to the floors above, and in the corner, a little lift.

There was a click on the intercom and a voice answered in very fast, almost indecipherable Italian. Vera answered in Italian, "I am Vera Pacitti. I have come from Scotland. I wrote to you about a girl called Marianne who comes from Palermo."

A pause, then the voice said, "*Uno momento*." A young woman with blondish hair and a striped T-shirt came tripping down the white stairway. She opened the outside door to the block of flats.

Vera stopped forward in front of Jamie. "You are Gina Giannelli?" and she held out a hand, which the pretty dark-haired girl accepted. They looked at each other, and Gina gave a half-smile. "*Si*, that is me."

"I am Vera Longhana Pacitti from Bagheria, Palermo. I wrote to you about Marianne Bernardino."

"*Ciao, Signora Pacitti*." Her smile widened. "I got your letter, *si Signora*."

"This is Jamie London."

Gina smiled again and shook hands with Jamie who found this meeting highly embarrassing. To Vera she said, "Come with me. Our apartment is on the first floor." As they went up she said, "You must have known my mother, Maria Corrina."

"Oh yes. Of course. I remember Maria well." Vera's face had become thoughtful, "We were good friends once. How is she these days?"

"Oh, you know. She's all right. We don't see a lot of each other. Dad and she live in Naples now. They're retired and are doing quite well. Please come in."

The room they entered had the same white tiling on the floor. It was light and pleasant, although the furniture was heavy and solid, many pieces chased with brass, quite obviously many years old. The walls were almost white contrasting with the heavily-framed pictures. In the corner was an expensive wooden chess set laid out ready to be played, and behind that an artistic arrangement of flowers.

"Please sit down." She indicated a formal hard-backed sofa of pale green damask, then said, "Please, if you will excuse me for a moment, I will make some drinks and we can take them up to the roof. It is pleasant up there at this time of day. Is coffee all right? My husband will be home soon."

They took the lift to the roof where they looked over the roofs of the area, and when they were seated around a little garden table, Gina started, as if primed for the occasion, to tell what she knew of Marianne. "I was a friend of Marianne Bernardino at University. She was a year ahead of me, but we lived in the same block of flats, and I knew she was from Bagheria." She handed out cups of coffee.

Then she continued, "Marianne had a job teaching English at San Giovanni School in Rome, but I know she has left that school now." She shrugged her shoulders and spread her hands, her expression registering the trials of life, "We just lost touch, that's all." She put down her cup. "It is quite sad I suppose." Then after a pause she went on, her face screwed up in her effort to reconstruct the past. "Her husband is Hugo Rossi. They have two children, Rosa and Eddy. But that was ten years ago."

Vera's face was flushed, "So the children will be what age now?"

"Let me see, Rosa will be about fifteen and Eddy will be about twelve, I should think." Stunned at this news, Vera fell into a reverie, sipping her drink and gazing out over the rooftops. She turned as she heard the door to the roof terrace open. A dark-haired young man entered and Gina rose to greet him. Then, taking his arm, she brought him over to them, saying proudly, "This is Mando, my husband. He works for the local government. He works very hard, you know." She shook her head teasingly, and caressed his back. He smiled broadly and shook hands with them with easy manners, while still basking in the glowing admiration he was getting from his wife. Vera chatted with the young couple in Italian, and then, for Jamie's sake, they switched to English.

The good-looking Mando plied them with nuts and biscuits and soon more aperitifs were produced. "Would you like to stay and share our evening meal?" he asked.

Vera was tempted to accept, but she felt they had imposed long enough. "You are very kind." Smoothing out her dress, Vera rose from her seat in the sun. She smiled at the two young people. "But we can't disturb you any more. I have enjoyed meeting you, and your help has been very precious to me."

Jamie too stood up. He felt a bit like a fish out of water, sensing his function there was unclear. "Yes, thank you for your hospitality. I enjoyed the drinks and seeing your nice apartment and your beautiful view here from the roof."

Vera closed her little notebook, where she had jotted down Gina's information, and replaced it in her handbag. "Perhaps we can meet you two kind people again before we leave Rome. We would like to buy you a drink."

"Oh, yes!" Gina's cheeks were pink now with all this unexpected excitement, "I would love to hear... Mando and I would really like to know if you are successful. And I should love to see Marianne again."

As they made their way out, Vera said, "What a lovely apartment you have here!" and she and Jamie stopped momentarily to survey the carefully chosen ornaments, and the peaceful, very Italian air of the cool living room.

"We have no children, yet, so it is easy to keep the house looking nice." Mando put his arm round his wife, "Maybe someday, eh, Gina?"

When they were leaving he shook hands, and his face became serious. "I must beg you to be careful of the traffic when you go out, please. Cars come very fast around the corner."

A taxi took them to the Excelsior Hotel where they dined quietly, exhausted after the events of their first day in Rome.

"I must have an early night, Jamie, you don't mind, do you? How about we have breakfast at around eight-thirty. Is that all right with you?"

"Yes, I'm tired too. I wonder what Gina and Mando made of me. They probably thought I was your boyfriend."

"Don't be silly. I said you were a friend, and so you are. I tell you I wouldn't have had the nerve to do this on my own. I have been trying to persuade Mario to come with me for years. But he wouldn't. Your presence gives me confidence, you know that." She smiled up at him, little lines wrinkling on her tired face. "I am very grateful to you, and remember, it is also a holiday, and I want you to enjoy yourself while you are here."

"Well the first day has been interesting. I wish I spoke some Italian." He looked down at the cutlery on the dining table, and fixed his eyes on the little candle, which burned there giving a romantic glow to their meal.

"You are still cut up about Maggie, aren't you?"

He flushed. "Things are a bit tense between us. You know, as soon as she got to London, I felt she'd changed. She seemed to be on cloud nine all the time. Not the same girl at all. And going off to Paris with him without even letting me know. That was the last straw. I felt she… she just didn't care about me once she got away from her home." His face was twisted with his effort to articulate his hurt.

"I bet she still feels the same for you, Jamie. You will have to give her a chance. She's very young and impressionable. Give her time. She'll come down to earth."

Jamie's face was closed and his eyes were hard. "Oh, we'll see."

"Tomorrow we can seek out this school, San Giovanni's, and see if we have any luck, and maybe we'll have time to do some of the tourist things as well."

"Yes. That would be great. I'd love to see St. Peter's Basilica and, of course, the Michelangelo ceiling in the Sistine Chapel. I've heard so much about them."

"Yes, of course. You shall. I want to see them again, too. But bear with me, Jamie, if first we go this school and try to find out about Marianne."

The principal of the school was cultured and charming, a balding man in his fifties. He offered them tea in his room. "Yes, I remember Marianne Rossi. She was a good teacher, very reliable. Her husband was a teacher, too. He taught mathematics. She was here for about three years, I think. A nice girl. She is a relative of yours?"

"Yes, my cousin's daughter. I would like to see her again. We have come for a holiday in Rome, and I thought while I was here I would look her up."

"You left Italy a long time ago?"

"Yes, over thirty years ago. I was born near Palermo in Sicily. Jamie here's from Scotland. He has kindly offered to help me to look for Marianne."

"Ah, Scotland! I know it for whisky and football, and he mimed playing the pipes."

"Yes, bagpipes." Jamie smiled.

"I was in Edinburgh once, many years ago. A lovely city with the castle and everything. I have a cousin who runs a restaurant in Edinburgh." Suddenly he became serious. He tapped his fingers together and looked down at his papers. "About Marianne Rossi…"

Vera got fidgety during this pause. "To tell you the truth, Signor Lembo, Marianne Rossi is not my niece, she is my daughter." The bald head was raised and he flashed her a surprised look. "Yes! It's true. She was brought up by my cousin in Sicily. I haven't seen her for… since she was a baby. There was the war and everything, you know, and I just lost touch." She broke off speaking then, and looking down began to search for her handkerchief in her handbag.

"*Mamma Mia! Signora!* This is very sad for you! But I know there are lots of stories like this. Those were dreadful times. The war was terrible." He shook his head sympathetically and then began bustling about the room. "Excuse me, *Signora, Signore.* I will have to check up on this, but I will have to go and look in the files in another room. There will be a record of Marianne's period here, without doubt. Excuse me." He left the room, calling to his secretary.

Within half-an-hour they were leaving the building with the name of a school in another part of Rome, the EUR district. It was on the *Viale di SS. Pietro e Paolo*, and they had instructions to take the Metro B to the terminus.

Jamie, looking at the nerve-wracked face of Vera suggested, "Let's have lunch and a drink to freshen us up. You've had enough excitement for one morning." She agreed and they took a taxi to the *Via Conciliazione*. There the Romans carried on with their noisy daily round without concern for tourists or thought for past history. They sat down thankfully at a pavement cafe to eat a simple pasta meal, with a bottle of red wine to warm them, for there was a cool breeze blowing. Through the tourist-thronged street the pilgrims and visitors made their ways chattering enthusiastically, either going across the great square to the Church of St. Peter or coming back full of wonder at the grandeur of the buildings, and the awesome works of art to be seen there.

The temptation was too much for them. Vera gave in to Jamie's eager face as he viewed the magnificent building, unable to conceal his curiosity, and they joined the stream of people, and soon found themselves passing the immense bronze door into the interior of the great church. Such majesty and grandeur left them for some minutes speechless. Jamie wandered from chapel to chapel, trying to take in the overpowering beauty of the sculptures and decoration. He was totally absorbed by the great Chair of St. Peter and the spectacular dome. Sadness filled him as he thought of Maggie and wished she were there to see it with him.

"We might as well see the Sistine Chapel while we're here," Vera said. She felt like a mother treating a fond son. After standing in line for some time they were allowed in to see Michelangelo's magnificent frescoes and she watched Jamie's face as he drank in the mastery of the paintings.

Without taking his eyes off the splendours around him, he whispered, "This is just terrific, Vera. I wouldn't have missed this for the world. It's fantastic."

"Well, tomorrow you can throw a coin in the Trevi Fountain, so some day you will return. That's what they say happens if you throw a coin in the water. I will, too. Then we can come back." She looked at him slyly, "And bring the one you love. And so will I."

"I wonder if she would be just as enchanted as I am."

"Oh, I'm sure she would. Or else she's not the girl I think she is."

A taxi took them to the Spanish steps, so Vera could renew old memories. There they rested with all the other tourists, soaking up the atmosphere of flowering azaleas and warm sunshine, amid the babbling tones of different languages and the remnants of past civilisations.

That evening, as night fell, they dined in the atmospheric *Trastevere* among the ordinary natives of Rome, where street lights illuminated the busy scene, and where little candle-shaped lamps made each table seem a romantic oasis. With a bottle of wine they relaxed, waiting to be served, and soaking up the ambience of the spring night. Between courses, a strolling accordionist entertained the diners, and they smiled and clapped enthusiastically when he came to the end of the song. Jamie leaned over towards her. "Tomorrow could be the big day, Vera."

"Oh, don't say it. I'm afraid to think of it. It's real scary, Jamie. I have to push myself all the time to do it. Just to lay eyes on her and to be able to say, "That's my child, my daughter..." she paused and became serious, "...but perhaps she won't want to know me. I don't know if she knows that I exist."

186

"Well, we'll soon know." He lifted his glass. "Here's to you. And thank you for bringing me here. It's a different world you've shown me. I'm stunned, quite knocked out! It's the first time I've been abroad, you know."

"Ah, Jamie. The world is your oyster now. Good times I'm sure are coming for you."

"I'll drink to that. Do you think we could sink another bottle of this vino?"

"Why not? I feel a little wild tonight." And Vera laughed her eyes bright and indeed a little mad-looking. Later she said tipsily, eyeing him through the flowers on the table, "You know, Jamie, before you had the rift with Maggie, I really fancied seducing you. When I first met you. When I heard you singing with the band in Mario's. You are very attractive, you know." Embarrassed he lit a cigarette. "But now that you're in mourning for your marriage, it's different. I can't feel that way any more. Strange isn't it?"

He was playing with the book of matches provided on the table, and looking thoughtfully at the smoke from his cigarette. "Your mind is on other things now. Just like mine, Vera. Who can explain their feelings?" A small band of players, two violins, and an accordion came to their table. They were playing "La Vie en Rose" with large plangent, romantic sweeps of their bows. Then, as he had seen other diners do, Jamie stuck a note in the pocket of the leader and bowing, the band moved on.

Their meal finished, and the second wine-bottle almost empty Vera shivered slightly in the cooling air. "See if you can find a cab, Jamie love. I feel a little sleepy now. It's been a long day." In the dim light he saw her face, softened with the wine and the music, and he could see shades of the beauty she had possessed in her youth.

"Of course, your majesty, but first you must join me in a brandy. It will put the finishing touch on the evening, what do you say?"

When they had sipped this last drink, and paid the waiter, they prepared to leave. "By the way, you look lovely tonight, Vera.

Mario should be here now to see you." He was leaning towards her smiling a little stupidly.

"Hush your mouth, Jamie London, and take me to my hotel."

He looked around. "How about one of those contraptions, a horse and carriage?"

"What an idea!" But she was persuaded. He put his arm around her and helped her into the seat behind the driver and they clip-clopped their way through the romantic city, back to the Excelsior.

Outside her room, he kissed her forehead. She looked close at his face and saw in his eyes the pain he was still trying to deal with. "Sleep well, Vera. Sweet dreams."

"You too, Jamie. Thanks for a lovely evening."

Next morning, the desk clerk assisted Vera by calling up the school on the front desk phone. He handed the instrument to her at the reception desk. Jamie stood watching her as she babbled into the phone.

"Yes, yes, that's right. Signora. Yes, Marianne Rossi teaches English, here in this school."

"Could you ask her to phone the Hotel Excelsior, Room 201, when she finishes at school today? What time will that be, please?"

"Signora Rossi will be finished her teaching duties at four o'clock. I will pass the message on to her. Your name is…?"

"Signora Pacitti. Thank you. Goodbye."

Using a map of the city, Jamie found the Trevi Fountain for them. They stood with the little crowd, taking in the spectacle of the wonderful, sculpted horses, and the great mythological god at their head. They spent fifteen minutes looking at the falling streams of water, and threw coins along with the rest, and for a second, to Jamie, the face of Vera changed to that of Maggie, the beautiful, laughing girl he first fell in love with. A stab of pain and jealousy pierced through him. The thought of her in the hands of the swarthy Dominic revolted him, and he had to work at putting the vision from his mind.

As they walked from the little enclosed square, Vera said, "I keep thinking of four o'clock and that telephone call."

"Let's go back then. You can rest and I'll join you later to wait for the call."

They waited until past the appointed time, and with the startling ring Vera jumped, then hesitated, afraid to lift the receiver.

"Go on, Vera."

"I can't do it." Then she lifted the phone and again he sat uncomprehendingly, watching her frowning face and listening to the babble of Italian as she tried to explain her position to the person on the other end of the line. It lasted about seven or eight minutes. When she put the phone down, her face was a mask.

"It was her?"

"Yes."

"Did you tell her?"

"No. I said I was her cousin from Britain, and that I would like to meet her."

"What did she say"

"She asked a lot of questions. Said she hadn't seen any family for years. Both her parents were dead. But she would meet me on Sunday morning in the Pincio Park."

"Goodness, that's three days away. It doesn't leave much time. We go back on Tuesday."

"I know. But I couldn't protest in the circumstances. I suppose she's busy through the week with her family and all. I said I'd like to meet them, and she said she would bring them along."

"Did she sound nice?"

"Yes. She was a bit wary at first. We have to meet her at — write this down — the park called the Pincio, near the Villa Borghese. They will be at the *Teatrino di Pulcinella* at eleven in the morning. And you won't believe this, I have to carry a red carnation so that she will recognise me. Oh, Jamie I can't bear it. My daughter? It's all too much. I must phone Mario tonight and tell him." She held her head with one hand, and could not stop the tears stealing from her eyes.

The sun shone through the trees casting shadows on the wide expanses of pale-coloured gravel, the great ochre pathway through the hill-top park. Couples strolled, their arms around each other, and smart Italian ladies, in knee-length skirts and short summer coats ambled along, their husbands close by them and their neat children dressed for Sunday followed behind. Many of the people had come straight from mass and were taking the air in the bright May sunshine under the tall, slim trees. Families sat on benches, some people reading newspapers, others just watching their toddlers run around on the stony ground. There was a leisurely holiday feeling in the air, and Vera and Jamie, having paid off their taxi, joined the moving throng. Soon they saw the crowd gathered around the puppet theatre.

Vera, her heart thumping, carried the red carnation, her face as pale as the oatmeal-coloured coat she wore, her rouged lips worried, mascara painted eyelashes stark in the strong light. She clung on to Jamie's arm for support. "Don't they all look so carefree, Jamie?"

"Yes, it's a slower pace they have here. They seem to have so much time. You'd think they hadn't a care in the world."

"It brings back memories of my childhood in Sicily. It's the Italian character. On Sundays they dress up. They have the sunshine and each other and probably a good dinner prepared ready for them at home, so they enjoy the moment."

"Yes, when you don't have to hurry indoors away from the wind and rain, it makes life less hassled, I suppose," he said.

Vera watched the little families as they passed them, so much care and attention was given to the little ones. Such indulgent smiles on the faces of the parents, and she bit her lip at the thought of her past, and what she had missed.

"Let's just stand at the edge of the crowd, Vera. It's not quite eleven, yet." Ten minutes passed and they were growing nervous. Then suddenly four faces seemed to loom out from the stream of pedestrians, four pairs of brown eyes were staring at them. The girl of sixteen was very pretty with long brown hair and a flawless tanned skin, and the boy too was olive-skinned and handsome. Vera was white and shaky with nerves.

"I am Marianne," the girl said simply. This is my husband, Hugo. You must be Vera."

Jamie felt the weight of Vera against his arm as the shock of the statement hit her. She stumbled slightly, her eyes riveted on the serious face of the chic young woman, and then recovering a little, she managed to say, "I am Vera Pacitti. How nice to meet you! This is a friend from Scotland, Jamie London."

They made their way to a vacant bench, and Gina said politely, "Have you come to Rome on holiday?"

"Yes, in a way." Vera sat down keeping the frozen smile on her face.

Hugo spoke now. "We were thinking, Signora Pacitti, it would be nice if you could join us for a coffee in the restaurant here. It's not far, and we can sit and talk there."

Still stunned from the shock of the meeting, and mesmerised by the children, Vera nodded. She could not take her eyes from Marianne, unless it was to stare wonderingly at the beauty of Rosa, the slim young girl, who was thoughtful and composed like her mother, or Eddy, the boy who resembled his father. As they walked along, Vera said, "I was sorry to hear about the death Violetta Bernardino, your mother."

"Yes. It was quite sudden, six years ago. Father died a year later, so we don't visit Sicily very often, now." Marianne looked closely at Vera as they sat down at the table "You were a cousin to my mother?"

"Yes, my name was Vera Longhana, before I married Mario Pacitti. I met him in London."

"And you left Bagheria many years ago?"

"Oh yes. Almost forty years ago. What age are you now, Marianne?"

"I'm thirty-nine."

"My goodness, you look like a young girl."

"Oh, no." Marianne blushed. "I wish I were still young." Her accent was very attractive, and her English was almost perfect. "But... for goodness' sake, what I would like to know is how on earth you found me."

"I got your friend's name, Gina Giannelli, and her address from someone at home, an old friend of the family. She knew that you and Gina were friends in Rome. So Jamie and I, we called on the Giannellis, and they were very kind and gave me the name of the San Giovanni School where you used to teach. Signor Lembo, your old boss kindly put me on to your present school, and we traced you from there."

"Goodness. That is unbelievable." Marianne looked from Jamie to Vera. "I can't get over it. It's a shock, you know." Then she added, "However, it's very nice to meet you both, and good to have old family friends come to see me. Isn't it Hugo?"

"Oh sure! Sure!" He smiled obligingly at everyone in general. "Can I get you something else, Signora Pacitti? Signor London?"

"Yes, I'll have another coffee, please, Hugo. It's very good."

Marianne politely filled in the lull in the conversation, "And how long will you be in Rome, Signora Pacitti?"

Vera looked at Jamie. "Our flight is on Tuesday morning at eleven-thirty. So, really, alas, we have only one more day."

"Oh, if I had known that, I would have arranged to meet you earlier." Marianne looked genuinely sorry.

Jamie nodded, "Yes, I'm sorry we didn't meet you before this. And I would love to have seen more of your lovely city. There are so many beautiful things to see. I must come back some day."

Hugo's English was not as good as his wife's, but he managed, "Everyone wants to return to Rome. Its magic casts a spell on people." His brown eyes sparkled as he looked around proudly.

"Yes." Jamie offered a cigarette to Hugo and they both lit up. "It's a shame but I must return to Scotland without seeing even half of the sights of Rome. But I have to start a new job next week, so I can't delay my flight." Hugo nodded in sympathy.

After a pause, Marianne, looking at them seriously and sounding a little stilted, said, "Hugo and I would be honoured if you could come to our house to join us in an evening meal tomorrow. Let's say around eight o'clock?"

Vera was delighted. "That is very kind"

Hugo held out a card. "Here is our address. The taxi driver will find it easily. We are on the second floor."

Vera's eyes now fell on the young girl who sat straight-backed, on her best behaviour. "And what age are you, Rosa?"

"I will be sixteen in three weeks."

"And what are you going to do when you leave school?"

"I go to drama college to be an actress." Her voice was pretty as she struggled with the English words.

Marianne and Hugo laughed. "That's this month she wants to be an actress."

But the girl was upset. "No, no. I mean it. I want to go to drama school."

"As you see, Signora, our daughter has big ideas. Expensive ones, too."

Vera addressed the boy in Italian, "And you, Eddy?"

"I will be a pilot and fly jets." He simulated a jet plane's noise. "I will fly all over the world."

"Will you come and see us in Scotland?"

"Sure I will."

"You must be very proud of them. Such clever children, and so good-looking!" Everyone smiled and then Vera ventured, "Did your mother ever mention me to you, her cousin Vera, do you remember?"

"Yes, she did. She once said, she had a cousin in London, and I should meet you one day. But it never happened. There was no money for that sort of thing in those days." Vera was mesmerised by the composure and refinement of the girl. She felt dizzy to think that this well-adjusted young woman could possibly be her daughter.

"Well, you have done well to get to university and to qualify as a teacher. You must have worked very hard."

Marianne shook her head, "Not really all that hard. My parents were good to me."

"You had an older sister. Maria wasn't it?"

"Yes, and I have two brothers still in Sicily. None of them was interested in going on with their education."

"Do you wear a kilt in Scotland?" Eddy was addressing Jamie. Everyone laughed, and Vera translated the question.

"No, not often, I'm afraid, Eddy."

Vera told them, "Jamie sings in my husband's restaurant in Glasgow. He's a very good jazz singer. Also he has a job as a commercial traveller for a large company. Isn't that right, Jamie."

Embarrassed, Jamie said, "I suppose so, if you say so, Vera."

"You enjoy living in Scotland, Signora. Do you miss your homeland?"

Hugo was trying his best to speak English.

"Oh, please call me Vera, Hugo. Well, really, Mario, that's my husband and I, we are Londoners; we've been in Scotland for only five years. And I think we will return to live in London in our retirement where we have some old friends. Maybe sometime you can visit us." Vera looked around the table at the little family, "We could show you around."

They had done well for strangers meeting for the first time. They had talked together for over an hour, and a little bond was growing between them. Vera was secretly enchanted by them. Beneath her smart coat, her heart beat a little quicker, and a glow of excitement suffused her face. She stood up, helped by Jamie to move the heavy chair, and she said, "It was nice to meet you. We will walk back to where we saw some taxis. Thank you, Marianne and Hugo. I can't tell how much I look forward to seeing you all tomorrow evening. It will be the highlight of our trip."

In the taxi, Vera was mumbling almost incoherently with excitement. "Isn't she charming, and pretty. Such lovely, thoughtful eyes! But she has obviously no idea about me."

Jamie nodded, "I think Hugo was getting some ideas about you. He was watching you fairly closely."

Vera breathed out a long sigh and sat back in the cab. "I'm shattered. To think I have two lovely grandchildren, so mannerly and good-looking. It's a miracle, Jamie!"

"Oh well, we could do with a miracle, you and I. Some good luck, anyway"

"Did you see any resemblance to me?"

"It's hard to say. Perhaps in her facial expression. Also the deep-set eyes. But her hair is much darker than yours."

"Ah, but mine was dark brown once," she laughed.

In the morning, they went shopping for souvenirs, and had a leisurely lunch in a smart restaurant. Jamie could see that Vera was growing tense at the thought of the meeting with her family in the evening, and the crisis that was looming up for her. He banished her to her bedroom to rest; telling her he would call her in good time for the evening.

Nervous as a kitten, Vera tried on three different outfits before she felt happy with her appearance. "I'm glad you're here, Jamie. I could never go through with all this without you."

He was drinking sparkling wine, getting slightly merry, and laughing at Vera's gathering panic. "Don't worry. The cost of... let's see... companion, guide, comforter and escort won't be too high. I'll try and keep my charges down."

She threw a cushion at him. "Drink your wine down, you rascal. And think yourself lucky to be here with such a charming lady, woman of the world, bon viveur as myself." She smiled as she turned round, her jewellery all in place, her make-up perfect.

"You look terrific, Vera. I am not worthy of such beauty, charm and graciousness," he teased while pouring her a glass of the wine.

"You're a great comfort to me, a real pillar of strength, Jamie London. And a shoulder to cry on." She laughed uproariously at her description, then as they left for their momentous dinner, she whispered from the doorway. "Your Maggie is a real fool of a girl, that she does not cling on to you, and keep you out of temptation's way. If it were me who was your wife, you wouldn't be let out of my sight."

After the first embarrassments, and when the formalities were over, the meal with Gina and Hugo and the children became an entertaining, quite noisy affair. With the wine, Hugo became expansive, and went out of his way to make his guests welcome.

They talked of their village in days gone by, of the fun it all used to be when they were young, the primitive way of life, the hills, the picnics, the wine-making and the feeding of the animals. They felt as if they had known one another for years, as the wine flowed and the food kept coming. After dinner, the children sang for them, and then Rosa showed how well she was learning to play the piano.

Towards eleven, as they sat with liqueurs, and the children had long been banished, Vera whispered to Jamie, "It's now or never."

"Would you let me have just a peep at your kitchen, Marianne? I'll bet it's more modern than the one I have."

"Of course. Come on, I'll show you. My latest acquisition is a washing machine. Also, Hugo bought me a little television set for my birthday, so that I can watch it while I am preparing the dinner."

"Gosh, you have two television sets? What luxury!" Then she said quietly, "It will be on 29th of this month, your next birthday. Is that right?"

Surprised, Marianne stopped stacking the dishes. "That's right. How did you know?"

"Let's sit down. I want to tell you a story. In Bagheria, there was a sixteen-year-old girl who fell in love with a student, Paolo Rivera. He was sent to America and his sweetheart found that she was pregnant, and she never saw or heard of Paolo again."

Marianne stopped her tidying up, and gave her attention to Vera. Slowly the older woman continued with the story. She didn't take her eyes off Marianne's face. "Shocked and horrified, her mother sent the girl to live with her cousin, Violetta, who was married with a two-year-old little girl. On 29th April, her baby was born. She called her Marianne."

Vera watched the startled expression that was forming on the face of Marianne. "The poor mother of the baby left for London to live with her uncle. When she had learned a little English, he gave her a job in his cafe."

Marianne's face was strained and serious. "This mother? She did not have any more children?"

"No. Those were hard times. Everyone was poor. If you had work, you were very lucky. Then, when she finally did marry a few years later, she and her husband were not lucky enough to be blessed with a family. They were very busy, working from morning until night building up their business. Then the war came. Separation from each other. Bombing. Upheavals. And when the war was over, everyone was exhausted. Just glad to be still alive."

The women looked at each other. "And you have no children in England, Vera?"

"No. No children in England."

"But you knew my mother. She was Violetta."

Vera did not answer for some time. "Violetta brought you up, Marianne. I thought she might have told you about… about me and about your birth, but it was her decision."

Marianne stared at Vera in disbelief. Then her face crumpled and tears streamed down her face. "I can't believe this. I miss Violetta. She loved me, and looked after me. She was so good." The distraught girl sat down heavily a dishtowel in her hands.

"Yes. I remember her as a good, kind girl. But you must understand, my situation was very bad. To have an illegitimate baby then was like a death sentence. A few people knew the story, but we lived deep in the country, and the truth could soon be buried. Did no one ever hint at anything to you?"

"No, not that I remember." Marianne's face was crestfallen. Vera sat upset and helpless as Marianne sobbed and sobbed. She sat at the kitchen table paralysed, longing to put her hand out to comfort the girl, but afraid of a rebuff. At last, Marianne dried her eyes and smiled weakly. "I wish I had known all this before now."

"I know. It's tragic. But you must realise, life was hard. There was no money. And my husband, he could take no holidays. I dreamed about it for years, and, perhaps if Jamie had not come along, come into our lives, I would never have got up the courage to come and find you."

Marianne rose from her chair. She put her arms around Vera. "I'm glad you came at last. But I will need some time to come to terms with all this." Vera's heart danced at the touch of the beautiful young woman who was her daughter.

"I don't think there is a happier mother in all of Rome tonight, Marianne. We will have to try and make up for the past." Now her eyes, too, were red with emotion.

"I must tell Hugo and the children. I think they'll be pleased. It's so unbelievable. Like a fairy tale." They were both in shock. "You could stay here in Rome with for a few days if you want to. Although I am out at work, if you can pass your time during the day, we can talk in the evening and get to know each other." Vera's handkerchief was out of her handbag, now. She choked out her thanks and mumbled something about her grandchildren. They embraced each other, and a great joy filled Vera, so that her spirits soared.

When the two women returned to the sitting room, one look at Vera's face told Jamie the whole story. "I suppose you won't be going home with me tomorrow, then?" he said, a soft smile lighting up his good-natured face.

Chapter 15

The congregation gathered in the old stone-built St. Mark's church to the sound of organ music. Jamie, directed to the side of the church for friends of the bride, felt stiff and trussed up like a chicken in his new white shirt and dress-suit. The waves of his hair were slicked back, and his usual carefree expression had been exchanged for one of abstraction, almost wariness. Four weeks had passed since he and Maggie had separated. He knew she had been busy with Diana and the wedding plans, and he had heard through Gregor and Prue that she was otherwise leading a quiet life at home with her mother and younger brother.

An atmosphere of expectancy was growing in the church. There were whispered conversations between wedding guests, and there was much head-turning as people sought each other out. Where were Gregor and Prue? *Late as usual*, he thought. And where were Mario and Vera? Since she had returned from Rome last week, Jamie had been avoiding Vera. According to Mario, Vera was a changed woman. The trip to the continent, and the joy of finding her daughter had totally rejuvenated her. She was irrepressible with her plans, and the fact that Marianne and her family were coming to Scotland for a visit in a few months' time was her greatest pleasure.

Still, he mused, he had enjoyed the trip and all the excitement, so that his melancholy and chagrin over Maggie had been dispelled, but he felt he didn't want to see too much of Vera. In their unspoken way, they both knew how close they had come to sharing a bed. Another few days together might have been enough. All the same, he wouldn't mind seeing her and Mario now, among this sea of strangers. He clasped his hands, as if in prayer, and stared straight ahead, steeling himself for the coming meeting with Maggie.

Would she be able to read his loneliness in his face? Would she see the hurt he felt, and how miserable his life had become? He would be inscrutable. Not to be hurt again. That was the answer. As the music changed to the wedding march, and the muffled conversations of the congregation stopped in anticipation of the entry of the bride, Jamie's eye caught the tanned face, the opulent figure of his *bête-noire*, the hated Dominic. He was ensconced just three rows behind him. Looking away quickly, he felt a flush of anger and hostility rise up in his chest. Swine! What was that fat Italian doing here?

Then the bride's slow procession, Diana, pale and lovely and so shaking with nerves that the cream roses of her bouquet almost rattled as she passed. Her young face partly hidden behind a veil, she passed down the aisle on the arm of her father whose face just burst with pride. This great show of a wedding was costing him at least a year's salary, but he judged that it was worth it to see his daughter dressed like a queen, radiant with happiness, and with a church full of witnesses to see proof of his position of affluence and success.

Let's hope it turns out to be worth all the bloody fuss, was the bitter thought on Jamie's mind. Then he felt a rush of nervous adrenaline as the slim figured Maggie brushed past him. The blue of her dress contrasted with the rich brown waves of her hair. She looked beautiful in a cold, closed-up way. No smile crossed her face. Following her were two flower girls also in pale blue. They made a stunning picture as they advanced slowly towards the altar. There stood the groom, John, and his best-man, Jay McLellan, broad-shouldered footballers both of them, resplendent in their kilts.

To the exclusion of almost everything else, Jamie's eye fastened on to the retreating figure of his wife. Her shapely waistline and hips where the folds and pleats of her dress lay, the pale slenderness of her arms and the sweep of her hair where it fell sweetly on her shoulders. How he ached to hold her again, to beg forgiveness for his coldness and for his unyielding judgement of her. He gripped the pew to prevent himself from sinking down with emotion. He felt himself to be in the centre of a vortex where people whirled around him, never impinging on his distress. *We are all sad, serious actors in some mummer's play. Nothing anyone says seems to have real import. It's such a game!* he thought. *What are these ladies doing in their showy hats, and these men in their morning suits? Is the minister in on the great joke? Will he tell us all to go home and behave better in future? What absurd ceremonies people put themselves through!* He longed for an end to the charade-like behaviour of the principals, and thought with a nervous dread of the gathering at the local hotel, which was to follow.

In true Scottish fashion, a fine reception had been prepared for the wedding guests. Here the atmosphere was warm and celebratory. The already-poured whiskies and sherries soon warmed the guests as they arrived and tables were laid with places for at least one hundred people. Almost as soon as the meal and the customary speeches were over, the floor was crowded with happy, half-tipsy couples determined to have a good time. The band was good. They played Scottish country-dance music and people were soon whirling and skirling to eightsome reels, and Dashing White Sergeants and the like. Sometimes they changed the mood and played popular music, modern tunes and old favourites so that the dance floor was seldom empty and an air of festivity and gaiety took over the room. Maggie had come to sit with Mario and Vera, and inevitably the talk turned to the big event of finding Marianne.

"What's she like, Vera. Does she look like you?"

"Oh, Maggie, she is very pretty, but so sensible and serious. She's older than you — in her thirties." Vera's face glowed. "She has two children of her own — Rose who's fifteen and Eddy is twelve. And they're coming to visit us at the end of next month!" Her voice rose and her eyes widened with excitement, conveying her disbelief at the wonder of it all.

"That's marvellous, Vera!"

"Hello, folks." A slight click of heels. Maggie looked up and with a start she saw that it was Dominic who was gazing down on her. "You make a very pretty bridesmaid." He beamed at her.

Heart pounding, she opened her mouth but no sound came out. Luckily Mario, seeing how stunned Maggie was, intervened, "Well, hello, Dominic. I didn't know you were coming today. You're looking very prosperous. Isn't it a lovely wedding? We're all proud of Maggie and Diana today."

"May I sit down?" and he sat down close to Maggie as he spoke. The familiar expensive aroma of his aftershave swept her memory back to Paris, and she felt her cheeks burn.

Vera said, "They didn't tell us you were coming, Dominic."

"Well, I heard about the wedding, and got myself invited. I wanted to see everybody again."

Vera smiled up at him, her face full of charm, "That's nice. Did you know I'm just back from a trip to Rome? Jamie came with me to help see if I could find my family. Have you heard about it?"

And so they became engrossed in conversation about Vera's new-found family and how amazing the story was. During a lull in the talk, the music swelled into a modern waltz tune, and Dominic asked Maggie to dance. She hesitated but had not the presence of mind or words to refuse. As soon as she felt his powerful arms around her and his broad body close to hers, the old spasms of excitement returned and she had to force her mind to concentrate on the dance steps.

"I've missed you, sweetheart." She did not answer. "You knew I would be here. I told you I was coming."

"I have put you from my mind, Dominic."

"Every night I thought of you, and your sweet love. You've no idea how often I've thought of you."

"Please, Dominic. I'll have to sit down. I can't dance with you if you carry on like this. And, you know, Jamie's here. It's too much. It's not fair."

"I know he's here. But I also heard you two have split up."

"It's just for a trial period." She tried to keep control of herself, and think of a way out of this intolerable situation. The music had stopped and she made to get back to Vera and Mario.

He pulled her arm gently to detain her, "I'm still crazy for you, Maggie. I'm still waiting for you."

"Please, Dominic. Please!" She pulled away.

Standing by the side of the table, talking to Mario and Vera was Jamie. His face was shocked and crestfallen. Had he heard what Dominic had been saying? Had he seen them dance together? They smiled hello to each other, and he held the chair back for her to sit down.

Then Vera filled in the pause in the conversation saying, "Isn't this just too bad, Maggie. Jamie's had bad news. He has to hurry off to the hospital to see his mother. She's very ill."

Staring at Jamie serious face, Maggie felt a rush of sympathy for him. His eyes met hers, "Yes, Iris phoned me. She and my sister, Betty, are hurrying to the Royal Infirmary now. It seems Mother's developed a chest infection. We half-expected something like this. I don't know if I told you, but her health has deteriorated over the past month or two."

"I didn't know. I'd no idea she was ill, Jamie. You should have told me. I'm so sorry." Maggie's distress and guilt were evident. She looked miserably back at him.

He looked down. "Yes, well, I have to go." He gave a quick glance round. "I'll say goodnight." And he quickly strode across the dance floor to the door. With a sore heart Maggie followed him with her eyes.

"It's rough on Jamie, this bad news. Poor fella." Dominic said this to no one in particular, and no one found words to answer him. As the conversation picked up again, Maggie was becoming more and more upset. Her head was down as she stared at the tablecloth, and her fists were clenched. "I think, if you'll excuse me I'll go to the hospital, and see Mrs London." She stood up, looking round for her hostess.

Dominic had stood up too. "I'll drive you there, honey. But you'll have to show me the way."

"Maybe I'll catch up with Jamie and go with him. Tell Diana and John what's happened, will you Vera? I'm sorry." She rushed for the door, holding up the skirts of her dress and Dominic followed like an attendant knight of old. She reached the front of the hotel, where some guests were smoking and taking a breather, just in time to see Jamie's car shoot away quickly.

It was eleven o'clock by the time Maggie and Dominic found themselves climbing the old shallow marble staircase of the infirmary. Built in the last century, an ancient pile whose days of serving the great city of Glasgow were coming to a gracious end. An air of vastness, of height and space was the first impression of the place to the visitor. And at night, secretiveness was all pervasive as ward doors were closed, and serious nurses hurried along quietly, their faces set to their tasks.

Maggie found herself whispering to the ward sister, "I'd like to see Mrs London, please."

"Are you family?"

"Yes."

"There are a few people in there now. Please wait here." She indicated a bench set against the white tiles of the corridor.

She sat with Dominic, too abstracted to bother about the incongruity of her clothes or his presence. In some way, it was a comfort to have him at her side. Presently Iris and Betty came out and gave her a grave, restrained greeting, so that she felt some disapproval. They hardly gave Dominic a glance. "She's hasn't got long to go, Maggie. I've sent for Phyllis to come up from Arran. But she has been asking for you."

"Yes, can I go in, now? Yes, Aunt Lily is just coming out. We're going to get a cup of tea, and come back. The doctor thinks she'll not last through the night."

Maggie stood quietly beside Jamie looking at the parchment skin and sinking eyes of the old lady. Jamie gently pushed her into his seat and stood behind her.

"Maggie. You came. I'm so glad to see you." The old eyes lit up, and she put out her hand for Maggie to hold. "You've always been my lovely girl. I'm so proud of you and Jamie. He loves you so much." Tears rendered Maggie speechless. Sadness, regret, guilt all welled up inside her.

"Don't cry, Maggie. You usually cheer me up with your smile. Let me see it now."

Maggie smoothed the covers on the old woman's bed. "Come on now, it's you who usually cheers me up, Mrs London. Isn't this a great hospital? They look after everyone so well."

Jamie patted his mother's hand. "We'll go and have a cup of tea now, Mother, and come back and see you in a little while." He gently drew Maggie up from the bedside seat. The sad eyes of the mother followed the pair, Maggie her handkerchief to her eyes, her face tear-stained, her shoulders slumped, and Jamie, his face hard, and little muscles at the sides of his cheeks working overtime as he sought to control his pain.

Then he had the shock of facing the shorter, broader Italian man who awaited Maggie in the corridor. They made an incongruous trio against the ancient walls, two men in dress suits and a young woman in a long bridesmaid's dress. Dominic's position was uncomfortable, but he stood his ground. "I'm sorry about your mother, Jamie."

Jamie nodded, his face livid. He turned to Maggie. "Don't cry, Maggie. Please don't cry." His arm was around her. "Shall I take you for a cup of tea in the hospital canteen?" He made as if to guide her away, and she looked at Dominic.

"Look, Jamie. She's had a long day. I brought her here to see your mother, but she's really tired, so I think I'd better get her home. She's dropping with exhaustion."

Jamie took his arm from Maggie's shoulder and he stood back. "If you want to go home, now Maggie, maybe that's best. I have to stay here. I can't leave. The doctor says she won't last the night."

She nodded, "Yes, I think I'd better go. My own mother wasn't too well at the wedding. I'd better make sure she got home all right. She will wonder what's happened to me. It's after midnight. I'm so sorry Jamie, about all this. I'll phone you in the morning."

He longed to call out, "Stay! Stay with me. I love you." But the words were choking inside him and would not be said. With a small smile he kissed her cheek and then kissed her pale, soft hand. "Goodbye Maggie. I'll be in touch."

The dark blue BMW purred its way through quiet, damp streets through long parallel lines of blinding street lights. Within ten minutes, Dominic's car stopped, and she saw they were in the car park of a city hotel. "What's this, Dominic?"

"It's the Carlton. Where I'm staying. The bar's still open and I feel like a drink. How about you?"

She glanced through the heavy glass doors at the uniformed doorman and the deep red carpeting. "All right. I could do with something. And Mum doesn't keep alcohol in the house. But I'll have to phone her, Dominic."

"Sure, you will, of course. There's a phone just outside the cocktail lounge."

When she returned from telephoning, he stood at the door of the bar.

"She's all right. Lawrence took her home, and I've told her I'll be back quite soon. I really think I'd better go, Dominic."

"I've told them to bring the drinks up to my room. You can freshen up there and fix your face. Besides I want to talk to you. After all I'm flying to America tomorrow. Yes. I'm afraid this will have to be our goodbye."

In his suite of rooms, she kicked off her shoes and used the bathroom to freshen up and sort her make-up. Then she sat down to sip the drinks he had ordered. "You're a dark horse. First you turn up unexpectedly at the wedding and now you tell me you're off to America tomorrow."

He smiled enigmatically and sipped his drink. "Maria, my wife and Nicki, they don't know that I'm coming to New York tomorrow. I'll take them all by surprise. I've almost finished winding up my business interests in London. Retirement of a sort looms ahead. Today… tonight… is a last throw of the dice. I've come to Glasgow to ask you to come with me."

"Dominic! How can you do this? This is crazy." To herself she thought, *Is there to be no end to this day?*

"So, my wife may be glad to see me. Then again, she may not. I will surprise them anyway when I arrive. I want to find out if America excites, if I want to live there or if I want to stay in this country. I have that option — and so have you."

"No, Dominic." her small voice was exhausted. I have plans for the future. I want to study. Anyway, I couldn't take another woman's husband."

Moodily he regarded her. "She hardly seems like a wife. She hasn't noticed my absence for the past few years, anyway. We are almost like strangers. Come to the window, my dear, so that I can smoke. I have some cigarettes here. Would you care for one?"

"Oh, all right. I can't resist. I love a cigarette, but never get one nowadays. Everyone is so goody-goody nowadays, or so it seems. My mother moans at me if she sees me with a cigarette." Then lost in thought she watched the smoke spiral upwards and said quietly, "Poor Jamie!"

They stood smoking and sipping their drinks and looking out at the thinning traffic as the small hours of the clock took over. Then they sat down opposite each other in deep armchairs. Dominic lifted the phone. "Bring two more gin and tonics to room 203 please."

"No, Dominic. I should go home. Please…"

"Hush, my dear. We do not always do what we should. Anyway your mother will be fast asleep by now. And after all, I'll be on the plane in a few hours."

When their drinks arrived, he broached the subject again. "Well, what do you think? What's your answer? Do you follow me to New York? What do you say?"

"You're out of your mind, Dominic! You know that?" She giggled in spite of herself. "I'm still married, you know, and I have applied to go to university. To build some sort of career for myself."

"And I am an old has-been, nearing sixty. Yesterday's lover."

"Don't be like that, Dominic."

"Listen, Maggie. I've got plenty of money. More than you realise. I can buy anything you like. Houses. Any car you would like. You could have anything you want. And I..." He came and sat on the arm of her chair. "I'm bloody crazy about you. You know I am." She giggled and he pulled down the top of her low-cut dress and kissed her breast.

"I have to go, Dominic. Please don't do this!" But she did not push him away, and soon he had moved her compliant body to the bed where he caressed her, his breath becoming rapid with passion and desire. He covered her pretty lips with hot kisses, his hands teasing her neck, caressing now her arms and breasts, now her thighs, so that she felt the old desire rise within her. In a last valiant effort, she pushed him away. "No, Dominic. I shouldn't do this. We shouldn't do this."

"Why not? Have you ever wanted to, more in your life?" He had her long skirt above her knees now. Then he stopped and held her soft hips in his strong brown hands. "Come on, Maggie. You want me, don't you?"

She did not answer.

"Answer me. You want me?

"Please. This is wrong!"

"Is it wrong, Maggie? Is it wrong?" But now he had entered her and her protests were too late. "Well, is it?" He was moving with ecstasy to her moans.

"No, Dominic. No. Dominic!"

They climaxed together in a great shudder of passion, Maggie writhing beneath him, speechless with the pleasure he had brought her. He sat up and looked at her giving a satisfied little laugh. Then he kissed her upturned nipples. She did not open her eyes. "Well," he said, "are you coming to New York with me?"

After a while, she moved herself from the bed, rolling over and standing up. "Dominic. This happening tonight — we just shouldn't have done it." She sat down on the bed and kissed him. "I just know my life is here in Scotland. I want to go to university. Cars and clothes and fancy houses? Sure it would be great, but don't tempt me any more, Dominic, please. I'm only human, after all."

"And what about my love for you?"

"If you love me, you'll let me follow my own path."

"I'm too old for you? Is that it?"

"Well… when I'm forty-four, you'll be eighty-four."

He put his hand on her thigh, and started to rub her body through the thin lawn of her underskirt, "But I'll still love you. I love you so much."

"Dominic, "I'll always love you. Always. You have been wonderful to me. I will miss you terribly. But I have made up my mind."

"Then before your leave me, let's have just one more embrace." His love was now sweet and gentle, so that she fell almost into a stupor as he caressed her. At last she pushed him away. "Dominic, I must go. Please take me home. I'm a bit ashamed of myself. Coming straight from the hospital and the bedside of Jamie's dying mother, and ending up here with you. What has become of me? I feel I am losing all track of reality. I'm not the same girl you met in Mario's."

He smiled ruefully, "Yes, you are. This passionate woman was always there. I knew it the evening I first saw you."

Smoothing down her dress, she gave him a steady look. "Are you saying you knew you could get me into bed if you wanted?"

He laughed, "Something like that." Then when he saw the mounting anger in her face, and her stuttering to find an answer to his remark, he threw his head back and rolled on the bed in great amusement.

"You swine!" She shoved on her shoes and searched for her handbag.

Restraining her from rushing out the door, he held her to him. "All men think that way, honey. It's how the world works."

"And I was very obliging to you in London. Easy meat."

"No, you're wrong. You were what you are. A perfectly nice, good, well-brought-up girl. You just lacked experience — and I fell in love with you." She scowled at him. "And I like to think you fell a little bit in love with me."

"And when you asked me to work for you in London? Had your plans to seduce me already been made?"

He was serious now. "I knew it was a possibility. But if it hadn't happened, it would have been all right. I liked you, and knew you would enhance my restaurant. I didn't want to interfere with your marriage. Now it's a little different. It's a lonely old man who will take the plane for New York tomorrow." She couldn't find the words to reply and stared at the door. "Say you'll miss me, Maggie."

"You know I will."

"And you will think of me sometimes?"

Her face softened, and she touched his face tenderly, "I will think of you." She felt drained and saddened. "I wish you luck in New York."

He drove her home through the deserted streets in silence. At her mother's house, they kissed briefly and he waited until she closed the door of the house before he drove off at speed.

In the infirmary, Jamie sat by the bedside with his two sisters as his mother passed peacefully away.

Chapter16

Only a day like today could drag Phyllis away from her beloved Arran — a call to the bedside of her dying mother. It must be three months since she had seen the old lady, who like herself, lived widowed and alone. *Poor old soul, I should have gone to see her before now. Why did I have to wait until she was terminally ill? Why do families treat each other this way? I'm a self-centred, heartless person. A disgrace! I enjoy my life of peace and of being by myself, but I know she hated it, and missed us all.*

This was true. Phyllis London, tall, spare and weather-beaten from her long country walks, had embraced her lifestyle calmly and with a measure of contentment. She had her two dogs, Rajah and Farah, both English pointers, lithe and bursting with energy, and with them each day, for hour upon hour, she wandered the hills and shores of her beloved island, needing no other thing. One other physical pleasure she had was the bright coal fire, set ready to be lighted on her return. Then as darkness drew in, she could sit looking over the grey waves of Ryan Sound to the Mull of Kintyre, and watch the sun go down over the hills. Or when the dogs had been fed, take her supper to the table in front of the warm glow of the fire. Then she would spend some time reading or watching television, and then a last trip out for the dogs, before calling it a day. Quite early she would retire to her warm bed, in the room in that part of the house at the back, partly cut into the rock of the hillside where her cottage snuggled away from the wind.

Summer days were long and happy. Then, usually, people came to visit. Her daughter, Daphne, came with the children to spend their time on the rocky shore, sailing boats, climbing hills, making fires, having barbecues, until their perpetual motion ceased and they collapsed after supper with exhaustion. It was in the summertime that Phyllis found herself popular with nephews and nieces and all sorts of friends and relations looking for a few days holiday in the wilds of the island away from the city.

However, it was the winter that the local inhabitants, including Phyllis, liked best. Then the island belonged to only a few. They could do what they liked, spend weeks in isolation if they wished. If they wanted company, they could have cosy fireside conversations or games of cards with neighbours, while the thick velvet darkness fell outside, and the only noise was the background music of the unceasing water on the shore.

For ten years Phyllis had found refuge in her seaside cottage. At first she had come with her husband, Cecil, who, after a lifetime of wild living, had agreed to trim his sails, give up drinking, try to give up smoking, and generally retire, settle down and reform himself. So the two had escaped the rat race, packed up all their worldly goods, sold their house on the mainland and come to live in Arran. Previously, this had been their regular summer holiday haunt, so it seemed a natural bolthole for them where they would try to get a new handle on life before it was too late.

Phyllis had met Cecil Bates when she was directed to work in the Munitions Factory during the Second World War. There, Cecil had been the manager and had fallen madly in love with the nineteen-year-old Phyllis. She fell for his dashing ways although he was already showing the results of his dissolute lifestyle, and was nearly twenty years older than her. She ran away with him, partly to escape the unhappy household where her mother had been left widowed and penniless.

Through years of unhappiness, she watched her husband spend all his money without thought for the morrow, and bitterness entered her heart. She brought up their one child, vowing that she would get her own back on this Don Juan of a husband one day. Then she had been very attractive and indulged in a few brief affairs and the odd weekend away from him, as an evening-up of the score. But she seemed unable to escape from her ageing husband who watched her jealously. But fate caught up with Cecil, and he did not live even five years into their retirement. He died of emphysema, and Phyllis found herself a widow in her thirties.

At first she had occupied herself, helping out the owner of the little village tea-room serving teas to tourists, just really to pass the time. Then for a spell, she had worked behind the bar in the hotel in the next village round the island. But now, with her dogs, and her old banger of a car, she was quite content to be a bohemian, beachcomber, and semi-recluse.

Now, she sat watching the white water of the wake of the ferry to the mainland, calculating that on landing, the train she would catch should get her to Glasgow Central. She would take a taxi to the Royal Infirmary. God, she thought, to meet Iris and Betty again, both of them so much better off than she was, both non-smoking (for Phyllis still had the occasional cigarette) and practically non-drinking, with beautiful homes and perfect families and both having wonderful social lives. She would have to listen to all that guff about golfing holidays and dinner parties, and new kitchens, and what a wonderful course William was on at university.

And then there was darling Jamie. Spoiled rotten by Mother. He had always been the apple of her eye, the one she really cared for. Phyllis had been just nine when Jamie had been born. The joy of her parents at God's gift of a boy, after having three girls — at last a boy! Phyllis had always reckoned that the arrival of her brother had cast a shadow over the rest of her life. For when mother called, "Come here, darling" it was not she who was called but her blond, curly-headed chubby little boy. When new clothes were to be bought, didn't Jamie's cost twice as much as her own? At school and afterwards, his interests had always been her parents' first consideration.

Carrying her weekend bag, Phyllis moved from the open deck, and went downstairs to get some coffee. Seeing the bar practically empty, she changed her mind about the coffee and ordered a large brandy and lemonade, more befitting the awful occasion she mused. Sitting in the corner, she lit a cigarette. *Thank goodness I still had that black coat and hat in the wardrobe from Cecil's funeral...* her thoughts drifted on. She hated the idea of going back to the city with its tenements, its billboards, its thousands of pubs, and general air of exhaustion. She remembered too well, the daily grind of work, of jockeying for positions, of everyone out for money, status, and getting one over on the neighbours. *God, just let me get these few days over with!* Phyllis finished her cigarette, and pleading stress to herself, allowed herself another drink.

The funeral cortege drove through the dusty streets, six cars filled with family and friends. Then the little group standing round the open grave while the minister gave a service in doleful tones, knowing little of Mrs London but what he had been told by Jamie.

Phyllis had had time for only short conversations with her two sisters, but noted that their clothes were much better than hers, and that they left the hospital in expensive cars. Life had treated them well, it would seem. She knew she was the outcast, regarded as an eccentric, what people were now calling beatniks and dropouts. Strangely, it was only Jamie that seemed to have anything in common with her. After a lifetime of hating him for disrupting her place in the family, she now found him sympathetic. He had known illness, loneliness and bad luck, like herself, she thought.

The subdued party of sombrely dressed mourners all faced the grave as the coffin was lowered. Phyllis looked for Jamie's wife, whom she hadn't seen. Maggie stood apart from Jamie, and her answering smile to Phyllis was hesitant and a little rueful. Why were they apart? She had a soft spot for the pretty Maggie, always having found her full of life and with that daring streak that Phyllis knew was in her own make-up. Something, however, was obviously wrong between Jamie and Maggie.

She caught up with Maggie on the way back to the cars. "How are you, Maggie? Long time, no see."

"Oh hello, Phyllis. How are you? And how's Arran?"

"Great. You must visit me some time."

"Yes, well, maybe." Maggie looked around like a criminal caught in the act.

"Where's Jamie? Are you leaving him in the cemetery?"

"Oh, we came in separate cars." Maggie flushed as she saw Phyllis's surprise.

"Oh!"

"Yes, I'm staying at my mother's just now. I have to go, Phyllis. I'll give you a ring. Goodbye!"

In the taxi taking her away from the graveyard, Maggie's thoughts turned to the previous Saturday when she had visited Jamie's mother, so that she flushed at the thought of Dominic and the hotel in the early hours of Sunday morning. Her face screwed up in horror at the picture that she tried to blot out. After leaving her husband with his dying mother, not much more than an hour later she had been in bed with her ageing lover. She closed her eyes and shook her head in an attempt to erase the memory.

And then worse was to come — the phone call in the morning from Jamie, worried as to where she had been all night. She put her hands to her ears in the deep recesses of the back of the taxicab that sped her homewards through the town, as if Jamie were speaking to her now. "Are you all right? I phoned around half-past twelve last night, and again at one o'clock, to see if you had got to your mother's all right. You weren't home."

"I know. I... I went for a drink."

"You *went for a drink*? At that time?"

"Yes, I was upset at seeing how ill your mother was. I...I felt..."

"All right, Maggie." His voice was icy. "I have to go now. Mother died in the early hours of Sunday morning at three thirty to be precise. The funeral will probably be on Wednesday at her local parish church. I'm putting a notice in The Glasgow Herald. Goodbye!" And he had put down the phone.

Maggie emerged from the powder room, her make-up touched up for the fourth time. It was almost midnight at Mario's and she longed for the taxi to come that would drop her home at her mother's. Jamie had left the place at eleven o'clock on the dot, as soon as his last number was over. From somewhere he had resurrected "Smoke Gets in Your Eyes," and although things were frosty between them, the sentimental old song brought tears to her eyes.

The band had finished the song with a long dramatic chord, and Jamie had relinquished his hold on the microphone, and within seconds she saw the back of his head as he made for the door. And was she imagining things, or was that the pretty table-maid, Sukie following him? She, of the bouncy breasts that caught the eye, was following him with her clicking, high-heeled shoes.

"Okay, Maggie, sweetheart?" It was Mario. "You look like you need to be home in bed."

She slumped down on a chair, her jacket and handbag on her arm. "You're right, Mario. I feel like I need a tonic, I haven't been feeling too well recently."

He sat down opposite her. Now that the evening was nearly wrapped up, he was smoking a cigar. "No sign of you and Jamie making up."

"No."

"That's too bad." His kindly face smiled indulgently at her. "You're a good girl, Maggie, and I love you. I love both of you but you're in danger of making a mess of your lives."

"I know, Mario. This is a really bad patch. There's only one bright spot on the horizon."

"What's that?"

"I've been accepted for the M.A. course in the university. I start at the end of September."

"I don't believe it. Really, Maggie? I don't know what to say. And you'll be leaving me?"

"Yes, that's the only bad side of it." She played with the catch of her handbag.

"No, my dear, it's good. It's what you want."

"Well, yes. I think it is what I want."

"How long, before you'll be leaving?"

"Oh, it will be some time yet. I've been lucky, though. I've got a grant for my fees and living expenses."

"Are you going to continue to live at your mother's house?"

She nodded. "Yes, for the present."

"What does Jamie say about it?"

"Oh, he doesn't know. I don't think he'd be interested."

Mario moved to the chair alongside her. "Believe me, he would be. He still loves you."

"I don't know about that. I thought I saw Sukie following him out of the door tonight." Mario raised his eyebrows in surprise at this. "Oh, yes, I'm sure I did. Anyway, I know he can never forgive me for going to London, and all that." She shrugged. "And in a way I don't blame him. I deserve all I get."

"Dominic's in the States now."

"I know."

"And you can be sure Jamie still loves you."

She shook her head. "No, you're wrong, Mario. I think I disgust him."

They were interrupted by the arrival of the cabman. "Taxi! Taxi for Mrs London."

"Oh, yes." She rose and smiled. Then suddenly she bent down with an impromptu kiss for Mario's cheek. "Goodnight, Mario."

"Goodnight, Maggie."

In the months that followed, a new Maggie emerged — serious, less ready to laugh, hardworking, single-minded. Each evening she caught the bus home from the college, never lingering with the other students, for she had no great rapport with them, being as she was, in name anyway, married and a mature student.

The sound of a yearning love-song was usually what greeted her as she got through the door of home. Her brother, Lawrence, seemed to play records non-stop, Johnnie Ray, Tommy Steele, Elvis Presley, as soon as he got home from school. Lawrence was seventeen now, and he seemed aeons away from Maggie and her friends. Like a beam of light, their new youth culture, clothes and music, but above all their confidence showed the way to a new world. His generation were ushering in a new scene. They did not look back to the war, but forward to a different way of living, and the music just beginning to appear was a precursor of the great burst of energy and pop culture that was about to explode on the world.

"Had a good day, Maggie?" It was her mother, an inveterate worrier.

"Yes. But I've got quite a lot of work tonight. I've an essay to get finished for next week. It's quite important, so I'll start it after supper."

"I'll get Lawrence to turn off that music shortly, love. Don't worry."

"Oh, it's all right, Mother." Her voice was subdued and toneless. She missed Jamie terribly. She thought about him in his new job as traveller for Rodger and Russell, and she knew he spent a lot of his time with Gregor and Prue. Also, she had heard he was often in the Anchor & Chain, the pub close to the flat. She hoped he wasn't drinking too much. Once or twice she had almost phoned him. Then she had taken cold feet. He was the one who had made the chasm between them. He could not forgive her and who could blame him? As she ate her evening meal, Maggie felt her mother's covert and worried glances, and wished she could talk to her at times. But how could she explain her affair with Dominic. It would shock her beyond anything.

It was a few days later that the bombshell burst. The words of Doctor Ryan rang in Maggie's ears. "You don't need a tonic, Maggie. All the indications suggest you're pregnant."

"Pregnant?"

He smiled, "Looks like it. It's not so bad." Her mind was in turmoil. "You can carry on at the university after the birth. Your mother will probably help out. You won't be the first student to have a baby. I'd say you were near enough five months. You're still very slim, but there you are."

Stunned she made her way home. Five months? The date he had suggested for the birth was 20th March. The end of her second term. But the fact she had to face was that the child had to be Dominic's. He had been her lover five months before, and there had been no one else since.

Hiding the news of her condition from the family was not too difficult in those first few days. She was considered to be moody and unhappy by her mother and her brother because of her broken marriage. All that week she was in a daze, pushing the doctor's fateful words: "All the indications are…" to the back of her mind.

By the end of the week, riding home on the bus, setting her mind to face the weekend, Maggie knew the doctor's diagnosis was right, without question. She felt the pricking of her nipples and almost overnight her breasts seemed swollen and tender. What startled her most were the unmistakable small movements in her belly. It had taken her all her time to stop from crying out in panic when, at a literature lecture, she had felt the strange sensation when the baby moved in her womb. Too late now for an abortion. Too late now to make a choice between life with Dominic or marriage to Jamie. Now she had neither. And her degree course, her plan for a career? What could she do? Maggie sat looking miserably out of the bus window, as it trundled its stop-start journey through the streets to the other side of town.

Life is just so difficult. It is just too difficult for me. I can't seem to win. She looked unseeing at the darkening streets. What a fool she was! What an ambitious fool! She hadn't just fallen off the ladder. Someone had taken it away. Bewilderment and fear vied with each other to swamp her brain, and she frowned with the effort to cope with her plight. *Oh Jamie! Where are you now? You would know what to do.* But she couldn't turn to him. He had been hurt enough.

Her mother was in the front garden, tidying up the debris of leaves and twigs in the early winter sunshine and Maggie caught the expression on the thoughtful face, lined by a thousand past crises.

"Tea will soon be ready. I'm just coming in. Won't be two minutes." Mrs Fisher put the pile of leaves on the wheelbarrow and started to clear up the garden tools.

"It's okay, Mother." How could she shock the old lady with the news that she was pregnant, and the father was someone else, not her husband? And that someone else was hundreds of miles away and couldn't be told — probably living quite happily with his wife and family. Wearily she took off her coat and dropped into an armchair, staring at the walls, her mind in a turmoil.

For reasons she couldn't explain, the thought of Phyllis in Arran came into her head. Phyllis who had seen so much, had faced problems in her past — if anyone could understand her predicament, and perhaps be sympathetic, it had to be Phyllis. She would phone. Perhaps she could visit Phyllis. She was strong and would maybe have an answer. She knew there was a boat at ten on Saturday mornings. If Phyllis would have her for the weekend, she would go. Tramping the hills with Phyllis and the dogs, even in the rain, seemed an inviting prospect at that moment.

Maggie saw from the lounge of the boat that the boat was docking at the old pier in Brodick. There were few passengers, it being out of season, and lifting her bag, Maggie went up on deck. She searched for the face that should be there among the few people meeting the boat on the quayside. Her nerves were jangled by the screaming and squalling of the gulls that had followed them for the whole crossing. She watched the boatmen in their dark woollen jerseys tying ropes to the bollards, while others stood to take tickets, and the first of the cars and lorries emerged from the hold of the ship. The air smelled of seaweed here, and the people moved lazily, as if knowing there was all the time in the world to do anything. From the top of the gangway, she saw the greying blondish hair of Phyllis, tall and slim, holding her two dogs on leads.

"My! You're looking well, Maggie. Did you have a good crossing? It's quite calm today. Come along! Let's see if this old banger will start. We'll stop at the grocer's shop while I pick up a few things. It's great to see you."

"It's great to see you, Phyllis. And good of you to come to meet me."

"Well, I don't know how else you'd get round the island to my place. The bus is very unreliable in November."

Out of Brodick and on to the string road that cuts through the hills, they drove, the old car just making it, coughing and spluttering. Phyllis chattered inconsequentially about the weather, the price of petrol, the news of her daughter and new grandchild, while Maggie relaxed in the warmth of the car, turning to smile now and again at the good-natured dogs. They panted and sniffed from the back seat, their wet noses and tongues within inches of Maggie's face.

Within an hour or two, when they were seated in Phyllis's living room, overlooking the sea, Maggie had told the whole story. They were having tea in front of a well-burning coal fire. Phyllis had laid an embroidered cloth on her little coffee table, and had set out buttered scones and fruit-cake and had taken out her best china in Maggie's honour.

"The sixteenth of March?" Phyllis asked.

"Yes, it seems ages away."

"Oh, it'll soon go in. You're hardly showing at all, for five months."

"What will you do about university? Well — the doctor thinks I can keep on until the last few weeks."

"And then?"

"Exactly! I haven't told mother yet, so…" she broke off.

"And Jamie?"

"No… I… he doesn't know."

Phyllis put down the cup and saucer carefully. "He doesn't know?"

The younger woman's face crumpled and inevitably the weeping started. "I'm sorry, Phyllis. I'm sorry to inflict this on you."

"Hush now. Don't be silly. What are friends for? I knew there had to be a reason for your visit. Don't cry. I'm glad you felt you could come to me. Really I am."

"You always seem as if you could cope with anything."

"Well, I don't know about that. But you're right. I've had my share of trouble and come out the other end." She looked down at the sleek coats of her dogs. They, sensing her interest, raised adoring eyes at her, in case she just might be planning to take them walking. "Look, cheer up! I've a bottle of brandy in the pantry for emergencies. Hold on, this should help."

She came back with two generous glasses of brandy. "Sip this and take your time." Bit by bit, the whole story of Dominic, her time with him in London and Paris came tumbling out. Jamie's lack of ambition, his slow retiring manner, Maggie's frustration at always being short of money, of never seeming to get anywhere.

Her tears now dried she spoke earnestly, "But no, Phyllis, I don't want you to think I'm trying to justify what I did. I've been a fool, I know. And Jamie's too good for me."

"Look! You've been foolish, sure. A more experienced, harder type of girl would have foreseen what would happen with Dominic. I know the type. And Jamie is not quite blameless. He should have been more vigilant. He should have kicked up more of a fuss about the whole thing."

Maggie took a gulp of the brandy. "Now we're separated, and with this baby expected and it's not his, it's all such a mess. I can't take it all in. And I know I can never get Jamie back." Once more the uncontrollable weeping, so that Phyllis paced the room, only stopping to look at the choppy waves of the sound, as if an answer was to be found out there. She felt heart-sore for the young girl whose head was now bowed in anguish. It stirred up memories of similar dilemmas from her own past. But she had always managed to find a way out, a knowing friend, a willing doctor, these had got Phyllis out of her scrapes, but for Maggie things had been left too long. The pregnancy would have to be gone through with, now. Anything else was out of the question.

They walked and talked for much of the weekend, and by the Monday, when Maggie had to go home, they had settled on some sort of plan. First, Maggie would tell her mother the whole truth. If her mother did not wish to look after the baby, then Maggie would finish the first year of her studies with Phyllis helping out if she could, and then, Maggie could take a year out of her studies to bring the baby safely through its first year.

She should wait for Jamie to approach her, if he so wished, with enquiries about the baby. And then she would tell him the truth. Meanwhile she would balance out her life as best she could. They were both agreed that Dominic should not be told anything.

Chapter 17

From the window of the flat, Jamie looked out in sleepy surprise on a solid layer of white snow. The town was like a ghost town, as if the New Year celebrations had exhausted the citizens so that there were no longer people around to function normally. Jamie dressed carefully for Diana and John's house-warming party. As he surveyed himself in the mirror, he rubbed his chin thinking to himself, *Thank God, I got to bed reasonably early last night. I don't look too debauched.* Reflected behind him was the double bed and he allowed his mind to dwell for a few minutes on the memories of loving nights together with Maggie. A picture of her young face with the broad smile came to mind, and he almost heard her uncontrollable giggles when he said something to make her laugh. In those days they were always laughing.

Sadness soon filtered back through to him as he wondered how she was now. Did she despise him? Did she love this Dominic? His eyes swept over his shaving gear and toilet articles. He paused for seconds, considering the bottle of sleeping pills. How many would it take to do the deed? How many pills washed down with a bottle of whisky? He shook the momentary thought away. But he could not shake from his brain the thought of the Italian boss-man, money and confidence oozing from him, and lust in his heart. In his mind's eye he saw the podgy, middle-aged hands caressing Maggie's body. As the pain took up residence in his soul, he went on tying his tie and adjusting his collar, waiting for the hurt to recede, at least a little. He would get through this day, but he knew that later, perhaps in the dead of night, the bitter thoughts would return, like a great thorn that tore at him.

Approaching the house where the party was to be, he drove around piles of sand and bricks, each having an inch of frozen snow on top, gleaming under the street lights. There were half-a-dozen houses completed, boasting little balustraded balconies and porches with reproduction carriage lights, an enclave of affluence, in this western part of the city. Here and there, there were Christmas trees with fairy lights. A little luxury was stealing into people's lives.

Diana's dad had an interest in the property business, and had built this sprawling ranch house for his daughter and son-in-law. Flounced curtains were in every lighted window and as the front door was opened, music poured out into the frosty night. Jamie stood there, a refugee from the grey buildings of the worn-out city, taking in the opulence of the place, the fancy brickwork and the two-car garage.

"Jamie!" Diana squealed out his name. In her wide-skirted pink dress, her hair piled in curls on top of her head, she resembled the fairy on top of her own Christmas tree. Behind her came the bumbling Gregor carrying a drink for him, and Prue was there too, still plump from her recent baby, and they embraced him warmly. Inside there was a real party atmosphere. Couples were dancing, trying out the latest rock-and-roll steps, and to compensate for the chatter and noise, the music had been turned up very high. From the happy, flushed faces and bursts of laughter, this party looked like being a whale of success.

No one asked about Maggie, and after a time, he relaxed. With the help of the alcohol, Jamie's heart soon lightened, and he even thought of asking someone to dance with him. After an hour of getting quietly sloshed, he heard greetings at the door. It was Mario and Vera, and with them their granddaughter, the sixteen-year-old Rosa, he had last seen in Rome. She was dressed simply in a black velvet skirt and white lace blouse, slim as a reed and, with her dark hair and olive skin, she stood out from the rest of the girls.

"Keep an eye on her for me, Jamie. She is staying with us for another week, and tonight is to be a treat for her. We'll pick her up again in a couple of hours. Come on Rosa, you remember Jamie. You met him in Rome." The young girl, withdrawn and shy was experiencing a culture shock, as she tried to take in the noise and wild dancing that was going on. Jamie kissed her cheek lightly and handed her a glass of sparkling wine.

"Do they do this rock-and-roll dancing in Rome, Rosa?"

"I don't think so, but I've seen it in the American movies." She gave him a beatific smile, showing her fine teeth, and his heart gave a bump at the beauty of her. *God, she's young and tender! So unspoiled! And some wolf will come along and take that sweetness from her. She's too young for this wild place!*

As he looked around the room, some couples were embracing in corners, and almost everybody seemed to be well on the way to being a bit drunk. The place still smacked of newness, new paintwork, new curtains and new insubstantial contemporary furniture. Diana was rushing around, shepherding people into the dining-room, where she had prepared an impressive array of food. "Great party, Diana!" Jamie put his arm round her to hold her still and kissed the top of her curls.

"Well, it is our first party. Do you like our house?"

"Lovely house!" He waved his arm around the room. "I tell you, honey, it's really terrific." Rosa stood beside him, nodding and smiling politely.

Diana was pleased. "We're thrilled with the house, but you should see Daddy's own house. They have an indoor swimming pool." A little tipsy, her voice high with excitement, she enthused. "I must show it to you. They've gone to Spain for a couple of weeks."

"No, no, no! You can't take my best pal away from me." It was Gregor, quite drunk, a foolish grin on his face, swaying towards them. "I'm taking them to show them Stuart and Elaine's place, just across the street. Bob and Tina want to see it too. We won't be ten minutes, Diana, okay?"

Diana watched the breakaway party exit from the door into the cold snowy night. Kevin, a prat in a kilt, which clung round his hairy thighs, it being a little damp from spilled beer, swayed out the door after them. His arm was round the neck of a slim, heavily-made-up divorcee who was called Norma, a neighbour from further along the street. Stuart managed to unlock the door of his house, which lay warm and empty, dimly lit, and hanging with Christmas decorations. He and Elaine were a modern couple living together out of wedlock, Elaine being a girl he had brought back from South Africa to Scotland where his job as a geologist in the off-shore business had been. They were suitably unconventional, witty and very with it. They fitted in perfectly with Gregor's idea of a fun couple. "I must show you my organ, folks. It's a bijou antique," Stuart called back to them as he led the way. "Picked it up for a song at the auction rooms." There in the corner, a stranger among the modern furniture in the new house, stood an old nineteenth century organ complete with candle holders. The party sat down and Elaine quickly supplied some drinks, while Stuart lit the candles. He sat down in front of it and started to sing very loudly:

So I'll cherish the old rugged cross,
Till my trophies at last I lay down.
I will cling to the old rugged cross
And exchange it some day for a crown.

He sang with mock solemnity, a wicked grin on his face. Some of the others, nonplussed at this blasphemy, eyed each other, not quite drunk enough for this, and others joined with hearty voices. Jamie shook his head at Rosa and shifting Stuart from the stool, played a jaunty version of "There is a tavern in the town." Soon, they had a sing-song going around the old wheezing machine knocking out such drunken tunes as Nellie Dean and "Sweet Sixteen" which they sang with mock feeling.

Rosa giggled at their antics and at Jamie's soulful eyes as he sang to her. There followed other old-time favourites like, "If You Were the Only Girl in the World", finishing up with *"Plaisir d' Amour."* Then the kilted Kevin insisted on doing a sword dance using two rolled umbrellas, and the party sang along to his crazed steps, his hands raised above his head while his damp kilt swirled around him.

"Come on Gregor, leave the girl alone. She's just a child, and in my care." He had caught his amorous friend with his arm round the waist of Rosa and trying to whisper something in her ear. Gregor was protesting as he was pulled away from the girl when Diana burst into the breakaway gathering.

"Come on everyone. We're all going to look at Daddy's house. John's showing people the pool, and..." she was incredulous now, "Ben McCrae and Fiona are swimming."

They crossed the street, a line of couples, clinging together, jumping gingerly through the crisp snow in their party clothes, to the parents' house and soon joined the mayhem there. Inevitably, Kevin jumped into the blue, clear water where the ceiling lights seemed to swim dizzyingly, and the pleats of his kilt were floating incongruously around his waist. Screams of hilarity and disbelief echoed around the window-lined walls. A girl in her wide skirt shouted, "Here I go!" and threw herself into the water. Her boyfriend and several others followed like lemmings, each squealing out their abandon.

Loud pop music blared out from somewhere, and the whole scene was taking on an orgiastic air. Rosa clung to Jamie's arm, afraid that it would soon be her turn to land in the water. "Jamie, can you not stop them. They might drown!"

"No, no. It's okay. They're all just a bit tight. The water will soon sober them up." He looked for a few seconds into her troubled face, and drawing her into the shadow of the room, behind a large palm tree in a great earthenware pot, he kissed her full pink lips.

The result was electric. She stared back, her eyes astonished. "Jamie..." she started to say. He took her drink from her hand and put it on a shelf, and embraced her, smiling. He kissed her gently once more, the sweet pleasure of her lips together with the school-girlish perfume were heady, so that he found his hands moving down to her hips. Her face was disturbed, growing pink, her mouth slightly open, and her eyes shining darkly.

"Rosa, Rosa. You are a beautiful girl." But she was becoming agitated and her bosom strained as she tried to recover from his caress, and she began to push him away. "I know. I know... I shouldn't have done that." He stood back recovering himself. "I think it's time..."

There was a disturbance at the door and two very sober-faced policemen in chequered caps appeared, introducing a shaft of seriousness and sanity from the outside world. The revellers slowly wound down from their frenzy. Diana and John gravitated towards the door, while someone turned off the loud music, and people pulled themselves from the pool, their party clothes wrecked and heavy with water. They were given a warning about the dangers of what they were doing, and also about the level of noise in the street. Within minutes, the party was grinding to a halt, and when Vera and Mario arrived to pick up Rosa, they were not pleased at all at what they heard. They bundled her away into their car, and Vera was decidedly sniffy about the whole affair.

That night, Jamie's dreams were full of the sweet, young body and saintly face of Rosa. Then the picture would change to the beloved face and form of his estranged wife. It was an erotic nightmare, full of longing. He would doze for minutes and then would wake up, his body alive and aroused, but his heart dying inside. He almost prayed for morning to come and for peace to be allowed him. He was considering getting up, and making himself a large whisky when, at last, he fell into a merciful sleep.

Morning found him drinking strong coffee, and considering the day ahead, the last day of the holidays. Where was Maggie? Was she happy? When would he see her? Did she still think of him? He shook his head. No, she had known what she was doing. He had given her no cause to find fault in him. Had he not given her everything she had wanted. Everything he possibly could. He had loved her to distraction. He felt the old pain around his heart, and the anxiety returned.

The kitchen range fire needed stoking, and when he had dressed and put the flat in order a little, he walked around trying to find inspiration on how to pass the day. He thought of his mother, and guiltily remembered that she was no longer there for him. God rest her soul! Had he forgotten her already? He couldn't visit Gregor and Prue; they would be up to their eyes in children and probably visiting family members. Finally, he decided to take a bottle of whisky, and visit Mario and Vera. He might have a chance of seeing the tender Rosa even for only an hour. At least he would have company — he could bear to be alone no longer.

But as he drove the few miles to the Pacittis' block his confidence was slipping away again. "Push on, push on!" he told himself. "It's New Year. Everyone visits everyone else at New Year." He found himself stopping the car about a hundred yards from the building, and he eyed the bottle of liquor on the passenger seat. If he indulged in whisky drinking, he would have to take a taxi home. *Will they be glad to see me? Will Rosa have told them of his kisses? Maybe I should turn round and go home and get smashed in front of the TV. May be Maggie will phone to say Happy New Year.*

The noise from the pub on the corner attracted his attention. He locked his car and stepped across the street to check out the place. He found he knew a few of the men there from his football days, and almost immediately he had three glasses of whisky set before him. "Jamie, boy! Happy New Year! The best striker Glenfield ever had. Have a drink. Great to see you! What are you doing in town?" This felt good. They talked of past games with the football fans' instant recall of penalties, goal kicks, off-side and sending-off. A happy hour of reminiscing, of back-slapping and introduction to all and sundry passed, until Jamie feeling definitely woozy, if a lot lighter-hearted, refused to touch another drink.

It took almost half-an-hour to get out of the place and shake hands with all the serious drinkers who followed to the door of the pub, but at last he extricated himself. Looking at his watch, he decided he could still call on Mario and Vera and leave by taxi after an hour or so. He would park the car in the parking bays opposite their window. It would be safe there and he could pick it up next morning early and drive to work. He was just turning into the road when the accident happened. The car that crashed into his was red. It skidded too fast round the corner as he drew out to re-park his car. It struck the wing on the driver's side and he heard the sound of crunching metal and breaking glass, and darkness descended on him.

In the twilight of the accident ward in the Western Infirmary, Jamie opened his eyes. Immediately he felt the sharpness of the needle in his wrist. It pained him when he tried to move. The tube led to a bottle of blood being transfused into him. He swore weakly to himself. "Christ Almighty!" Then his eyes travelled to the foot of the bed where he made out three figures — Mario and Vera, faces drawn and worried, and Rosa her mouth crumpled, her eyes watery. Vera approached him softly. "Jamie, you're awake. You've been in an accident."

He laughed weakly. "I feel like a boxer whose just been carried out of the ring."

She leaned over him. "You're going to be all right, dear. Thank God! We got such a fright."

"Was the other man hurt?"

"Not as badly as you. He's got a broken leg. Your right arm and leg are both broken, and you have two cracked ribs. You lost some blood from a gash in your thigh, but" — she placed her hands on his shoulders — "you'll be all right. Thank goodness!"

Mario joined in. "It wasn't your fault, Jamie. He was going too fast and was quite drunk."

Jamie smiled and croaked out, "I was coming to see you. I had a few drinks in Madden's Bar. I met a couple of old pals."

"Yes, but you weren't drunk like him. And you were practically stationary when he hit you. You were just half-pulled out from the pavement when he crashed in to you. We heard the crash in our lounge, and we saw from the window that it couldn't have been your fault."

Rosa, childlike and petite had come up to his bedside and patted his hand tenderly, tears forming in her eyes. "We've waited for ages for you to open your eyes, Jamie." Her accent was sweet music to him and he wished in a weak-kind of way that he could bury his head in her scented brown hair. "I'm so glad you're all right."

231

"Sure, sure. I'm okay. This drip thing hurts a bit, and my bones ache, but I..." His eyelids were drooping. He forced them open. Now he saw another figure joining the others. Were there four people around him? He felt a strange racing of his heart as he saw that it was Maggie who had joined the other three. Her face was strained and contorted with emotion. She kissed his cheek. "Oh, Jamie. I got such a fright when Vera phoned. You're... you're an awful boy. What are we going to do with you?" The others retired to the waiting room, and she continued to smile indulgently at him, like a mother gazing on a wayward son.

"Hey, wait a minute!" He tried to sound strong and confident. "I'll be all right." She patted his hand and in spite of herself she felt the tears start. He was drifting off to sleep again, "Don't worry, Maggie. It's not your fault. I'll be fine." The last words were slurred as he lost consciousness again, and she was left to gaze on his broken, bandaged body. Stunned by events, she thought of the past few months and of her unfaithfulness until bitterness and guilt overcame her so that she began to sob quietly head bowed on to her chest. Then Vera and Mario came and took her away whispering to her to soften the great remorse that was overwhelming her.

It was decided, by Vera mainly, that Jamie should spend some weeks with Mario and herself while he recuperated. Rosa had to return to Rome, and Jamie could have her room. Weeks passed and Vera enjoyed her role as Florence Nightingale attending to his every need. Maggie visited once a week, interrupting her journey home to her mother's house to see how he was progressing.

Jamie improved a little each day, and began to wonder how he would ever repay Vera for her care of him. Tenderly she bathed his limbs and changed his dressings. Each day they lunched together while Mario was at work. They watched television or read until Mario joined them in the afternoons and again in the evenings after he could get away from the restaurant. Sometimes, Jamie felt a bit uncomfortable as he caught tender looks from Vera when she thought he wasn't watching her. He had always known, since their time in Rome, that she was a bit sweet on him, but he ignored this, putting it down to a middle-aged fantasy. In his weakened state he felt vulnerable, and hoped that she wouldn't do or say something silly that he couldn't deal with.

It was nearly February and he began to feel it would soon be time to move back to his own home. Testing his leg, he walked to the window to look down on the winter streets. He had to move gingerly across the deep-pile carpet, his arm, which had been broken in two places, was still in plaster and held in a sling.

Rosa had sent him a sweet little card from Rome, wishing him good health, and adding a couple of kisses. He picked it up for the twentieth time from Vera's sideboard where it sat beside a photograph of Rosa. The now familiar feeling of wistfulness, of unrequited longing filled him, and the face of Rosa metamorphosed into the face of Maggie, so that he closed his eyes in sadness and frustration.

"She's too young for you, Jamie." Vera had appeared at the doorway from her bedroom. She had been preparing for their going to Mario's that evening where he was to sing for the first time since the accident. Her perfume drifted over to him and she took the card from him, standing just too close to him for comfort. He saw beneath her housecoat, her cleavage, the wrinkled skin carefully oiled. Her teeth were good and her hair was carefully tinted and set in a young bobbed style. "I wish I were younger, Jamie. I would have given the girls a run for their money where you are concerned. I was very beautiful, you know."

"I'm sure you were — I mean, you still are."

She leaned against his broad chest putting her hand on the back of his neck. "Poor Jamie! You've really had a raw deal. First Maggie and now the accident." Her lips brushed his cheek, and he felt her protruding breasts against him.

"My shoulders hurt a little, dear. Do you think, with your one hand you could give them a little massage?" Her voice was thick and sexy.

Confused he stammered, "You want a massage?" Involuntarily he looked around to see who was watching. But Mario had left for the restaurant.

"Sure, my back needs rubbing and we have over an hour before we need to leave."

Panic filled him. She was giving out very sexy signals. Then like an angel from above, the doorbell rang. Quickly Vera hurried to answer it, and Maggie was there. He hadn't seen her for almost two weeks, and he was relieved and delighted when she walked in. He squinted at her from the plush armchair where he had taken refuge, a paler, lighter Jamie. From the way his sweater and trousers hung on him, it was quite obvious he had been ill. His clothes hung on him in a loose unflattering way. She too, looked different, dressed in jeans and a loose sweater, almost without make-up and carrying books in a great leather shoulder bag. With a concerned look she approached him, apologising for not coming to visit before now. She sat beside him, and seemed to scrutinise his face. Did she see his confusion or pick up the sexual frisson in the room?

Vera sat down opposite them, her slim legs showing as they escaped from her housecoat. She hid her annoyance at the way she had been interrupted, by lighting a cigarette and talking in a bright voice. "Sit down, Maggie. Our boy improves every day, as you can see. And tell us, how is your course going?"

"Oh, I'm enjoying it, but it's hard work. My brain's not as young as it used to be. I have to work harder than the young students." Her voice was strained and over-precise, her nervousness at her situation being carefully under control. She turned to look at Jamie.

He was a bit flustered, feeling guilty although he had no reason to. God, if Maggie had been ten minutes later! Where would he have been? At the same time he was trying to decide what face to show to this, his estranged wife, from whom he had to hide his love. He longed to embrace her and confess his misery and need of her, but she was so cool. This was another Maggie — older, serious

— even her clothes were different. She was composed, shut in. Gone was the eager ingenue he had married.

She's been through some unhappiness too, he thought, *but she's come out on the other side. Unlike me, she's dealing with her life.* "I'm fine, Maggie. Nice of you to think of me. Vera has been looking after me well." He smiled enigmatically and looked across at the inscrutable older woman. "I don't know where I'd have been if it weren't for the care she and Mario have given me."

Vera smoked on, her eyes narrowing as she weighed them both up. "You'll have a coffee, Maggie?"

"That would be nice, Vera." As the older woman rose gracefully in her expensive housecoat, and left the room, Maggie moved closer to Jamie on the couch. "I'm really sorry about how things turned out, Jamie."

"Oh, everybody gets their turn of misfortune. It was mine this time, that's all." He made an attempt at a grin. "It happens to the best of us."

"Well, it's real bad luck." She struggled for something else to say that wouldn't be too personal, and placing her bag on the carpet said, "Do you see much of Gregor and Prue?"

His heart ached for the serious girl she now was. Her carefully dressed hair and glamorous aura were no more. Gone was the girl-about-town image. Her thick brown hair fell around her face, and with her almost bare of colour she seemed more vulnerable than ever. "Yes, they've called couple of times when they can get out without the kids. They're just the same, always arguing about something. They're a laugh a minute, but happy enough." He paused, then added, "I envy them."

"So do I," she said simply.

"You've changed then. You used to think theirs was a living hell"

"Not now."

Vera came in with three coffees. "Here we are." She put down the tray. "Jamie's going to sing at Mario's tonight, and on Sunday he's going with Gregor to look at boats. They're thinking of buying one together."

"Really? You must be feeling better."

"Yes. I think I'll be going home in a day or two. Can't inflict myself on people much longer." Vera's eyes shot a surprised look in his direction. "Vera's made a new man of me."

"Not quite. You haven't changed that much, but you're getting better. She lit another cigarette using the table lighter. "So, Maggie, you're going to keep on your studies for three years, are you?"

"Yes. If they don't throw me out."

And when that's finished what will you do?"

"Oh, get a job. A good job, I hope."

"No more catering trade for you? No unsocial hours? You'll be a real career woman."

"We'll have to wait and see, Vera. I've a lot of bridges to cross. A lot of exams to pass."

When it was time to go, Maggie picked up her bag. "Mother will wonder what's happened to me. Take care, Jamie. I'm really glad you're getting back on your feet."

Vera stood up too. "So you're still at your mother's?"

"Yes."

Jamie walked to the door with her while Vera sorted the cups on the tray.

Limping behind Maggie, Jamie asked quietly, "And Dominic, how is he?"

"He's moved to the States."

She saw Jamie's eyes widen. "Goodbye, Jamie." She kissed his cheek and touched his face tenderly with her soft hands. "Sing well tonight."

"Goodbye Maggie."

Vera followed her outside into the corridor and closed the door to the flat. Her face was very serious. "I'll speak plainly, Maggie. You're pregnant aren't you?"

Cut to the quick, Maggie stared back, her face almost hard with the shock of the words. "Yes, Vera, that's right, I am."

"What are you going to do?"

"Mother's going to take care of it while I'm at university."

"Good gracious! How can you consider such a thing?"

236

"It's what I've decided, Vera."

"And the baby is Dominic's?" she whispered the last word.

Maggie balked at this frankness, but after a pause she answered, "Yes."

"And he doesn't know?"

"No. And I don't want him to know either. He and I are finished. That time in London. I shouldn't have happened. I know now that it was all wrong. I was, I suppose, foolish. It was just… just madness."

"What about Jamie?"

"Don't tell him. He has enough to cope with. He'll have to build his life again. I've ruined things for him."

Vera melted a little and put an arm around the unhappy girl. "You want this baby."

"I have no option, Vera. But I've got used to the idea now, and well… anyhow it's too late to do anything now. I'll manage somehow, with mother's help." Now, as they stood close in the corridor, Maggie, her eyes flashing with anxiety in the dim light, whispered to Vera, "Promise not to tell Jamie. Not just yet. He'll know soon enough."

"All right, I won't tell him. Poor Maggie!" Vera embraced the younger girl again sharing in some of her pain.

"Yes, poor, stupid me! Goodbye Vera. I'll see you some time."

Chapter 18

Darkness was taking over the winter streets of the city although it was not yet five o'clock. Maggie's mother turned from her kitchen stove as her daughter returned home for the evening.

"Sit close to the fire, Maggie. You look tired. Take off your boots. The meal is nearly ready."

Maggie eased herself into an armchair, grateful for her mother's never-failing cheerfulness. While she waited the call to the table, she read through her day's notes, trying to make sense of the scribbled pages, and promising herself to rewrite the stuff later that evening. The warmth of the coal fire gradually relaxing her, she found her eyes almost closing, and her thoughts turned from the American Revolution to Jamie and their days together. Life had seemed such fun then. Everything seemed to be something to find amusement in, and with Gregor and Prue, the four of them had giggled and laughed their way through the first year or two of marriage. Poor Jamie, how she had hurt him. And how she had hurt herself, landing herself back with her mother and brother in this little house in the suburbs. When Jamie divorced her, she would be just another unmarried mother, trying to study in her spare time, killing herself to build a career.

Ready emotion, always creeping up on her these days, made the smallest thing seem a reason for tears. Last weekend, at the cinema, watching the film, *Carousel*, with two friends, had thrown her into uncontrollable weeping, much to the chagrin of her student friends. Now she felt the child move quite violently inside her, and she feared for the future, and the great unknown territory she was moving into.

She heard her brother coming home. Almost six feet tall now, lean and handsome in an unformed spotty kind of way, he stood leaning over his latest girlfriend, he in narrow jeans and loud shirt, she in a calf-length straight skirt with long lanky hair.

"Hi, Maggie. This is Winifred. She's come round for supper. How are you feeling?"

Maggie pulled herself up from her reveries and managed a smile. "I'm okay, Lawrence. Is that a record you've got there, Winifred?"

The shy girl smiled. "It's fab. Have you heard it? It's Chubby Checker. I just got it."

The two disappeared into Lawrence's room and soon the smell of joss sticks and the noisy beat of rock-and-roll music were filling the house. Maggie fell back into a doze, her mind full of her lectures, then her thoughts moved on to what she would have to do for her confinement, and finally she ended up with the puzzled face of Jamie again filling her thoughts. Now and then, the intense face of Dominic, with its dominant, all-seeing brown eyes would interchange with that of Jamie. Was there an accusation in that face? What would he say if he found she was carrying his child? Maggie shook her head to dispel these persistent anxieties. She had made her decision, and she would have to stick with it.

That night she finished her second-last assignment for the term, her shoulders aching with the prolonged leaning over her desk by the reading lamp in her crowded little bedroom. Tomorrow she would really concentrate, she promised herself. She would keep her mind channelled on finishing the work set for the class by her tutors.

At lunchtime, next day, joined by her two friends, Morag and Lindsay, Maggie strolled out of the lecture room, animatedly discussing the points raised by the speaker that morning. She felt a few curious stares from some of the younger set, and she was aware that her dark, loose clothing was starting to cause them to speculate about her. They knew that she was separated from her husband, and that she was giving them some gossip to mull over during the break in the refectory. She felt her face redden as she sat down, her tray of canteen food looking unappetising.

Lindsay and Morag, mature students like herself, were aware of her plight and stopped their conversation on seeing her distress.

"Never mind that lot of silly girls. They've got all their troubles in front of them." Lindsay patted Maggie's hand in sympathy. "You'll get through it. Don't you worry. You've only a few weeks to go. Don't lose heart now. You're doing well, kid."

"Thanks Lindsay. I'll have to tell my mother, soon. Very soon. I don't know how she hasn't twigged yet." Maggie started on her lunch.

"I'm sure she'll be all right. You'd best get it over with, girl. You haven't committed a murder, after all. You'll get through it." As they ate their snack lunch, Morag continued, "God, I'm glad my two are at school now and out of harm's way while I'm here. Yours too, Lindsay?"

"Yes. My Tommy needs looking after for an hour before I get home, but that's all, so I don't feel too bad."

Maggie had made a close friendship very quickly with these two soulmates. She was glad of their support. "Do you think I'm doing the right thing, leaving the baby with my mother and coming back to university so soon?"

Lindsay lit a cigarette. "Of course you are. You've started out on this road, so don't go and fall off now. After all, the third term is the shortest one, and you'll have all summer to be with the baby."

Maggie's smile had a touch of melancholy in it, and the two other girls exchanged glances. They knew that there was a story behind their new friend, but didn't want to intrude on the troubled girl. Some day she would tell them, they felt sure.

"When is it due again, Mags?"

"Four weeks from now." Maggie grimaced. "I'm halfway through the essay for Hobbs on the Nineteenth Century Novel. Then the two exams at the end of next week, and I can relax."

"Relax?" Lindsay hooted. "That'll be the day!"

"Oh you know what I mean." Maggie had to join in the hilarity with them.

"Don't forget to ring us to let us know when it arrives. I can't wait to see it. Do you want a boy or a girl?"

Once more Maggie felt her face flush, but she said shyly, "Oh, a boy. I would love to have a little baby boy. But anything will do."

They were huddled close round the Formica table, so that their conversation would not be overheard by the noisy throng around them. "Anything?" screamed Lindsay. "I don't think so!"

"Well, you know what I mean. I try not to think too much about it. I keep hoping it will be all right, and not…"

"Everybody does that. It stands to reason. It's a lot to get your head round, another human being emerging from your body." Morag had become all dreamy. "Just think, you'll have a sweet little bundle to cuddle soon." Her face was near to ecstatic with remembered joys, and they all smiled, regretting the bell that signalled the time to return to their classes.

But during the history seminar, Maggie's mind wandered some of the time. Would she cope with just her mother to help her? No father for her baby! Had she made the right decision, or should she have told Dominic? How hurt was Jamie, or had he met someone else by now and forgotten her? In the end, when the class was finished, Mr Nichol asked her if she was feeling all right. She smiled and reassured him that she was fine, burying her fears in the recesses of her mind, not to resurface until the hours of darkness when sleep wouldn't come, and she walked smartly out of the classroom, her head held high.

That evening, after dinner, Mrs Fisher studied her daughter as she lay, half-asleep on the chintz-covered couch. Glad to have her living at home with her, and yet nervous of upsetting her, she tried to formulate the question that had been worrying her now for a long time. Soon, Maggie moved her position. Sensing her mother's eyes on her, she opened her eyes.

"What is it, Mother?"

"Well, you haven't told me, and I haven't asked you, but do you have something to tell me? Is there a baby on the way?"

"I was going to tell you this evening, but I see you've guessed. I didn't how to come out with it." She tried to keep calm. "Yes I'm expecting a baby."

"When is it due?"

"The end of March. At least that's what they say."

"The end of March?"

"Yes. I know I shouldn't have kept it a secret."

"You're hardly showing at all. What does Jamie say about it?" The older woman's face was strained with embarrassment and agitation.

Maggie raised herself up to a sitting position and looked down at her body, her face unreadable she said, "He doesn't know about it."

"So, it's all over with you and Jamie?"

Maggie hung her head, and mumbled, "I'm afraid so." Her face screwed up in misery.

"I know, my dear. I know. Just tell me. The baby's not Jamie's, is that it?"

"No. It's not Jamie's. So he won't be coming to see me." She lifted her eyes to her mother's face, and quickly dropped them again when she read the pain and disappointment that was there.

"My God!" was all her mother could say.

Maggie started to sob, tears blinding her. All the regret and pent-up emotion seemed to spill out of her.

Helen came and sat on the arm of the chair beside her daughter. "There, there, don't cry. You should have told me before now." She bit her lip, scanning her mind for solutions to this situation. "And so, the baby's father is… is this Dominic?"

Again Maggie nodded, her head thrust low, the tears still falling. "And does he know about the child?"

This time Maggie shook her head, and her mother unable to contain herself stood up and started to pace the floor of the bright little living room.

"And the bold Dominic's shot off to America."

"He hasn't shot off. I told him it was finished between us."

"Finish with him and you're pregnant to him?"

"I didn't know I was pregnant at the time."

God help us all, she thought, feeling sorry for herself as this new problem was thrown at her. First to be left a widow before she was fifty, then the worry of her arty son with his long hair and mad ways, his hair almost reaching his shoulders, and his school work worsening, and now her clever daughter she was so proud of, pregnant to a man who was not her husband. A tense silence filled the room, as each struggled with thoughts and emotion.

"What are we going to do? How are we going to manage? Maggie, what a mess!" But she regretted the words almost as soon as they were out of her mouth. She rushed over to the distraught girl and put her arms around her. "I'm sorry, love. Oh, I'm sorry. We'll manage somehow."

Momentarily, they clung together at the fireside, each desperately needing the other. Then composing themselves, feeling almost release that the story was out in the open, Helen Fisher wiped her eyes, her mixed emotion leaving her feeling weak. She was going to be a grandmother.

"I'll make us a cup of tea, Mum. Don't tell Lawrence about the baby not being Jamie's. Let's just keep it between us, okay?"

With a watery smile Helen looked up from the hypnotic burning coals. Her thoughts were of her late husband, and the sadness of it all. "Sure, we will. Sure, Maggie. It can be our secret. We'll just have to get on with things as they are."

They got through the next few weeks, and the morning came when Helen called Maggie for her breakfast, and there was no answer. She found the girl, lying in bed, her face contorted, her fists clenched around the sheets, trying to control the pain that was searing through her. Agitated, she laid her hands on Maggie. "You should have called me you silly girl. How long since the last pain?"

"I don't know. Quarter of an hour, maybe. Oh, Mum, it's like waves of fire or hot steel going through me." Maggie's face was pale and shocked. "It's unbelievable."

Her mother's face crumpled with sympathy as her own excruciating first labour came back to her. "I know, love. I know. I'll call the doctor. Just you hold on. You'll be all right." She straightened up the bed, then hurried out to the telephone.

When she came back, Maggie's eyes followed her mother as she took up her position with the watch. "You will help me with the baby, mother. You'll look after the baby for me, sometimes, when I have to study?"

Helen Fisher's face softened. "Of course I will. It's our baby. What do you think your mother's made of? Of course I'll look after it. Just you relax until the doctor comes. I'll see to everything."

The ambulance reached the hospital at ten o'clock in the morning and at one o'clock Maggie gave birth to an eight-pound baby boy, a lusty, perfect child. They gave her the child to hold, and she tearfully scrutinised the little angry face, love dawning in her heart.

Her mother was allowed in to the labour ward, and she tried to make up for the fact that there was no father there to praise her Maggie. "I'm so proud of you, my dear. The baby is lovely."

Maggie smiled. "A boy, Mum. Just what I wanted."

"He's beautiful, truly beautiful!"

Later, Prue and Gregor called, hiding their feelings at the baby not being Jamie's. "You look as if you had just gone five rounds with the world heavyweight champion." Gregor's good-natured face beamed at her.

"That's how I feel, Gregor. I ache all over."

"Oh, I was on my feet in no time after each of mine," Gregor said.

"Ha, ha! They've no idea about the agonies we go through, Maggie. It's a bloody unfair arrangement."

"Bloody's right!" Maggie pulled herself to a sitting position, and they chatted amiably. After a while, Maggie ventured, "How's Jamie, Gregor?"

"He's okay." His voice was guarded. "Saw him, let's see, last Tuesday. He's liking his job. Lucky devil, a new car every year, and paid to go and see people in businesses around the west of Scotland. God! Lucky bleeder!"

Maggie sat up in the bed, her shoulders slouched forward, her breasts engorged and tender, playing with a tissue handkerchief. She glanced over to the little scrap of a baby, rolled in white, hospital, cellular blanket, and the eyes of the other two followed hers. "He knows about the baby?"

Gregor answered seriously. "Yes he knows."

"You told him?"

"Yes. Couldn't very well not tell him, Maggie." Then to cover up the silence he said cheerily, "We're going out on the boat, soon. You know we bought a little sailing yacht, a twelve-footer. It's at Balloch right now. We're doing it up, ready for the warmer weather." Maggie's eyebrows raised at this new venture. "Yes. Taking old Benton out. That should be a laugh."

"Mr Benton! Can't imagine him in a sailing boat."

"Jamie and old Benton have become quite thick. He's a lonely old soul, and quite nice really, so we thought we'd scare him with a sail on the loch."

When they stood up to go, Maggie saw the pity in Prue's eyes. Having her husband by her side, was she looking down on her? "Goodbye, Maggie. We'll come and see you at your mother's, soon. You'll be back at university, you think, in a few weeks?"

"Yes, that's my intention." Smiling brightly, Maggie waved them goodbye, but when their figures disappeared, she slipped down under the stiff white coverlet pushing her fists into her eyes to stop the tears of self-pity that were welling up there.

Chapter 19

The hotel was called The Rosebank. It was on the Ayrshire coast and Gregor, dressed in Arran sweater, corduroy trousers and leather boots was ensconced there, happily lounging on the luxurious tartan-covered couch in the conservatory which overlooked the water. He was eyeing the large whisky, which sat on the low oak table in front of him beside some water in a jug that had the figure of Johnnie Walker painted on the side. Seated opposite him was Lewis Benton, still wearing his overcoat against the chill of the spring morning, now wiping his moist, red nose with his handkerchief.

Puzzled as to just how Gregor and Jamie had talked him into this unusual outing, Lewis felt shaken up and disorientated. Sunday morning usually meant a late breakfast in his landlady's dining-room, and with his third cup of coffee a cigarette, while he read the papers. Then later in the day, he would walk through the park, lunch in his usual pub in Byres Road, have some cracks about politics and the like, then back to his lodgings for supper and an evening of TV, with perhaps a few nips of whisky before bed. This was the usual course of events, that is, when he didn't go home for the weekend, back to his hometown of Aberdeen, to his sister's home.

But Gregor and Jamie had insisted he come and see their new boat, and he had felt like a change. The two boys were entertaining, and now that Gregor had left Rodger and Russell's, and Jamie was part of the management, he felt it was quite appropriate to meet them socially.

"Cheers, Mr Benton! Nice to see you in Civvy Street, so to speak. Here's to our day out."

"Cheers, Gregor!" Mr Benton, after drinking perhaps two thirds of his drink, put his glass down and smacked his lips appreciatively. "First today! Not a bad whisky."

Gregor said, "Drink up, Mr Benton and I'll get you another."

"Oh, no, not at all." And he waved his hand to indicate his dissension. "We must pace ourselves, Gregor. It's only twelve-thirty. Anyway, call me Lewis today, since we're both off duty."

"Right… er… Lewis." Gregor's glass was half empty, and the spirits were already making him woozy. He said, "God, this is living! What a brilliant idea of Jamie's! This sailing lark is a winner. Lovely view from these windows, Lewis, have you seen it? The water is calm today."

"Beautiful, Gregor. This beats my usual strolling through the park on Sundays, trying to avoid the kids and the prams."

"Too true! And don't mention prams. I've seen enough of them to do me for a lifetime."

Lewis smiled. "Your children must be growing. They must be getting big now. Three isn't it?"

"Yes. Two boys and a girl. Let's hope that all we ever have. I tell you it's no joke. It's a non-stop job, bringing up kids. I get pushed to the back of the queue, last in the pecking order when it comes to Prue giving out attention."

"Oh, come on!" Lewis looked amused. "It can't be that bad, Gregor."

"Well, let's put it this way. I feel as if I've really landed lucky just to be having a drink and out of the house today." Gregor pushed back the red curls from his forehead, and tried to rearrange his long skinny legs, so that they were less obtrusive. He surveyed the narrow country road looking for Jamie's blue Ford Consul, and then he pulled his attention back to the conversation. "Sometimes, Lewis, I think I must be just plain mad. Look at me. I'm thirty-two now. I have very little autonomy in my life. I have five mouths to feed, and just getting out for the day, today, was an ordeal. God, I had to pass the Spanish Inquisition. "What hotel? How long will you be away? Will you be drinking? Are you sure you're meeting

Jamie and Mr Benton? Will you want a meal when you come home?"

"Sounds formidable, right enough!"

Gregor stood up. "Here's Jamie!"

"Listen, Gregor. Before he comes in, what's the story about Maggie and him? He never tells me. I see him three times a week when he reports into the office, but he's a closed book."

Serious-faced, Gregor answered in a low voice. "Maggie had a baby boy, a week yesterday."

Baffled, Lewis said, "I see. He didn't tell me. That's nice!"

"No, not really." Gregor voice was almost a hiss now. "The baby's not Jamie's"

Lewis struggled to hide his confusion as he came to meet Jamie in the hotel doorway. "At last, Jamie. What'll you have? We're one ahead of you."

"Just a half pint, please. Driving you know."

They were the first party in the dining-room, a haven of beautifully set tables, rosy lighting, and smart waiting staff. It was a luxury for each of them, and Jamie began to drop the tense front he had been maintaining since the news about Maggie and the baby had broken.

Afterwards they ambled along in the sunshine, stopping to watch, with the fascination of city men, the water lapping around the old wooden jetty. In the air near the waterside the breeze was more apparent, and there was a feeling of renewal and rebirth in the air. They walked along to see the activity that the finer weather had brought to the lochside where the little boats had been moored through the months of winter. Perhaps a dozen people were there, fussing with their crafts. Some were hammering, some sanding down the woodwork, others varnishing or painting, and all seemed absorbed in their work.

Jamie said, "My cousin, Lachie's been down most of last week, working on the boat. It's that one, the fifth one along." He led the way, and when they reached the little motor launch, Gregor and he removed the tarpaulin. The three stood back to admire her.

There was pride in Jamie's voice. "There she is! The Queen Violet. A poor thing but our own."

"A very nice name, Jamie. And a nice-looking boat. Very impressive." Lewis was walking round the vessel, now and then rubbing the hull in appreciation.

"God, Jamie," Gregor's face was bright with pleasure, "Lachie's made a good job of her. She looks terrific."

"Ay, he's put three coats of varnish on her, and he's tuned up the engine. Let's get her in the water."

Lewis was rolling up his overcoat as they laid hands on the boat. "Are you sure you know what you're doing, Jamie?"

Jamie was already at the controls. "It'll be okay, Lewis. Lachie gave us both a few lessons. Don't worry. Just take a seat."

They set out gingerly at first, and soon the wind was in their faces, and the three were speeding out from the shore like schoolboys on a voyage of adventure.

Gradually relaxing, Gregor sat back in the boat taking in the performance of the other craft on the water, while he experienced the unaccustomed feeling of having leisure time — that is time not used to make a quick dive to the pub to find an anodyne to the daily the grind. "I could get used to this," he said.

"Who's this fellow Lachie, Jamie, who taught you to handle boats?" asked Lewis.

"Oh, he's a cousin of mine. Comes from Islay. Knows boats inside out. He used to run a little croft on the island, and part of the time he was at the fishing, but he's moved to Glasgow now, but he just loves to mess about down here when he gets any time. He's interested in real sailing."

"Real sailing?"

"Yes, with sails, you know. Sails without an engine. He's going to give me a few lessons, once he owns his own craft. That'll be a real challenge."

Gregor took over the controls of the boat next, and a silence fell on them as they moved slowly up the loch, each lost in his own thoughts. Involuntarily, Jamie's mind settled on Maggie, and the shock of the news of the baby's birth, so that the uncomfortable, demeaning position he was in, overwhelmed him. He mused on his past and his time in hospital. That illness that taken more than years out of his young life. He had been just twenty-four when the pain of his leg had finished him with football, and rendered him bedridden with no sure cure. The words of the doctor to his mother sounded in his ears. "I'm sorry to tell you, Mrs London, and you Jamie, that the tests on your leg show that you have a tubercular lesion. I'm afraid, you will have to stop work, and give up all sport. Rest is the only thing we can prescribe. You have contracted bovine TB, undoubtedly from untreated milk." This statement had been a shattering blow.

Jamie turned so that the other two couldn't see the pain in his face. He had thought Maggie, with her broad smile and loving nature, was in some way compensation from Fate or God. She had changed his life, completely turned it around. After living at home with his mother during his long recuperation, and being very tentative about his health, she had brought a new purpose to him. How untouched she had been! Once he told her. "God sent you to me. Do you know that?" She had laughed and dismissed his words as just a line. But he had been deadly serious. Now he thought ruefully if God sent her to me he didn't take long in taking her away again.

Lewis and Gregor exchanged glances as they saw Jamie's self-absorption. Eventually Lewis broke the silence. "The hills are quite breathtaking. Really we should do this more often. It's good to get out of the town."

"Yeah. Quite inspiring. What do you say, Jamie?"

Jolted out of his reverie, Jamie looked at them blankly. "Yeah. It's great. Best idea we ever had, Gregor. We must take Lachie up on his offer to give us lessons in sailing."

Lewis did not want the day to end. "Oh, let's make a night of it, boys. Once you get back, Gregor, Prue'll never let you out again. What about it? You can leave your car and walk home. You, too, Jamie. It's not too far, or you can take a taxi. You're not in a rush are you?"

Tempted, Jamie looked thoughtful. "Well, I suppose I could. What do you think, Gregor?"

Lewis pressed his case. "We'll have a bite of supper, a sandwich or something at The Crown in Houldsworth Street, and a drink. You'll be home by eight or nine. Go on, Gregor, give Prue a ring."

Afterwards in the bar, Lewis said kindly, "I'm sorry to hear about you and Maggie, Jamie. Really sorry." Jamie did not answer.

Gregor stood up quickly, "I'll get another round in. Same again?" and he hurried off to the bar.

Lewis leaned over saying, "I just heard this afternoon, I had no idea you and Maggie had parted."

Jamie shrugged his shoulders miserably, "Yes. A few months ago."

"That's too bad. She's a nice girl. I liked her."

"Yes, she's a nice girl." Jamie looked away, unable to meet Lewis's eyes.

"Here we are boys!" Gregor was back. "Phoned Prue. She's not too chuffed, but as you say, Lewis, once you're out, you're out. It's the getting out that's the problem." They laughed and then after a pause, Gregor said, "I went to see Maggie, yesterday in the hospital." He took a sip of his beer. "Prue and I went together."

Jamie paused with his glass halfway to his mouth, then said nonchalantly, "She was all right?"

"Well, you know. Yes, okay, I suppose. Nice baby." Gregor was eyeing a short-skirted teenager who was swaggering past while Jamie, his heart racing, stared at his friend trying to read his thoughts.

Lewis had knocked back his glass of whisky, and his voice showing evidence of alcohol consumption announced. "Well, you know, if it was me, I'd go and see her, for... for old-time's sake, you know. Yes, I would."

Jamie's eyes flashed. "Go and see her? The baby's not mine. She had an affair with someone else. The kid is someone else's."

On seeing Jamie's cheeks redden, and his anger rise, Lewis was afraid to make any further remark. Gregor spoke quietly straight to Jamie's troubled face. "You still love the girl, Jamie. That's obvious."

"What do you mean?"

"Would you be as miserable as you are if you didn't care."

Jamie dragged the words out of himself. "I'm just disappointed," he said in a low voice, "hurt, gutted, deceived. How could she do it?" They saw his emotion rising, and they were silenced, each lost in his thoughts.

Presently Gregor put down his pint. "I still think Lewis is right. You should go and see her. I think she wants to see you. She asked about you from Prue and me. And that Dominic's gone for good, you know. He's gone to America. She finished with him long ago. He doesn't know she's had a child."

Rage and frustration suffused Jamie's face at the mention of Dominic. "I wish he'd drown, the bastard, or his plane would crash. He ruined my life."

"Yeah, I'd hold him while you knock his teeth out," Gregor patted Jamie's back. "I'm right in there with you. The swine knew what he was doing, seducing a girl just past twenty. Dirty old man! But think of Maggie for a minute, Jamie. She's made a mistake, and she's not half paying for it. She looked so woebegone all alone in that hospital."

Lewis nodded quite drunk by now. "Gregor's right, Jamie. I know you feel you've been deceived but… well, anyway, how would like to be me with nothing, and no one to love me? I wish I'd had half your chances in the game."

"Chances? Chances, Lewis? What chances? My young life cut short with serious illness. Two years hospitalised with a gammy leg, and my beautiful, young wife's unfaithful to me with a man old enough to be her father! Chances? You must be joking!" Jamie lifted his beer and threw it back.

"You'd rather be me, Jamie? Straight from school to Rodger and Russell's. Banished to another town where I knew nobody. I hardly see my family. As for women I just can't talk to them. Can't relate to them." Gregor and Jamie were stopped in their tracks by this unaccustomed soul-baring.

Gregor was fiddling with a beer mat, embarrassed. "Come on Lew! There must have been a girl in there somewhere, sometime in your life."

Swaying slightly forwards and backwards, and trying to sort out his muddled brain, Lewis looked down, saying, "Well, yes. When I was twenty or so, there was a girl. I treated her like a princess. We did in those days. No funny business. We were going out for about a year, but..." his eyes became troubled as he remembered. "She ditched me, I suppose. I must have been a dull fellow. She married one of my friends — a farmer. She's a grandmother now, would you believe, and very happy, I think." His eyes misted over as he delved into his thoughts "She's still bonny. I saw her about a year ago in Aberdeen town centre with two grandchildren; Audrey Fitzpatrick is her name. She was well... she really was the one, the only one for me."

Now both Jamie and Lewis looked miserable, and Gregor tried to lighten things up, "Well, maybe it's not so bad. No constant financial crises. No trying to get on the right side of her all the time — trying to sweeten her up. You know what women are like, always trying to make you fit their pattern, always nagging"

"It's time you stopped smoking, Gregor. Stop drinking, Gregor. When are we having a holiday? And so on." He was getting into his stride.

"Well," Jamie said. "That's all over for me. I've fallen out of that situation. I've lost the knack of following what makes women tick." He looked up ruefully. "A born loser, that's me."

Lewis accepted a cigarette from Gregor. "I think I take first place in the league of losers, boys."

Gregor mumbled, "Well, anyway, neither of you is short of a bob or two. I'm permanently boracic lint." He pulled out the pocket linings of his jacket to illustrate his plight, and they had to smile at his doleful face.

Jamie said, "We'd better call it a day. Look at the time."

"Lewis, Jamie, it's been a pleasure. Best day I've had in ages." Gregor's eyes had a glazed look as the drink took effect. "And I'll look out for a woman for you, Lewis. Millions of them out there. Just looking for a man."

At the door Jamie had stopped a taxi. Turning he said, "Goodnight, goodnight. See you in the morning, Lewis. Love to Prue, Gregor."

Gregor stumbled over to the door of the cab. "Just think about going to see Maggie, my son. She's very… well, vulnerable… you know, conscience-stricken, I think."

"A bit late for remorse, Gregor, a bit late. Thanks for a great day. Goodnight."

For weeks, Jamie wrangled with his feelings. Plagued by thoughts and tender memories of Maggie, and repelled by her behaviour and by the idea of her bearing another's man's child, his face bore the signs of inner turmoil and confusion.

By eight o'clock each evening he was anchored in front of the television set, whisky bottle to hand, his sorrows halfway drowned, and the lonely evening slowly passing. On one of these nights of debauchment, the phone rang, and, as he'd half-expected it was Tillie, the waitress from Mario's. He'd taken her out once but had not really enjoyed it, and had made no advances to her.

"How are you, Jamie? I was just sitting here thinking about you. How are you coping on your own?" Her voice was bright with forced gaiety.

"I'm fine, Tillie. Just sitting here watching television."

"You'll be singing at Mario's tomorrow night, as usual?"

"Yes. I think so. All other things being equal." He hoped he didn't sound too intoxicated, and struggled to keep hold of the conversation.

"Well, Frank and Beryl are having a party after work. They asked me to ask you too."

"Oh. Where is it?"

"They have a second-floor flat in Ruthven Street, off Byres Road."

"Well, thanks for thinking of me… might be all right. We'll see how it goes, Tillie."

"Oh, great! I'd love you to be there."

He said goodbye and rang off. Tillie was about thirty-five, slim, attractive, blonde-haired and divorced. He knew there was a kid somewhere, but he didn't ask too many questions, trying to keep his distance from her. She was tireless in her flirting with him on Saturday evenings as she weaved her sexy way round the tables. He knew what she wanted, and up until now he had managed to resist her advances.

On Saturday evening, at eleven o'clock, she stood by the door of Mario's, glamorous in mini-skirt, low cut top and too much make-up and jewellery. Jamie collected his coat and joined her. "Lead the way, Tillie, lead the way."

She giggled and shimmied down the stairway on her high heel shoes. "George and Rita are waiting for us. Come on."

It was the usual sort of affair, sedate and orderly at first, with drinks and snacks. There were polite introductions, forced laughter, until the drinks started to take effect. Then the girls became less inhibited, they moved more seductively, the men smiled foolishly and the dancing started.

After another hour or so there were little skirmishes as partners strayed, to whoever they fancied was sexier. Jamie grew weary of it. He planned to slip away when no one was looking and grab a cab for home. His brain was numb and the scene bored him. Tillie had given him the come-on all night and now she was trying to make him jealous by dancing extremely close to the party host.

The music blared out some smaltzy tune about unrequited love and Jamie quietly stepped through the hallway, but Tillie had spotted him. Tipsily she threw her arms around his neck. "Where are you going, lover-boy?

"Home, Tillie. I'm tired."

"I'll get my things, and you can drop me off. Will you darling? It's on your way." Her face was very close to his, and she smiled seductively.

Guardedly he shifted his coat to the other arm. "If you like," he said.

In the cab she pushed close beside him and drew him into a long passionate kiss, her curves against his tense body, her perfume almost overpowering. "Let me come home with you. I'm crazy about you, Jamie."

"Tillie, I don't know." Gently he pushed her back against the leather seat.

She thrust herself even closer and caressed his hair, moving down to his body.

"Come on, it'll be great. I'll make you very happy."

"Tillie, I'm a married man."

"Are you? That's not what I hear."

He couldn't find an answer, realising that it was common knowledge about his marriage. He felt sad at the thought of Maggie's name being bandied about. In a few minutes the taxi was drawing up at his door and Tillie got out. Feeling like a fly caught in a spider's web, he let her into the flat. They had a drink and sat chatting, she giggling seductively all the time, while he eyed her slim legs and provocative pose.

"I'll get you another drink." He rose to take her glass.

"We don't need another drink." She took his hand and led him to the bedroom. He was in her power now, and he succumbed to her hot caresses. Their lovemaking was quick and passionate. Jamie fell back exhausted on the bed.

"That was great, Jamie. I knew it would be. I could stay with you tonight if you like."

"No, Tillie. I'm off early in the morning." It was a lie but he wanted to see her out of the door, so that he could get back to his thoughts of Maggie. He watched her fasten her brassiere and adjust her clothing, putting on her panties. They hadn't even undressed properly. I'll get the car out and take you home. It's not far, so it should be all right. I'm sober now."

"You're taking me home already?"

"It's almost three in the morning." The smudged make-up showed the roughness of her skin. Her hair was messed up. In the light of the bedside lamp she looked hard and common, and Jamie turned away from her. He averted his eyes from the photograph where Maggie eternally smiled, fresh and innocent. In the hallway he said, "On second thoughts, I'd better not drive. I'll call another cab." She looked up unsmiling. He could see he was not pleasing her one little bit. He tried to look pleased. "It's okay, Tillie, don't worry, I'll pay the driver before he leaves."

Her expression was sour, "You're sorry we did that, aren't you? I can see it in your face."

He hid his thoughts. "No, I'm not sorry. Don't be silly."

"That's okay, then. I really like you, you know." Seeing his face still non-committal, she shrugged, "I'd better get home." As she reached the door she turned to him, "Still carrying the torch for Maggie, eh?" He did not answer. "Well, you're a fool. She's a good-time girl, that's all there is to it. She's way out of your league. After the big-time, she is."

"You're wrong. Don't say that about her. It's not true." They were at the edge of the pavement in the cold damp night, and the driver waited impatiently for her. Jamie gave him a couple of pounds, and raised his hand to wave.

As he met her eyes she did not smile or wave, saying only through the cab window, "We'll see, my darling. Goodnight."

The cab drove off, and he returned to the flat, going straight to the whisky bottle. Next morning found him wakening in the chair where he had crashed out. Creakily he raised himself, his mouth rough and dry, his eyes bloodshot and shrunken. He felt awful.

The phone rang. It was Gregor. "How are you this morning?"

"Deadly."

"Thought you might fancy a round of golf. Guess what, Prue's allowed me out today."

"I'm a bit rough for that, Gregor."

"Nonsense. Cheer up! Take an aspirin and some bacon and eggs. We'll have a pint before we set out. You'll be fine."

The fresh, moist air of the course lifted the deadliness of the hangover. Gregor was in good form, and by the end of a couple of hours, Jamie felt better, vowing never to drink so much again.

"It's my game, Jamie, so you're paying for the drinks at the nineteenth."

"Okay. You win. You have to be good at something, Gregor"

They strolled off to the bar installing themselves by the window. Jamie fell into his seat. "Christ, I'm exhausted. I think I'm getting old."

"Thirty's not old." Gregor was full of the joys of spring. "Prue's gone to her mother's for the day. It's so great to get a round of golf. Sets you up for the week."

"Weak — that's how I feel." Jamie shoulders were slumped and he stared at his pint of beer.

"What was she like?"

"Who?"

"The bird you were with last night."

"How did you know?"

"You look knackered. And just a trifle, you know… guilty."

Jamie took a sip of his beer. "Don't ask."

"Was it the waitress?"

"Yeah."

"Hot piece is she? Fancies you, does she?"

"Oh, drop it, Gregor."

"You'll hate me for saying this, old son, but you'd better get a grip of yourself."

"How?"

"One of those tarts on the loose is going to get her claws into you and you won't get away."

Jamie looked disgusted. "And what would you do if you were me, Einstein? How would you solve my miserable situation?"

"Well—"

Jamie broke in before Gregor got started. "Listen, chum, it's all a game, this man-woman thing. She's divorced and I suppose lonely, so she gets a fancy for me. It's human nature. Women are extremely devious. They have a way of getting what they want. Look at you and Prue. She's very maternal and wants children. So she keeps you, the provider, tied to her apron strings, lets you out just enough to keep you placid. Relationships, marriage, you can keep them! I hear John and Diana are having rough time."

Gregor's eyebrows were raised at this new bitterness in Jamie. "Yeah? John and Diana, surely not having trouble already?"

Jamie lit a small cigar and seeing Gregor's envious face, he offered him one. "Yeah," he continued, "I hear he's always out with the boys, or training, or playing football. He gambles. There's talk of another woman. Her father is never off his back, trying make him fit into the mould of a good husband. And as for poor Diana, she's hardly had time to put her wedding dress away before the whole stupid business falls apart. It's a game, Gregor."

"Come on, it's not always like that. You haven't half got the blues today. Really, Jamie. Sometimes marriage can be great. Prue and I are happy really in spite of all our money worries. And we're both crazy about the kids." Jamie did not answer, and Gregor gazed around the bar, thinking how he could be a help to his miserable friend. He loved Jamie, loved his usual happy-go-lucky, fun-loving personality. In Jamie's company he had had such good times. It was distressing to see how hard he had been hit, but what to do, he didn't know.

After some time, Jamie snapped out of his despondency a bit to ask, "How is Prue settling into the new house? Do the kids like it?"

Gregor's face lit up. "Prue loves the new kitchen, and the garden is great for the kids. We're very happy, really. I suppose money will always be a problem, but the kids are just terrific. This morning when Prue dressed them up for the visit to her mother's, they looked cute as buttons. You know, Jack's turning out to be a real smart kid." His enthusiasm and earnestness wrung a smile from Jamie.

"You're a lucky man."

"Look, Jamie. Why don't you go and see her?"

"Who?"

"You know who. Maggie."

An expression that was almost a sneer came on Jamie's face. "No, I don't think so." Gregor gave up and a silence fell between them. "She made her decision."

"Not every decision we make is the right one. And some decisions, some actions, have untold repercussions that we didn't foresee. Look, Jamie, this'll cheer you up. You know it's your birthday next week. How about Saturday afternoon we have a barbecue? We got a beautiful big grill and all the tools, in a present from Prue's mother when we moved to our new house. And I know someone who would help me to organise things. It's a walk-over; we went to a barbecue party last week, which a neighbour gave. The guy showed me how to deal with the fire and everything. The women prepare all the food. It's terrific fun, and if the weather's not good we can move inside. What do you say?"

A hint of Jamie's lost charm came back to him as he said, "For you, Gregor, anything!"

Chapter 20

An October Saturday evening, and the street was quiet. Maggie looked down from her bedroom window, only half-seeing the shiny black of the wet road under the street lights, and the occasional falling leaf from the neighbourhood trees. Now and then a car would pass usually carrying a couple, dressed for a night out. Everyone seemed to be going somewhere. Her mother and Lawrence were both out, and there was only the baby and herself in the quiet house. A wave of melancholy filled her as she started picking up the detritus from the baby's bath time — a toy rabbit, a rattle in the shape of a baby lamb, talcum powder, socks and shoes and baby clothes. In the corner of the room, on the other side of her bed, was her desk, the books piled in a disorderly fashion, some lying open, others with places marked. Her English Literature essay lay hardly started, and she felt the half-empty page accusing her as she passed.

Another late night of brain-cracking work. How to develop her argument? God! Twentieth Century Poetry? Who needs it? She leaned over the cot to gaze at her sleeping son. "Edward McPherson, you are a beautiful boy," she said. And, to be sure, with his pink cheeks and rosebud lips, the baby was an angel. Her heart turned over with love. She held her wristwatch up to the sleeping child. "Look, Edward, nine thirty," she whispered. "I'm going to have a cup of tea, and then two hours or so of writing before your grandma returns from her day out. And Lawrence will be back from his pub night or whatever. So you better be good and let me get on with my work."

She placed a kiss on his little podgy fist and thought of Jamie. How different things would have been if this were Jamie's son, and if instead of this fine, dark hair, brown eyes and olive skin, his hair and skin had been fair. How Jamie would have loved his own son! But she must not torture herself. She would have to be mother and father to this child. And Dominic? What would he say to this sleeping beauty? His old heart would have been touched, she thought, and she could not stop the confused emotions filling her breast. Dominic's love seemed ages away, and she missed that adoration. But that episode was closed. Totally all over. She now considered that it had been a dreadful mistake, a false step. She shuddered when she remembered that torpid affair in London and Paris. What had possessed her? How she had hurt everyone who loved her — her mother, her friends, but most of all, Jamie — level-headed, good-natured Jamie. His sadness now brought a dreadful guilt. *I'm just a born fool!* She glanced down at the sleeping child and the little face calmed her. *I must snap out of this. I am sinking into self-pity. I must be strong. The past is past.* Soon she had settled down to her writing, blocking everything else from her mind.

After an hour or so, voices on the stairway disturbed her concentration, and her fingers still buried in her hair as she tried to make her brain come up with some original thoughts, she looked up from her little circle of light. Quickly she rose to warn Lawrence and his two friends to move quietly, because of the sleeping baby. They smiled sheepishly and Lawrence put his finger to his lips, and they ascended the stairs in exaggerated fashion.

"Don't wake the baby, boys." But it was too late. A loud crying came from Maggie's bedroom, and resignedly she picked the warm bundle from his cot, and stood at the top of the stairs for him to be admired.

"That's my boy! This is little Edward — little Teddy. Hello, how's my favourite little fellow?"

"It's all your fault, Lawrie. He might have slept until morning." But she was smiling, and Lawrence ignored her words. Like Maggie, he had dark hair. Just an inch taller than his sister, he was five years younger, the baby of the family. His two older brothers, Willie and Jack were fair-haired like their mother, but Maggie and Lawrence both had the looks and temperament of their father, physically finely-made, sensitive and artistic. The absence of their father from the family was felt by Maggie more than by the others, for she had been his favourite. Thomas Fisher had adored Maggie. She was clever at school, and quick and witty like himself. He thought his youngest son too sensitive and introverted, and shook his head in puzzlement, as when most boys were out playing some sport, Lawrence would be sitting, picking out chords on the piano or trying to teach himself to play the guitar.

Just past fifty-five when he died, in his last long illness, Thomas Fisher had given way to despair, hating himself for his failing kidneys, and for the heartache he was causing his wife and family. The older boys had been married before they had to face the loss of their father, and although they had attended the funeral with sadness, their lives were away from the family home now and they had other worries of their own to cope with. Lawrence had taken the event badly and had become more silent and remote. At the funeral, he tried to relate to the many family mourners who filled the house, but felt like a raw, inarticulate boy among them. Some of the near relatives seemed to be there for days, praying and weeping, and recounting endless stories of Thomas and his many escapades.

Maggie had been quite strong then. Apart from a hysterical breakdown on being taken to view the body, set up in a coffin in the front room, she had managed to be composed during that awful time. Joining the long line of neighbours and workmates of her father she walked sadly behind the hearse to the little chapel where the body was taken. She had taken her mother's arm as they left the church after the service, and was shocked when her mother slumped down heavily in a faint, almost pulling the young girl down with her. It had been the number of mourners, people from all walks of life, many unknown to the family, that had overwhelmed Helen's mind, and made the occasion one of great sadness. They had had no idea how much Thomas had been loved.

But that had been over six years ago, and now Lawrence was almost grown to manhood. He hoped for a career in art or music and although Helen Fisher worried about his long hair, and his lack of application at school, he was turning into a well-adjusted fellow, never happier than when listening to records. He was fond of his sister, and sad that she had made a mess of her marriage, as Jamie had been a hero of his. Now he was telling his friends about the wonderful trumpet solo of Bunny Berigan. "It belongs to Maggie's husband, Jamie, this record. It's called "I Can't Get Started." I'll play it to you. It's sensational." The three boys in their woolly pullovers and earnest young faces crowded around the record player while Maggie stood at the open door holding little Edward. "You don't mind me playing this record, Maggie?"

"No, don't be silly. I love Bunny Berigan." But as the familiar warm gravelly voice started, she felt a sinking feeling as she remembered the nights long ago when Jamie had played this same piece, and sang along with the record.

She left the little group and took the baby downstairs, her feelings getting the better of her. As Maggie fussed with the baby, changing his nappy and then trying to make him smile, her mother appeared, surprisingly accompanied by a white-haired, gentlemanly man who had been on a church outing with her. This was a turn-up for the books, a totally new departure for their mother, and she confounded them further by animatedly asking Lawrence and his friends to come downstairs to join them for a drink, and to bring their music with them.

They played Johnnie Ray records, and some Count Basie, and even some Elvis Presley, while they ate cheese and pickle sandwiches and drank mugs of tea. Later, Helen got quite tipsy on port and lemon, and became very emotional when, at her request, they put on a record of "Smoke Gets in Your Eyes." It was a strange, impromptu party.

When the guests had gone and they were clearing up, Maggie told her mother that she was going to a college dance with Barney, a student on her course.

"He's very bright. Gets an 'A' for nearly every essay. You would like him, Mum."

"So what if Jamie hears about this?"

"What if he does?"

"You're closing the door to him? You're not taking him back?"

"He doesn't want to come back."

"Oh, I don't know." Helen was at the door now, about to retire to bed.

"You know nothing. The baby would always come between us. Let's just drop the subject and get to bed." Maggie folded the dishtowel and turned to go.

Lawrence standing now, holding his records said, "You know, Maggie if you start fooling around with another guy, you're leaving the way open for Jamie to do the same."

"So?" she sounded angry.

He ventured another remark, "I like Jamie…"

"Please, Lawrie. Leave me alone. I have to get through this degree course, so I can build a career. I have a child to bring up. You lead your life and I'll lead mine."

Their mother had started to go upstairs and Lawrence said quietly, "But you still love him, don't you?"

Maggie did not answer immediately. Then she whispered, "It's all gone. I made a mistake and I've lost. That's it." He was appalled at the finality of her words. "Someday, Lawrie, you'll see what I mean. You'll join the rest of us soon in this game."

"What game?" A frown was on his handsome young face.

"Falling for someone. Being in love. Trying to sort your feelings out. You'll find it's not so easy. At least not unless you're half-dead to start with or very lucky to find the perfect mate."

"The perfect mate? That's a good phrase."

"Yes, words and phrases is all I'm good at now." She had reached the door of her bedroom, and opened the door quietly, so as not to disturb the baby. "See you in the morning, Lawrie. I enjoyed the music."

"Yeah! So did I. Goodnight, Maggie."

Thankfully the sun had broken through the clouds, and in Gregor's garden smoke was filling the air as he grappled with lighting the charcoal on the two barbecue grills he had set up. A few neighbours, drinks in hand, had established places on the seats laid out on the little lawn. Children ran around the garden in high excitement at the unaccustomed festive air, while Prue full of driving energy, fussed with bowls of salad and baked potatoes. She was helped by a neighbour, Sheila, and the now pregnant Diana, blooming in her pretty maternity dress.

"How many are coming, Prue?" Diana was counting out plates and cutlery.

"About twenty, I think. I hope I haven't forgotten anything."

"What have you got in your oven in the kitchen?"

"Oh, it's roasting chickens, just in case Gregor's barbecued sausage and burgers are a failure. Jamie promised to be here early to help him. I wish he'd hurry up. Gregor hasn't a clue."

Diana hurried off saying, "I'll get John to go and help. He's done barbecuing before. He'll know when the charcoal's ready."

Tables had been placed beside the grills, and Diana directed John to the cook's side, and then tripped back inside to help Prue with the punch. "I'll add another jigger of gin to this brew, give it a kick. Here, try a sip."

"Mmm! That's better. Even the aroma's intoxicating now." Diana filled some glasses and took a trayful out to the garden.

"Thanks for all your help, Diana. I couldn't have managed without you."

"Don't be daft, Prue. You've done wonders with the new house and garden already, considering you've got three kids so young."

"Let's grab a glass of punch and slip out to the seat at the other her side of the house for five minutes, away from the children. Do you fancy a cigarette, Diana?"

"Oh, I've stopped because of this." Diana patted the bump on her stomach. Besides it makes me feel sick, but I'll join you with a drink."

Prue lit up. "You're looking great. How are you and John getting on? He's settled down a bit, has he?"

"Well, Dad gave him a dressing down. An ultimatum really. You know two different people phoned me to tell me that they had seen him with someone else."

"God, the bastard!"

"He denies it of course. And I don't know who to believe now. But this pregnancy has made a difference. He does a bit of housework, now, hoovering the carpets and so on, and he's started to take an interest, a little interest in the garden. Yes, he's been a lot better recently. Still plays football, of course, but he comes straight home afterwards."

A car drew up. Prue stood up and got rid of her cigarette. "Oh, goodness. It's Jamie!" While he was getting out of the car, Prue whispered to Diana, "Listen, don't say anything, but I've invited Maggie along." Diana eyes popped at this news. "She didn't promise to come, but I hope she does. With having the baby, she doesn't get out much, but don't say anything to Jamie."

Jamie was carrying records and some cans of beer. "Is this where it's at?" He grinned at the girls.

Prue said, "You're looking smart. I could fall for you myself today. You'd better hurry if you want to see Gregor as chef of the year. Come on, I'll get you a drink."

Mario and Vera, and some of the staff from the restaurant arrived. Frederico produced a tall chef's hat for Gregor, and the food soon started disappearing almost as soon as it came off the grill. The fun was good as Gregor hopped about in front of the hot coals, his handless efforts at cooking being a constant a source of laughter. Soon Frederico took over, and as the punch and beer began to take effect, the atmosphere took on a festive air.

The late autumn sun was throwing slanting shadows across the garden, and people were settling down to their food when, suddenly, a new shadow appeared, and eyes turned to see Maggie arrive and stand tentatively on the patio among the still-flowering geraniums. She had come quietly round the side of the house, and looked as if she wondered if she were in the right house. Mario and Vera were the first to greet her. Then Gregor rushed over to hug her warmly. "Welcome, Maggie. It's great you could make it." She accepted a glass from Prue, and smiled around her, slightly startled at how many people were there.

"Your house and garden are really nice, Prue," Maggie said. "Aren't you the lucky ones?" The old friends smiled and talked animatedly, delighted at seeing one another again, but it didn't take a great observer to notice that her eyes were searching the garden for Jamie.

"He's over there, Maggie," Gregor said. Her eyes followed Gregor's pointing finger, and as she spotted Jamie, just as he turned around. Startled momentarily on seeing her, he thought her paler and more subdued than he remembered. He felt foolish when it was obvious that the shock of her appearance had thrown him off his stride, so that his conversation with John about football petered out. He couldn't remember what he had been saying.

She walked over and joined them. John looked round in surprise, "Well, hullo, stranger. Good to see you, Maggie. How are you?"

"I'm fine, John. And you?"

"Just great. Oh, I think Diana wants me, excuse me."

"Hello, Jamie."

"Hello, Maggie."

"You're looking very prosperous. I like your sweater."

"I'm all right. How are you? You look a bit pale. Did you drive here?"

She sipped her drink. "Yes, I did," she said.

He was stuck for what to say next. His heart was racing at her nearness. He kept staring at her luxurious dark hair, and breathed the familiar flowery perfume, but he avoided her eyes as much as he could. Shooting surreptitious glances at the others around, he felt foolish and gauche, suspecting that the two of them were now the centre of interest of the afternoon. He managed, "I didn't realise you'd be here."

"Well I almost didn't come. It took a bit of doing, you know. But Gregor and Prue were very keen, and they are old friends." They walked to the furthest corner of the garden. "Beautiful shrubs," Maggie said.

"Yes." He stood just behind her, tightly holding on to his beer glass.

"Gregor and Prue are lucky."

"Yes, they've not done too badly. Your baby all right?" The last question hung like ice crystals in the air.

"Yes." She was supremely cool. "Mother's looking after him."

"That's good."

"What's his name?"

"Edward."

"Oh, an unusual name, nowadays."

"It was my great-grandfather's name."

"And you're back at university?"

She gave an almost carefree laugh, "Yes, nose to the grindstone, shoulder to the wheel, you know." She picked a late flower and sniffed it. "How's your job? You like it?"

"Oh, yes. It's not really like work. Not like the office drudgery. You know old Benton. There's no pressure to sell or anything. It's just a question of being nice to the customers."

"You've landed lucky."

"Do you think so?" How's young Lawrence, he must be, what, eighteen now?"

"Yes. He's great. Wants to go to art school. He's become quite good at the guitar." She smiled. "Would you believe he has started his own skiffle band. You know washboard, tea chest. It's really quite good. Red Lawrie and the Boppers, they call themselves."

Jamie remembered Lawrie fondly. "He still has some of my old records. He always had taste in good music. God, time doesn't stand still, does it? Good for Lawrie!" They had reached some other guests in their wander round, Frederico and Luigi made a great fuss of her when she reached their party, embracing her and complimenting her so that she felt her tension ease, almost happy for the first time in months.

Twilight was falling and the children were rounded up by Prue's mother. A garden light was switched on and music was playing. Some couples started to dance on the little terrace. Gregor approached Maggie where she sat chatting to Vera and Mario, and pulled her up to dance with him, his long ungainly legs going all ways as he attempted ballroom dancing. She giggled as he teased her in a strong mock French accent. "*Chérie*, you are so beautiful. How wonderful to haf you in my arms! You must know that I luff you madly." And he threw her around, her hair flying. Jamie, feeling Gregor had regressed into an immature schoolboy, watched his friend's antics in pique. Upset and frustrated, he lit a cigarette and stood, one hand in his pocket, wishing he could get drunk. When she sat down still laughing, he could not approach her, nor could he ask her to dance.

Then he saw she was saying goodbye to people, and eventually she came and stood beside him. "It's been good to see you, Jamie." She held out her hand to him.

He shook hands with her, and then, squinting into her eyes said, "I'll walk you out to your car."

"Oh, thanks. I'm sorry to leave early like this, but I have to hurry back. It's not fair on Mum, as she has the baby most of the week while I'm out."

"Yes. He must be six months, now."

"Yes." She stood by her car, and looked up into his troubled, screwed-up eyes. A stab of pity for him hit her chest. "Take care, Jamie," she said and he nodded. With a hand laid gently on his arm she said, "Jamie, I'm sorry the way things have turned out. You must blame me. It was my foolishness."

His face was almost expressionless. "Who can tell where faults lie? It's not always straightforward. It's life, I suppose," he said.

"I have no excuses for what happened." She felt the blood rush to her face.

"No," he said his face dark red with emotion, and his cheek muscles working overtime. "I just wish I could figure out where I went wrong."

She caressed his arm. "It was me who went wrong, Jamie." They looked round as a few of the others had come to the front door to wave goodbye to her. Maggie held his right hand in both of hers, then turned to the car. In seconds she had started the car, and waving to them, drove away.

Gregor handed him a stiff whisky when they got inside. "You can sleep on the couch tonight, mate. You need this."

Shaken, Jamie slumped on an armchair, and took a gulp of the drink. "She's still beautiful, Gregor."

"Yeah, and you still love her."

"I always will."

Students were filing out of the great wrought-iron gates of the university. At four o'clock on an icy December day the sky was heavy with the threat of snow. Jamie sat in the warmth of his car idly watching the procession of young men and women who emerged, college scarves swathed around their necks, their carefree young smiles mocking his feeling of worthlessness. His mind wandered to the book by Albert Camus, he had been reading the night before. He mused on the thought that man's life was, in a way, like that of Sisyphus rolling his great, heavy stone uphill. Then, on reaching the top, he had the small consolation of snatching a view of another life, before the stone rolled back down the hill and he had to start the whole gargantuan struggle over again. *Perhaps I'll see her face. Perhaps she'll see me, and come over. No, I don't want her to see me. If she's alone I may talk to her, and I may not. I'll wait and see.*

Jamie thoughts ranged on, *Better get back to the office with my orders if she doesn't hurry up.* Old Benton would be on his first snifter from his desk bottle, ready for his adjournment to the pub for his pre-supper consumption of drinks, and would be in his usual persuasive frame of mind, seeking companionship — presage to another disastrous evening. Jamie moved his position, straining his eyes to pick out Maggie. Several times he thought he saw her, but he was mistaken. Had he forgotten what she looked like? Never. Not when every night her face filled his head as he tried to find sleep. She hadn't picked up many of her things, from the flat. Half her clothes were still there, her books, make-up. Did she mean to come back? He must talk to her. Perhaps she would like to go with him to the Humphrey Lyttleton concert in Edinburgh next week. She used to love traditional jazz when they first met.

He examined his watch. Four fifteen. Nice suit, well-shaped hands, signet ring — good leather brogue shoes, beautiful car interior — he thought he saw her, but once again it was her double. That day had started off well. Convivial talk and coffee with customers in the morning. An invitation to a golf-club dinner, through a chance meeting with a friend at lunchtime. Then between calls, as he negotiated the traffic, the anguish of the break-up with his wife had overwhelmed him, and the old sick sadness was on him again. He knew that he had to see her, had to find out what the score was. Since meeting her at Gregor's house, a small flame of hope was burning again in his heart. Yet he was afraid to acknowledge it, terrified of hurt and rejection.

God, I'm like bloody Romeo, hoping to catch a glimpse of the girl who has captured my whole being, the only person who can make sense of my life! He drummed his fingers on the steering wheel, then watched the grey of the old sandstone building turn darker in the evening light. The surge of students had fallen off to a trickle and, his excitement too falling off, he eyed his car keys stuck in the ignition, deciding to give the idea just sixty more seconds. Then he saw her. She looked slim and young, like a schoolgirl with her dark duffle coat with striped scarf and long boots, a bag slung over her shoulder.

As he made to open the car door he saw that she was laughing and talking to a tall fellow with dark curly hair, young and fresh-faced and also dressed in dark duffle coat and college scarf. They looked good together. They swung to the right and strode down Gilmorehill, down the avenue towards Sauchiehall Street and public transport. Should he call her, offer her a lift? But she was absorbed in her conversation, his courage failed him and the moment had passed, and the two students were unaware of his little drama as his car sped past them.

He decided to give the office a miss that evening. He would drive straight home and explain himself to Benton the next morning. He felt he had to run for cover, had to retrench, consider his position. Who was this guy who seemed so familiar with

Maggie? He would have to find out. *Am I a wimp or something? For Christ's sake!* he thought, *She's still my wife.*

In the newsagent's shop he saw a poster for Friday evening in the Railwayman's Arms — Red Lawrie and Boppers. Folk Night and Skiffle. That was tomorrow evening. Maybe he'd go. It would be some place to go.

After his lonely evening meal, Jamie considered his position. He stared at the telephone, daring himself to phone. If her mother answered, what then? "All right," he told himself, "I enquire after her health. Her mother always liked me. And the same with Lawrence." He could talk to him. But if Maggie answered what then? He could not bring himself to lift the receiver.

I'll write down what I want to say — always a good ploy. A piece of useful advice he'd once been given, and he found paper and pen and wrote:

1. How are you?

2. How is your mother and Lawrence.

3. How is the baby — Edward?

4. Do you ever get out at night?

5. I see Lawrie is playing in the Railwayman's Arms tonight.

6. Did you know that Humphrey Lyttleton was doing a concert in Edinburgh? On Saturday? Would you like to go?

He phoned and she answered. "Jamie? How are you?"

"I'm okay. Listen, Maggie, Humphrey Lyttleton's playing in Edinburgh on Saturday. Would you like to go? I could try and get tickets."

"Oh! I'd die to hear Lyttleton in the flesh, but... I'm going out to hear Lawrie play tomorrow night, and that would be two nights running I'd have to ask Mum. Hold on..."

After an eternity and she came back to the phone. "Okay, Jamie. She says okay."

"That's great. But would you mind if I came to hear Lawrie tomorrow night? I saw the poster about it on my way home."

"If you like, Jamie." Did she sound unsure?

"By the way, I saw you coming down University Avenue after four o'clock today."

"Really? Why didn't you say hello."

"You were with someone."

"Oh, that would be Barney. He'll be there tomorrow night to hear Lawrie."

"I'll be there about eight-thirty. Will you keep me a seat beside you?"

"Yes. I'll try. It gets pretty crowded, but—"

"See you then on Friday, Maggie. We can talk about Saturday night then. Bye!"

He came off the telephone and blew a great sigh of relief that the deed had been done, and for the first time for months a smile of something like happiness crossed his face.

Chapter 21

Lewis Benton looked around the comfortable office, his glance stopping on the small pages of a personal letter that lay on his desk. Friday afternoon, four o'clock, and he'd had four nips of whisky already. Where the hell was Jamie? He hadn't reported in as usual last evening. Now the office staff were busily clearing up the correspondence and so on, ready for the weekend. Why didn't Jamie phone or call in with his orders?

He wondered if he should take the seven-fifteen to the north, or spend the weekend in Glasgow. Who would care? His sister, Isobel was involved with the church nowadays, but this letter from Lorna, his sister-in-law was a bit of surprise. It lay like an accusation on his desk, hand-written on blue paper.

42 Academy Street,
Inverness.
(Tuesday afternoon.)
Dear Lewis,

I am sorry that since your brother, Robert, died we seem to have lost touch. This letter is just to remind that the house in Dochart, on the Black Isle, is now your property, as according to your mother's will it was to revert to you and your heirs, if Robert died first.

Morag, my cousin who lives with me now, and I moved out of the house three weeks ago to the address above. We are in a flat down near the river and find it quite suitable for us. I know I should have written before but must plead that I have been very busy with packing and so on. The house is, as you know, on a beautiful site with lovely views of the hills, and you could perhaps rent it out as a holiday cottage. I have left some of the old furniture there but you will have to attend to that side of

things. Also, the paintwork on the outside is needing attention.
If you could pay us a visit some time to talk about this and
collect the keys, I should be very pleased.
  Hoping your health is good,
  Yours affectionately,
  Lorna.

Lewis dropped the letter on the desk. Robert had been twelve years older than himself, and he had seen him only about twice a year, if that, usually at funerals or weddings. A fine upstanding country doctor, straight as a die, content with his devoted wife, Lorna, his work and the countryside. And what countryside, too! The house set on a little rise outside the village of Dochart had an incomparable setting among the hills with spectacular views on three sides, the large garden backing on to a small forest. It was a stone-built property, bought by their father as a weekend retreat for the family, and then Robert had moved there permanently with Lorna and started his country practice. He wished he had visited more often, and now it was too late.

Lewis opened the drawer and looked at the whisky bottle, thinking that perhaps he could take a week off and go and look at the old place. He could wander among the hills and along the banks of the river. He shut the drawer again. Where the hell was Jamie? He rose and looked into the warehouse yard, just in time to see his car pull up. "Thank God!" Lewis muttered. He'd ask his advice and decide whether to go or not.

With his hands behind his back, pacing up and down behind the door of his office, he waited for the younger man. Jamie pushed open the door, chuckling at some throwaway remark to the girls in the office, "Well, Lewis, Friday again!"

"You're cheerier than usual. Did your horse come in first?"

"No, no," he laughed, "just glad it's the weekend. Sorry I didn't manage to the office last night. I got tied up." He placed some papers on the desk. "Not a bad week of orders. Over three thousand pounds worth, in all. Stevens & Co., are needing a lot of tubing." He stopped as he sensed the atmosphere. "Something wrong?"

Lewis was still standing with his hands clasped behind his back. "No, no. That's good about the orders. It's just that I'm undecided about whether to go up north tonight or not. It's a long, cold journey. I thought you'd help me to make up my mind." He went round the desk. "Will you have a tot of whisky?"

The carefree expression momentarily left Jamie's face. "No, thanks. Better not. Got to drive home and I'm going out tonight."

"Oh, where?"

"Going to hear young Lawrence playing at the Railwaymen's Arms. He's started up a band, you know." He looked shyly at Lewis. "Maggie'll be there."

Lewis's face almost broke into a smile as he poured himself a whisky. "Does she know you're going?"

"Yes." Jamie beamed.

"That's great! A very good turn of events. I'm so glad, Jamie." He meant it, too. In his way, he loved Jamie and had always had a soft spot for Maggie. He poured a second drink. "Well, that's just about the best news I've heard all day, and this is the best I've felt all day." Looking at the pages of the letter, his head bent, the greying hair showing his advancing years, he scanned the words again, "This is from my sister-in-law in Inverness. It seems that she's moved out of the family holiday home in the Black Isle and now it's mine. I've inherited it. So Lorna wants me to come up and do something about it."

"Sounds like a nice bit of luck. I wouldn't mind a cottage in the country."

"Oh, trouble is I don't really feel like going all that way tonight. I'm not in the mood for a journey. What do you think?"

"I'll can drive you to the station, if you like."

"No, no. You're going out. You've got something special on."

Jamie sat down in the chair opposite still looking at the troubled face of his boss. "Why don't you come out tonight with me instead, Lewis? You're very welcome. How's that for an idea? It might cheer you up and you'd see Maggie."

Lewis looked a bit thrown by the suggestion, but Jamie was now in full flood. "I'll take you to your lodgings now. You can pick up some shirts and so on. We'd have a bite to eat at my house, go and hear the band, then you could stay in my spare room afterwards, and I'd put you on a train on Saturday morning. You could stay up there for a few days, or a week, even."

"What about the office? And the warehouse?"

"Oh, Mina would manage the office. And Flannery is very good in the warehouse. I could call in every day."

Flushed from the whisky now, Lewis's eyes swivelled himself around from the window, "By God, Jamie, you've talked me into it." He got up. "Let's get out of here."

As soon as they went through the swing doors of the Railwaymen's Tavern, Jamie caught sight of the band, a foursome with long-haired Lawrence, acting as guitarist and lead singer. They could just be heard above the din. It was a very old pub with a long mahogany bar, a glass-shelved gantry filled with different whiskies and other drinks, and four large beer pumps. Cigarette smoke was everywhere, and the level of noise was startling.

To the uninitiated in the culture, stepping in from the street to a busy public house on a Saturday evening was a complete eye-opener. Voices were raised in political argument, laughter, was breaking out here and there, and men crowded four deep downing pints, or trying to catch the attention of the barmen. There were a few women sitting between the males trying to listen to the skiffle band, but mostly the place was dominated by typical end-of-the-week drinkers, the reward for a hard week of manual work.

Jamie and Lewis tried to ease their way through to the bar. Looking over to the corner, Jamie saw a big bass, a pianist, and a guy with a washboard behind Lawrence. His voice was quite good, and the sound they made had a decided beat.

"Can you see her?" Lewis asked, craning his neck in the same direction as Jamie.

"Don't think so." They got their pints of beer, and squeezed their way towards the band. She was seated with a party of young people who were really into the music, clapping and moving to the tune. Jamie watched her for a minute, and Lewis watched him watching her. At the end of the song, she saw them and came over.

"He's very good, Maggie."

"Yes, he's got some talent, I must admit. Come and sit with us and meet some of the others."

Jamie pulled her gently back. "You're still on for tomorrow night?"

"Of course, I'm looking forward to it."

When they had found seats close to the music, and briefly nodded to the people Maggie indicated the two newcomers relaxed and soon each found another pint of beer in front of him from someone in the party. The evening went on in this noisy fashion, Jamie now and then noting how Maggie related to the chap from the university, the one he had seen her with that day. But they all seemed to be friendly and carefree, so that there was nothing to do but go with the flow and enjoy the moment.

A cold Saturday in December found Jamie in his car, parked outside Mrs Fisher's house. He was freshly shaved, dressed in dark blue shirt with new sports jacket, a white cotton tie done up in a large Windsor knot. He looked down at his highly polished brown brogue shoes and checked his fingernails. *I'm like a lovelorn teenager*, he thought. Melodically he sang to himself, keeping time on the steering wheel,

He was a bit worried about his hair. He'd had it cut short all over, just that afternoon, in a crew cut. He knew it altered his appearance, and wondered what Maggie would say. Eyeing the front door, he knew he should go in and say hello to her mother, perhaps even take a glance at the baby, but he had said he'd wait outside, so he was sticking to that.

When she finally came out, ten minutes later, she too had changed her hairstyle. It was shorter and styled close to her head. She looked a million dollars in a fitting grey two-piece suit and drop pearl earrings. He drove off after a minimum of greetings and she sat quietly in the passenger seat until they were well on their way along the Edinburgh Road.

"Baby all right?" he said eventually.

"He's fine. Mum's giving him his supper. He'll be all right. You should have come in to see him."

"I know. Why don't you remark on my hair," he said. "It's the latest fashion."

"Yes. It's nice. A crew cut?"

"Yes. Yours is nice, too. In fact you look terrific. Will you be hungry enough to eat at seven when we get to Edinburgh? The concert is in the Usher Hall. I thought we could try the new Indian restaurant that's opened beside it."

"Sounds good. Did you have trouble getting tickets?"

"A little, but it was worth it. Humph is great. But there is such a following for jazz nowadays. You wouldn't believe it."

"I do believe it, Jamie. In fact, some of your records from the past might be worth money someday. I used to love it when you played them."

"Those were the days!"

"Do you remember when we used to rush home from work at lunch time for a snack, and play "Lullaby of Birdland" and bebop around the flat.

"Yeah," he laughed or Johnnie Ray singing "Somebody Stole My Gal." Then his amusement evaporated and he said, "Ironic. Just the right song for me, eh, Maggie?"

She was hurt. "Don't Jamie!"

"Okay, let's enjoy this evening."

The Usher Hall was crowded and the music had the audience enraptured, riding every note of this New Orleans style jazz. At the end, the band got a standing ovation, Maggie and Jamie clapping and cheering Humphrey Lyttleton along with everyone in the packed house. Jamie breathed a sigh of relief as he steered her to a pub for a drink before they set out for home. The evening had gone well.

They diced around subjects, talking about Lewis, about her course, and about Prue and Gregor, until he said, "What do you hear from Dominic?"

"Well funny you should ask, but I heard from Diana that he might visit Mario's during the New Year holidays. It appears he's in London now."

"That's only three weeks away. He'll hear about the baby."

"How will he? I won't tell him."

"Someone will."

He sat at looking at her grave, intelligent face. If anything, he thought, her looks had improved. She had removed the jacket of her suit, and he saw the sweet rise of her bosom and the beauty of her slender neck. On her left hand were still the rings he had given her.

"Yes, that hair-cut suits you, Jamie. I like it." She changed the subject.

He said, "I'll get you another drink, then we'd better go."

Arriving back at her mother's door, her perfume was flowery as she leaned towards him, "Why don't you come in for coffee. Mum will probably be in bed."

"Why not?" he heard himself say.

They lit cigarettes and talked about the concert and some of the old beatniks in the audience. They were, for a little while young again, carefree as they once had been.

"What will you do if Dominic finds about little Edward?"

"Look, Jamie… let's forget about it. I enjoyed this evening…"

"I still love you, Maggie." She looked down, deeply moved by his words but somehow unable to reciprocate, then a baby's cry sounded from upstairs and the spell was broken. "I'd better go. Maybe we could do this again, next Saturday, see a film or something. I'll be busy because Lewis is away for a week, so I'll phone you, say on Wednesday?" With a brief, tentative kiss on the lips, he parted from her.

At four in the afternoon on Wednesday he phoned.

She sounded agitated, "Listen, Jamie. I'm terribly sorry. I forgot I had to go to the Christmas Ball at the Union with Barnie on Saturday — I promised weeks ago."

"Tell him you can't go." No answer. "Tell him you're a married woman."

"Okay! I'll tell him."

"I'll pick you at six o'clock Saturday. We can eat at Ferrari's."

"Oh! Big-time James!"

"That's me!"

It was another good evening together. Some of the old ease and familiarity was returning between them, and Jamie's ready wit was reviving, so that Maggie found herself laughing as she had done in former days. "Not sorry you missed the ball?"

"No, not sorry at all."

"Listen you used to love green Chartreuse, and I've a bottle at home. Also I have a package for you to open. A surprise!"

"Oh, I love surprises."

"Right, let's go now. I've set the fire in the lounge."

It felt strange to her to be back in the old surroundings. The place seemed so spacious, and arty. She'd forgotten all the trendy posters and pictures, and the polished wood of the floor in the low-ceilinged sitting room, covered here and there by a bright modern cotton rug. She'd forgotten the seat built into the bow window with its yellow linen cushions. Jamie put on some soft music on the record player and then she watched his face as he mixed drinks for them. *He's more serious now than he was, less ready to joke. He's lost some of his good humour.* Dropping down on the hearthrug she held her hands up to the heat of the log fire, turning when he neared her. He held her drink in one hand and a jeweller's box in the other. With his anxious eyes on her face she took out a pretty gold chain bracelet from its red plush background. Her eyes widened as she held the gift up to the light. "It's beautiful, Jamie!"

"It's one of your Christmas presents."

"Oh, I don't deserve it!" she said, throwing her arms around him.

"Well, I think maybe you do." His strong arms were placed gently around her.

Still holding each other she whispered, "I've missed you so much."

"Me, too." After a few minutes in front of the fire, he held her even closer, saying. "Can you stay a little longer. I'd like to show you my etchings. I keep them in the bedroom."

They were both smiling widely now, and she pulled gently away. "I'll give Mum a phone call. I'm sure she's all right with the baby."

All bitterness went from Jamie as he held her. She could not doubt his love for her, and afterwards, Maggie felt happier in his arms than she had ever felt — even in the first days of their marriage. "I've been such a fool, Jamie," she whispered tearfully.

"You are not the only one, Mags. I was so stupid not to see what was happening when you worked in that place. Maybe I was a bigger fool than you. Someone should have kicked my backside. It's so wonderful to have you here with me."

"Mum has asked me to invite you for Christmas dinner."

"Oh? That's very nice of her." They lay together on the bed, he not wanting to move and lose this moment of closeness, his lips close to her hair.

"Lawrence and his girlfriend will be there. And Mum has a friend who takes her out sometimes, so it should be good fun."

There's just one problem. "I'm a bit concerned about Lewis over the holidays. He's going to his cottage in the highlands, and I said I would go up for a few days, and maybe spend some time there."

"If you're worried about him you could invite him to Mum's for Christmas dinner. She won't mind at all. She's ordered a big turkey. And if he still wants you to go up north, you can go afterwards."

"If I go, would you come, too? To the Black Isle, I mean, with us after Christmas, and maybe stay over New Year?"

"Oh, I don't know. What about the baby?"

"Of course. I mean you and the baby."

"Lewis will have a fit. He won't want a messy baby in his cottage."

"I don't think so, Maggie. I don't think he'll mind at all."

Helen Fisher was delighted with the new turn of events. Maggie had packed all her books away for the holidays, and Jamie slept with her in her bedroom. With little Edward in his cot, the room was a bit chaotic, but they didn't seem to mind this. Jamie often held the child tenderly at his bath time or while Maggie prepared his food. Once Maggie caught him looking closely at the plump, naked baby, stroking his ears and the fine dark hair that was coming in quite fast now around the chubby face. "He's like one of those baby Jesus paintings you see in Italian Renaissance pictures. He's really beautiful. Almost as beautiful as his mother."

Seeing them together like that touched her heart. "I don't know if boys should be beautiful, Jamie."

"Of course they should. Everyone should be beautiful."

Lewis came on Christmas day, and he too was relieved that his favourite people had put the past behind them and were once again loving and caring with each other for all the world to see. It was a happy, family time, and after two days Maggie had managed to pack all the paraphernalia for the baby, and she and Jamie and Lewis set out for the six-hour drive to the highlands.

At just forty or fifty miles an hour, Jamie negotiated the winding road northwards up through Perth. They stopped twice for food and to attend to baby Edward. He bounced about on his mother's knee, wanting to move around the back seat, so that when, swathed in his woollen clothes, he fell asleep, on the last stage of the trip, Maggie sat back with relief. When they reached Dalwhinnie, a Christmas card scene of falling snow and white hills greeted them. Their car was the only one the road, and an eerie silence surrounded them as the snow fell.

They were glad they had started out early, as the road was often closed if there was a heavy fall of snow. "The gates are closed! They've closed the gates!" the locals would tell each other in perturbation as great iron gates were closed and locked barring further travel. For, in the past, cars had been stuck in snowdrifts on the road overnight, long lines of them, and had to be dug out next day by snowploughs. Each winter amazed the highland people afresh. With great excitement they would talk of getting out the snowploughs and of the red-tipped snow poles along the sides of the high places being almost covered, and of the possibility of their town or village being cut off from the south.

Lewis sat beside Jamie in the front of the car. He felt good being with them, as if part of a family, close and concerned for each other. "We'll be staying at the Glen Achilty Hotel tonight, I've told them to keep us rooms, and perhaps we'll stay for a few days because, I think the cottage will be too cold for us. It needs the Aga to be lit, and the heating to be switched on. I want you to see the cottage first, Maggie, before we take the baby there. It might not suit you, and I need to get in some food and the like. And remember, the hotel bill is my treat."

"That's very thoughtful of you, Lewis," she said, "And generous. I really am dying to see your house. I had no idea it was so beautiful or so, sort of remote up here. I've never been up this way before. I'm sure your house will be lovely."

"Yes. It is nice, and the views are very good. Mind you I've never seen it in the snow."

They drove on, silenced by the beauty of the falling white flakes of snow which were painting the dark mountains white, making them loom even closer to the road, and making hills in the far distance seem nearer. Snow fell on the rivers, and the stands of fir trees, and on the remote little groups of houses on the long narrow road, and as the afternoon passed and the light started to fade, the road glinted and glimmered before them. After steadily watching the direction of the road, as they rounded bends and went over low hills, it was with a sigh of relief they suddenly saw, stretched out before them, like a prize, the choppy waters of the firth and the lights of Inverness. The plump baby woke up, pushing himself up out of his shawls and turned his gaze out to the snow, his dark eyes wide, and his little podgy finger pointing. Jamie turned on the car radio, and everyone laughed as the song came over the airwaves. "I'm dreaming of a white Christmas."

Lewis said, "You wouldn't believe it. So appropriate! This drive has been like being in a Hollywood movie, or in one of Grimm's Fairytales. What a beautiful sight! It really is like a picture postcard, but thank goodness to be nearly in sight of the end of the road."

"I think I'll always remember this journey, the snow and everything," Maggie said. "It's all so breathtakingly lovely," and she pointed out of the window. "See the snow, Edward. Look at all that beautiful snow."

After another twenty minutes round the side of the waters of the Beauly Firth, with the snow swirling now in the wind, Lewis pointed to the side road. "Just down there. That large house that's all lit up. That's our hotel. And very well done, Jamie! Excellent driving! Thank you for getting us here safely."

A warm highland welcome awaited them in the comfortable old country hotel, almost full to capacity as it was with people from the south having a New Year break. Christmas decorations and holly and a happy holiday spirit were everywhere. The maids, for the most part cheery highland girls, were still in the uniforms of the earlier times, black dresses and little white aprons trimmed with lace. They were entranced with little Edward, offering to hold him, and to look after him, so that Maggie and Jamie often had time to stroll around the grounds, while Lewis read in the hotel lounge, usually indulging in a warming brandy with his coffee. The owners knew Lewis, and they were pleased to see him and to hear news of his family in Aberdeen, and from his business in Glasgow.

It was a wonderful break. Each morning, after breakfast, the three of them set out for Lewis's house, some five miles away, Jamie carrying the baby. They saw to the heating, and lit a fire in the old lounge fireplace to warm the walls of the house, while Maggie prepared lunch in the large kitchen, although she was unfamiliar with the great hot rings of the farmhouse stove.

Built on to the front of the house was a sun lounge, from where there were spectacular views of the hills and mountains. A wide stream could be seen from the windows eternally flowing through the valley between the hills, a grey-blue line on the whiteness of the fields. Around the house was a large garden, now white like all the countryside, which sloped down southwards, and became a little orchard on one side. On the north side the vegetable garden backed on to an ancient wood, a remnant of the Caledonian forest. There the trees hung heavy with the newly fallen snow, and it was there that they went walking each day, marvelling at the crisp fresh air, and silence and secretiveness of their surroundings. They saw not a single soul on these meanderings.

All week it was sharply cold but the sun shone and it was perfect for walking as no more snow fell. On the day before Hogmanay, the second-last day of the year, as they returned to the hotel after tramping through the woods, Lewis and Jamie, and Maggie carrying the baby, were stopped at the hotel entrance by Ronnie Farquarson, the owner, to say that there were people in the lounge, just arrived, who were asking for them. Maggie leading the way, the fat baby balanced on her right hip wandered towards the lounge doorway, glancing backwards at Jamie and Lewis, making a puzzled face at them. She came to an abrupt halt as she saw the three dark-suited men who sat by the fire. It was Dominic and his son, Nicki, with his friend, Michael, from America.

Dominic was smoking a cigar and they had drinks set on the table in front of them. They were the only people in the lounge. For a second or two, Maggie stood frozen, clinging tightly to the baby, unable to move a step forward or backward. When Dominic stood up, the spell was broken. He covered the space between them, and with the fat cigar in his hand, his eyes slightly hooded, she heard that distinctive voice again, "I have travelled a long way for this moment, my dear! It is wonderful to see you." His eyes were on baby Edward.

Maggie sank into an armchair, the baby struggling to be on the floor so that he could crawl around. Jamie and Lewis stood, one either side of her, staring at the three men. "Well, Jamie, so we are all in the North of Scotland for the New Year celebrations!"

A mixture of nerves and anger was rising up in Jamie. "How on earth did you get here?"

He indicated Nicki, who was looking ill at ease, as he stood a little behind his father. "This is my son, Nicki. He drove us here. It's a very nice place." Once again he was looking at Maggie and Edward.

"But who told you where we were? Nobody knew but my family." Maggie managed to find a voice, and sat holding the struggling baby, and pushing back her hair from her pink, wind-burned face.

"Mario phoned your mother for me and she told him the name of the hotel." He flicked the ash from his cigar into the ashtray. "Why don't we all sit down?" He was an expert manager of situations. There was nothing else for it and the two parties sat facing one another. "I am in Scotland with Nicki for business reasons, and to spend some of the festive season here. So I thought I would look up my old friends. No harm in that is there?" Maggie could see he was struggling too. He was doing his best to be persuasive and placatory, the dark eyes in his mobile face almost pleading. Like all Italians, he used his hands to put over his points.

Jamie said through tight lips. "Don't tell me you intend to stay here for the New Year."

"Why not? It's a nice place with nice people." Smilingly he turned to Lewis. "You are Mr Benson, are you not? I've heard a lot about you." Dominic leaned over and held out his hand to Lewis who was more or less forced to shake it.

The baby was now standing holding on to Maggie's skirts, bouncing up and down delighted in himself. "What is his name, Maggie?"

"He's called Edward."

"Nice name, Eduardo!" And he smiled down at the child.

"No, Edward." said Jamie. "Edward London."

"Look. I'm sorry if I have inconvenienced you, and I can see you three are tired. And so are we. We've just arrived, and left our bags in our rooms. Why don't we have our dinner and then meet for a chat later?"

Jamie and Lewis were standing up. "Come on, Maggie. Let's go. The baby needs his bath, and you look exhausted."

"Yes. I am tired." Her voice was small and strained.

"Won't you even shake my hand, Maggie?" his eyes were hurt and his face was crestfallen. "I am so happy to see you again."

She looked into the liquid brown of those, oh so familiar eyes, and held out her hand. "You look well, Dominic." She nodded to Nicki and Michael. "I'll see you later on. Goodbye." Lifting the child, she walked slowly to the door, leaving the room without looking back.

Upstairs, Lewis joined them in their room carrying a bottle of whisky. "I think you could both do with a drink." They sat for a while stunned by this visitation. Jamie's face was white with suppressed anger.

"How dare he come here?" Jamie got out eventually. "How could he spoil our holiday? And how could you shake hands with him?"

"Look, folks. I think I'd better go and get changed for dinner," Lewis murmured.

"No, Lewis. There's nothing to hide. You know the story." He turned to Maggie who looked tired and miserable. "He's come to see the child. That's why he's here."

"How do you know that?" she whispered. "He has never been told about Edward."

"I know it. I can tell by the way he looks at him. It's quite obvious."

Lewis stood up unsteadily. He felt too old for this high drama. "I'd better go. I look forward to our little party tonight. It's nearly six-thirty. I'll be ready to go down in about an hour." And he was out the door leaving the bottle behind

"So has he got your stupid hormones going again, my dear — Dominic, the demon lover?" Jamie poured himself a drink.

"You're being silly."

"He must think there's a chance for him, or he wouldn't have travelled all this way, don't you think?"

"You should know there's no chance for him." She looked straight at him. "I've told you often enough, it's finished between him and me."

"And I'm supposed to believe that?"

"I'm going to put Edward in his bath. Will you go down to the kitchen and have his bottle made please? I can't do everything myself, if we are to join Lewis for dinner." He came and stood close to her and the baby. Anguished, he put his arms around the two of them, still holding the glass in his hand.

"Put the whisky away, and come and help me, Jamie. I have to have a bath, too, and wash my hair."

"You are my beautiful wife, and I love you very much." His voice was tearful.

"And this is our beautiful son, and I love you very much."

When the meal was over and they were strolling to the bar for a last drink, Dominic approached them. "May I have a word with you, Maggie?" Jamie scowled but did not stop her. He and Lewis walked on into the bar. "I'd like to see the baby in his cot, asleep." He'd had a lot of wine, and his speech was a little slurred.

Her blue eyes were guarded as she said quietly, "Why, Dominic?"

"He's my child, isn't he?" She felt the blood rush into her face. "Don't lie to me, Maggie. I know he's mine. I was your lover when he must have been conceived. Of course he's mine." She didn't answer. "Anyway, I could tell the way Mario told me about him that he was not Jamie's."

She felt giddy and held on to the newel post of the banister to steady herself. "Dominic. Please. You shouldn't have come here. You and I have caused enough pain."

People were strolling past them and they had to keep their voices low to avoid being heard. "I had to see you," he hissed. "I had to see you while I was in the country. And when I heard about... about the child, I had to come."

"I have to go. I have to go and check that the baby is all right. One of the maids is keeping an eye on him, but I—"

He took her hand. "You are still my lovely girl, Maggie, but I see you have changed. You have grown up, I think, while I have just grown older. Have you and Jamie decided to make a go of it again? You are back with him?"

"He is my husband. He is a good person, and he loves me and Edward very much."

Dominic looked down at his feet, his face stern. "Let me come up with you to see the baby."

"If you are staying on to bring in the New Year then you'll see him tomorrow. Won't that do?"

"I want to see him now."

"Are you drunk, Dominic?"

"Have you ever seen me drunk?"

"Yes." she said and their eyes met as they both remembered Paris. "You can come to see him if Jamie comes with us."

"All right. Go and ask him."

Stiffly and formally the three of them mounted the stairs. The maid, who sat in the room quietly watching television, was amazed to see them and made herself scarce. They gazed down silently at the sleeping child, so deeply asleep, sweat glistening like dew on the velvet skin of his cherubic face. Maggie and Jamie turned away and left Dominic for a few minutes staring with disbelief at the infant.

Saying nothing the three of them returned to the bar where Dominic said politely, "I must join Nicki and Michael. They'll wonder what's happened to me." Now his face was grave. "I congratulate you, Jamie on your good fortune, you are a lucky man." Jamie did not smile, but he felt a shaft of sympathy for the older man who continued, "Tomorrow evening, I would be honoured if you and Maggie and Mr Benton would join us for dinner. We are leaving directly after breakfast."

Maggie looked quickly at Jamie for a reaction. The muscles in his cheeks were working as he held his face taut. He said, "Would you like to do that, Maggie?"

She clutched the strap of her little evening bag, and biting her lip said, "I think that would be all right. It's the last night of the year. But it is up to you Jamie."

For a second they held their breath, then Jamie held out his hand saying, "That is very kind of you, Dominic. We will be happy to have dinner with you tomorrow."

When the atmosphere built up for the ending of the year, emotions ran high in their little party. Like everyone else, they had been drinking wine and inhibitions were thrown to the winds. When the bells rang out to announce the ending of the old year, they shook hands and embraced each other, and sang Auld Acquaintance joining hands with the rest of the guests. When out of Jamie's hearing, Dominic whispered to her "Was it a good year for you, Maggie?"

She was tipsy by now, "I wouldn't like to go through it again, mind you, but it was a year that brought me little Edward… and I got Jamie back."

"Ah," he stuck his cigar in his mouth, and put his arm around her. "And I got to see you again, but I tell you, the year before last was better." She looked around to see where Jamie was, before she laughed. Then he said in a low voice, "Are you happy, my darling?"

"I'm happy, Dominic." She kept her gaze steady under his scrutiny.

"I'll miss you, sweetheart."

"And I'll miss you."

This made him happy. "Can I come and see my son, sometimes?"

"You are going back to America. You'll have other things on your mind. You'll forget us all soon."

"I don't think so."

She saw Jamie turn round from the bar where he stood with Lewis and Nicki, then turn back again. She took Dominic's hand. "If you write to me with your address in New York, I'll send you photographs of him, and if you want to come to see us, then you come. Let's go over to the bar now and join the others. We'll say goodbye tomorrow."

As they approached, Jamie called out, holding up his glass, "Happy 1961, Dominic!"

"A toast!" shouted Lewis. "Here's to 1961 and my retirement!"

"Really, Lewis? You're giving up?" Jamie was surprised.

"Yes." He swayed a little. "After I've seen how nice it is here, and what with falling heir to my brother's house, I think I'll give up work in the spring." Everyone was taken aback. "And," he held up his glass of whisky, "you are all welcome to come for a visit to my home in Loch Achilty, anytime you wish."

"You'll feel different in the morning, Lewis." Jamie steadied his friend as he slipped along the bar.

"No, no. I'm retiring from the game with my spoils. No more striving. No more competing for business."

"Not a bad idea, Lewis." Dominic affably put an arm around Lewis. "All this working your way up the ladder, it's a game for young people."

Jamie held his wife close. "Sorry to break up the party, folks, but we have to go now. We have to check on Edward. We'll see you all in the morning."

Lewis and Dominic watched them go up. "Two lucky young people. Got everything going for them," Lewis murmured.

"Everything!" Dominic agreed.